Praise for Maya Linnell

'When a new Maya Linnell novel lands in the office, we pretty much draw the curtains and shut up shop until it's read . . . [*Magpie's Bend*] is imbued with such deep empathy for everything country, we can't get enough of Maya's fictitious McIntyre family.' *Australian Country Magazine*

'Maya's books reek of authenticity and celebrate everything that's wonderful about small-town living.' Cassie Hamer, author of *The Truth About Faking It*

'Comfortable and so very much like returning home to help out, Maya Linnell has once again transported readers into the very essence of country living.' Blue Wolf Reviews

'In a fitting tribute to regional Australian and the strength of community ties, *Magpie's Bend* is another heart-warming rural tale from former country journalist Maya Linnell.' Mrs B's Book Reviews

'A delight from start to end . . . don't tell Penny and Angie, but I think Lara's story might be my favourite yet!' Bookish Bron

'Immersing yourself in the country characters and spirit of Bridgefield is a delight. Just the thing to while away some summer hours.' CWA Ruth Magazine

'A ripper of a read with something on nearly every page that rang true to me—the Australianisms, the landscape, the characters and their language.' Sueanne, Done and Dusted Books

'So much delicious baking in this book you'll be ready to fire up your own oven and whip something up as soon as you finish reading. Enjoy!' Australian Romance Readers Association

'Beautifully written from the opening pages . . . A story about learning to love and trust again.' Tanya, @Read by the Librarian

'Magpie's Bend is a heartfelt, winsome and satisfying rural romance, a delightful read I enjoyed over a long weekend.' Shelleyrae, Book'd Out

'Reading this book is like getting a warm hug, it's true escapism in every sense.' Merc's Book Nook

'Always a joy to read Maya's rural romance stories . . . so authentic and well written' Michelle @SheSociety

Praise for Maya Linnell and *Bottlebrush Creek*

New Idea *Book of the Month, June 2020*
Sunday Age *#3 Bestselling Romance, June 2020*
Top 10 Aus Fiction Bestseller, June 2020
Weekend Australian *#4 Bestselling Romance, July 2020*
Shortlisted for Favourite Australian-set Romance in the Australian Romance Readers Association Awards, 2020

'Two big thumbs up for an authentic Aussie story.' Mercedes Maguire, *Daily Telegraph*

'Loved this book . . . such a delight from beginning to end.' Emma Babbington, *New Idea*

'Charming and enjoyable ... fans of Maya's first novel will keenly enjoy this latest outing.' *Canberra Weekly*

'Pure escapism, with a plot twist you won't see coming.' *Lifestyle1 Magazine*

'A natural warmth oozes from the pages ... a truly heart-warming read.' *Western District Farmer News*

'Engaging and distinctly Australian. A great country read.' Rick Whittle, ABC Wide Bay

'*Bottlebrush Creek* will keep you turning pages into the early hours of the next morning.' Bestselling author Tabitha Bird

'Everything you want in a rural romance: relatable characters, farm life, the sound of the ocean ... and the perfect fixer-upper.' Bestselling author Fiona Lowe

'Maya's deep understanding of living in country Australia and down-to-earth good humour give her story great authenticity. *Bottlebrush Creek* is a ripping good read.' *Australian Country Magazine*

'A beautiful story that illustrates the loves and lives of rural Australia.' Tanya Nellestein, *Hearts Talk* Magazine

'Heart-warming, funny and poignant, *Bottlebrush Creek* will capture your heart and imagination. An absolutely delightful and enjoyable read.' Blue Wolf Reviews

'A stellar follow-up ... an incredibly modern and relatable tale.' 6PR Perth Tonight Book Club

Praise for Maya Linnell and *Wildflower Ridge*

MAYA LINNELL

Paperbark Hill

ALLEN&UNWIN
SYDNEY·MELBOURNE·AUCKLAND·LONDON

First published in 2022

Allen & Unwin
83 Alexander Street
Crows Nest NSW 2065
Australia
Phone: (61 2) 8425 0100
Email: info@allenandunwin.com
Web: www.allenandunwin.com

A catalogue record for this
book is available from the
National Library of Australia

ISBN 978 1 76087 969 3

Internal design by Bookhouse, Sydney
Set in 12.1/16.6 pt Sabon LT Pro by Bookhouse, Sydney
Printed in Australia by McPherson's Printing Group

10 9 8 7 6 5 4 3 2 1

Bestselling rural fiction author Maya Linnell gathers inspiration from her rural upbringing and the small communities she has always lived in and loved. *Paperbark Hill* is her fourth novel, following *Magpie's Bend*, *Bottlebrush Creek* and *Wildflower Ridge*. A former country journalist and radio host, Maya also blogs for Romance Writers Australia, loves baking up a storm, tending to her rambling garden and raising three young bookworms. She writes to a soundtrack of magpies and chickens on a small property in country Victoria, where she lives with her family, their menagerie of farm animals and the odd tiger snake or two. For a regular slice of country living, follow Maya on social media or sign up to her monthly newsletter at mayalinnell.com.

@maya.linnell.writes

To Harley, Tom and Zoe,
three of my very favourite Linnells

1

Diana McIntyre swiped a dusty sleeve across her damp forehead, tucked her trowel back into her tool belt and proudly assessed her day's work.

Six long garden beds ran the length of the paddock, two with freshly turned soil. In all her years of gardening, these were the patches she was most excited about, planted with tubers for her first commercial dahlia crop.

'Two down, four to go,' Diana said, fanning herself with her straw hat and trying to recall the last time they'd experienced such a spring heatwave in the western Victorian town of Bridgefield.

It wouldn't look like much to a visitor. Heck, if she hadn't spent the day on her knees, with her hands in the dirt, even she wouldn't be able to tell there were thousands of dollars of dahlias buried in the first two patches.

Pete will be impre . . . Diana pressed a hand to her heart. She'd lost count of the times it still caught her unawares.

She dusted her hands on her overalls, as much to remove the dirt as to shake off the sudden stab of loss. The mob of corellas that had been watching her all afternoon swooped down and began picking through the soil. Diana started towards the birds, waving her hat, covering just a few steps before her body reminded her she'd used up her quota of energy for the day.

The gate hinges creaked as she walked from the dahlia paddock into her house garden. Diana snipped a bloom from the flourishing Abraham Darby rose bush, willing the scent to distract her. The last thing she needed was the boys to arrive home from school and find her in tears again.

Fresh starts, she reminded herself, cradling the bloom as she ascended the steps to her weatherboard farmhouse. Starting the flower farm was a step in the right direction, darned if she was going to let grief swallow her now.

Despite the early hour, Darwin's oppressive heat had sweat trickling down Ned Gardiner's back as he squeezed the final boxes into the moving van. He took a quick look over his shoulder to see his ten-year-old daughter Willow striding towards him.

'Morning sleepyhead,' said Ned. 'Ready for adventure?'

Willow pushed her glasses back up her nose and lifted an eyebrow. 'Are you *sure* Stan's going to make it through the red centre?'

Ned turned and met Willow's doubtful stare. He crouched down, smoothed her jet-black hair behind her ears and unfolded her scrawny arms.

'Sure as eggs,' he said. 'Has Stan the Van failed us yet?'

'I'll miss the fresh mangoes,' Willow said, nestling into his embrace.

'Me too. But maybe not the neighbours,' he stage whispered.

A giggle escaped and, just as he'd hoped, Willow's face brightened.

'Mrs Neilson was a little bit mean, wasn't she?'

It was Ned's turn to grin. That was probably the nicest thing in years that anybody from the apartment block had said about the disapproving resident in number five.

Seven-year-old Doug yawned as he ambled down the steps, his T-shirt on backwards. 'Ready to rock, Dad?'

Ned nodded, feeling his shirt sticking to his body. He wouldn't miss the Darwin humidity.

Doug jumped into the van. Willow farewelled the mangy tabby cat weaving between her legs.

'He'll fool someone else into feeding him before the day's out,' Ned assured her.

'Mrs Neilson might feed you if you're a good boy, Flopsy,' Willow crooned, scratching under the cat's faded flea collar.

Ned's eyes went to the twitching lace curtains. Mrs Neilson was more likely to dance naked in her front yard, but kind-hearted Willow didn't need to know that.

'What about the mango tree, Dad? Are you sure we can't take it with us?'

Willow's pensive gaze stayed on the tree she'd lavished with attention during their stay, just like the tabby cat and the semi-translucent geckos that frequented their balcony.

'I wish we could, sweetie. How about one last water?'

Ned looked over his shoulder as he uncoiled the hose and sprayed a jet of water towards the tree.

'Dad!'

It was worth risking the wrath of the water conservation-nuts on the apartment board, just to see the children's delight. The curtains twitched once more as he finished watering, latched the van's back door, climbed inside and clicked his seatbelt on.

'Mrs Neilsen saw you doing that,' said Doug, his eyes wide.

'She'll report you to the water authority. Or . . . or the police,' added Willow.

Ned gave them a wink and waved to their nosy neigh-bour—*former* nosy neighbour—before coaxing the van into gear and pointing it south.

Diana rebraided her strawberry-blonde hair as hoots and hollers floated down the driveway.

By the time she'd reached the window, the twins were halfway down the gravel track. Harry was in front this time, his curls whipping back from his face and lanky legs pumping madly as he raced his bicycle past the hay shed.

His twin, Elliot, wasn't far behind, leaning forward like a Melbourne Cup contender hoping to win by a nose. *Competing for sheep stations again.*

Diana's eldest, Cameron, rode at the back with little Leo, still her baby at eight years of age. Despite the large age-gap, or maybe because of it, they chatted away, leisurely cycling home.

She headed outside with a container of lamingtons, warding off the inevitable 'I'm starving' and 'coconut on the floor' dilemma in one swift move. Bickering over who was today's driveway derby winner, they skidded to a halt at the dog kennels.

Diana's heart felt full as they unclipped the sheepdogs and made a fuss over their canine friends. Cam and Leo joined the fray, covering the final stretch of the driveway as a team.

My beautiful boys.

'Hi Muu-uum.'

'Lamingtons!'

'You should hear what Harry did at school today.'

They shoved their bikes haphazardly against the garage, gave her a quick hug and launched themselves at the food.

'Good day, Mum?'

Diana had to reach up to tousle Cameron's fair hair. 'Sure was, buddy. Notice anything different over there?'

The teenager took a lamington and followed her gaze. 'You got all the dahlias in?'

'I'm not a machine. I was pretty darn pleased to get *two* flowerbeds planted out today.'

Cam chewed thoughtfully. 'Reckon we can do the rest over the weekend. Might even rope those ferals into service.'

He nodded towards Harry, who was balancing a lamington on his nose. Paddy, the young kelpie, was glued to the sight, just waiting for a slip. Leo and Elliot were trying to copy him, much to the delight of their elderly border collie, Bonzer, who was feasting on the fallout.

Diana shook her head, biting back a grin. It was a circus, but it was *her* circus.

The road sign lit up under the glare of the van's headlights, telling them it was another 150 kilometres until the next town. Ned glanced across at his little passengers beside him on the bench seat. Doug had fallen asleep two hours ago, full of roadhouse burgers and ice cream, while Willow had fought to keep her eyes open, only dropping off half an hour ago. Her hands were still curled around the paperback she'd been reading for most of the day, and her glasses had almost slipped off the end of her nose.

Ned reached across and gently removed the tortoiseshell frames that were a smaller version of his own. She stirred, murmured, and settled back to sleep. His kids had always been good travellers.

The phone danced on the dashboard and a photo of Ned's little brother appeared on the screen.

Bit late for Jonno . . .

He put the call on speakerphone and slipped it into his top pocket, beside Willow's specs, expecting a jet-lagged catch-up but instead hearing panic in Jonno's voice.

'Colin's in hospital.'

'What? How bad?' Ned drew in a quick breath, mentally calculating the kilometres between him and his father's property in western Victoria. Almost 3000 clicks. He automatically pressed the accelerator a little harder.

'I'm on my way there now,' said Jonno, 'but from what I've heard, it doesn't look good.'

Jonno shared what little he knew about the accident, all second hand from the nurse who'd called him. Ned listened in quiet disbelief, straining to hear as the phone conversation dipped in and out of reception.

'What the hell was he doing? Resheeting the roof in gale-force winds?'

'You know Colin. The roof would need to be replaced entirely before he'd ask for help. Apparently he was trying to fix a loose sheet of tin before it got worse.'

'Worse is an understatement,' Ned murmured.

He looked at the clock on the dashboard. Time was against him. Even if he drove through the night and got the first plane out of Alice Springs tomorrow morning, there was still a four-hour drive from Melbourne to Bridgefield. At best, they'd be back in the Western District around sundown tomorrow.

Ned listened to the medical terms Jonno used, knuckles white against the steering wheel. His mind flew through the possibilities, but each new option required more dicking around than he had time for. What he'd gain in catching a flight, he'd lose in making arrangements for the van.

He slapped the steering wheel with his hand.

'Thought you were only back in the country for forty-eight hours?'

'I am,' said Jonno. 'The icebreaker's all set to sail from Hobart. I'll let you know how he is when I get to the hospital, but I reckon I'll cancel my trip.'

'Don't be a bloody idiot. A research trip like this doesn't come along every week. Colin will be fine. He's too stubborn to die.'

Ned called the hospital as soon as Jonno hung up, but the nurse's grave update didn't instil any faith in him.

'I'll get the doctor to call you back, he's arranging a transfer to a city hospital as we speak.'

Staring into the dark night, Ned rubbed the bridge of his nose, trying to smooth out the indent made by his glasses.

'What a bloody mess.'

A little hand wrapped around his.

'What mess, Daddy?' Willow's sleepy lilt was followed by a yawn.

Ned looked at her, glad his little girl didn't realise quite how many answers there were to that question. The mess they had found themselves in when his now ex-wife, Fleur, decided parenting was 'too hard'. The mess they lived in for a week or so each time they unloaded the van at a new rental. The mess of paperwork each new school required for the kids' short-term enrolments.

'Shhh, go back to sleep,' he said, keeping his voice low.

He drove into the bleak night, reluctantly stopping at a motel in Tennant Creek and getting an earful from the owner when he knocked on the reception door.

'You know what time it is, mate?'

Ned apologised and paid handsomely for a seedy-looking room with an op-shop aroma.

Willow stirred but Doug barely flickered an eyelid when he carried each of them into the motel and tucked them between the mothball-scented sheets. Ned didn't have the same luck. Even after a quick shower, sleep proved elusive. After a decade of avoiding trips to Victoria, he couldn't get back to his home state fast enough. Would they make it in time?

2

Dim light crept in around the edges of the motel curtains as Ned twisted his head towards the bedside table. The alarm clock read 4.49 a.m. *Close enough to morning.*

He tugged his phone from its charger.

Jonno's text message update was brief and to the point.

Not good, they've transferred Colin to Geelong for surgery.
Don't take the scenic route.

He crept out of the motel room, closed the door softly behind him and called his brother. Straight to voicemail. Jonno was either out of battery or snatching some sleep.

Ned phoned the new hospital, working his way through the automated menu as he unlocked the van and pulled his backpack from the passenger footwell, and was finally connected to the correct nurse's station.

'The operation didn't go as planned, I'm afraid. We can't do anything more for your father, Mr Gardiner, except make him comfortable,' the nurse said gently. 'If you're travelling from interstate, I'd recommend you get here sooner rather than later.'

Ned thanked her woodenly, swallowed the lump in his throat and walked inside. He turned the shower to scorching and let the needle-like droplets do their thing, watching the water run down the riot of inkwork on his chest. The tattoos had been there so long he barely noticed them unless he was standing in front of a mirror, or if the children tried to replicate them on paper.

Willow and Doug were starting to stir by the time he'd pulled a clean set of clothes from his overnight bag.

'Morning, munchkin,' he said, smoothing the hair away from Willow's face.

She rubbed the sleep from her eyes. 'Is it early?'

'We'll catch the sunrise if you get your skates on.'

She scrambled out from under the quilt, slipped on her glasses and was ready to go before Doug was even upright.

'Can't we sleep in today, Dad?' The little boy wrapped his arms around Ned's neck and allowed himself to be carried to the bathroom.

'Quick shower, then we'll hit the frog and toad, right?'

Ned ushered Doug into the shower, then headed outside again. He found the van's front door wide open, with Willow neatly arranging her journal and pencils on the bench seat.

'What time do you think we'll get to Uluru tomorrow? Does it change colour when the sun sets on it? Or when it rains? I heard it's like an iceberg, with only a tenth of the rock above the surface. Uncle Jonno told me that, and he knows all about icebergs, doesn't he, Dad?'

Ned quickly weighed up which of her queries to answer first, knowing there would be an avalanche of questions to follow no matter how many he answered.

'Uncle Jonno does indeed,' he said, deciding to level with her. He held up a hand before she launched into a running commentary of Antarctic facts and figures. 'Speaking of Uncle Jonno, he called last night to say your grandfather's really sick.'

He felt uselessly light on details, but when he'd finished explaining, Willow laid a gentle hand on his arm, her big eyes brimming with sympathy. She nodded sagely and reached for her notebook. With a steady hand, she put a line through the itinerary she'd so carefully written and illustrated and tucked the book back into the glovebox.

'Well, what are we waiting for, then?'

Ned pressed his lips together, wondering how he'd got so lucky to raise such a kid, and pulled her into a hug. *Fleur doesn't know what she's missing . . .*

'I'll drag your brother out of the shower. You grab the tucker bag,' he said.

Doug was still standing under the shower, half asleep, when Ned stepped back inside the motel room. *Like chalk and cheese,* he thought, switching off the taps and pressing a towel into his son's hands.

He'd just hoisted the backpacks over his shoulder and scoured the room for errant socks when a squeal came from outside. Ned dashed out to the parking lot, terror turning to relief when he saw that Willow wasn't being loaded into the back of a Torana. She beamed over her shoulder. He groaned when he saw what she was holding.

'Look who was hiding in the back of the van! Isn't it lucky I found him?' said Willow, cuddling the squirming tabby cat.

'You've gotta be joking me. Did you put Flopsy in there?'

Willow shook her head, eyes wide with innocence, tightening her grip on the feline stowaway.

'Flopsy!' Doug went from semi-comatose to wide awake in two seconds, sprinting out of the motel room to embrace the cat.

'We'll have to leave him here,' said Ned, crossly.

'You bloody well won't,' came a shrill voice. A lady in a khaki uniform stepped out of the room beside theirs and stood next to a 4x4 with the same logo as her shoulder patch. A parks and wildlife ranger! Ned cursed under his breath.

'He's not our cat,' he explained. 'Just a stray.'

The ranger folded her arms and looked at the children, who turned on their biggest puppy-dog eyes, fawning over the cat.

No, no, no, thought Ned. This was not a war he wanted to wage at this very minute.

'We don't have a cat carrier,' said Ned.

The lady looked smug as she pulled a cat trap from the back of her car.

'I don't know where you come from, mate,' she said, peering at their number plate, 'but it's an offence to abandon cats in the territory. I suppose you could surrender it to the local pound . . .' Each word was drawn out in that territory drawl he'd noticed during their four-month stint in the Top End. 'I've got their number on my phone somewhere,' she said, trawling through her phone at a snail's pace. 'But they don't open until 10 a.m.'

Blowing out a frustrated breath, Ned loaded the cat into the cage. 'We don't have time for that,' he said. 'We'll deal with him when we get to Victoria.'

Doug scrambled onto the bench seat.

'It's okay, Flopsy,' crooned Doug, patting the cat through the wire bars. The tabby threw itself against the wire door in a kamikaze attempt. Willow piled in beside him.

Ned reversed out of the tight motel car park and pointed the van in the direction of the highway.

'Will Grandad be at the farm when we get there or will he still be in hospital?' asked Willow.

Ned thought of the update from the ICU nurse in Geelong.

'I'm not sure,' he said, truthfully. 'We'll have to wait to hear from Uncle Jonno.'

'Isn't he on his way to the South Pole?' said Doug. 'Will there be polar bears? And reindeers? And killer whales?'

Willow launched into an explanation of the differences between the north and south poles as Ned watched light creep across the horizon.

Doug listened carefully, then scratched his head. 'Do you think Mum's gone on one of those big icebreaker ships?'

Ned inhaled deeply. This day was going from bad to worse, and it wasn't even 7 a.m. Last he'd heard, their mother Fleur was living in an ashram near Mumbai, with no plans to return to the family she'd started and quickly abandoned. Not a subject he felt like rehashing today.

Pushing her dark hair away from her eyes, Willow shook her head. 'Uncle Jonno's ship doesn't leave for a few days yet. They don't have icebreakers in India. That's got nothing to do with teaching yoga.'

A herd of feral goats grazing in the scrub proved the perfect distraction. While they were out of phone range, the children's endless questions were on full throttle, and continued well into the morning. Ned answered as best he could, a third of his attention on the road, a third on their chatter, and a third on what lay ahead.

By the time the next town came into view, they were all ready for a pit stop. He pulled up in front of a weatherboard store that had been fashioned to look like a miner's hut. Ned's stomach grumbled as a customer came out the front door. The aroma of baked goods was too good to resist. He handed Willow $10.

'We'll be in the playground,' he said, nodding to the stretch of grass and newish play equipment.

'Right, Dougo, that cat's going to want a toilet stop,' Ned said. After looping a belt though the cat's collar as a makeshift lead, he scanned the park for a discreet spot where Flopsy could relieve himself.

'Come on, pretty kitty,' said Doug, carrying the cat across the grassy knoll, just as a Jack Russell bounded up to them. Flopsy wrenched himself backwards and Doug was left holding a belt, and empty collar and a handful of tabby fur.

Saturday dawned as a replica of the day before, tempting Diana outside with her morning coffee. Even though it was a whisker off 7 a.m., the garden was full of life. Bees zipped between the roses, grass parrots fossicked for seeds and the pair of wallabies that lived in the back paddock stopped for a drink at the water trough.

'As long as you keep your big clod hoppers off my dahlia patch, we'll get along just fine,' she said, raising her mug in their direction.

Diana loved it when the backyard was chock-a-block with the boys, the trampoline heaving with their bodies and the animated soundtrack to their fun, but there was something special about the dewy mornings before everyone else was up. She'd tried journalling and meditation after Pete's death, but the mindfulness tasks had felt like a chore after the months passed and the sharpest grief receded. Early-morning starts, on the other hand, had been a constant for her two years of solo parenting. The sunrises grounded her—they were a reminder that each day was a fresh start.

Diana looked across to the new dahlia paddock. The flower farm was another fresh start in the making, a chance to turn a long-held passion into an income.

Sitting her mug on the fence post, she fished her phone from her dressing gown pocket and snapped a picture of her progress. She opened Facebook, uploaded the image to the Micro Flower Farms Facebook page, and watched as a handful of comments popped up. She sipped her coffee, smiling as she scrolled through the messages.

Denise from Wagga Wagga said it all: 'Look at those mountains. Heaven on Earth.'

'Smashing view, Diana! I'd spend all day in the garden too with that backdrop,' commented Michelle from The Gap.

Diana laughed at the next comment from Phil in Linton. 'Reckon the dahlias will be brave enough to try to compete with that vista? LOL.'

By the time she'd finished her coffee, Diana had browsed a dozen different posts within the group, liking them and also dropping comments of encouragement to her fellow farmers, just like they'd done for her. They'd been united by a common interest, shared goals and a determination to turn a patch of dirt into something special.

She scrolled a little more, landing on Sadie Woodford's gorgeous page. Inspiration struck as she scrolled through photos from the flower guru's in-person workshops and teaser posts about her forthcoming book, which was already slated to be a bestseller.

I need something big to get Darling Dahlias off to a flying start, and what better person to ask than the biggest name in the Aussie flower industry?

Diana typed a quick text to her friend Bron, who lived in Melbourne and worked at the agency that handled Sadie's PR.

You know how Sadie's scouting out venues to launch her new coffee table book? Reckon she'd consider a fledgling flower farm run by one of her very first students? x Diana

Diana caught her bottom lip between her teeth, feeling a tingle of excitement as three dots appeared on the screen. If there was an opportunity to nab Australia's favourite flower grower and bestselling non-fiction author, she wanted to chase it.

Worth a shot! If you don't ask, you don't get. xx Bron

Diana pushed aside the fear that after so many students and several years Sadie had probably forgotten meeting her. Instead, she plucked up her courage and sent an email to the woman who was inspiring a new generation of flower farmers, one workshop and book at a time.

3

The tall branches swayed every time the cat scurried higher. Ned pulled a wrinkled hanky from his shorts and squatted down next to Doug, and brushed the tears from his cheeks.

'Here, buddy, blow.'

Doug did as he was told, his eyes welling as he looked up at the tree.

Willow tore another strip off the sweet bun and handed it to her brother. 'Eat this,' she said, hands on her hips like a mother hen.

Ned tried again, more gently this time. 'We need to leave, mate. Flopsy could play this game for hours.'

Doug's bottom lip quivered. Ned's lips thinned. Jonno's phone call had briefly distracted him from the cat rescue mission, but his latest update had been grim. Their father's organs were steadily shutting down and the doctors estimated another few days at best. It took every skerrick of his patience not to bundle the kids into Stan the Van and tear off down the highway until they reached Colin's bedside. Yet here he was thousands of kilometres away in outback Northern Territory playing chasey with a stray cat.

'Unless you can climb up the tree and grab him, we have to leave.'

Doug took another step towards the ladder they'd borrowed from the bakery.

'It's now or never, mate,' said Ned, looking at his watch again. Their ten-minute pit stop had stretched to an hour. He steadied the ladder against the base of the tree and gave Doug an encouraging smile.

'Just stop before the branches get too bendy,' he said.

Flopsy meowed from the top of the tree. Doug called him as he climbed, and for one joyous moment, the cat started moving towards him.

About time, thought Ned.

'He's coming, Dad,' called Doug. He twisted, relief written across his little face right up until his hand slipped.

Ned swore, his heart lurching. He'd have a son *and* a father in hospital at this rate. Doug scrambled to get a grip. The branches whipped back and forth, dislodging the cat.

'Flopsy!' Doug shrieked, clinging on like a koala.

Ned positioned himself under the tree as best he could, but the cat twisted and turned in the air as he fell, a mass of yowling fur. Ned closed his eyes as claws slashed in every direction.

Gotcha. 'Willow! Get the cage before I lose an eye.'

Flopsy squirmed and hissed in his arms, still swinging like a prize fighter. By the time Ned had wedged the cat into the cage, plucked Doug from the tree and returned the ladder to the bakery, his patience was well and truly zapped.

He caught a glimpse of his face in the rear-view mirror as he reversed out of the parking lot. *Freddy Krueger, eat your heart out*, he thought, dabbing at the thin, bloody scratches. Nothing like making a good impression on his return to the Western District.

Bron must have been sitting on her phone because she answered immediately when Diana called that afternoon.

'Guess who's going to be working with *the* Sadie Woodford?' Diana said.

Bron giggled. 'Fancy that.'

'She just replied. You must have put in a good word!'

'Maybe just a little nudge,' Bron admitted. 'What's the point of running a PR agency if I can't help old friends every now and then, and leak exciting news? I'm looking at the early pages of her new book as we speak. This one's all about dahlias.'

'Dahlias,' Diana breathed. While most flower farmers stayed incognito, the talented Sadie had an almost cult-like following. It didn't hurt that she had the Midas touch with a range of linked products.

'In fact, I can't believe I didn't think of it first. You, as a graduate of her inaugural workshop, it's marketing gold. I just added my ten cents, and as soon as she saw the photos of your beautiful Grampians backdrop, she loved the idea!'

Diana suddenly felt nervous. Darling Dahlias was only a micro-flower farm in its infancy. What if she couldn't get it up to scratch in time, or the dahlias were all wiped out by a virus or an army of hungry grasshoppers? She found herself breathing a little faster.

'I can hear you hyperventilating from here, Diana. The book's not out until next March and—' Bron cleared her throat triumphantly, 'it's a win–win situation. You'll get Darling Dahlias plastered across all the media, and Sadie's got that gorgeous setting to work with.'

Diana stayed outside after the call had ended, slightly starstruck. Sadie had not only remembered her, but was also keen to launch her new book and business venture in Bridgefield.

Diana looked back at the rows of freshly turned dirt and tapped out a quick message to Colin Gardiner. While Sadie was the national queen of the floral world, Colin was the local equivalent. A similar age to her father, Colin had a lifetime of breeding and showing flowers under his belt, and he happily shared his expertise with anyone who chose to listen. It was one thing to be growing flowers for sale, but another kettle of fish to host a launch party. And if there was anyone who knew how to make her property look its best, it would be Colin.

As she checked her phone, Diana realised Colin hadn't replied to her last text. She checked her Facebook page. He hadn't logged on that morning either. She typed up a quick message.

> Hey, Colin! You still dropping the last crate of tubers off today? I can collect if you like, wait till you hear our news. We're going to be flat out getting this garden media-worthy.

Diana composed a new message, adding her sisters Penny, Angie and Lara, and their father Angus into a group text. *They'll be just as excited.* As her finger hovered over the 'send' button, she could almost hear Pete's voice in her head, reminding her about counting chickens before they hatched. *Maybe I should wait until Sadie's event is confirmed until I shout it from the rooftops.* And while the idea excited her every bit as much as it scared the pants off her, she knew her mentor Colin would help her every step of the way.

Diana pocketed the phone and headed inside, straightening photo frames as she went and rubbing fingerprints from the family portrait taken before Pete died. Diana's hand hovered at the edge of the frame. Pete was never one to act spontaneously. Would he have considered hosting an event before they were a hundred per cent ready? She shook her head, knowing if it hadn't been on their five-year plan, it wouldn't have got a look in.

She pulled out her diary and counted ahead. Five months until Sadie's launch in March. An opportunity to showcase the flower farm to such a great audience didn't come around every day and she was ecstatic that she'd made it happen.

Ned drove on autopilot, pausing only briefly at each stop, as they made their way south.

The sign to Whyalla and Port Lincoln flickered past on their third day of travelling. On any other occasion, Ned would've pointed out the sign, told his kids a story about the road leading to the world's best oysters, and maybe even a story or two about the time he and Jonno had made the interstate trek to attend Oyster-Fest, but his hands stayed gripped on the wheel. The nurse's latest update repeated in his mind on loop.

'Your father's asking for you . . . making him comfortable.'

Flopsy—who was still distinctly unimpressed with the cage—occasionally let out an indignant meow, but the children stoically accepted the ten-hour driving days. Ned guiltily conceded their requests for fast food, barely tasting the chicken burger or chips on the way through Bordertown.

'C'mon, Stan my Man,' he muttered, urging the van into Victoria. After what felt like forever, the sign for Geelong finally loomed on the horizon.

'Nearly there, kiddos,' Ned said, managing a weary smile for Willow and Doug. 'Half an hour, tops.'

The phone's musical ringtone cut through the silence in the cabin. He'd only spoken to Jonno an hour earlier. With a sinking feeling in his stomach and the lights of Geelong just visible in the distance, Ned pulled the moving van into a parking bay to answer his brother's call.

'I'm sorry, mate. He's gone.'

Ned squeezed his eyes shut. *So close. If we hadn't spent an hour getting the bloody cat from the tree. If we'd switched to a hire car and worried about moving our stuff later. If we'd got on a plane in Alice Springs and flown down. Hell, if I'd just made the effort to visit.*

Shoulda, coulda, woulda.

'Did your dad die?' Doug asked quietly when Ned ended the call.

Willow threaded her arms around him, gently squeezing him closer. Doug offered up the last of the Caramello koalas from his stash. Their small gestures, when they had barely known their grandfather, were nearly his undoing. The best Ned could do was nod.

4

Diana pulled into the cricket ground, glad they were playing an away side this weekend. It would have been torture keeping her exciting news to herself if her family were at the game.

'You look as proud as punch,' said the coach as Diana walked into the clubrooms. She followed his gaze through the windows to where Cameron was taking his place on the pitch.

'I've seen a few cricketers come through the ranks, but that boy's something special,' said the coach. 'He makes it look easy—no wonder the premier league wants a piece of him.'

Diana nodded, not correcting his assumption. Yes, she was proud of her son—of *all* her boys—but the coach didn't know why she was really brimming with excitement.

'Cameron's head will be so big he won't be able to walk through the door at this rate.'

'As long as he doesn't forget his country roots when he's wearing the baggy green,' insisted the coach, not deterred by Diana's gentle reprimand. 'He can come back and teach the youngsters about what it takes to make the big league.'

The coach gave her a wink and smoothed his grey moustache. 'I can feel it in my waters, Diana. Pete knew that boy was destined for great things as soon as he put a cricket bat in his hands. With his natural talent, and all the hard work you've put in, he's got it in the bag.'

And sure enough, Cameron barely seemed to break a sweat as he led the local A-Grade side to victory again. Everyone was in high spirits on the drive home, Diana listening with one ear as the boys talked cricket stats, batting techniques and run averages. Colin was yet to reply. He was the only person she could share the launch news with, aside from Bron, and it was all sorts of strange that he hadn't texted back immediately. *Something's up.*

Diana slowed as she crested the hill and turned when the thick stand of paperbark trees parted for their driveway. As they unloaded the four-wheel drive, she made up her mind.

'Who wants to take scones to Colin's place?'

The three younger boys cheered their approval. Cameron grabbed the lion's share of the cricket equipment and nodded in the direction of the shower.

'I've got to scrub up before Georgie gets in,' he said, heading up the steps. Cameron's girlfriend had been spending more and more time at their house, and even though she'd had a talk with Cameron about respect, consent and birth control, she still worried about the logistics of leaving a teenage couple alone in the house. *Better under my roof, where I know they're safe, than sneaking around behind my back, I suppose.*

Diana watched Cam's muscles flex as he swung Leo up onto his shoulders and carried him into the house. *He's seventeen, not a toddler,* she reminded herself, shelving the thought.

After a day in the sun, Diana was keen to wash off the sunscreen too.

'Any volunteers to help with scones while I jump in the shower?'

'I'll measure,' said Harry.

'I'll crack the eggs,' added Elliot.

Not to be outdone, Leo tugged on an apron and started leafing through the recipe book. The handwritten scone recipe was easy to find, with smudges of flour and egg white reflecting its popularity.

'I'm cutting the scones out,' Leo said.

She left them in charge of prepping the scone dough, a job they'd helped with countless times.

The oven was humming when she strode back into the kitchen shortly after. A layer of flour covered the benchtop, with a big white blob of dough in the middle. Elliot jumped up from the couch, looking guilty, and Harry flicked off the cartoons.

'I thought you guys were making the scones?'

'We couldn't find the scone cutter,' said Leo, jumping up from a beanbag and promptly spilling a bowl of popcorn on the carpet.

Diana pulled the dustpan and brush from underneath the sink and traded the TV remote for the cleaning tools.

'Righto, I'll get them in the oven while you guys clean up. Elliot, you're whipping the cream. No licking the beaters until you've turned them off at the power point this time, though,' she warned, shuddering at the memory.

Twenty minutes later, she filled the car with three out of four boys, a warm basket of scones and all the trimmings for the type of impromptu afternoon tea Colin loved.

Ned woke to light glinting in through the tatty net curtains. The sounds of the farm floated in through the window he'd cranked open last night when they'd arrived, stunned and travel weary.

The frogs from the dam sang a familiar chorus. If Ned strained his hearing, he could make out the soft clucking of his father's chickens in the paddocks beyond, but no amount of soothing rural sounds stopped the sudden barrage of grief. *An hour too late.*

Wakefulness brought more regret as he recalled their rush to the hospital, the condolences from the nurses and their brief reunion with Jonno.

No sense trying to sleep now. Ned walked down the hallway, checking on the children. After the night they'd had, he hoped they'd get at least another few hours of sleep.

A meow came from behind him and he turned to find the tabby cat trailing in his wake, uncharacteristically friendly— probably because of the possibility of breakfast. Ned's fingers skimmed the thin, red welts on his face that had raised more than one eyebrow at the hospital last night, but for some inexplicable reason, he was comforted by the stray's presence.

Closing the kitchen door, he called Jonno.

'You get any sleep?'

Jonno had looked as shellshocked as he felt at the hospital last night. He had stayed with the van, watching his sleeping niece and nephew while Ned said a final goodbye to Colin. It had been hard to correlate the quiet, hard-working man with the still, shrunken figure in the hospital bed.

Jonno gave a wry laugh. 'I probably got more sleep than you. Don't know why you didn't spend the night here in Geelong.'

Ned shook his head and looked around his father's house. It had never felt like home to him, but after seeing Colin last night he'd wanted to come back to Bridgefield.

'I don't know either,' Ned replied, his voice cracking. He closed his eyes and leaned against the sink. They were both quiet for a beat. Birds twittered outside the window, and the bellowing of a speaker came down the phone line. Jonno was already at Melbourne airport, ready to fly to Hobart and join the rest of the research crew. Ned took a shaky breath as he filled the kettle, rifling through several cupboards before he located the mugs.

'What time's your ship sailing?'

'This arvo. I would've stayed if Colin hadn't . . .' Jonno trailed off, also struggling to find the right words. 'It's the last expedition heading south until summer, and the grant funding's tied to this trip.' Ned heard the indecision in his brother's voice. 'Bugger it, I'll cancel.'

'Don't be daft,' said Ned. 'I can keep an eye on the farm for a week or so. I'll track down a local who can watch it until you get back.'

Ned's phone buzzed and he pulled it away from his ear to see a text message.

'I've just sent you a number for a guy named Butch,' said Jonno. 'I made a few calls yesterday while I was waiting around the hospital. Butch should be able to keep the farm ticking along until we work out what to do with it. I've asked him to come as soon as possible.'

Ned's guilt and regret stirred together in a nasty combination as he heaped a bigger than usual spoonful of instant coffee into a mug. He'd failed at keeping in touch with Colin, and missed saying goodbye by a measly hour, and it stung that his little brother didn't think he could handle the farm for even a short spell.

'Jeez, anyone would think you don't trust me,' Ned joked.

'Let's just say, I can't imagine you tossing in pharmacy for free-range eggs.' His brother's voice might have been shaky, but it wasn't mean.

'Course not.' Ned took a swig of coffee, burning his lips on the strong brew. 'My next two contracts are all lined up,

starting with a discount pharmacy in Mount Gambier next
week.'

'That's what I thought. Lock up when you leave. And maybe
suss out the tenant in the hut.'

Ned frowned, turning to look out the kitchen window. He
set his cup down on the bench, coffee slopping over the rim.

'That old shearers' hut is still standing?'

'I think so. Not sure if Colin goes through a real estate
agent, but you'll want to let them know.'

Their mother had been the last person to stay in that little
fibro box, before she'd left for Queensland. Ned didn't realise
it'd been rented out since. He looked around and reluctantly
faced the fact that there was probably a lot he didn't know
about the workings of this place.

Ned sat at the dining table long after Jonno had rung off.
From inside, he watched the sun make its ascent across the
eastern horizon. The loose roofing tin responsible for Colin's
accident was still flapping noisily overhead, but that wasn't
the only issue. Even from where he sat, he could see that the
post-and-rail fence between the orchard and the potting shed
was sagging, a branch rested half on top of the old pigsty and
sheets of rusted tin were scattered around the closest paddock.

What kind of storm had swept through here? It looked like
more than one storm's worth of disarray.

He opened the glass door and stepped outside. Butterflies
swarmed on the flowers. Birds called. Plants bloomed in every
corner of the garden, in the pots that lined the verandah, and
in the baskets that hung from the eaves. The flowers would
keep blooming, and the chickens would keep laying, but all
Ned could think of was the man who'd never again tend to
this garden or collect the eggs from his beloved chooks.

He stepped back inside as laughter echoed down the hallway.

'There you are, Dad! This place is so cool. Did you see the chair in the kitchen? It's got a pumper thing that moves it up and down,' said Doug, clutching Flopsy in his arms.

'Colin's had that old dentist chair for years,' Ned said as he followed his son inside to show him how to work the mechanism on the back. Willow gasped as the chair reclined until it was parallel to the ground. 'Perfect for ripping out wobbly teeth.'

'Let's get cracking, kiddos. The hens will be pecking through the doors of the chook tractors if we don't let them out soon,' he said.

'Do the chickens drive tractors?'

Ned laughed at his daughter's incredulous expression.

'They're hen houses on wheels, that can be towed around the paddock. I'll show you, get your boots on.'

The keys to Colin's old Land Rover ute were in the ignition, just as he'd known they would be. Ned tried to see the property through his children's eyes as he drove down the laneway, unlatched gates and pulled up outside the first chook tractor.

'You're right, Dad. It's like a caravan. Or a shed on wheels,' said Willow. She jumped out of the ute and circled the tin structure, eager for the first glimpse of her grandfather's hens.

'They're so noisy,' said Doug, clamping his hands over his ears. The clucking intensified as Ned unlatched a side panel and swung open the awning. Doug hopped from foot to foot as the hens ravaged the grass at his feet.

Willow stood stock still, fascinated by the birds. 'Can I name them, Dad?'

Ned lifted one steel awning after another until the entire northern side of the chook tractor was exposed.

'All of the chickens? There's quite a few flocks on the property, you'll run out of names pretty quick. Also might be tricky to tell them apart,' he said, watching the near-identical ISA Brown hens spread across the grass like a creeping chestnut carpet.

He opened a side door and stepped up onto the wire-mesh platform, cranking the manual conveyor belt.

'Wow!' Willow's eyes grew wide as the eggs wobbled towards them. 'That's so cool.' After showing her how to fill the egg trays, Ned left her to it. He found Doug on his hands and knees, digging for worms.

'They love them, Dad. Look at this.' Doug tossed the worm in the air and giggled as a handful of chickens raced to it, fluffy bums waddling and wings flapping.

Should've brought them here years ago.

Diana smiled as Colin's gardens came into view. They were always a kaleidoscope of colour, distracting visitors from the eyesore of old sheds, piles of scrap metal that Colin joked were his retirement plan, and the dilapidated granny flat in the distance.

'Now remember, no touching all the stuff,' she said. Diana pulled up next to an old van and pointed to Harry. 'You especially. Those vases are more fragile than they look, and Colin's got enough to do without replacing another one,' she said sternly.

'I get first dibs on the dentist chair,' called Leo, racing through the jasmine arbour before Diana had a chance to remind them to knock. She hurried past the new variety of sweet peas Colin had been so excited to share on her last visit, catching the boys just before they barged in.

'Steady on, you lot,' Diana said, rapping on the glass door. 'I think Colin's poorly. Mind your manners.'

The boys fidgeted as they waited.

Diana knocked again.

Harry peered in through the glass.

'There's a cat on the bench. I thought Colin didn't like cats?'

Diana heard children's voices. Maybe coming unannounced was a bad idea. She looked again at the unfamiliar van parked in the drive.

Visitors?

'Colin? It's Diana,' she called, following the pavers around the side of the house.

As she rounded the corner she bumped right into the barrel-chest of a man who was definitely not Colin. The scones went flying. A deep voice matched his solid build.

'Ten-second rule?'

'Always,' she replied.

Their knees bumped as they both knelt. Together they returned the scones to the basket. It was only when they stood up that she noticed his glasses, the sadness in his bloodshot eyes and the thin red welts running from his forehead to his chin.

Stop staring, already.

'Ned Gardiner.' He relinquished the last scone and held out a hand. Diana shook it, finding his hand warm and his grip strong.

Gardiner . . .

She spotted the bowl of cream Elliot had dumped beside Colin's pot plants and realised the boys had bolted into the backyard as if they owned the place.

'I'm Diana McIntyre, and those little blighters have completely forgotten their manners. We don't normally go skulking around people's backyards. You haven't seen Colin, have you?'

Diana glanced around the yard, then back at the tall man before her. Her smile faltered at the pained look on his face. He gestured towards the wicker chairs. For a moment, she was reminded of the day her father arrived at her door to tell her Pete had collapsed at the saleyards. Diana started making a mental tally of what might have gone wrong as unease welled in her stomach. Car accident? Farm accident?

'You might want to sit down.'

She sank into the chair closest to the sliding door and braced for news she knew she wasn't going to like.

5

Ned wished he'd delivered the news with more panache and felt at a loss as to how to comfort this stranger, when he'd barely processed the shock himself.

'I should've come yesterday,' Diana said, balling up the colourful fabric of her skirt. 'It wasn't like him to ignore my messages, especially when he had more dahlias for me. Oh, Colin . . .'

He heard the catch in her voice. Had she known Colin well?

The sound of laughter and yahooing from the backyard was answer enough. Her boys looked at home swinging from the rusty old monkey bars with Willow and Doug. He could just imagine Colin deep in conversation with this petite woman, with her home-baked deliveries and shared interest in dahlias. *Just like Jessie . . .*

Ned clenched the arms of the chair. Memories of the little sister he'd lost years earlier felt fresh again when mixed with his grief at his father's unexpected passing. Colin and Jessie had both loved flowers.

'Can I get you a tea? It'd be a shame to let the scones go to waste,' he said gently.

He slid open the door and gestured for her to go first, surprised when she slipped her shoes off at the door mat. Now there was something he hadn't seen in years.

She set the basket of scones on the bench.

'So are you the marine biologist or the pharmacist?'

'Jonno's on his way to Antarctica for a research trip. I'm the pharmacist. Milk? Sugar?'

Diana's long hair caught the light when she nodded.

'Both please.'

Flopsy wandered into the kitchen and splayed out on the patch of sunshine warming the slate floor. Diana crouched beside the cat, and Ned watched in surprise as he stayed put, lapping up the attention.

'This guy must be a good traveller. Colin said you spent a lot of time on the road?'

He shared the tale of their stowaway stray, pleased when the story brought a little comic relief to the kitchen. And a little colour to her pale face.

Most of the children came running when they carried the tray of food outside to the table.

'Not hungry, Harry?'

'Nah, not yet,' the boy said, swinging upside down on the monkey bars.

Crumbs and dollops of cream went everywhere as they filled their plates, making Ned glad he'd served up outside.

'They look like ones from a shop,' said Willow, piling her scone high with cream.

'*Better* than ones from a shop,' said Ned, taking a bite. But instead of the sweet taste he'd expected, Ned almost gagged, trying to chew without screwing up his face in disgust. A giggle came from the monkey bars.

He glanced across the wooden table as Doug spat his mouthful onto the lawn. Willow shot him an incredulous look—*Grosssssss!*—as she put her barely nibbled scone back on the plate. Diana looked up from spreading jam on her youngest son's scones, alarmed.

Ned washed down the mouthful with scalding tea. *She seems nice, but these are the worst scones I've ever tasted.*

Diana felt her face getting warm. Nobody had ever reacted to her scones like that before. They'd won more blue ribbons at the Bridgefield Show than any of her sponges, yo-yo biscuits or fruit cakes.

She could see Ned was trying to be polite, but the kids weren't such good actors. Leo looked like he'd sucked on a lemon.

'Ewwww!'

Diana broke a small piece off and nibbled it. 'Ergh! It's like eating a salt shaker,' she said, pushing the plate away. She glared at Harry, then rose from the picnic table and strode across to the monkey bars.

Not hungry, my foot! That sentence alone should've set alarm bells ringing.

'What on earth did you do to those scones?' she said, frogmarching him back to the table.

'Nothing, Mum.' But his shifty expression told a different story.

Not only had they gatecrashed a house and imposed themselves on a man whose father had just died, but they'd also nearly poisoned him and his children.

Too mortified to even look in Ned's direction, Diana picked her plate up and forced it into Harry's hands.

'Eat one, then. Go on, finish that one with cream and jam on it. And if you can't do that, you'd better come up with a darn good apology.'

Ned's son shook his head. 'I don't think you want to eat it,' Doug said sagely.

Elliot hooted with laughter and nudged Leo, who was now wiping his tongue on the hem of his T-shirt.

What must this family think of us?

'Colin said he liked salt. So, I added a few spoons instead of caster sugar. I thought he might like it.'

'Big spoons,' added Leo, knowingly.

Diana thought back to previous visits, trying but failing to remember a conversation about salt. Ned stood and began piling the terrible scones back onto the tray.

'That's true,' Ned said. 'Colin put salt on everything. Reckon that dose may have been a bit heavy even for him, though.'

After an apology from Harry, the children ran off, eager to see who could throw the salty scones the furthest.

Diana helped clear away the jammy knives and cream-covered spoons.

'He'll send me to an early grave, that boy . . .' Diana stopped sharply as she realised what she'd just said, and winced.

'Next time we'll bring decent scones, I promise. I really am sorry about your dad.' Diana rubbed her nose, hoping to ward off the prickling tears, and smoothed down her skirt. Looking at the floral fabric reminded her of the news she'd been so excited to share with Colin. She bit down hard on her lip.

How can I even think about the flower farm when Colin's just died? She berated herself as she rounded up the boys and headed to the car.

Doug and Willow stood by their father's side at the edge of the driveway, their deep hazel eyes and dark hair were evidently a strong Gardiner gene. She felt another wave of sadness for her friend and mentor.

'Thanks for keeping my boys company. I'm so sorry about your grandfather.'

'We didn't really know him,' Willow said, simply.

Ned's cheeks flushed.

Diana looked away, hoping to spare him any embarrassment. *How long since he'd last visited?* Although their conversations had revolved around flowers, not family, she knew Colin had never been overrun with babysitting duties or visitors.

Her gaze landed on the garden shed where Colin stored his dahlia tubers. Would it be tacky to ask Ned about the last crate of dahlias? *If you don't ask, you don't get.*

'I know it's not perfect timing, but Colin had another crate of dahlias for me. He was going to drop them off this week,' she said. 'I can grab them now, save me barging in on you again.' *Or, worse,* she thought, *letting them waste away in the shed when they could be in the ground, blooming in Colin's honour.* If Pete's death had taught her anything, it was that wishing, denying and pining wouldn't bring anyone back.

'Knock yourself out. Do you want me to help you find them?'

Diana shook her head, looking towards the garden shed Colin had been so proud of. His son Ned was holding it together, but something in his manner made her suspect the shed would be a step too far today. It was like her mum's sewing room in those weeks after she died—too much to handle when the grief was so fresh.

'It's fine, I know where he kept them.'

'Just make sure the door's latched on your way out,' said Ned. 'The brown snakes were always pretty fond of that shed.' His voice was thick with anguish. She offered a small smile before he turned abruptly and headed back to the house.

Oblivious to the emotion behind his father's silent exit, Doug followed Diana and the boys to the shed. Willow was torn, but curiosity won out. The bright young girl's eyes widened as they entered.

'It's the prettiest shed ever,' Willow said, studying the wall of faded posters, different colours for each month of sowing suggestions, A3 charts with moon cycles and huge prints of different dahlia varieties. Doug gravitated towards the rows of trophies and sashes that Colin had won with his show flowers. Diana went in search of the plastic crates, finding them by Colin's workbench.

'Look at this, Doug!' Willow whooped. 'It's Dad. Check out his hair.' She bounded over with a framed newspaper clipping. Diana leaned over for a look and smothered a grin.

Teenage Ned was weedy and sporting a mullet. His delighted grin as he collected a trophy was worlds away from the reserved and weary man she'd met earlier.

'What flowers are these?' said Doug, toying with the plastic seed trays on the workbenches. Tiny green shoots poked out of the trays, searching for the light, unaware that the green-thumbed man who'd potted them up so lovingly wouldn't be there to see them in full bloom.

'Not sure.' Diana managed as she swallowed and herded them out of the shed and shut the door firmly behind her.

She'd been so excited to share her good news as she had driven down the driveway an hour ago, but as she left, she had the distinct sense that the future of her business was now a lot like the future of the little seedlings on the potting table. Although eggs were Colin's enterprise, dahlias were his passion. His gentle guidance, combined with Sadie's workshops, had been instrumental in making her flower farm a reality, and he'd promised to work beside her as the business evolved. Would Darling Dahlias bloom and flourish, or wither away without Colin's expertise and guidance?

The chickens were already roosting by the time Ned drove to the first paddock that evening.

'I'm winding the first one, Dad,' said Doug, reefing the car door open before Ned had even pulled the handbrake on. Willow wasn't in such a hurry, slipping her hand into his and walking with him. She'd been quiet since they arrived, exploring the house, all its nooks and crannies.

'You can do the next paddock,' he offered.

Willow shrugged, while Doug bounded ahead, delighted by the conveyor belt mechanism that streamlined the egg-collection process.

'Slow down, mate,' Ned called out as Doug cranked the conveyor belt handle enthusiastically. Dozens of eggs jolted towards the small boy. *This will end in disaster if we're not careful.* 'Steady on, the customers don't want them scrambled.'

'I don't think Dougie realises we'll have months and months of eggs to collect,' Willow said.

Ned's step faltered. His plan to call Butch had gone out the window when Diana McIntyre had arrived.

Tomorrow, he told himself. He'd arrange things with Jonno's mate Butch, get in touch with Colin's solicitor, speak about the will and finalise the cremation details.

'We won't be staying long,' he said, kneeling so he was at eye level with his daughter. 'Besides, Victoria isn't on our special map.'

Willow considered that. The map of Australia was one of their most-loved possessions, covered in stickers, one for each place they'd travelled as a tight-knit trio.

'What about the flowers? That lady said Colin's flowers were the best in the district. Who's going to look after them? And the chooks? Uncle Jonno won't be back for months, will he?'

Ned scooped her up into his arms.

'Your little head must be bursting with all this thinking you've been doing, my girl.' He told her about Butch, who would likely step in until Jonno returned. 'How about you leave the worrying up to me?' he said, piggy-backing her to the chook tractor.

'Nice work, Dougie.' Ned watched the smile creep across his son's face. Piling into Colin's dusty and dented Land Rover, they criss-crossed the property, collecting eggs from the remaining chook tractors and shutting the fowls up for the night. The sun had almost set by the time they got back to the house.

'Righto, grommets. Fill up the bathtub and scrub yourselves clean,' he said.

'There's a bath?'

They hit the ground running heading for it, just like he'd known they would. There hadn't been a bath in their last three apartments.

Ned ducked outside before the light completely disappeared and unloaded several plastic stacking containers from the back of their van. He thought about their visitors as he added the food supplies to Colin's pantry. *Colin's never taken on a protégé before.*

Diana unloaded the crates of tubers the next morning, unable to shake a sense of dread as she looked at the dahlia paddock she'd been so excited about just two days earlier. She heard the squeaky gate creak open. Cameron was shower-fresh, with a clean shirt and expectant look on his face.

'Are we still heading to Mac Park tonight?'

'Course we are,' she said. 'I sent Aunty Pen a message and told her about Colin.'

Everyone looked forward to Sunday roasts at McIntyre Park, or Mac Park, as it was also known, the family farm where the four McIntyre sisters had grown up. If there was ever a sympathetic sounding board, it was her family.

'I've got a few things to drop off for Lucy, and I promised Claudia a Book Week costume,' she said. 'Be an angel and pop the dress-up box in the car, will you, mate?'

Diana selected an upbeat playlist to accompany the day's work in the patch. After Pete's death, when the days had been long and the nights even longer, she'd gravitated towards the maudlin tunes of Jeff Buckley, Augie March and U2. It was only when the healing process kicked in, and getting out of bed wasn't quite so hard, that she switched to upbeat eighties' hits. Songs like 'Walking On Sunshine' and bands like Bananarama and The Bangles lifted her spirits, and she hadn't budged from the peppy tunes since. The music did its trick as she worked through the day. She felt marginally better by the time she drove her boys to McIntyre Park.

'Oh, Diana,' Penny said, taking the steps two at a time and meeting her in the driveway. 'I'm so sorry about Colin.' Penny's voice was calm and soothing, similar to the tone she'd used to coax Diana out of the pit of grief after Pete's death. Lara swept out of the house in a cloud of aromatic roast lamb and met them on the deck.

'What a shock! How's Colin's family holding up? I remember Jonno from high school, though I can't picture his older brother. He was a few years ahead of us, wasn't he?'

Diana nodded. Here she was worrying about her business when poor Ned Gardiner was grieving for his father.

'He's just driven down from Darwin. He seemed pretty shell-shocked,' she said, looking around for her eldest niece. 'Evie not home this weekend?'

Laughing, Lara shook her head. 'Tough gig for some. She was at the theatre last night with Edwina and Karl, and apparently they've got tickets for the Melbourne Symphony Orchestra tomorrow. It'll be a reality check when school holidays come and she's back to volunteer shifts at the general store, or lamb marking with Penny.'

'Very versatile, your Evie,' said Diana. 'Just like her mum.'

Lara shrugged off the compliment, but Diana could tell she was pleased.

Their father Angus came across from his cottage and they went inside to the kitchen. Penny's husband Tim Patterson ambled in with their toddler, Lucy, then Angie and Rob 'Jonesy' Jones pulled up in the driveway with Claudia in the back seat.

Angie McIntyre, the youngest of the four sisters, was a whirlwind of curls and a cheerful dress with bold floral patterns as she stepped out of the car. Seven-year-old Claudia, who was a mini-Angie in an equally bright skirt and even wilder curls, rushed up to Diana.

'Did you bring the costume, Aunty Diana?' She slipped a warm hand into Diana's and beamed as if her aunt was her fairy godmother, ready to make all her swashbuckling dreams come true. *Any sweeter and she'd burst*, thought Diana.

'Claud, at least wait until you're inside before you start hassling Aunty Diana,' Angie said, grinning as she hugged her big sisters.

Diana squeezed Claudia's hand. Transforming her niece into a pirate was better than dwelling on Colin's passing. Together they fetched the sewing supplies from the car, carried them inside and set to work pinning and adjusting Leo's old pirate outfit. Even though the two cousins were almost the same age, Claudia was stouter than Leo and it took some rejigging to get the fit right.

The little girl pointed to Diana's hands.

'Your fingernails are like mine!'

Diana glanced at her short nails. Despite her quick once over with the nail brush, evidence of her gardening lingered.

'Worth a bit of dirt for all those flowers though, isn't it?'

Claudia giggled and nodded. Diana hugged her tight and breathed in the little girl's strawberry scent. A daughter would have been nice, but four healthy boys and three beautiful nieces were a pretty good compromise.

Before long, the outfit was ready.

'Ahoy there, me hearties,' Claudia growled in her best pirate voice as she swept into the kitchen. Diana felt the world right itself momentarily as her niece modelled the refreshed costume, receiving an appreciative applause from the extended McIntyre family.

When they all sat down to dinner at the lovingly worn pine table an hour later, conversation filled the room, then laughter, as Leo told them all about the salty scones incident.

Angus waved his fork in her direction. 'You get all those bulbs in yet, love?'

Diana nodded at her dad. 'Done and dusted.'

Angie chimed in. 'They're tubers, not bulbs, Dad.'

'Whatever they're called, I think they'll be marvellous, love. They'll sell like hotcakes at the general store, won't they, Toby?'

Lara's partner Toby Paxton nodded. 'I'll make sure of it.'

Like a tongue probing a sore tooth, Diana couldn't help her eyes tracking across the table to where Pete used to sit. Would Ned be doing the same thing across town at Colin's dining table at this exact moment?

Angus followed her gaze and rested a hand on her forearm, sensing her thoughts.

Who would be comforting Ned through the loss? His brother was on a slow boat to Antarctica and from what Diana had heard around the traps, there wasn't much love lost between the Gardiner boys and their elusive mother, Maeve.

6

Diana's slippers scuffed along the carpet as she went through the house, switching out lights and shaking off the melancholy. Nights were the worst for moping. One little detour down the rabbit hole of grief and—*boom*—suddenly it was 3 a.m. *Not tonight, sunshine. There's too much to think about,* she decided, making her way down the hallway.

It wasn't until almost all the lights were out that she noticed the shaft of yellow under Leo's door. She found him with a photo album in his lap.

'Way past your bedtime, little lion,' she said. Pete's twinkling eyes smiled at her from the album, still wearing the blue hospital scrubs, with newborn Leo in his arms.

'Big Ted had a bad dream,' said Leo, hauling the bright green teddy bear off his pillow and onto his lap. 'I think he's forgetting what Dad sounds like.'

Had Colin's death brought the grief racing back for him, too?

'Scooch over.'

Diana hitched up her dressing gown and nestled beside him and Big Ted. As she stretched out beside her youngest, she was surprised at just how long his legs had become. He was going to be tall like his brothers. Tall like Pete.

'I think Big Ted, and all of us, for that matter, will remember him forever.' She placed her hand on his flannelette pyjama top. 'He's in here.' Diana moved her hand to his head and stroked the spiky bits of hair that defied gravity. 'And in here.' She unfurled his hands and eased the photo book from his grip. 'And in here.'

His gentle sigh tickled her cheek as she continued. 'And, if you can't hear his voice—'

'Big Ted can't,' Leo interrupted.

Diana began again. 'And if *Big Ted* can't hear his voice when he closes his eyes, he can always look at the videos on my phone. Or on the laptop. If that video of Dad busting the trampoline mat doesn't make you laugh, nothing will.'

A small giggle erupted, followed by a yawn. Diana dimmed Leo's bedside lamp, tucked him in and stroked his fair hair until his chest rose and fell in a smooth rhythm. She picked up the photo album Penny had made after the funeral, with photos from everyone's phones. The album wasn't coffee-table quality. There were fingers over lenses, blurred shots and the type of candid pictures that never made it into the annual photo album. But since Pete's unexpected stroke, the collection was priceless.

She checked on Harry and Elliot next, their lanky limbs splayed at all angles in their bunk beds, and then Cameron.

A familiar tune caught her ear as she opened Cam's door. He was fast asleep, with Pearl Jam crooning about not finding a 'Better Man'. She smiled at the memories and entered the dark room just as a Crowded House track came on. Picking up the phone, she opened Cameron's playlist and scrolled through, finding it full of Pete's favourite tunes.

There was a Pete-sized hole in all their lives, and while Leo wore his heart on his sleeve, she worried Cameron was feeling the loss of his dad the most. She squeezed her eyes shut for a moment. What she wouldn't give for one last hug, one last kiss, the feel of his hands on her.

Diana packed the school lunches on autopilot.

'Don't forget we're off to Geelong for Cam's cricket tonight, guys,' she called as the boys wheeled their bikes out of the shed.

'Onto it, Mum.'

'And remember the lunch order forms for Miss Kenna,' she called, waving them off with a 'love you'.

The morning passed quickly in the rose garden, and it was a surprise to hear the mailman's enthusiastic toot carry down the length of the driveway. A flock of corellas flew out of the trees in the driveway. She dusted off her knees and walked to the mailbox, stopping by the kennels to unchain the dogs. They followed her up the driveway, chasing grass parrots and peeing on every second fence post.

A letter caught her eye among the bills, magazines and tractor catalogues. It was a brown envelope with a set of golf clubs printed in the top corner. There was only one golf fanatic she knew. With a groan, she ripped open the envelope.

Ned was at the rickety clothesline, knee-deep in laundry, when a big white van came down the driveway and pulled up beside the egg-grading shed. The bouncy brunette looked familiar, and as she climbed out, he knew why.

'Imogen?'

She pushed a pair of sunglasses to the top of her head and beamed back at him.

'Bugger me dead, if it isn't Ned Gardiner. I haven't seen you since uni,' she said, throwing open her arms. He wasn't sure what he expected from his little brother's ex-girlfriend, but it was the first hug he'd had since Colin's death and he hadn't realised how much he needed it.

'You must be devo about your dad. I tried to call Jonno when I heard, but he must be screening his calls,' she said, leading the way to the grading shed. 'Are you manning the fort?'

'Jonno's just left for a research trip down south. And I'm only manning the fort until Butch gets back from holidays,' he said. 'Didn't seem fair to make the bloke cut his honeymoon short.' Butch had given his apologies and instructions to keep the egg farm humming along.

They carried the eggs to the delivery van, and when she opened the door, he saw it was already half loaded with rural goods destined for city buyers.

'Just in here?'

'Yep, next to those organic veggies. Not sure whether Colin's told you much about his customers, but he sells most of his eggs to Ballarat.'

Ned studied the vibrant array of produce. It was better than admitting he knew nothing about the running of his father's business.

'You're keeping well, Imogen?' Ned asked.

'Can't complain. How about you? Do you have a whole tribe of rug rats? A brainy pharmacist wife that shares your passion? Or are you still married to your job?'

He laughed, shaking his head. Jonno's other girlfriends had always seemed dull and timid in comparison to Imogen.

'Just me and two kids. They're around here somewhere.' A quick scan of the backyard proved fruitless. 'A boy and a girl, seven and ten.'

She seemed pleased.

'My Oscar's a similar age. They're always looking for fresh blood at our small school—you thinking of staying?'

Ned dismissed the suggestion.

'I wouldn't know what to do with a farm; Jonno's a much better candidate. I can't even keep a houseplant alive.'

'Pffft.' Imogen put her hands on her hips. 'Says he who won nearly every flower category of the Bridgefield Show for three years running. My Nan still hasn't forgiven you for upsetting her winning streak. Speaking of flowers, you know Colin was helping at the new dahlia farm on the other side of Bridgefield?'

Ned thought of Diana McIntyre and her cheeky sons.

'So I heard.'

She hopped in the van and leaned out the window.

'I'm friends with Diana, she must be gutted too. When's the funeral? Want me to spread the news?'

He swallowed hard, trying to chase away the memory of Colin's thin white hair and the hand that was cold and clammy when he held it in the hospital room.

'Colin didn't want a fuss. He's being cremated this week and, according to his will, we're to sprinkle his ashes by the creek.'

'Sounds like your dad. And how's your mum taking it?'

Ned felt his lips press into a tight line. 'No idea.' Even if it had been his job to notify her, he wouldn't know where to send the letter.

Imogen glanced across the paddocks. Her hand flew to her mouth as she looked back at him.

'Oh God, she probably doesn't even know . . .'

Ned followed her gaze back to the shearers' hut in the distance, shadowed by the hay shed. 'You're kidding . . . Colin let Maeve move back again? *She's* the tenant?'

He hadn't seen any sign of life there in the days since he'd arrived, apart from a light in the window last night, but Imogen would know what was happening in this tiny town better than him.

Imogen fixed him with a sympathetic look.

'You and your mum still haven't built that bridge? Want me to go and break the news to her?'

He caught sight of Doug and Willow climbing on the monkey bars and shook his head. As much as he didn't relish the idea of seeing Maeve Gardiner-Guthrie again, not after the way they'd left things, now that he was here in Bridgefield, he owed his mother the courtesy.

'Thanks, I'll take care of it.'

Diana tucked the letter into her apron. It was just like the one she'd received a week after Pete's funeral, and it conjured up the same feeling of 'ugh' as she recognised her father-in-law's handwriting. She ripped at the envelope while marching down the driveway, but had to pause halfway to decipher Reg's blocky lettering.

The timing couldn't be worse. Diana turned to look at the dahlia patch she'd just planted. Not only had she lost Colin, her right-hand man, but she was going to be saddled with extra work in the form of a 70-year-old armchair umpire with a history of mansplaining. She felt Jinx winding herself around her feet.

'Lucky us, hey Jinx,' she said, collecting the cat for a cuddle.

The sound of her phone ringing startled them both. Jinx jumped out of her arms. Diana patted her field apron, trying to work out which of the many pockets the phone was in. Her father's cheery greeting came down the line.

'How're things, love? You weren't yourself last night,' Angus said.

Her sigh was apparently all the answer he needed.

'Pop the kettle on, I'll be there in five.'

The jug had just boiled when Angus's ute rumbled down the driveway. Kicking off his boots at the door and placing his Akubra on the table, he drew her in with his good arm.

'Sometimes it's the other deaths that jolt it back into focus, remind you of what you've lost, isn't it?' he said kindly. He made his way to the pantry, lifting the lid on several Tupperware containers before finding something he liked.

'These'll do the trick,' he said, setting a container of Diana's homemade monte carlos on the table.

'Righto, hit me with it. Is it the flowers, Cameron or Colin? Or something altogether different?' Angus leaned back in his chair and took a sip of tea, as if he had all the time in the world for her.

Diana passed her father-in-law's letter across the table and watched as Angus read it.

'Reg's not a bad sort, love. He's probably missing Pete, too, in his own way. Maybe he'll drive the boys to sports, or help out with the flowers?'

The snort of laughter almost sent tea spurting from Diana's nostrils. 'Help? The closest he gets to helping is taking his dishes to the bench instead of leaving them at the table.'

'Then tell him you're too busy, or that you've got other plans.'

'I can't fob him off a second time.' Diana shook her head. 'It'll be easier to get it over and done with at this time of year, instead of during peak dahlia season.'

Angus gave her a wink. 'Let me know when he arrives and I'll try to take him off your hands for a few days. Surely he can't be that bad.'

'Thanks, Dad.'

'How's the man hunt?'

A biscuit crumb lodged itself in Diana's throat and she spluttered. 'Man hunt?'

'You'll be needing a new right-hand man to help with the flowers, no?'

Diana gulped down a glass of water, her cheeks flushed. Why had Ned Gardiner chosen that particular moment to pop into her thoughts?

'Yep, I'll definitely need to find someone down the track. Cam pitches in when he can, but between his cricket schedule and school, he can only do so much. I'd rather he was out hitting a ball in the nets. He needs to be in fine form if they're going to choose him for the premier side.'

'All those weights and cross-fit sessions, he'll start looking like the Incredible Hulk. I bet Bradman never pumped iron,' he said.

'There's more pressure on elite athletes these days, Dad. Cam's determined to give it everything he's got.'

'Wonder where he gets it from,' said Angus with a grin, picking up the flyer she'd stuck to her fridge.

Diana was front and centre of the marketing poster. Lara's partner Toby had taken the photo several summers earlier with dahlias from her trial patch, and she could still recall standing in the paddock, feeling proud and happy as Pete clowned around behind the camera lens, trying to make her laugh. The sun was setting behind her, bringing out the ginger undertones in her fair hair, and adding an ethereal tone to the armful of café au lait dahlias. She'd thought about throwing in the towel when Pete had died, but as Colin had explained, a project made grief easier to bear.

But now Colin was gone, too . . .

Angus cleared his throat, bringing her back to the present. 'As much as I like the idea of Darling Dahlias, maybe you might be better skipping a season and launching the following summer instead, love? People would understand,' he paused.

'It's not like you've got any wedding orders locked in or brides getting married in the gardens.'

Diana stared out at the paddock full of tubers and thought of the event she'd somehow wangled her way into hosting. The event that she'd been so excited about until she heard about Colin.

'No weddings . . .' Despite promising Bron she'd keep the news under wraps for now, Diana confided in her father, and while Angus preferred wheat and canola crops to flowers, he still managed to sound suitably impressed.

'That puts a different spin on things then, doesn't it? I wouldn't know this Sadie Woodford bird if I fell over her, but I've heard you girls talking about her books. What are the chances of getting one of these, these . . .' he clicked his fingers, grappling for the right word.

'Influencers?'

Angus grinned and winked. 'That's the one! You were obviously in the right place at the right time for this influencer to consider it. You can't knock it back now, love.'

Diana thought about the conversations she'd had over glasses of wine with Bron, bemoaning the difficulty in pitching events outside the big cities.

Angus's confidence was soothing. 'If anyone can make it happen, I'd put my money on you.'

Diana thought about the website Penny had helped her make, the brochures, business cards and flyers she'd had printed, the contacts she'd made from Sadie's workshops. She remembered Colin's words, when she'd first told him about her flower farm plans: 'You put all this energy into these plants, starting small like a seed and hoping it'll pay off in the long run. And eventually, just like the flowers, you'll bloom into the person you were meant to be.'

Diana looked across the paddocks and to the Grampians, where her mother's memorial stone sat at the top of Wildflower Ridge.

What if all wasn't lost? What if I employed a helper, just for one season?

Ned eventually found Willow and Doug inside the tractor shed, climbing over an orange Chamberlain tractor that Colin had always talked about fixing up, but never got around to.

'Who's up for a mid-afternoon movie?'

Delighted at the rare treat, they followed him inside, choosing a dusty DVD from Colin's ancient collection.

'Want to watch *Space Jam* or *The NeverEnding Story*, Dad?'

'I've got a few more jobs to do,' he said, glancing out the window. 'Start the film without me and I'll be back in a minute.'

But even after they were settled on the couch, Ned still lingered.

Cross the paddock, break the news and it's done, he told himself.

Unanswered questions swirled as Ned forced himself out the door. It was over two decades since he'd watched his mother unravel after Jessie's death. Would she weather the sudden loss of her ex-husband better than the painfully slow loss of her daughter to cancer, or would it push her back into the darkness again? She hadn't accepted the help she needed from the counselling services back in the mid-nineties, it was hard to imagine she'd speak to someone now.

He skirted around a pile of roofing tin in the paddock, haphazardly secured by a pile of steel posts. *Snake paradise.*

Knee-high grass grew around a rusting trailer, and as he approached the sheep yards he saw they were worse for wear too. Gripping the top rail, he gave it a little shake. The whole section wobbled. One end looked like it was hanging together by baling twine. *What a shemozzle.*

When had it got so bad? And why had his father let it go, after years of being fastidious about every paddock on the property?

The closer he got to the shearers' hut, the more questions he had. The small transportable hadn't aged well either, he noted, eyeing the paint peeling off the door. Ned knocked, wary of the cobwebs that clung to the cladding.

Maeve Gardiner-Guthrie opened the door, her beige top, wan complexion, and milky-grey hair matching her faded surroundings.

'Edward.'

Even though it had been seven years since he had spoken to Maeve, and even longer since he'd set foot in Bridgefield, she looked infinitely older. He glanced into the dim quarters.

'Mind if I come in?'

The lino floor creaked underfoot as Ned followed his mother down the hallway. A glass-topped dining table sat in the middle of the basic kitchen, crowding the small space, and even with Maeve's obvious attempt to brighten up the interior, there was no hiding the sad state of the building.

Ned sat down at the table and waited for her to take a seat. 'Has anybody told you about Colin?' He wasn't surprised when she went straight on the defensive.

'I stay out of his business and he stays out of mine. Is he crook?'

Ned swallowed. 'There was an accident. He passed away a few days ago.'

'What? Oh, no . . .' Maeve wrung her hands, her eyes downcast.

He pushed back his chair, giving her space to process the news. He expected wailing and keening, like in the hospital room after Jessie died, but the only sound was Maeve's deep, measured breathing. Eventually she moved to the sink and filled the kettle.

'And that's why you're back.'

Ned nodded.

'What happened?'

He outlined the accident as the jug boiled. Maeve opened and closed cupboards. Like the old sheep yards, the hinges looked like they were hanging by a thread, a world away from the glass-fronted Cairns apartment she'd been renting when they last crossed paths.

'Been back long?' Ned finally asked.

'It's only temporary,' she said. 'I've got a few veggies out the back, your father brings me eggs and whatever I can't grow, I get delivered.'

She's been in this dump long enough to have a vegetable patch . . . ?

Ned caught himself scanning the cupboards as she moved about the small room. He hadn't smelled alcohol on her breath or her skin, and it was only early afternoon, but still there had to be a reason she hadn't erupted into tears already. Before Jessie had fallen ill, Maeve had laughed and parented and handled setbacks without hysterics and vodka, but that felt like a lifetime ago.

'You won't find any bottles if that's what you're looking for.'

She set the mugs down with a thump. Tea slopped over the side, pooling on the glass surface. Another memory came to Ned as he sipped the scalding brew, one of the many occasions Maeve had promised she had a handle on sobriety. Ned had believed her that time, right up until she arrived at his graduation ceremony and accidentally slammed her hand in the car door, in front of all his uni mates and their parents, then threw up, either from the pain or the vodka.

Ned could almost smell the bleach and feel the shame washing over him as if he were in his early twenties again, rinsing his mother's blood and vomit off his hired graduation gown. What was it a friend had told him years later, after he'd severed ties with Maeve?

Once an alcoholic, always an alcoholic.

He felt a sudden urge to be snuggled on the couch with Willow and Doug. He should be with them now, where the lines between parent and child were clear, and their world was full of fun, not haunted by bad memories and disappointment.

Ned carried his now-empty mug to the sink. He'd done what he came to do, it was time to leave before things went pear-shaped.

The mess of old timber and scrap metal was the least of Ned's worries as he crossed the paddock. What would happen to Maeve now that Colin wasn't there to pick up the pieces?

He was almost at the sheep yards when his name rang out through the air.

'Edward. Can't we at least try?'

Ned shook his head as he turned.

'We *have* tried, Maeve.' His sigh felt like it came from the bottom of his guts. 'The rehab clinics tried. Jonno and I tried. Colin tried.' None of it had stopped the merry-go-round of sobriety and alcoholism from spinning.

'If you'd been in touch, you'd know I haven't had a drink in years. It hasn't been an easy life, you know.'

Ned threw his hands in the air.

'We've done this before, Maeve. Colin might have fallen for it, but not me. Not again.'

'Nobody's perfect, Edward. I can only do my best.'

This is her best? He looked from his mother's washed-out appearance to the run-down hut. She'd burned her bridges with friends, as well as her sons, long ago. Even if she wasn't drinking anymore, it didn't look like anyone's version of a great life, and who knew how long it would be before it all came tumbling down again.

7

As tempting as it was to put his feet up when the afternoon drew to a close, Ned's dinner suggestions hadn't gone down well.

'But we don't like baked beans,' said Doug. 'Can't we have pizza? Or tacos?'

'We should go out for tea. I feel like Thai food,' Willow declared, looking crestfallen when Ned explained the lack of culinary options in Bridgefield.

'It's not a restaurant kind of town, munchkin. And we'll go grocery shopping soon, but not tonight.'

Ned pulled out his trump card, the one he hoped would save him further arguments. He wasn't sure what the general store offered, but he took a punt they'd still stock fresh bread and ice cream.

'What about scrambled eggs on toast? With ice cream for dessert?'

The compromise hit the mark and the children piled into the old Land Rover, debating Paddle Pops versus Bubble O'Bills.

Ned followed his nose into town, noticing new houses along the way and signs for businesses that hadn't been there when he was a teenager.

'Why's everyone waving to us?' Willow asked, her suspicious expression making Ned grin.

'It's a country thing. These people know your grandfather's ute, not us.' He mirrored the next car's greeting by lifting a finger off the steering wheel. The drive into town only took a few minutes and soon enough they were pulling up in front of a bluestone building with a striped bull-nosed verandah.

The general store was brighter than he remembered, with a couch by the window and fresh display cabinets showcasing regional produce. *Locally baked sourdough?* Maybe he'd underestimated Bridgefield. He chose a multigrain loaf, studded with seeds.

'Good choice. Made fresh this morning,' said the bloke behind the counter, sliding the loaf into a paper bag. A similar age to Ned, he had an easy manner and waved away Ned's apology for arriving right on closing time.

'No worries, take your time,' called the shopkeeper, leading them through the shelves to the freezer cabinet. The old-fashioned doorbell rang out as another customer slipped into the shop.

'Glad I caught you, Toby. I've just dropped a birthday gift on the terracotta tiles. Smashed to smithereens. Tell me you've still got a bunch of flowers. Or even better, is Diana McIntyre selling her flowers here yet?'

From behind the shelves, Ned's ears pricked up.

'Nope, Diana's won't be ready for a while yet. We've got one bunch of Woolsthorpe natives left though.'

'You're a lifesaver. Losing Colin will throw such a spanner in the works for poor Diana. I bet she's gutted.'

Ned felt his cheeks burn at the unintended eavesdropping. He moved a little to his left, peering past a rotating postcard display for a glimpse at the front counter.

'She's bearing up well. But she'll miss his help, that's for sure,' Toby said, wrapping a bouquet of proteas and eucalyptus.

'Such a kind soul, Colin, always saw the best in people.' The lady lowered her voice and leaned across the counter. 'Especially letting his ex-wife come back to the farm like that. I heard her second husband wasn't as understanding of her issues.' Her tone oozed judgement, and although it had been a long time since his mother's behaviour had impacted Ned directly, the associated shame was as uncomfortably familiar as ever. He ducked his head, studying the ice creams as intently as his children.

The shopkeeper changed the topic with effortless diplomacy before walking the customer to the door, but still the woman's comments stuck in Ned's mind as he drove back to Colin's. It was an echo of conversations from the past, gossip they'd left behind in Gippsland.

Once an alcoholic ...

No matter how long she'd been sober, Maeve's battle with alcoholism had left an unforgettable legacy. Ned struggled to compartmentalise the memories as he scrambled eggs and toasted sourdough. The lure of eating dessert in a hot bath had the children racing through dinner and the dishes. Lukewarm sudsy water lapped at Ned's elbow as he removed the bath plug afterwards. Watching the water swirl around the plughole, he found his thoughts returning to Maeve.

She'd lost a daughter through no fault of her own, but didn't she care that in her maelstrom of grief and hurt and self-destruction, she'd lost two sons and thrown her life down the gurgler too? Apparently not.

Diana looked at the paperwork spread out on the coffee table in front of her. There were notes in Colin's precise cursive, spreadsheets with projected growing timelines, and detailed notes on repeat customers and florists.

But of all the paper on the table, it was the handwritten list of flower subscriptions she was most proud of. It had been filled out over several weeks, on the front counter of the Bridgefield General Store, by locals keen to sign up for the weekly, monthly and fortnightly bouquet subscriptions.

'Coming to read me a story, Mum?'

Diana turned to see Leo with his book under his arm. 'In a minute, mate, I'm just working out the next planting schedule,' she said.

'You've already got millions of dahlias, Mum. And the fox socks and the cosmos and the sunflowers.'

Diana laughed. 'Foxgloves,' she corrected. It probably did seem like a lot of flowers to a little boy. She had enough tubers and seedlings to fulfil the bouquet orders in front of her. With a strategic approach, and an extra set of hands, she was confident there'd be enough blooms to make a stunning backdrop for Sadie's launch party, too. *Well, pretty confident.* She just needed to kick Plan B into action.

'And there's no such thing as too many flowers, mate.' She moved the paperwork into a pile, careful not to mix it up with Cameron's homework, which was spread across the other half of the dining table.

Cam buried his hands in his head as she crossed the open-plan living room.

'I'll be back with Milo soon,' she said, patting his shoulder.

Leo's bedroom was all ready for their nightly reading session—lamp on, pillows propped up and teeth freshly brushed. He climbed into Diana's lap as soon as she sat down and snuggled in with the second Harry Potter novel. Jinx joined them halfway through the chapter, her tail twitching as they turned the pages.

Diana thought of the many kittens Jinx had given them over the years. She was a good mother, and although they always found homes for Jinx's babies, Diana had been meaning to get her desexed.

Maybe one last litter of kittens . . .

After kissing Leo good night, she wandered down the hallway to the twins' room, and by the time she'd listened to them each read a page from the latest *Guinness Book of Records*, she was ready for something sweet.

Diana pulled a bag of Maltesers from behind the bread bin—one of her many hiding spots around the house—and offered them to Cameron.

'You winning?'

'This is impossible, I'll never pass next year's exams if I can't even work this out,' he said, frowning at his workbook. He leaned back in his chair, folding his arms across his chest. Diana collected a few stray pieces of paper from the floor. Maths had never been her strong point. Just looking at the intricate algebra equations hurt her brain, she could only imagine how he felt.

'I wish Dad was here,' he said, softly.

'Me too, buddy. Me too.'

Pete had been the one to sit with him and muddle through the technical maths problems. She drew her son into a brief hug, then made them a hot drink.

'You'll be thrilled to know we have a visitor on the way.' She told him about Reg. 'Remember how Dad had to rearrange the lounge room last time Gramps stayed, because he wasn't happy with the TV reception?' Cam said.

Diana crunched her Maltesers.

'I remember. Promise me you'll keep him entertained at least some of the time. I'll be flat out in the flower patch, especially without Colin's help.'

An idea formed as she looked back at the flower farm paperwork, then checked her watch.

'Hey, Cam, I'm just ducking out for a bit. I'll be back in an hour, tops.'

Before she could talk herself out of it, she gathered up an impromptu basket of supper, slipped on a cardi and grabbed her keys.

Willow and Doug met Ned in the lounge with a tattered Paul Jennings book later that night.

'An oldie, but a goodie,' he said, leading them to the couch. All three of them chuckled at the whacky characters and predicaments.

'One more?'

Ned looked at the clock and gave a quick nod. It was earlier than their usual bedtime, but the fresh air and hours spent exploring the property had both children yawning as they returned from the bookshelf.

'Can we have a chapter from this one, Dad?'

He traced the embossed lettering on the cover of *The Magic Faraway Tree*, knowing instantly whose it was.

'Nah, something different, Doug,' he said. He'd had enough trips down memory lane for one day.

'But this one's got your name in it,' said Willow, opening the book. It was inscribed with a message.

Happy 10th birthday Jessica, from Mum, Dad, Edward and Jonathon.

'Look, someone's crossed out the names.'

Ned looked at his messy handwriting, where he'd updated their names to Jessie, Ned and Jonno.

'You told us not to write in books.' Doug's tone was a mix of awe and indignation.

'I got a thrashing for it, don't you worry,' Ned said under his breath. 'Time for bed, quick sticks.' He rose and held his hand out for the book, trying to channel the firm but patient voice Diana McIntyre had used after the salty scone incident.

'But who's Jessica?'

'Doug,' hissed Willow, grabbing her little brother by the pyjama sleeve and tugging him towards the hallway. But Doug wasn't giving up.

'Nobody tells me anything,' he said, snatching his arm back and folding his arms across the book.

Ned sighed, knowing Doug wouldn't settle if he was worked up. It was times like these he almost wished their mother was around to help simplify complicated explanations or bounce tactics off. If only Fleur hadn't buggered off to 'find herself' when it all got too hard.

'Jessie was my sister, buddy. We'll talk about it more tomorrow, okay?' he said finally, drawing the little boy in for a hug.

Doug wriggled out of his grip and stomped down the hallway, clinging to the book. Willow frowned, opened her mouth and then shut it, knowing her dad well enough not to pursue the subject.

'Tomorrow,' Ned promised, folding Willow's glasses for her and tucking them both into bed.

He flicked on the lounge TV and was halfway through an ABC show when a set of headlights shone down the driveway.

Who normally visits Colin at this hour?

❀

Ned slid open the door to see Diana McIntyre ducking underneath the jasmine arbour, her long strawberry-blonde hair aflame in the light.

'I wasn't sure how well stocked Colin's cupboards were,' she smiled. 'Thought you might need some fortification. I can leave you to enjoy it in peace, but if you fancied some company . . . ?' She let the sentence trail off, smiling as she pulled a bottle of wine from the basket.

'I could do with a drink,' he admitted, stepping aside. She moved through Colin's home with a distinct familiarity, while he opened several cupboards in search of wine glasses.

'These okay?' He returned with a pair of goblets with grapes and fruit etched into the side.

'Those were your father's favourites,' she said, locating a chopping board under the sink and dividing the fruit into two piles. He looked at the small bowl, then back at the platter she'd started making.

'One for the children tomorrow,' she explained, confirming Ned's impression that mothering was as natural to her as breathing. *She could teach Maeve and Fleur a trick or two, that's for sure.*

Diana studied him as they settled at the dining table.

'How are you managing?'

Ned took a sip, savouring the wine as he worked out how to answer.

'Had better weeks, to be honest.'

'Can't imagine why,' she said, leaning back against the chair.

He felt some of the tension ebb away at her wry tone and sampled the quince paste, soft cheese and biscuits she'd brought. *Top notch.*

'Has the casserole brigade beaten a path to your door yet?'

Her description made Ned smile.

'They might have if we were in Gippsland still, but most of my teenage years in Bridgefield were spent at boarding school, so nobody knows me from a bar of soap.'

'Probably for the best,' Diana said, twirling the wine in her glass. 'There're only so many meatloaves and lasagne you can accept before you start mixing up Corningware containers and returning the wrong Tupperware lids to the wrong houses.'

'Spoken from experience?'

He felt like kicking himself when her smile dimmed.

'It was a big help when my mum died. Anything was better than Dad's burned toasted sandwiches, but tastes have changed in the last few decades. The casseroles and soups were great, although my boys lost their appetites when my husband Pete passed away . . .' She set her glass down, automatically twisting a slim wedding band around her finger. 'And I barely had the heart to turn away all the beautiful home-cooked meals, so I offloaded things like lamb's fry to my dad and your dad. Irene's ox tongue stew and steak and kidney pie are still lurking at the bottom of my freezer, if you're keen?' she said with a laugh.

Her words were raw and her attempt at a joke wasn't quick enough to mask her sadness. *Recently widowed?*

'We're good for stews—and scones—thanks.' He smiled weakly. 'But losing your mum *and* your husband . . . that must have been crap.'

Diana nodded and reached for her wine. 'It's completely crap losing somebody you love. And Colin was a special chap.'

Ned wasn't sure how he felt about Diana grieving his father's loss as much as—possibly even more than—him. He looked up to see her blinking hard.

'Sorry, I didn't mean to turn this into a pity party. He was a good friend, that's all. And I know how rough those nights are after such a tragic event. I bet your mum and brother are pretty shaken, too.'

Ned studied his glass, trying not to bristle at the mention of his family. If the woman in the shop had known about Maeve, it was only natural that Diana would too. He wondered how much the locals knew about Jessie's fight with cancer and Maeve's battle with the bottle.

He swirled his glass, waiting for the gentle prying. It was one of the many reasons he preferred life on the road. No lying about the reasons he avoided trips home. No explaining his mother's alcoholism, then her struggle for sobriety, or his father's dogged 'forgive and forget' approach.

Diana could feel Ned retreating. *Was it the comment about Maeve?* She hadn't been judging him, but from the storm passing over his face, it was obviously a sensitive subject. She finished her drink and reached down to pat the tabby cat who was twice the size of Jinx. *Time to head off.* But as she pushed back her chair and went to stand, Ned surprised her with a question.

'So how did you and Colin start working together? He never took on a protégé before. Well, at least, not that I know of.'

Diana crossed her legs, leaning back in her chair.

'We met at the local Anzac Day wreath-making session. I'd held off getting roped into another committee, but the flu knocked out most of the usual suspects and Pearl Patterson was sick of me moping around. She'd sell ice to an Eskimo, Nanna Pearl. She dragged Colin in, too, and as soon as he heard I was recently widowed, with big plans for a flower farm, he took me under his wing.' She laughed fondly at the memory. 'My sisters thought it was hilarious. I'm normally the one taking people under my wing. I'd done a course on flower farming a few years earlier, and your dad helped revise my planting design, shore up suppliers for bulbs and tubers and introduced me to a network of green thumbs I never knew existed.'

She watched his face. He thought before he spoke, like Colin, but he didn't have the same easy conversational manner.

'He always said his veins were half-blood, half-chlorophyll,' Ned said with a tight smile. 'Never could quite walk away from his flowers.'

'You weren't tempted to follow in his footsteps, though?'

Ned shook his head. 'I helped in the garden when I was younger, but I haven't grown anything since. Mind you, I can see the appeal of having a few rose bushes in the backyard. I bought red roses for Valentine's Day once, and nearly had to sell a kidney to pay for them.'

She laughed, amused by the confession. 'You *do* know how many red roses are flown in from South Africa, dipped in chemicals to get through quarantine and a whole slew of other nasties so they don't open prematurely, right? And they come wrapped in metres and metres of plastic, and that's not even taking the carbon miles into account. Your dad would have been livid!'

He sat back, grinning at the notion, but it was only fleeting before the sadness returned to his eyes.

No matter how old you are, there's never a good time to lose a parent. She thought of all the advice she'd received after her mum's accident and then Pete's death. It was the doing, not the advice, that had made the most difference. The flower farm had given her focus and purpose. Colin's guidance had offered structure and clarity, but it was the act of putting things in the ground and watching them grow—the promise of new seasons and fresh blooms—that had been the very best therapy.

Diana considered the question she'd intended to ask him tonight. She'd learned so much from Colin in such a short space of time and could only imagine how much knowledge Ned would have absorbed from his father when he was growing up. She looked at him again, catching his eye through his black-rimmed specs.

Bugger it. What's the worst he can say?

Pulling the Darling Dahlias brochure from her handbag, Diana pushed it across the table before she could change her mind.

'This is totally random, and I completely understand if you tell me to go jump, but your dad was going to be my main helper when the dahlia season was in full swing. He was a godsend, more than just a set of extra hands. I know you haven't done much with flowers recently, but I'd love your help on the farm if you were staying.'

Ned looked at her with such disbelief that Diana immediately regretted her rash suggestion and, in the colossal silence that followed, she realised she must have insulted him. She looked down.

It's a stupid idea. He's a pharmacist, for God's sake. Not a farm labourer. Maybe an ad in the shop window will be a better bet.

8

Ned was as surprised by Diana's suggestion as he was by the prickling in his eyes. Had she known about Colin's requests for help, all those years earlier, and how he'd dismissed them every time? Was she trying to retrospectively make things right, or did she genuinely need a hand? For a moment he feared she might catch him getting teary for a second time. Keeping it together outside Colin's gardening shed had been one thing, but there was nowhere to hide at the dining table.

Pull it together, man.

Swallowing hard, he pushed his glass away and surveyed the lounge room and kitchen. The house was full of little mementoes from Jonno's polar expeditions, postcards Willow and Doug had sent Colin from their travels, an article Ned had once written for the university newspaper. If he looked carefully, he was sure he'd probably find something relating to Maeve, too—maybe a recipe she'd written down in the days before cooking was replaced with drinking. The woman in the general store was right: Colin had always looked for the best in people, even when they might not deserve it. Why hadn't he been able to do the same?

When he finally looked up and saw the discomfort and flush that had spread across Diana's face, Ned realised she'd misinterpreted his response.

'Sorry . . . I wasn't dismissing the idea—'

He grimaced, unsure how to admit what was really going on inside his head.

'Grief's a sneaky bugger,' he said eventually, studying the wood grain on the table.

He felt the warmth of Diana's hand covering his own. Her long, pale fingers and thin wrists looked fragile against his olive skin.

'Sure is,' she paused and waited for him to look up. 'You know, sinking my hands into the dirt was the best therapy after my husband died. I know you didn't get a chance to see your dad much with your work, but I do need a hand, and you look like you could do with a little downtime to process things?'

Shame coursed through Ned's body for the second time that evening. *Didn't get home as much as you wanted . . . Was that how Colin had worded it?* It was much more generous than the reality. He hadn't tried hard enough. Hadn't wanted to return to the home where ghosts had as much a place at the dining table as the living. And when he'd finally got over himself, and diverted from his precious schedule, it was too late.

'I can't, I've got a job lined up in Mount Gambier.'

'Hey, no judgement here. You've got to follow your passion, right?'

Ned thought about the job he was shifting his kids across the country for. Filling prescriptions at a chain-store pharmacy wasn't so much a passion as a convenience, something that paid well and allowed him to have a hefty bank account and a generous share portfolio. And all for what? So he could prove his smarts with a weekly paycheque that rivalled his father's monthly takings. Show his loyalty to his sister Jessie by honouring each and every sparkly sticker on their beloved travel wish list? He'd set himself up in the last decade, he'd shown his children more of the country than many adults saw in their lifetime. But as he nursed his wine, those two accolades failed to bring their customary comfort. Diana's suggestion was left field, but he found himself turning it around in his head.

'And you reckon working as a farmhand will be a miracle cure?'

She shrugged. 'Saved me going under.'

He agreed to think about it, but found his mind dwelling more on Diana than her offer after she drove away. As he locked the sliding door, Ned picked up her brochure: Darling Dahlias, 19 Paperbark Hill Road, Bridgefield, and a mobile number. The street name wasn't familiar, but it had been a long time since he'd puttered around the back blocks of Bridgefield. He flipped through the brochure.

Damn.

Maybe it was the halo effect of the sunshine behind her, or perhaps it was the full, uninhibited smile, but the result was breathtaking.

The photos were stunning. *No.* He mentally rephrased that. *Diana* was stunning.

Little footsteps sounded on the slate floor, and he turned to see Doug by the dining table, Flopsy in his arms, his hair a cockatoo's crest of mess. 'Why didn't you tell us you had a sister?'

Ned's gaze went to the pale square above the fireplace, where a family portrait had once hung.

'Let's talk about it tomorrow, Dougie.' He put a gentle hand on his shoulder, steering Doug back down the hallway. 'It's time for you to get some sleep. I'm counting on you to be my chief egg collector tomorrow.'

Willow was already snoring and didn't even stir when Ned repeated the elaborate routine of checking under the beds, behind the door and inside the wardrobe for boogie men before Doug would crawl between the sheets.

As Ned washed the day away with soap and hot water, he told himself he should've been upfront and told them the sad truth about his mum and his sister a long time ago, like he'd done when their mother Fleur left. But then the Gardiners had always made a habit of keeping secrets, hadn't they?

The next morning, Doug, Willow and Ned visited each of the paddocks, moving the chook tractors to fresh pasture and topping up the supplies.

It wasn't long before the last flock of chickens were settled in a new corner, close to a shelterbelt of gums, orbiting their mobile home on wheels.

With the hens clucking contentedly and the early-morning sun casting a rich sheen over the green pasture, Ned told his children about Jessie and the fast-moving cancer that had changed his family forever. Willow seemed to read too much between the lines.

'So after your sister died, then your mum became sick? Is cancer contagious? Is that why we don't see her, because you don't want us to get sick? Is that why Colin died too?'

Ned removed his glasses and rubbed his eyes. It was so much easier when they accepted their grandparents were interstate.

'There are all types of illness in the world, and medicines of all shapes and sizes to treat them. It's what keeps blokes like me in a job,' he said, tweaking her nose to lighten the mood. 'And if you want to be a pharmacist, too, you'll learn all about them at uni. Cancer's definitely not contagious, but sometimes you get so sad when someone dies that it makes you unwell.'

Willow brightened up but Doug wasn't convinced.

'Will you get crook, now that your dad has died?'

Ned put his glasses back on and hugged his little boy. 'Not a chance, buddy, you can't get rid of me that easily.'

A chook ran across the paddock, tiny legs going like the clappers as it chased a butterfly. They all erupted into laughter. *Perfect timing.*

They were almost back at the ute when Doug came out with another question. 'Is your mum still sick?'

Ned opened the rusty door, choosing his words carefully. 'She's not as healthy as she could be.'

'We could send her a card, like we did when Uncle Jonno broke his wrist,' Willow said. 'Do you have her address? She lives in Queensland, doesn't she?'

His heart ached at their excited response when he told them she wasn't just living in the same state, she lived on the same property.

'Can we see her today then? Let's go now!'

He deflected the question and instead promised to show them photographs of Jessie.

Back at the house, Ned fossicked through the dusty book-shelf until he found the collection of leatherbound photo albums. Doug and Willow settled on the couch, and Ned found himself holding his breath. Home haircuts and Mickey Mouse T-shirts filled the first page, then a random elephant.

'You had a pet elephant?' Doug shrieked.

Ned laughed.

'That was the zoo,' he said, turning the next page to show giraffes, gorillas and alligators. Willow leaned over his shoulder, softly touching a photo of Jessie.

'She's got the same hair as me.'

Ned's smile faded as he recalled the chunks of hair littering the shower after Jessie started her treatment. Time had frozen his sister but, as he studied the picture, he spotted the similarities between Jessie and Willow. Dark wavy hair, fierce smile, freckles on the bridge of her nose. How had he not noticed before?

Ned turned the page to find a photo of his mother, in her neatly pressed jeans and smocked shirt, cheerfully oblivious to the illness that would soon tear their family apart. She was hamming it up for the camera, one hand on her hip, the other holding Jessie's hand, both grinning, unaware that Jonno was making rabbit ears in the background.

And what would he do if he lost Willow, just like they'd lost Jessie, all those years ago? Not turn to the bottle like Maeve had done, time and time again, long after the neighbourhood empathy and assistance had morphed into pity.

Doug reached across, sensing Ned's hesitation, and turned the pages for him.

'Sounds like everybody who lives here is either sick or dead. Aunty Jessie, Colin, your mum.'

Ned looped an arm around each of their shoulders and squeezed them to his sides.

'You two ratbags look pretty alive to me. Maybe the three of us can breathe a little more life into this place?'

Willow rested her head against his and he felt her hand slide into his own. Even Doug sat still, almost reverent, as they got to the end of the album. *This was what families should do. Draw together when there's sadness, not shatter.* Diana McIntyre popped into his mind again. A close-knit bunch. And for a woman who'd recently lost her husband, she seemed to be weathering the storm well. She'd asked for his help with the flower farm, and she seemed to think he'd find solace in gardening, too.

Ned took another look at Maeve before closing the album and sliding it back onto the shelf.

Diana eased a chocolate cake into the oven, then thumbed through the recipe book until she came to a page with little blue smudges on the corner. She ran her eye down the ingredients, confident she had everything she needed, then put a book-mark in and kept flicking to find a third and final recipe for the day's bake-up.

While the blueberry muffins and choc cake would be perfect for the boys' lunch boxes, she needed something different for tonight's sewing group. None of the ladies would want to risk staining their fabric. She decided on a simple slice, the same one she'd been making since she was Leo's age. She made the muffins first, added them to the oven, and was melting butter and honey for the slice when Penny called.

'Hey, sis, any chance we can switch the sewing circle to tomorrow night? Sarah Squires has something on tonight—I said I'd do a ring around.'

Diana stirred in coconut and mixed fruit, then turned her attention to measuring the sugar.

'No can do. Reg is arriving tomorrow. What's Sarah's problem this time? Another horse emergency?'

Penny laughed.

'If today's Facebook check-in at the hairdressers is any indi-cation, I'd say it's more likely a hot date. Don't stress. I'll tell her it doesn't work. We'll never get any sewing done if we're always rescheduling.'

Their suspicions were confirmed when they arrived at Lara's house at 7 p.m.

'I see Miss Squires got a better offer tonight,' Winnie Beggs said, the moment she set her sewing basket down. 'All dolled up when I bumped into her at the shop. I wonder if she'll let him hang around longer than the last fella.'

Diana looked away, but not before Lara spotted her grinning. Sarah had a wicked sense of humour and, on the sessions she attended, she happily regaled them with tales from the online dating world.

Pearl Patterson, who most in the district referred to as Nanna Pearl, looked up from the ironing board, where she was pressing the seams on a nine-inch patchwork block.

'Sarah changes her mind as often as she changes her underpants, I don't know where she finds the energy.'

'Me neither,' said Diana. Dating apps and websites weren't her cup of tea and, while she enjoyed Sarah's anecdotes, she wasn't in any hurry to experience them for herself.

The chatter continued above the whirring of the sewing machines and eventually ended with supper and a glass of wine.

'Great slice,' said Lara, helping herself to a second piece.

'Best way to use up the Weet-Bix crumbs,' Diana agreed. By nine p.m., the sewing machines were all packed up, the date and host were chosen for the next sewing circle and Lara's place looked less like a sweat shop and more like a home.

Diana and Penny were the last ones to leave.

Lara walked them down the hallway, pausing by the door. 'How're things? Hard without Colin?'

'Just let us know if you want any help, or even if you simply want to chat,' Penny said, pulling on her shoes. They walked out of the house together and Penny climbed into the vintage red Holden that Tim had restored for her.

'I'll be fine, honestly,' Diana said, waving her off.

And as she followed her sister down the driveway, their headlights illuminating the donkeys in their stables, Diana thought again of how lucky she was to have such a supportive network of friends and family. The man who owned the donkeys, Clyde McCluskey, had been so lonely when his wife Edna died that he sprinkled his misery around like glitter, rebuffing any well-intentioned visitors. She didn't know much about Colin's wife, Maeve, except that she tried to drink away her pain, pushing her sons away in the process. And then there was Sarah, whose bed was rarely empty as she attempted to date herself out of a post-divorce slump.

The odd block of chocolate and bout of tears are nothing in the scope of things.

'*Today* can we meet your mum?' Willow asked, climbing onto Ned's lap to steer the Land Rover down the laneway.

Ned rested his chin on Willow's head. Just like the pocket money that burned a hole in their pockets until they spent it, they weren't satisfied just knowing about their grandmother. Willow had asked the same question nearly every day that week and the puppy dog eyes were wearing him down as much as the knowledge that the children would probably strike out across the paddock without him if he didn't agree sooner or later.

'We'll see,' he said.

After the eggs were graded, boxed and set out ready for Imogen to collect, he settled the kids down with sandwiches and flicked on the television. 'I'll be back shortly. You guys wait here.'

Ned pulled on a pair of Colin's elastic-sided boots, walked to the shearers' hut and knocked on Maeve's door. He studied his mother's face when she answered. The photo album had reminded him that she'd been beautiful once, and even during the darkest days of her alcoholism she'd always made an effort with her appearance. But now . . . she looked worn down by the years of bad decisions.

'If you've come to give me another lecture, you can save your breath,' she said quietly. 'If your father, rest his soul, had no trouble with me staying here, I shouldn't imagine you would either.'

Ned held up his hands.

'I don't want to argue. I'm not here to throw you out.' He looked around, noticing wheat sprouting from the gutters and a hole stuffed with steel wool. 'But this is a dump, Maeve.'

'Damn sight better than a car, or living under a bridge,' she said stiffly, straightening her shoulders. Ned hated to think these were situations she'd already found herself in. He saw all manner of customers in his line of work, from ice addicts to high-profile politicians, and he'd always made it his mission to treat each customer with kindness, regardless of their social standing or ailment. But somehow, he found it infinitely harder to bestow that same impartial kindness on his own mother.

'Why do you care, anyway? If Colin hadn't died, you wouldn't have given two hoots about where I was living. Hasn't seemed to worry you too much before.'

Ned refused to take the bait. He'd wasted too many years trying to help, and then feeling gutted when she slipped back down. But with Colin gone . . .

'We're staying a while. The kids keep asking about you and I want—'

Her face softened at the mention of her grandchildren. He cast around, trying to sum up all the things he'd ever wanted for her.

I want you to look after yourself.

I want you to be a normal mum.

I want to be able to answer questions about my family without having to censor the bad bits.

Ned took a deep breath, his promise to Willow and Doug fresh in his mind.

'I want you to get help.'

9

Maeve gripped the doorframe, then snatched her hand back as a big huntsman spider scurried across the dusty window.

'I am getting help,' she shot back. 'There's a guy near Natimuk.'

Ned's breath came out in a frustrated huff. Natimuk was hardly Harley Street.

'Someone whose qualifications don't come from a cornflakes packet. Colin might have played along with this whole circus, but you need to see someone properly qualified to deal with . . .' He faltered, remembering what the alcohol support counsellor had said, when he'd called the free helpline for advice earlier in the day.

No accusations, no blame and no finger pointing.

'I want you to get help dealing with grief,' he finished quietly.

He expected many reactions, and even braced himself for a slap across the face. It wouldn't be the first time, though she'd been three sheets to the wind when it happened before. But her burst of laughter caught him by surprise.

'You don't believe me, do you? I really haven't had a drink in years.'

Ned lifted his glasses and pinched the bridge of his nose.

'Grief seems to be a pretty common denominator, though. If you could commit to counselling, I think we'd have a better chance of moving forward.'

The wind picked up, making the nearby hay shed creak and groan.

'It's hard to believe,' Maeve said, 'given the state of this lovely mansion, and the Porsche parked in the hay shed over there, but I don't have endless buckets of cash to throw at fancy shrinks.'

Her smile took the edge off her sarcasm. He'd been prepared for that one.

'I can handle the cost. Will you go if I make an appointment?'

'Can I see the children if I do?' Maeve's question came out quickly.

Ned nodded, hoping he'd made the right decision. Would a good father barter his children like that?

'If you agree to getting help.'

He heard Maeve gasp and he turned to see two dark heads bobbing across the paddock, coming in their direction. Willow and Doug must have followed at a distance.

Gah! That wasn't how it was supposed to work.

He strode towards them, meeting them at the worn sheep yards.

'I asked you to wait back at the house.'

'Is that her, Dad?'

'It is, but she's not up for visitors today,' he said. 'We'll see her later in the week, okay?'

'Can't we see her now?'

Ned looked back to see Maeve still standing by the door. For a moment he almost wavered. But he needed to see how bad things were first, and at least get her on the right path before he let his children anywhere near her.

Having been blessed with a father who was both low-stress and perceptive, Diana had never quite understood her father-in-law's talent for turning a simple visit into a military-style operation, with no stone left unturned.

In the lead-up to Reg's arrival, he'd bombarded Diana with phone calls about the weather, the state of the mattress in the spare room, whether he needed to bring the passwords for his pay television subscriptions so he wouldn't miss any of his favourite sports shows during his stay, and the availability of his special brand of almond milk at the local supermarket. All things they'd covered on previous visits.

'It's like having another child to worry about,' she told Angie, the phone pressed against her ear as she dashed around the supermarket in Hamilton. 'Hold up a minute, Ange. No, not that one, Harry. We already have lollies. Put them back,' she scolded, guarding the trolley closely as Harry, Elliot and Leo emerged from the confectionary aisle.

'I bet you're already counting down the days until he heads back to WA?'

'You'd better believe it,' Diana groaned. She finished the call, rushed through the checkout and packed the groceries around the boys' feet, knowing from experience that Reg's suitcases would take up most of the boot. They pulled into the Hamilton depot just as the bus arrived.

Diana checked her phone again as the boys clambered out of the car, hoping there might have been a message from Ned. Nothing. She'd resisted pestering him, perhaps it was time to put a poster in the general store window . . .

Her father-in-law Reg had a pep in his step as he disembarked the bus. She shoved the phone in her pocket and went to greet him.

'Boys, boys, boys,' he said, throwing his arms wide.

The boys allowed themselves to be squeezed tightly before Reg turned in her direction.

'How's my Annie-girl? Bearing up all right, old duck?'

In all her married years, she'd never warmed to that nickname. Diana silently counted to five and reminded herself of her father-in-law's good points. Primarily, the fact he lived on the other side of the country.

The drive home was full of stories about Reg's various travelling companions, his latest theories on the Australian cricket umpiring and a detailed, spoiler-heavy review of the new John Grisham novel.

Cameron was at the clothesline when they arrived home, pegging up the sheets and towels.

'Still got him earning his keep, I see,' said Reg, smoothing down what was left of his hair before donning his hat. 'Shouldn't he be at cricket, warming up?'

Diana tugged on the handbrake.

Breathe.

'All under control, Reg. We'll get you settled in first and make it to the cricket oval in plenty of time.'

She slipped out of the car and gestured for Cameron, who had always been the apple of his grandfather's eye, to help unload the luggage.

It wasn't until after she'd arrived at the oval an hour later, dropped Reg and the boys off at the clubrooms with a promise to be back before the match started, that she noticed two missed calls on her phone. A smile spread across her face.

Ned wasn't sure what he'd been expecting from Jonno's friend Butch, but if the bloke was annoyed about the chopping and changing of plans, or being contacted while he was on his honeymoon, he didn't show it.

'Too easy, mate, no worries. You guys sort it out among yourselves and let me know. If you need someone to run it temporarily, I'm happy to pitch in. If you want to sell or lease it out, then I'll chat to the bank about scrounging up a deposit. And if you're stuck on anything, just give me a call. Anytime! Colin helped me out of a pickle or two, I'd be chuffed to return the favour.'

The conversation threw Ned a little. He was used to the health-care industry, where timeframes, measurements and motivations were precisely planned. He listened and made notes as Butch briefed him on the farm's essentials, making plans for an in-person meet-up as soon as Butch returned to the Western District.

Ned headed outside, in search of the children. They weren't in the orchard, with the fragrant apple blossoms, and there was no sign of them in the old pig pen either. A noise came from Colin's flower shed and when he peered through the window, Ned found himself shaking with laughter.

Willow sported a pair of earmuffs, full-length khaki overalls and oversized gardening gloves, while Doug wore a huge straw hat that covered his eyebrows, with a tool belt slung over his shoulder like an artillery belt.

Ned tapped on the dusty glass. They spun around, their guilty expressions making him laugh even harder.

'What are you supposed to be?'

'We're Igor and Ernest, the best snail assassins in the country,' said Doug, picking up a box of snail bait and shaking it theatrically.

Colin's potting shed was dim inside compared to the clear sunny day, but Ned could see it was much the same as always. Gardening equipment crammed onto every shelf, benches packed with pots, pest sprays and potting soil. He took in the limp seedlings and the framed photos, knowing he wasn't quite ready to step inside just yet.

He beckoned the children outside.

'How about you grab those plants and we'll whack them in the ground, then we've got a special job to do.'

It was the first time in years he'd sunk his hands into the dirt, and even though the plants looked likely to turn up their toes, he found himself talking the children through the steps as he put them in the ground.

'Like tucking them into bed,' said Doug, proudly patting the soil.

'Now water them in and we're done. Willow, grab the hose.'

'We're *not* done yet, Dad. And you have to call me Ernest when I'm in my assassin gear, not Willow,' she said, sprinkling bright-blue snail bait pellets in her wake.

Their sense of humour was a welcome reprieve from his worries about Maeve, and the sombre task ahead.

'Righto, kids, Igor and Ernest need to step aside, because I've got an important job for Willow and Doug.'

Willow and Doug raced to the driveway, while Ned ducked inside to collect the ashes, which had arrived by registered post a few days earlier. Staring at the two matching canisters on the mantlepiece, he carefully carried one to the car, leaving half of Colin's ashes for Jonno.

He glanced at the shearers' quarters as they drove into the paddock. No sign of Maeve.

Driving through several gates, he eventually pulled up by a small creek. A flock of chickens followed them halfway across the paddock, and their clucking merged with the chorus of the galahs perched in the gums.

'Is this the spot, Dad?'

Ned nodded and eased the Land Rover door open. At least Colin would have a bird symphony year-round.

Tucking the crematorium tin into the crook of his arm, Ned took one small hand in each of his and together the trio made their way to the tree trunk.

'I still think Colin would rather be with the flowers,' said Willow, picking up a stick and tossing it into the water.

'See that bend over there?' Ned gestured to where the creek narrowed and then twisted to the south. 'Your grandfather used to trap eels there every Easter.'

'He must have loved it here. I'd come down here every day if I lived here. Maybe twice a day,' said Doug, with a nod.

'Yep, he called it his thinking spot.'

Ned opened the tin.

'You ready for this?'

Willow nodded. Doug clapped his hands, as if expecting the ashes to amalgamate into a lifelike Disney-style version of the grandfather he barely knew.

Ned waited for a light breath of wind before he tilted the tin. The magpie in the tree warbled, a fitting send-off as the ashes settled on the water and floated away. He hesitated and assessed the small amount of powder left. *Maybe Maeve would want . . .*

Ned rubbed the back of his neck. *Fat chance. She's more of a 'get smashed and avoid reality' type of griever than a 'scattering ashes in a special location' person, remember?* Still, something made him seal the lid to return the not-quite-empty cannister to the ute.

He sat down on the bank and patted the dry grass beside him.

'Pull up a pew, guys.'

Doug tossed stones into the water, interjecting occasionally with a question as Ned explained they were diverting from their carefully mapped-out trip.

'But if we're staying here to help your mum, then why haven't we met her yet? And why don't you call her Mum?'

While he hadn't told them their grandmother was a recovering alcoholic, ripe for a relapse in the wake of Colin's death, he'd made it clear they shouldn't expect a close relationship with Maeve.

'Families can be complicated. We haven't had a good relationship for a long time, and sometimes people don't want help. But with Uncle Jonno on his way to Antarctica, and your grandfather gone . . .'

Ned ran a finger along the soil of the creek bank, unearthing little rocks and watching them tumble into the water. 'I just want to keep an eye on her, make sure she's coping with all this . . .'

They nodded and he let out a deep breath, drawing them close.

'And I think maybe we can make it fun, spend lots of time outdoors.'

'I'm in,' Willow said, eyes twinkling behind her glasses. 'It's been ages since we've lived in a house instead of an apartment, and we've never lived on a farm.'

'Do you think we can go camping and toast marshmallows?' Doug asked.

'I know for a fact that Colin's shed will be brimming with tents and swags,' said Ned, tickling Doug under his chin. 'Probably even a bicycle or three?'

'I'm in, too,' Doug said, scrambling to get up. He bounded over to the ute, the lure of a bicycle trumping any uncertainty about their stay. Ned held out a hand to Willow and helped her up, hoping he'd made the right decision for them all.

Diana stood outside the Bridgefield General Store as she listened to Ned's voicemail. Although it wasn't a definite 'yes', he was open to hearing more. The second message was from Bron, confirming the launch party date and giving her the green light to discuss the event locally.

'No leaks to the national media, though. Leave that to us professionals,' Bron said.

As if I have time for harassing journalists between kid wrangling and flower farming, Diana thought with a smile.

The doorbell jangled as she went inside. Eddie Patterson waved at her from the shop kitchen.

'You look happy for a lady who's just been gate-crashed by her father-in-law,' said Toby, popping out from the kitchen. He wiped his hands on his apron and grabbed Diana's newspaper.

'It's hard to be miserable on a day like this. Sun's shining, kids are at cricket, and I might have *just* found myself a farmhand.'

'Ah, that'll do it. I'll pop these back on the bench then, will I?' Toby reached under the counter and pulled out a wad of Darling Dahlia subscription brochures.

'You're a gem.'

Diana flipped through the *Herald Sun* as Toby heated milk for one of his to-die-for lattes. 'So, who's the lucky worker? Did you hear back from the employment agency?'

'Those guys?' Diana shook her head with a snort. 'They couldn't organise their way out of a paper bag. No, Colin's son Ned said he might help out. Not confirmed, but I'm optimistic.'

Diana glanced around the shop, suddenly itching to share the news about the launch.

'Lara in today?'

Toby tipped his head towards the storeroom.

Taking her coffee out the back, she found Lara knee deep in boxes, baskets and industrial-sized bags of flour.

'Are you hiding from Reg already?' she said.

Diana laughed. 'Not yet. But I've got some hot goss if you're in the mood for good news.'

She could almost see Lara's ear pricking up, then drew a deep, dramatically suspenseful breath before telling her sister about Sadie Woodford's launch event.

'This is huge,' said Lara, her eyes bright with pride. 'How did you manage that?'

'You remember my housemate from uni, Bron?'

Lara nodded.

'She tipped me off and I contacted Sadie at the exact right time. But then with Colin's death, I didn't think I could get the place ready without his help.'

'We would have pitched in.'

'Of course . . .' Diana nodded. 'But you've got your own things going on. I thought I needed someone who knew what they were doing in the garden and could commit to it.' She told her sister about Ned.

Lara lifted an eyebrow. 'And this Gardiner bloke fits the bill? I heard he was a pharmacist with itchy feet.'

'If he's anything like Colin, he'll be a jack-of-all-trades. He needs a break while he gets Colin's affairs in order, and I need a worker.'

She couldn't help the defensive tone that crept into her voice as her good mood dipped a little, and suddenly wished she'd broken the news to Penny or Angie first. Natural-born optimists, just like her, they'd be cheering her on, not poking holes in her plan. Lara had the strongest bullshit radar of all her sisters and she'd never been afraid to ask difficult questions.

'Keep your hair on,' Lara said with a grin. 'If you're sure he'll be great, then I believe you. Imagine how much free publicity you'll get from this launch. You'll be hosting celebrity weddings before you know it. Hey, do you think they'll need a photographer for the event? Toby would be perfect.'

'I'll make sure I mention it to Bron,' Diana promised. As she left for the cricket oval, Diana felt her excitement returning. Darling Dahlias was going to start with a bang, no ifs, buts or maybes.

10

Ned crawled out of bed at sunrise, and squinted at the phone, rereading the email he'd sent to the locum agency in the wee hours of the morning. Cancelling the six-month contract at the Mount Gambier pharmacy had been easy, it was his decision to try and help Maeve that was harder to face in the soft light of day.

Ned opened the laptop and called Jonno on Zoom, bringing him up to speed on their decision to stay longer.

'Just because Colin obviously fell for Maeve's latest sob story, doesn't mean you need to. When did she even move into the shearers' hut? I can't believe I missed that.'

'Not sure,' said Ned. 'All her furniture's jammed into the place. It's in the same state it was fifteen years ago. It's a miracle the hay shed hasn't fallen on it.'

'It's a miracle she hasn't burned it down, more like it.' Jonno tugged a thick beanie down over his ears, and when he shifted position, Ned could see the porthole window in his cabin. 'Remember that time I got home from footy early and she was passed out on the couch with the fire door ajar?'

Ned nodded. For a time, Ned had dreaded phone calls from Jonno, and although his brother and father continued trying to help Maeve after he'd left for university, he felt both guilty and relieved that he was three hours away.

'Even if she says she's sober now, what if she falls off the wagon for the umpteenth time?'

'Trust me, I don't think it's a perfect set-up either but with Colin gone . . . and Jessie, too.' Ned sighed. 'I've decided to stay. It doesn't feel right washing my hands and skipping off into the sunset. Not until I've worked out what's the best thing to do and tried to sort everything out.'

Jonno's face softened as he nodded. Ned signed off with a promise to keep his brother updated and opened the email that had pinged into his inbox while they'd been talking.

It was the first locum contract he'd ever reneged on, and the agency rep was neither impressed nor overly sympathetic.

The text from Diana McIntyre was in stark contrast, and even though he had only agreed to meet and discuss further, she sounded delighted. He wasn't sure how much help he'd be, or why it felt like some type of IOU on his father's behalf, but if he was sticking around to keep an eye on Maeve, he may as well pitch in to help Diana.

When the delivery van rumbled down the driveway the next day, Ned had the egg trays waiting in the shade of the large shed.

'Fast learner, aren't you?' Imogen climbed out of the van with her notepad at the ready.

Ned picked up the crates and started loading them. 'It's not rocket science.' He didn't mention how good it had felt to be working outdoors again. 'I've started looking over Colin's paperwork. From the looks of things, these eggs mostly go to cafes?'

'Yep, they sell like hotcakes. I thought you were leaving?'
Imogen closed the back of the van and studied him curiously.

'Staying—just for a bit.'

'You know Maeve's not your responsibility, don't you?'

Ned nodded. 'I keep telling myself that. She's not exactly
good in a crisis though, is she? And there's more to do with
sorting out Colin's estate than I expected, so we'll cool our
heels until things settle down and Jonno gets back.'

'And I hear you're getting your green thumb on again?'

Ned looked across to Colin's garden and the cheerful riot of
spring blooms, wondering what he'd find at Darling Dahlias.
'I haven't said yes, yet.'

'Diana's so lovely you'll be hard pressed to say no. And you'll
be eating better than ever if she's serving up smoko every day.'

A shriek from the orchard drew their attention. Willow and
Doug weaved in and out of the fruit trees, then scrambled up
the ancient trunk of a blossoming granny smith.

Imogen watched their tree-climbing antics a moment longer
before climbing into the van. She leaned out the window. 'Your
kids will fit in great around here, too. What did you tell them
about Maeve?'

'Just the Reader's Digest version. Don't get me wrong, I was
tempted,' he said, shoving his hands in his pockets. 'Just so
they didn't think it was going to be a soapie-style reunion,
or anything like that. But they don't need the details.' Doubt
stirred in Ned's stomach. 'I just hope it doesn't backfire.'

'Kids are more resilient than we give them credit for. My
Oscar bounced back pretty well after my divorce.' She nodded
to Willow and Doug. 'It's been a long time since I dated Jonno,
but you guys seemed to manage the unique family dynamics.
I'm sure your pair will follow your lead; however you choose
to handle this.'

Ned tried to channel Imogen's enthusiasm as he loaded the children into Colin's Land Rover and drove them into Bridgefield.

'Did you go here, Dad?' Doug asked as they arrived at the primary school.

Ned shook his head. 'Nope, we didn't live here when I was in primary school. Uncle Jonno went here, though.'

'Did Aunt Jessie go here before she died?'

Ned faltered. It was hard to hear her name mentioned so casually. He thought about their conversation by the creek, his promise to be more open with them from now on.

'Your Aunt Jessie died before we moved to Bridgefield.'

A school bell sounded and children began filing out of classrooms. He looked at his watch. Lunch break, by the look of things.

Doug and Willow stuck close to him as they walked through the gates.

'Hey, I see the twins,' said Doug, pointing to the playground. Sure enough, two familiar blond boys were striding across the yard, laden with cricket bats, stumps and lunch boxes. They called out a cheerful 'G'day' as they set up the pitch.

Leo sprinted across the oval a moment later, abandoning his cricket bat as he rushed up to them. Ned felt a surge of gratitude for Diana McIntyre, as her youngest boy greeted them like long lost friends, proudly leading them to the front office.

'The Gardiner family, right on time.' The lady manning the desk took off her glasses, thanked Leo and introduced herself as the principal.

'You've already made friends, I see,' she said, as Leo skipped out, off to the playground. Willow and Doug nodded. 'Good choice, we all adore little Leo.' She looked at Ned as she began the tour. 'Their mother Diana used to teach here too, and all the McIntyre sisters attended when they were younger, of course. Such a great family, always volunteering and lending a hand where they can. They've had some tough times, but they're a lovely lot, those McIntyres.'

The comment stayed with Ned long after they'd seen every nook and cranny of the small school, met the teachers and signed enrolment forms.

Would the principal refer to *them* as 'a great family'? Single father, absentee mother, a hermit grandmother with a drinking problem . . . Fleur and Maeve might've stopped them ticking that box but as Ned waved goodbye to the principal, he knew he'd be doing his best to ensure Willow and Doug fell into the 'great kids' category, regardless of their family ties.

The kitchen looked like a bombsite when Diana got home. She heaved an armload of groceries onto the kitchen bench, doing her best to avoid plonking them in the middle of the half-unpacked lunch boxes and slick of honey beside a barely eaten sandwich that was attracting ants.

'Harry, Elliot, Leo! I need a hand in here,' she called out the window. The boys jumped off the trampoline and loped across the lawn, still in their training gear. 'Hey, Reg, how was cricket?'

'Not bad, Annie-girl, there was a lot of excitement in the clubrooms. Everyone's keen to see Cameron go all the way to the top. I told them our side of the family were all natural sportsman,' he said, sucking in his belly a little.

Diana cleared the bench and put away groceries as Reg proudly relayed the comments and praise from coaches and parents.

'We'll be watching him on the big screen before we know it, and it's probably time to upgrade his kit. Can't have my boy dragging around his equipment in a poxy old cricket bag.'

My boy? She looked at Cam's faded Grey-Nicolls bag. She'd tripped over it, dragged it inside when Cameron had forgotten, and fished grotty clothes from it countless times, but she knew it was special to him.

'That was Pete's old cricket bag,' she said softly. 'Cam's had it since he first started playing.'

Reg shook his head.

'It looks tatty lined up beside the other bags in the clubrooms. He probably doesn't want to upset you by asking for a new one.' He lowered his voice and tapped the side of his nose. 'Surprise him with a new one for Christmas, Annie-girl.'

The boys ferried the rest of the groceries inside and Diana started on a stir-fry. Reg uncapped the sherry and raised a glass towards Diana.

'Aperitif?'

'Bless you,' said Cameron, wandering into the kitchen with his dirty cricket kit in hand and a towel slung around his waist.

Reg laughed and poured himself a drink.

'No, it means pre-dinner drink, lad. When you're a bit older, I'll offer you a nip, too.'

He pulled up a stool at the island bench and flicked to the back of the *Herald Sun* as Diana prepared dinner. By the time she had the veggies diced, the meat marinating and all the ingredients for a chocolate pudding ready, Reg was squinting at the classified section, lips moving as he traced the fine print.

'Looking for someone?'

'Everyone's rolling off the perch, it's a rarity to finish the classifieds without finding school and sports chums in here.'

Diana listened with one ear as she added her secret ingredient —a tablespoon of coffee—to the pudding mix and then a pinch of salt. Her thoughts drifted to Colin.

'That reminds me, Reg. Colin was a similar build to you. I'm not sure what Ned plans to do with his clothes and shoes, but I can ask if you like?'

Her father-in-law nodded and kept reading. Clearing a lost one's wardrobe was a daunting task. Penny, Angie and Lara had helped her sort Pete's belongings into 'keep', 'donate' and 'discard' piles, and there'd been tears and laughter as she sifted through the outfits and the memories assigned to each. Knowing his clothes would be loved by someone else had made it easier and she made a mental note to ask Ned when she saw him next. Maybe he'd appreciate a helper for sorting through them, too?

11

Ned walked around the shearers' hut, spotting more of those steel-wool filled holes as he went, and found Maeve weeding a small veggie garden. He hadn't seen her in a set of gardening gloves his entire childhood. *Colin's influence?*

She waved away the sticky black flies and nodded a greeting. 'Edward.'

'I've booked that appointment in Hamilton next week. The kids made you these, too,' he said, handing her two get-well cards.

'Next week will be fine,' she said, studying the children's drawings. 'Did your wife put them up to this?'

He turned, shaking his head. 'Ex-wife. Last we heard she was at a yoga retreat in India.'

'Yoga?'

Maeve tilted her head, as if trying to figure out an appropriate response.

Ned looked out to the mountains, bracing himself for the pot calling the kettle black. 'I can't take any credit for the cards. When I told them you were unwell, they were disappointed they couldn't see you until you were better.'

Her gaze fell. Was she wondering what else he'd told them about her? Whether he'd outlined the many ways she'd failed as a mother over the years? He hadn't, but it was for their sake, not hers. She seemed to sense what he was thinking.

'I've been seven years sober, Edward. I'm not perfect, but I'm not the monster you seem to think I am. So, I can visit after the appointment?'

He kept his eyes on the paddocks ahead. Even though he'd committed to staying in Bridgefield to keep an eye on her, he couldn't deny he was wary. Eventually, he nodded. 'You've agreed to get help and if you can commit to regular sessions with this counsellor, then we can find some middle ground.'

'You don't look too thrilled about that.'

Ned thought of the regret he'd felt when he sat by Colin's hospital bed, an hour too late. He scratched his neck, trying to think ahead, not backwards.

'I'm dealing with it,' he said quietly.

He returned to the house to find a sea of Lego spread across the lounge room floor and Willow bickering with Doug over whose job it was to tidy it up. Clapping his hands, he spoke over the racket.

'Who's up for a quick spin? I'll call Diana and see if she's free to give us a farm tour.'

Doug and Willow had piled into the Land Rover before the phone call had even connected.

'Ned?' said Diana over lively conversation in the background. 'Hang on a minute!'

The phone went quiet. He heard a door shutting, and when she spoke again, he could hear the smile in her voice. It felt like a burst of sunshine.

'Hey, I'm glad you called. What's up?'

'Sounds like you're in the middle of something,' he said, apologetically.

'Not at all, it's just Sunday lunch.'

Just.

'I was hoping to drop in and check out the farm, but if it's not a good time—?'

Diana cut over the top of him.

'Absolutely. Everyone's on their way out. Come round now,' she said, brushing off his protests.

As he drove, Ned thought of the chatter he'd overheard in the background when Diana had answered the phone, the ties she had with her family and the bond she'd formed with his dad. None of his family had been together in the same house in twenty years. Did she know how lucky she was to have such a tight family?

It only took ten minutes to drive from Colin's farm to Darling Downs, and he saw the flower farm as soon as he reached the top of a hill.

Doug giggled as the Land Rover rattled over the cattle grid. While the roadside leading to Diana's property was flanked by paperbark trees, the gravel driveway that delivered them to the house was decorated with leafy ornamentals. Bees flitted in and out of the neatly trimmed hedges of rosemary and lavender that ran the length of the whitewashed weatherboard house. The grass was freshly mowed, and the clippings had been caught, rather than scattered across the lawn like at his place. The expansive rose gardens were mulched to perfection, each bush bursting with colour. Cars and people filled the driveway, and Ned soon found himself in the middle of flurried greetings.

No doubting the family resemblance. Even if Diana hadn't explained they were her sisters, he would have been blind to miss the similarities in their ginger hair, broad smiles and warm manner. The sisters hugged goodbye before rounding up their children, who were blond like Diana's tribe. Their

partners—Jonesy, Tim and the chap from the store, Toby—
followed, and Diana's father, gave him one last handshake.

'Condolences again, Ned. Colin will be sorely missed,' said
Angus.

Diana's family drove away and Harry, Elliot and Leo
commandeered Willow and Doug, keen to show them around.

'Sorry for interrupting your family get-together,' he said.

'No worries at all.' Diana led him towards the deck, the sun
dappling her green dress and dangly earrings. 'We do it most
Sundays, so it's no big deal. Don't suppose you're hungry?'
she asked. 'There's masses of leftovers.'

Ned started to object when a lanky lad rounded the corner.
He was a head taller than Diana, with the same blue eyes, but
his greeting wasn't half as warm.

'Welcome to the madhouse,' he said briskly. 'I'm Cameron.'

Ned returned his handshake and then remembering Diana's
shoes-off preference, slipped off his shoes, leaving them next
to a pair of pink sneakers and four pairs of Rossi boots. An
old border collie smiled at him from a basket by the back
door, tail thumping out a 'hello' and grey-flecked ears pricked
to attention.

Colourful paintings, woollen throw rugs and vases of flowers
gave the interior a warm and cosy feel. Magazines cluttered
the coffee table between two plump leather sofas. Ned cast
an eye over the photos on the wall. He could see where the
boys got their height from—Diana's husband looked at least
six foot four, a full head and shoulders above his wife.

'I'm Reg,' said an elderly gent, emerging from another
room. 'You probably knew my son Pete,' he added, sticking
out a hand and nearly shaking Ned's shoulder from its socket.

'I didn't, but I've heard good things about him,' Ned said.

'Not a local lad, then?'

'I think you've got to be three generations born and bred before you can claim that status.'

The old man laughed in agreement, unmuted the television and turned his attention back to the sport. Cameron settled down on the couch near his grandfather, but Ned sensed his attention was only half on the game.

Diana pulled a platter out of the fridge, piled with an assortment of fruit and desserts, and offered it to the children, who had all swarmed inside.

'We're fine thanks—' said Ned, just as the children galloped inside.

'I'm starving,' said Harry.

'Us too,' added Willow and Doug, smiling sweetly.

Ned grimaced. 'I fed them, I swear.'

Diana checked that the children were settled with snacks and water before showing Ned the flower farm. For some reason, she felt almost nervous, and found herself rattling off plant names and flower varieties as she took him through the rows.

She turned back, pleased to see Ned admiring the set-up. Her nerves disappeared, replaced with pride as she explained her supply agreements with the local florists. He watched and listened, pausing every now and then to pose a question, his considered sentences again reminding her of Colin.

'Hard to beat views like these,' he said, doing a slow spin to take in the mountainous panorama to the north and the gardens she'd ploughed so much love into. 'But I reckon the flowers will give the Grampians a run for their money when they hit their stride.'

He gets it. Maybe this could actually work . . .

'And you're planning to supply bouquets year-round?'

Diana harvested flowers as they went, dropping them into a bucket of water. 'Well, spring, summer and autumn, but even more exciting, I'm hosting a huge book launch here.'

She told him about the event, Sadie's books and the excitement of being singled out.

'You've probably heard of her?' He shook his head and even though she tried not to gush, she knew she probably came across as starstruck, as she rattled off the names of Sadie's coffee-table books and several of the awards she'd snapped up in the last few years.

'Now the pressure's on,' Ned said. 'You sure you want to trust a hack like me to help you prep for the floral event of the year?'

'Four hands are much better than two. There's loads to do beforehand if you're still keen?'

'You seem pretty capable. Sure you can't manage this place on your own?'

Diana shook her head.

'The boys pitch in when they can but I was really counting on Colin's help in the main dahlia season. Even more so now that I need it picture perfect for Sadie's launch in March. Plus, my eldest boy, Cameron, has been training with the premier league, so we're in Geelong all the time now,' she said.

He gestured to the flowers she'd picked.

'Mind if I . . . ?'

Relinquishing the bucket, she looked at his big hands, noticing how they clasped the fine stems. He gently laid the flowers onto the weathered table by the garden's edge, sorting them into type, then stripping the stems. She struggled to string together a sentence as he deftly drew them together, crossing the stems and rotating the bunch this way and that until it was a proper bouquet. *God, he's good with his hands.*

'Five or six months, you reckon?'

Diana dragged her eyes away from those long, nimble fingers and nodded.

'That would get us through the peak picking period, Valentine's Day and Sadie's event. If you were around for digging all the tubers up for storage in late autumn, that'd be brilliant, but I'll take what I can get.'

Diana found herself holding her breath as she awaited his response. *Please say yes.*

'There're a few things that need fixing up at Colin's, and the eggs to see to, so the flower farm mightn't always be at the top of my priority list. And it's been years since I've done anything with flowers, you might not want me.'

She laughed, assessing the posy he'd made. It looked like it'd been put together by a florist, each carefully placed bloom contradicting his words. She'd practised for months and created many terrible posies before making something half as good.

'If you're happy with award wages, I'll take you.'

He laughed and raised an eyebrow.

Remove foot from mouth, Diana.

'Deal!' Ned stuck out a hand, Diana took it, liking how firm his grip was. Not rotator-cuff shattering like Reg's, but no namby-pamby limp-fish handshake either.

She grinned all the way back to the farmhouse.

Diana took her morning coffee and a plastic bucket outside to the garden, watching the golden light transform the trunks of the gum trees to a rich ochre colour. She'd slept better last night than in weeks.

Diana bustled the boys out the door to school, dropped Reg off at McIntyre Park to spend the day with Angus and now home again, she slipped her gardening gloves on. The dirt had settled on the rows of dahlia tubers, with a mid-week rain smoothing the soil and erasing all traces of their work. It wouldn't be long before little leaves would push their way up through the soil.

Diana made her way past the dahlias and stooped down to inspect the sweet peas. The slugs had given them a hammering a fortnight ago, and she was pleased to see her dark o'clock pest-hunting expeditions had done the trick. Diana set her mug on top of the post that supported the sweet pea trellis, slipped the gardening shears out of her back pocket and snipped off long stems bursting with pink, purple and cream flowers. The fragrance was glorious, better than any perfume.

Time slipped away as she harvested from garden beds she'd created with Pete, patches she'd planted with Colin, and plots she'd worked on with help from her sons. Then she moved onto the newer sections of the garden that she'd made entirely on her own, when the shovelling, digging and planting provided an outlet for her grief. Before long, she had a dozen buckets of flowers lined up in the shade of the gum trees. Sky-blue cornflowers, sprays of boronia and carnations. She looked back at the house as she lugged them to the shed.

'Wish we had one of those wire trolleys like the nurseries use,' she said to Jinx, who was curled up in a pile of leaves. The cat's tail twitched in response.

At least when Ned started she'd have someone else to talk to other than the cat. The thought made Diana smile. She loaded the bouquets into the back of her four-wheel drive.

Cricket commentary on the car radio jolted her memory as she drove into town: *I need to book accommodation and confirm our tickets for the club function in Geelong.*

Pulling out of the driveway, she connected the phone to the car audio and breathed a sigh of relief when the city coach answered.

'Diana, I'm glad to hear you can make it. And after showing such talent in last weekend's practice match against Frankston, your young batsman's looking good for selection in the third elevens' side next weekend.'

'He is?' Diana let out a whoop of excitement. The twice-weekly 600-kilometre roundtrips were finally paying off.

'We've been watching his stats, and a spot's just come up in the side. We'll know for sure next week, but I thought you might like to know. Make sure he's all rested up.'

Diana hung up, beaming from ear to ear.

Several phone calls later and she'd secured them seats for the function. A phone call from Bron came through as the road dipped through gullies and curved around hills.

'I hope you've got some fancy flowers in bloom. Your friend Sadie's pulled a few strings. A magazine team is heading your way next Friday for the inside scoop on your flower farm.'

Diana's heart felt like it skipped a beat. *My friend Sadie.* But the joy was short-lived.

'Oh no, Bron! Cameron might be playing cricket for Geelong next weekend.'

'He plays cricket for Geelong every weekend, doesn't he?'

Diana exhaled loudly. 'Not for the third elevens, he doesn't. This could be his big break, then it's onto the second elevens and the firsts, then the state ranks.'

'God, you lost me in the thirds' and seconds' mumbo jumbo. I can hardly work out the difference between test cricket and one dayers.'

Diana laughed. It had taken her quite some time to differentiate between the levels, too.

'Just know it's the biggest break he's had so far. Can't the magazine reschedule for the following week? Or, even better, make it earlier. The irises are at their peak right now and—'

Bron hooted with laughter.

'This is a national magazine, lovely. They tell you when they're coming, not the other way around. Sadie called the editor specially and gave up some of her valuable page space for a mini feature on your flower farm. You'd be mad to turn it down.'

Diana tapped at the steering wheel distractedly. What to do? She'd never dared to dream of seeing her property in the pages of *Country Home* magazine. And here was a team of photographers and journalists, handed to her on a platter.

'Which edition's it for?'

'February, so every Tom, Dick or Harry will be thinking Darling Dahlias this Valentine's Day. I'd love to take the credit for this coup, but it's all Sadie's influence. Midas touch,' Bron added.

The dilemma played on Diana's mind as she delivered most of her flowers to the florist, then whipped into one of her favourite stores in town, the little Lifeline op shop. She carried the small bouquet in, along with a bag of clothes the boys had outgrown.

'Now here's a sight for sore eyes,' said the shopkeeper Malcolm, his arthritic hands shaking as he cupped one of the first season's roses and leaned in for a deep sniff. The older gentleman, who had been battling Parkinson's for as long as Diana had known him, thanked her again.

'I know I say it every time, but these beautiful flowers are better suited to the fancy stores. They'd pay you a pretty penny for them too, I'm sure.'

Diana waved him away.

'My pleasure, Malcolm. Really, it's just me being a flower snob and shuddering every time I see that hideous plastic arrangement.'

'I know it's not dollars and cents, but I spread the word where I can,' he said, turning the vase so the best flowers were customer facing, before tidying the stack of business cards he'd insisted she display. 'If only there was a better way to get more customers to your farm gate,' said Malcolm.

Diana thought of the magazine spread that had fallen into her lap all the way home. Just like the launch event, she knew it was an opportunity she needed to grab with both hands.

Diana was woken on Sunday morning by the twins bounding through her bedroom door before the sun was even up.

'Mum, where's my cricket uniform?'

'I can't find my helmet.'

She prised her eyes open gingerly, regretting her decision to stay up late working on the Darling Dahlias Instagram page. It had seemed like a perfectly good idea to update it last night, but she was now paying the price for burning the candle at both ends.

'Good morning to you, too.'

She dragged herself out of bed, bleary eyed, to help get them ready, and was pleased to find all four boys at the kitchen table.

'Just the lads I wanted to see,' she said, heaping coffee into a mug and loading up the toaster while the jug boiled. 'Time for a quick family meeting.'

Cameron caught her glancing down the hallway to the guest room, where Reg was still snoring his head off.

'I wanted to run an idea past you.'

The boys watched her curiously.

'You know how I've been a worried about how I'll manage the flower farm without Colin?' They nodded. 'And you remember Colin's son, Ned?'

Elliot piped up: 'With the crazy cat scratches down his face!'

'Willow and Doug visited school on Friday,' added Leo.

'Ned might give me a hand for a while,' Diana continued. 'And you know the best bit? A really famous author wants to have a huge launch party at our flower farm, and a magazine's coming to do a photo shoot for it.'

'So we'll be famous?' Harry said.

Cameron cuffed him around the ear. 'They wouldn't put you in it, Hazzie. They want people to buy the magazine, not have nightmares. I'd say they'd prefer a fit pro-cricketer.'

'Steady on, hotshot,' Diana said. 'There's a slight problem standing between you and your centrefold. You boys will be at school when the magazine comes, and Cam, you're heading to Geelong straight afterwards for the players function.'

Cameron's smile slid right off his face. 'What? But how's that going to work? Are they just taking photos of the flowers while we're away? I'm not missing cricket.'

'Course not, mate,' Diana said. 'I'd never ask that. But we need to work out Plan B, so you can still make the game and the dinner. I could ask Aunty Penny and Tim to take you, or I could ask your grandfather to drive you down?'

A loud yawn came from the hallway and they all looked up to see Reg in his tartan pyjamas, the wisps of his comb-over dangling across his ear.

'I *do* love a road trip. Who am I driving where?'

'I was thinking of my dad, actually,' she said, finishing her coffee and mixing up a quick batch of biscuits. 'To take Cameron to cricket next weekend. There's a past players' dinner Friday night and then—' She stopped, remembering the coach's request to keep quiet until Cameron's spot in the team was confirmed. 'Then there's cricket on the Saturday.'

'Brilliant, Angus and I could share the driving. We'd make a boys' weekend out of it, right Cam?'

Diana didn't miss the look of disappointment on Cam's face as he dragged his cricket bag through the laundry. The oven timer sounded and Diana turned to pull the batch of nutties from the oven, scalding her fingers as she flicked the hot biscuits onto a wire rack. She left them to cool as she collected a quick garden posy, then loaded the boys, biscuits and blooms into the car.

Harry, Elliot and Leo carried their gear into the clubrooms, keen as mustard, while Cameron stalked off without another word. Reg followed after Cam. Diana headed to the familiar white ute parked by the clubrooms.

'What's up Cam's nose?' Angus asked.

'Bad timing on my behalf,' Diana said, filling her father in on the magazine–cricket weekend conflict.

'Course I can take him. And it'll get Reg out from underfoot. You can't let an opportunity like that slip between your fingers.'

'You sure, Dad? I was thinking of asking Penny and Tim.'

'Don't give it another thought. Penny's got plans, last I heard, so Tim will be on dad duties. We can fly the McIntyre flag at the dinner and settle in for a good day watching cricket on the Saturday. It's a much better game than this level of country cricket. Too easy, love.'

Thank goodness for small mercies, she thought, giving him a kiss on the cheek. Diana fetched the bouquet from her car and continued around the oval.

'I hear you've been crook, Patti,' Diana said when she reached a pale blue sedan.

The older woman in the passenger seat clucked her tongue. 'Oh, you shouldn't have.' Unable to hide the delight, Patti buried her nose in the flowers and let out a little sigh.

I'll never get sick of giving people flowers.

'My nan used to grow sweet peas, rest her soul,' said Patti, blinking fast as she brought the bouquet up for another deep sniff. 'And it's just a few lumps and bumps scraped off my insides and a night in hospital. Not enough to make me miss the game.'

A little girl with freckles waved at them from the pitch.

'Our Lizzie will be captaining the Aussie women's team at this rate,' Patti said. A crack rang through the air as the girl smashed the ball into the field.

Patti, who had comforted Diana as they planned Pete's funeral, looked back from the cricket game to study Diana carefully.

'You're looking well. All that fresh air and hard work seem to be agreeing with you. I've signed us up for one of your bouquet subscriptions, too,' Patti said. 'I quite like the sound of fresh flowers every week, and if Gordon kicks up a stink I'll remind him they're tax deductible. People expect pretty flowers in funeral parlours, don't you think?'

'Absolutely. And thank you, it's been good having a focus.' She told Patti about the magazine spread and the launch event she was hosting.

'I know Pete and Colin would both be proud to see you soldiering on in their absence,' Patti said. 'I hear you've got the next best thing to Colin starting next week, too.'

'I think it'll be good for both of us.'

'Such a shame Ned Gardiner didn't follow in his father's footsteps a little sooner. Colin did well with the hand he was dealt, that's for sure. Better than many would have done.' Patti lowered her voice and leaned in a little closer, even though the dog on the back of the neighbouring ute didn't seem too interested in eavesdropping.

'You never get over losing a child, and I don't think Bridgefield was the fresh start they'd imagined. What with the boys leaving home the moment they could, and Maeve's struggles. Maybe now that Ned's home . . .'

'His kids seem happy with the decision,' Diana said, remembering the way Willow had quizzed Elliot on the bus schedule, the nearest library and school excursions. 'They might help ease the loss?'

Patti nodded. 'Things are different with grandchildren. It's almost like a reward for surviving parenthood. I can't say I know Maeve well, seeing she's lived away on and off over the years, but perhaps some time together will be just the ticket.'

12

Ned eased open his eyes to see a furry mound on the pillow beside him.

Flopsy.

The tabby cat stirred, his flicking tail conveying his annoyance at being woken as Ned climbed out of bed.

'Just make yourself at home, mate. Don't let me interrupt your busy schedule.'

Doug and Willow's voices came down the hallway, then the *thunk, thunk, thunk* of the foot pedal on the dentist chair pounding the floor. He detoured via the laundry, where he emptied dry food into the cat's bowl and topped up the water bowl. The sound in the kitchen grew louder. He needed to get in there before they broke a tile.

'Hey, ratbags,' he said, dropping a kiss onto Doug's forehead and slipping a newspaper under the foot pedal to deaden the sound. Both children were dressed in their new school uniforms, and if the milky bowls on the table were any indication, they'd finished their breakfast before playing dentists.

'All excited for school?'

Willow nodded.

'When's the bus coming, Dad?' Doug said as he jockeyed the old-fashioned hydraulic controls at the back of the chair. The chair made a 'psssst' noise as it descended. Willow jumped off the chair and grabbed her backpack.

'Steady on, it's only just 7 a.m.,' he said. But he was pleased by their enthusiasm. It was the first time they'd gone into a new school knowing anyone and it had obviously put a spring in their step. The dentist chair went up and down as the kids worked off their nervous energy.

'Righto, you lot, let's check the chooks before that dentist chair gives up the ghost.'

They finished their egg rounds quickly and headed back through the paddocks to grade the eggs and prep them for Imogen's pick-up. Willow dashed back to the house as soon as they'd finished, but Doug's little face was poised in such concentration that Ned could almost see the cogs turning inside his brain. Was he thinking about his first day at the new school? Or why they'd suddenly diverted from their travelling plans? Was it the aunt he'd only just learned about or the sick, elusive grandmother?

He nudged Doug.

'Penny for your thoughts, mate?'

Doug scratched his head, and by the big intake of breath, Ned wondered what doozy of a question he was about to come out with. *Not Fleur again, surely?* They rarely asked about their mother these days, but maybe all the revelations about the women in their family had stirred things up.

'Can I take a chook for show and tell, Dad? Leo said he's taken in lambs and kittens before.'

Ned threw back his head and laughed. Of all the comments he'd been bracing for, it wasn't that one.

'Why not, buddy, why not? Perhaps check with the teacher first, though.'

They packed their lunches and Ned waved goodbye as the bus pulled away from the old shelter shed at the end of Colin's driveway. The next job on his to-do list was clearing out his father's wardrobe. He'd been ignoring the task, but Diana's gentle query had spurred him into action.

Standing in front of the dark timber shelves, he'd been relieved to see everything was neatly ordered. Work shirts and jeans filled the bulk of the cupboard, with good clothes in the bottom drawers and Colin's only suit hanging on the back of the door in a canvas suit bag. He started stacking the clothes into piles on the bed, like Diana had suggested.

Although every piece smelled like his father, it was the collection of thick winter woollies that packed the biggest emotional punch. Ned's grandmother had carded and hand-spun the wool in Gippsland, knitting the brown fibre into jerseys she knew would keep her family warm long after she was gone. Who would wear them now? And would they know the history behind each garment, the love that had gone into them? Diana's father-in-law could have all the striped rugby jumpers, checked shirts and knee-length twill shorts he wanted, but Ned felt a wave of sadness at the thought of parting with the homemade knits.

He gathered them up in his arms and returned them to the cupboard, surprised to feel tears running down his cheeks for the first time in years.

Diana drove to McIntyre Park as soon as the school bus left. Penny looked up from the sink, her hands full of half-peeled potatoes, when Diana presented her with the wet-weather gear she'd spotted at the op shop.

'Forgot to bring these last night. Aren't they sweet?' she said, pulling out a pair of pink overalls. Penny cooed over the waterproof jacket, covered in butterflies, just as Diana had known she would.

'Thanks, Diana, they'll be perfect for Lucy next winter.'

'And did you look up that book I sent you the link to? Apparently, it's the new bible on toddler sleep training.'

Penny nodded. 'And this is why you're my favourite sister.'

'Piece of cake,' Diana said, waving her hand. 'Now, before I dash off, tell me what you know about magazine photoshoots. I don't have time to pressure wash the weatherboards, will they photoshop them afterward?'

Like the flick of a switch, Penny slipped back into marketing mode, running through likely scenarios and outcomes.

'You'd better buy your friend Bron a great Chrissy present. Putting Darling Dahlias in front of 37,000 readers . . . From a marketing perspective, that's amazing exposure.'

It was years since Penny had traded her corporate wardrobe and jet-setting jaunts for life on the merino sheep farm, but she still knew her stuff. Walking Diana to her car, she rattled off tips and tricks from shoots she'd been involved in previously.

'Don't worry about weeding the daggy garden beds either,' Penny advised. 'They'll only shoot the best angles, and they can photoshop any fingerprints off the glass or cobwebs off the weatherboards, if necessary.'

Diana and Penny looked towards the Grampians, fanned out along the horizon and, as they watched, a pair of wallabies hopped past the water tanks. It was nearly identical to the view from Diana's property.

'Let's be honest, they'll probably be swept up with capturing that view too. And the gorgeous woman behind the flowers,' said Penny.

'You need your eyes checked,' Diana laughed, as she climbed into the four-wheel drive and started the engine.

'So, when does Ned Gardiner start? Perfect timing if you've got to get it magazine perfect.'

'Next week,' Diana replied. She put the car into gear then paused. 'Hey, have you heard anything about Maeve Gardiner recently?'

Penny shook her head. 'Nope. Why?'

'Colin rarely mentioned her, and I only know her well enough to wave hello. Patti said something at cricket, and I don't think she has much of a support network. I don't want to put my foot in it with Ned, either.'

'All I know is she's a bit of a hermit.' Penny's tone turned serious. 'Not everyone processes grief the same way,' she said softly. 'Some people get lost in their work, some turn to drink, others start a flower farm, right?'

Diana nodded. That she could relate to.

The first week of school was a success, but Ned quickly realised, as he upended the washing basket on the dining table, that they were running out of school uniforms.

'I'll get some more in town today,' he said, using a cloth to wipe toothpaste from Doug's already worn shirt.

After the bus had pulled away, he headed to the shearers' hut and rapped on the front door. A mouse scurried for cover.

'All ready to go?'

His mother adjusted her shirt and gave a curt nod. The green top was the first bit of colour he'd seen in her clothing.

The drive into town was quiet, with the old Land Rover's rattling filling the conversation void.

'Looks like this is it,' Ned said, peering at the neat mailbox in front of the immaculate weatherboard cottage by the lake. 'Want me to come in?' He was relieved when Maeve declined but waited until the navy-blue door had closed behind her before he drove off. Setting a timer on his phone for an hour, Ned dashed back to the main street and crammed in as many errands as he could. School tunics, trackpants and a couple of warm jumpers each were easy enough to find, but Ned drew a blank at the school polo shirts.

'They'll be back in stock in a week or two,' said the chirpy shop assistant. 'Perhaps try the op shops.'

He found a Lifeline tucked between a florist and a book shop. There, among an assortment of clothes, were five blue polo shirts. And as luck would have it, they all had the Bridgefield logo on the chest. Ned checked the sizing and hurried to the counter. He looked at his watch, willing the volunteer at the back of the shop to walk a little faster. The older gentleman whistled, stopping to straighten a display as he ambled towards the counter.

'Fine weather, isn't it?' He removed the $2 tags and checked each shirt carefully.

'Sure is,' said Ned with an encouraging smile, pushing a $10 note across the polished counter.

'Great little school in Bridgefield,' said the man, folding each polo as if he were auditioning for a job at David Jones. *Hurry up.* Maeve's appointment would be finished shortly, and he wanted to be there before she came out, to ensure another appointment was not just discussed, but booked.

'And these are from the lovely Diana. Her donations are always in the best nick, freshly washed and ironed.'

Ned's impatience fell to the wayside as he looked down at the school shirts. Sure enough, there was a label with 'McIntyre'. And he bet if he lifted the polo shirts to his nose, they'd prob-ably smell like fresh cotton, not the trademark op-shop scent. The man pointed to the giant arrangement by the register: foxgloves, hybrid tea roses, eucalyptus foliage and cornflowers.

'She makes marvellous bouquets too. Bunch of those will get you out of the doghouse quick smart, if you know what I mean.'

The chap slipped the shirts into a bag and added a colourful flyer.

'You'll meet her if your rug rats are heading to the same school. Prettier than any of her flowers, and kind-hearted to boot. She sells to the florist next door and slips us the odd bouquet. And baked goodies if we're lucky. I'd marry her myself if I weren't already accounted for,' said the man, tapping his wedding ring.

Ned thanked him for the clothes, knowing the conversation would blow out if he mentioned he not only knew Diana, but would soon be working for her.

Diana McIntyre to the rescue again, Ned thought, pulling up outside the cottage. *This is almost becoming a habit.*

The receptionist flashed Ned a kind smile when he entered the counselling practice.

'There're plenty of resources for carers,' she said, passing a brochure across the counter. Ned hesitated, then accepted it.

'Thank you.'

Shaking off a strong sense of déjà vu, Ned studied the leaflet in case anything had changed in the twelve years since he'd last tried to help his mother. While the literature was similar, with perfectly practical paragraphs about boundaries and support, recovery and relapse, he realised that this time they were focusing on grief, not battling the depths of addiction at the same time. And he'd learned a thing or two about expectations in the interim.

'How was it?' Ned asked when they were outside.

Maeve pocketed the card for her follow-up appointment.

'Standard box of tissues on the coffee table, muted furnishings, questions about the deep, dark depths of my soul. Least it wasn't all preachy.'

'She's the best in the region, apparently.' He wasn't sure why that was important to him. Throwing money at his mother's addiction hadn't made much difference in the past but now . . . Ned swallowed. Now she seemed more of a willing participant.

They stopped at the supermarket, going their separate ways and meeting back at the car park. Maeve loaded her bags into the ute tray, then knotted the plastic handles together.

'Don't want the lightweight stuff flying out on the drive home,' she said quietly, intercepting Ned's quizzical look.

Soon Ned was turning into their driveway. After collecting the mail, he idled outside the shearers' hut. It looked even dingier in the bright sunshine. The ute door creaked open and Maeve hesitated. Ned knew what was coming—hell, he'd been the one to lay the ground rules—but he found himself swallowing a sudden reluctance. She'd made an effort, now he needed to uphold his end of the bargain.

'You can come tonight, if you like?' he said.

In Maeve's brief smile, he saw a hint of the woman she'd once been. She nodded, then climbed out of the Land Rover and accepted Ned's offer to help carry the groceries inside. He sat the bags on the bench, noticing extra details he'd missed on previous visits. The stack of paperbacks by the toaster, the striped tablecloth, and the way the vase of gum leaves added a subtle scent of eucalyptus to the room. The bones might be run down, and the pedestal fans in each room suggested it was also a sweat box in the height of summer, but it was obvious Maeve had tried to make the best of it.

The sheer curtains near the window stirred. He was surprised Colin hadn't fixed the draughts. In fact, as he surveyed the hallway with fresh eyes, it seemed the air leaks were as common as the steel-wool-plugged mouse holes.

Ned returned to the main house, unpacked his groceries, and opened a letter from his father's lawyer. Although he already knew what the will contained, Ned felt a sense of sad finality reading Colin's last wishes in black and white. The Bridgefield property, free-range egg business and Uncle Ray's Byaduk land were left to Ned and Jonno. Superannuation account balance and the acre surrounding the shearers' hut to Maeve. The extensive collection of gardening books to Diana.

The lawyer confirmed it would take around six months to wind up the estate. After everything had been finalised, they could each do what they liked with their inheritances. Ned refolded the will and sank into a chair. Six months in Bridgefield had seemed an inconvenience at first, but now he had the feeling it would pass quickly.

Ned pulled out his phone and typed the Byaduk address into Google Maps. It had been years since Colin had taken them camping at the bush block, the perfect venue for rolling out a swag on a long weekend, rabbit hunting and fishing. It was an hour's drive at most, and he knew one of the many keys on the Land Rover fob would open the gate.

One thing at a time, he reminded himself, glancing around the house. There was plenty to be tidied up before Maeve came for dinner.

13

Diana wasn't surprised when Reg stuck his head around the kitchen door and announced he was turning in early.

'Old blokes like me need our beauty sleep, Annie-girl. Still not used to those little tackers waking me up at sparrow's fart.' He yawned, then glanced around the kitchen. 'Bit late for cooking, isn't it?'

'They're growing boys, Reg,' she said, well aware that he was partial to the homemade biscuits and cakes too. As he left the kitchen, she finished unpacking the dishwasher, then added eggs, flour and milk to butter and sugar she'd just creamed. Jinx wound in and out between Diana's feet, as she filled the patty pans.

'How about you, kitty?' she said, stooping down to pat the cat once the cupcakes were in the oven. She wasn't sure whether Jinx was pregnant or not, but she gave her a generous saucer of milk anyway. Stroking the smooth fur, Diana's mind jumped from the possible arrival of kittens to the two lovebirds canoodling on the deck. Cameron and his girlfriend Georgie sprang apart when she tapped on the laundry window.

'How's the studying?'

Georgie picked up the book in her lap, while Cam ducked his head at the sight of Diana's raised eyebrows. She rolled her eyes. They'd be covered in mozzie bites out there, but at least they weren't draped over the couch, oozing hormones and locking lips in her direct line of sight.

Giving Cameron a final 'I've got my eyes on you' look, Diana headed down the hallway and tucked the younger boys into bed.

The oven timer dinged at the same time as her phone started ringing.

Diana pulled the cupcakes from the oven then answered her sister's call.

'How's my almost-famous sister?' said Lara.

'The photographer just emailed to confirm their arrival time on Friday but I'm still anxious about the whole thing,' said Diana. 'Cameron's barely speaking to me because I'm not going to see his first premier game.'

'Nonsense, Cameron will get over it. He'll have Dad cheering him on. Not like you've forbidden him to go or asked him to hitchhike there. Make sure you're giving yourself a break too, sis.'

Diana signed off with a smile and returned to her baking, pulling the ingredients for yo-yo bikkies out of the pantry.

The knock at the sliding door was quiet, but it had everyone standing to attention.

'Remember what I said, guys,' Ned warned, turning down the heat on the stovetop before following Doug and Willow to the door. And despite an earlier promise to keep their cool when their guest arrived, the children were a box of birds the moment Maeve stepped inside.

'I'm Doug, but you can call me Dougie, or Dougo, or D-man, like my new friend Leo does,' said Doug, underfoot like an eager puppy.

Willow scooped up Flopsy, presenting him as if they'd been lifetime friends.

'I'm Willow, definitely not Will and never EVER Willy. This is Flopsy. Dad didn't want to keep him but he was a sneaky little kitty, weren't you, Flopsy boy?' She waved one of the cat's paws in greeting. From the expression on her face, Ned got the feeling Maeve wasn't sure whether to laugh or turn around and run. *It's been a long time since she's had anything to do with kids.*

'And I'm Maeve, though I'm not quite sure exactly what you'll call me,' she said with an apologetic smile.

He put a hand on the children's shoulders, steering them out of the way.

'Let your grandmother inside, guys,' he said, sliding the glass door shut behind her. 'Grab a seat.'

'Smells good,' Maeve said, settling down at the table. Willow and Doug tussled for the chair beside her, not bothering to hide their curiosity, eyes darting from her salt-and-pepper hair to the voluminous handbag on her lap. Willow eventually gave in and let Doug have the closest seat.

Ned stirred the boiling pot of pasta, then the creamy sauce.

'Just an easy carbonara.'

'And garlic bread too, that's our favourite bit,' added Doug, beaming so his missing tooth showed.

'It was your dad's too, when he was little.' Maeve pulled two small paper bags from her handbag and passed them to the children. 'I brought a little something, I hope that's okay?'

Nodding, Ned watched as colouring books and pencils spilled onto the dining table.

'I didn't know what you liked . . .' She knotted her hands in her handbag straps.

Ned knew it wasn't easy for her. *She's making an effort,* he reminded himself. And she wasn't slurring her words or heading straight for the drinks' cabinet either, which was a dramatic improvement on the last time he'd sat down for a meal with Maeve.

'The books look great. What do you say, guys?'

Doug looked at him, a question on his lips. He glanced down at the *Bluey* colouring book, then up at his grandmother and across to Ned again, who recognised his thought: *But I'm too old for Bluey.* Ned gave him a subtle 'don't mention it' look just as Willow elbowed him in the ribs. It had been a long time since she'd played with My Little Ponies too, but she was cluey enough to accept the gift graciously.

Maeve's face flushed as she looked from Willow's over-the-top 'thank you' to Doug's mumbled response.

'Oh, they're all wrong, aren't they? The girl at the shop assured me—'

'They're great,' Ned said firmly, turning at the sound of hissing to see a volcano of salty, starchy water bubbling out of the saucepan.

He reached for a cloth, nearly scalding his hand as he mopped up the boiling liquid. 'This back element's either stone cold or flat out, more temperamental than the old Land Rover.'

Maeve laughed and he felt the tension ease as Willow elaborated on some of their cooking failures over the years. He'd always been proud of their ability to carry conversations with strangers, a skill they'd had plenty of practice at while travelling, but tonight he felt an extra sense of pride as they remembered their table manners and kept the conversation flowing.

If anyone had looked in the window, they mightn't have noticed anything other than three generations sharing pasta and garlic bread, stories and smiles, but to Ned it was a sight he'd never expected to see. Certainly not in this lifetime. And as he looked over the vase of roses Willow had picked from her grandfather's garden, and his eyes met Maeve's, Ned suspected she hadn't allowed herself to imagine it either.

Crossing his arms behind his head in bed that night, Ned watched the ceiling fan circle lazily overhead and conceded it had gone smoother than he'd expected. Flopsy padded across the room and settled on the spare pillow, a spot he now considered rightfully his.

'Bit different to the last family meal at that table,' he told the cat, who barely glanced his way before curling into a ball and shutting his eyes.

Ned realised he'd been so focused on Maeve's failings as a mother, he'd ruled out the possibility of her being a good grand-mother. It wasn't easy to imagine them building a relationship with her, but for the first time in his adult life, he no longer thought it was impossible.

It was 10 p.m. when Diana finished rolling the biscuit dough into balls. She dipped her fork in water and pressed each of the yo-yos, getting an inordinate sense of satisfaction when the biscuit dough rose between the tines to the perfect height of its neighbouring biscuit. Slipping the final tray into the hot oven, she set the timer and settled on the couch with a cup of tea.

Headlights flashed on the driveway. *Georgie's mum.*

Cameron waved them off, then wandered in, homework in hand.

'Sorry I was grouchy, Mum,' he mumbled, settling down beside her. Diana leaned back into the couch and watched as he opened his laptop.

'I'm sorry, too, I was looking forward to joining you at the players' dinner and watching you play.' She peered at his laptop screen. 'What are you working on?'

Cameron angled the screen her way. She blinked at the glare, then smiled as a slideshow of pictures flashed across the screen.

'You updated my website.' She looped an arm around her son's shoulder, accepting the olive branch.

'A little,' he said, though she could see the pride written across his face. She oohed and aahed over the 'contact me' and online order forms.

'When did Toby take this picture?' She pointed to the panoramic photograph that was now the website header on the 'About' page. 'It's beautiful.'

And it was. The shot had her and the three younger boys working in the garden, with their backs to the camera. Jinx was in the foreground, lazily sunning herself on the edge of the rosemary patch, and the jagged outline of the mountains stretched above them.

'Toby took it the other week. I was going to get it framed.'

The scent of buttery yo-yos filled the open-plan room, and when the timer went off, Diana reluctantly dragged herself away from the new website.

'I love it, Cam,' she said. 'Your dad would be so pleased with you, too.' She ruffled his hair—heavens forbid she land a kiss on his cheek—and rescued the yo-yos from the oven.

Her thoughts returned to Pete as she iced the last of the biscuits. What would he make of the launch event and the magazine spread? She wasn't sure, but before she crawled into bed, she swapped her pyjama top for one of his baggy T-shirts. It wasn't anywhere close to the support she wished he could offer, or the comfort of his arms wrapped around her, assuring her it would all be fine, but it was the best she had.

14

Diana waved the boys goodbye as the school bus departed Paperbark Hill, then walked back down the driveway. She had just reached the dog kennels when Ned's Land Rover arrived. Walking towards him, she was impressed with his careful reverse parking near the archway of climbing roses.

'Morning,' she said, smoothing down her lilac work top. *I can't imagine him in one of those white, high-necked pharmacist uniforms*, she thought, appreciating the snug fit of his jeans and light shirt.

'Beautiful day for it,' he said, surveying the yard. She tried to see the property through his eyes as his gaze moved from the roses to the garden beds brimming with sweet peas, zinnias, cosmos and wallflowers. 'Who could complain about this office, though?'

'It always makes me smile, too,' she admitted, opening the gate and leading him into the house garden. 'But the weeds grow twice as fast as flowers this time of year. Colin and I—'

She looked across to see if he minded her dropping Colin's name into conversation so casually. He nodded for her to continue. 'We had big plans for this place.'

'Do your kids live and breathe the flowers, too?'

She shook her head with a laugh.

'I wouldn't quite put it that way, the most interest Harry has shown was when he found out we're starring in a magazine photo shoot.' Ned's double take was almost comical and she realised she hadn't mentioned it to him yet.

'Book launch one day, magazine shoot the next. Never dull around here.'

'Trust me,' Diana said. She fetched the tools and together they walked the wheelbarrows towards the mulch heap. 'It's not the norm, all this media attention.'

'You've been planning this photo shoot for months then?'

'Nope,' she said, loading her shovel. 'Lady Luck was shining on us.'

Ned stopped shovelling, his wheelbarrow full in half the time as hers, and started filling hers.

'Hard work puts you where good luck can find you. I'm sure there's more than luck involved.'

Diana grinned. She liked him already, an impression that solidified as they worked together. She explained the different areas of the garden, outlined her planting, watering and harvesting schedule, and the breadth of her business plan while they topped up the mulch throughout the gardens. The morning went quickly and by the time the sun was high overhead, and the southern end of the garden was fully mulched, Diana was well and truly ready for lunch.

'You coming up for a feed? Nothing fancy, but unless my father-in-law's eaten us out of house and home, there should be plenty for salad sandwiches. Colin and I usually ate on the deck.'

Ned gestured to the ute. 'I've got a few calls to make, but thanks for the offer. I'll just fetch those clothes for your father-in-law.'

Diana was pleased that Ned had followed her suggestion. She returned inside the house with the two bulging plastic bags.

'Ned's got a heap of clothes for you, Reg. You might need another suitcase to get it all back home, though.'

He looked up from the TV screen with a distracted nod.

'Advantage point! Look Annie-girl, Federer's about to thrash the pants off this cocky young English player.'

Diana assessed the lounge room with a grimace. Chip packets and empty glasses littered the coffee table and the washing basket with Reg's shirts and jeans still sat by the ironing board she'd set up that morning, as wrinkly as ever. She sighed, then caught sight of herself in the mirror and sighed again. How long had she been walking around with dirt smudged underneath her nose? And how hard was it for Reg to pick up after himself? She washed up and started slicing cheese, tomato and lettuce for sandwiches.

'No pickles on mine thanks, Annie-girl,' said Reg, filling the kettle with water. 'Your new worker isn't joining us?'

'He's got a few calls to make. But you should see the progress we've made this morning. Ned's worth his weight in gold,' she leaned against the bench, feeling grateful again for Ned's willingness to pitch in. 'And this afternoon, while I'm doing the deliveries, he's going to start planting out the new seedlings. Exactly what I needed.'

Diana turned to see Reg fishing around in the dishwasher for two clean plates. How many times had she scolded the boys for taking one or two things from the dishwasher instead of unpacking the whole darn thing? She was about to say something when a slice of cheese slipped off the bench and onto the floor.

Bonzer snuck out from under the dining table and scoffed the cheese.

What the . . . ?

'One man's trash,' Reg laughed.

'Out, out, out!' She caught the dog by the collar and ushered him towards the door. 'He's an outside dog, Reg.'

'Poor old chap looked woeful on the deck, watching the cat stretched out on the sofa like Lady Muck.'

Diana groaned. 'The cat doesn't roll around in stinking sheep carcasses or chew the cushions.' She turned around and mumbled under her breath. 'What day's your flight again?'

But she mustn't have been as quiet as she thought because Reg let out an indignant snort.

'So that's what this is about, is it? Shuffling the old things out as soon as they become an inconvenience?' He sucked on his false teeth. The sandwich plates clattered as he set them down.

'Reg, it's not like that,' she said. 'Maybe two weeks is a better timeframe next trip.' *Especially when you don't lift a finger.* She tried a different tact. 'Or, we could set up the caravan. Wouldn't you be more comfortable in your own space, with no one interrupting your sports shows or waking you early?'

His eyes tracked to the family portrait hanging above the fireplace, taken when Leo was a newborn.

'I can tell when I'm not wanted,' he said, with a wounded air, his slippers shuffling across the tiles. 'I'll pack my bags, then.'

'Reg . . .' Diana trailed off. Surely, she wasn't being unreasonable? Angus and Colin were the same vintage, and they'd never expected to be waited on hand and foot. Reg paused outside the spare bedroom, panting from the effort of lugging Colin's clothes.

'Never thought I'd see the day when I wasn't welcome in my son's home, but here we are. I'd hate to think it was to do with that Gardiner lad, given Pete's barely cold in his grave, but from the number of times I've heard Ned's name these last few days, it's clear you're moving on to a replacement.'

A replacement?

Diana felt her cheeks flame.

Ned wasn't sure what had happened while he'd been eating his lunch in the Land Rover, but the next thing he knew, Diana's father-in-law was dragging his suitcases onto the deck.

'Going already?'

Ned's question was met with a curt nod.

Diana was nowhere to be found inside and by the time Ned finished his sandwich, Angus McIntyre was driving off with Reg in the passenger seat, luggage in the ute tray.

Not a happy camper.

'Reg's going already?' He asked when Diana joined him in the garden.

'He was supposed to stay another fortnight . . .' From the way she trailed off, Ned got the impression she was cut up about whatever had transpired between them. Diana shook her head.

'It's never smooth sailing with in-laws, is it?'

'I haven't had much experience in that department, I'm afraid.'

Diana glanced up. 'Yours didn't get involved?' She seemed happy for the distraction, and he found himself elaborating.

'Fleur was estranged from her family. It was one of the things we had in common. I didn't realise it was an ingrained habit until she left us, too.'

The conversation shifted to the school and sports clubs, and after inspecting the array of seedlings in a small hothouse, they moved to the cosmos patch. Diana showed him how she pinched out the central shoots to encourage vigorous growth. Her hands raced across the garden beds, tossing snails into a bucket as she went.

The next two hours flew past and soon the cosmos patch was all pinched out, the new seedlings were watered in, and Diana had left with a boot-load of bouquets.

Ned considered what he'd learned about his new boss as he
drove home. He knew she liked eighties' music, loved paperback novels but couldn't get into audiobooks, preferred jigsaw
puzzles over cards and nachos over tacos, but as he pulled up
at Colin's he realised he had no idea if she felt the same spark
as he did when he was around her.

Diana called Lara as soon as she'd finished her deliveries.

'Hey, sis, I just saw the bouquets you dropped off at the
shop. They're gorgeous! Toby sold three bunches in an hour.
Did your first day with Ned go well?'

'Ned was brilliant,' she hesitated. 'Though you won't believe
what Reg came out with today.'

'Reg?' Lara laughed. 'Let me guess, he raided your walk-in
robe again for something of Pete's?'

Diana thumbed through a recipe book as she described the
conversation with her father-in-law. She needed something
sweet to go with her cup of tea.

'So, he's checked himself into a motel?' Lara chuckled. 'It
might be a blessing. You can't please everyone, Diana. He's
old enough and ugly enough to fend for himself.'

'But he's probably telling everyone I threw him out on his
ear. Pete would have conniptions.'

'You did invite him back, so it's not like he didn't have
options.'

'Dad said he still plans on doing the boys' trip to Geelong
for Cameron's cricket,' Diana conceded.

'Hopefully, Dad can talk some sense into him, smooth his
ruffled feathers.'

Diana tapped the walnut desk. 'Touch wood,' she said.

'You were way too polite in the first place. I can't believe
he had the nerve to suggest you were shuffling him off so

you could take a lover. I'd be dropping him off at the motel myself.'

She was grateful Ned hadn't asked why Reg was leaving in a huff. It didn't help that Reg's insinuation had prompted all manner of wayward thoughts. She felt her cheeks warming as Lara drew her back into the conversation.

'Your love life is nobody's business but your own. I can see why you would, though, if big arms, a deep voice and brooding is your type.'

'It's not. He's not,' said Diana, a little quicker and sharper than she intended.

'The lady doth protest too much, methinks,' quipped Lara. 'Seriously, though, you could do worse than Ned Gardiner. You know what they say about a guy with big feet . . .'

Diana rolled her eyes as Lara laughed down the phone line.

'He's got big shoes?'

'Exactly! Look, I know what it's like to be lonely, but good things can only happen if you let them, trust me.'

'It's hard when you've lost your perfect half. I mean, luckily the boys eat like horses, otherwise I'd be the size of a house with all the baking therapy.' Diana snapped the recipe book shut, remembering she still had muffins. She cut one in half, added a slither of butter and warmed it in the microwave.

'Just say the word and I'll confiscate your recipe books,' Lara teased. 'But seriously, that's a mighty fine pedestal you're putting Pete on. Have you forgotten the snoring? The massive get-togethers with other stock agents that had him running late for sports and Sunday roasts? It wasn't always perfect.'

The muffin was warm, sweet and buttery, exactly what Diana needed, and she prepped four more. The boys would be riding down the driveway at any minute, ravenous as always.

'Not perfect every minute,' she conceded. 'But pretty darn close.'

15

The sun was just poking over the horizon when Ned tugged
on Colin's boots. A new pair for himself had been high on the
priority list when he'd first decided to stay, but the more he
wore them the less it seemed to matter that they were flogged
out, with buckled elastic around the sides. Colin's belongings
were all around him, but there was something Ned especially
liked about the boots, as if a little piece of his father was with
him each step of the way. He'd also kept a number of Colin's
work shirts as well as the knits. The rest had gone to Reg and
the little Lifeline op shop.

'Wait for me, Dad,' called Willow, careening down the
hallway as she pulled a hoody over her pyjamas. Flopsy
bounded behind her, squeezing through the gap in the flyscreen
door and then out into the garden. Ned narrowed his eyes as
the cat disappeared into the bushes.

'Off to decimate the local bird population again,' Ned said,
shaking his head. The birds that congregated in the grevilleas
and wattles launched into a musical warning system, fluttering
to higher branches as they alerted their avian friends.

'He hardly ever catches any,' said Willow, giggling as a honeyeater swooped close to the cat's tail, flushing him out from under the shrub. 'Doug's still asleep, shall we leave him here while we get the eggs?'

Ned looked at his watch and then back at the house.

'We can do a few other jobs until he's up. The old pigsty needs some work, but that's more of a weekend job. What else can we do around here?'

'Can we get pigs, Dad?'

'Wouldn't even know where to find a breeder, missy. And we've got enough on our plate already, don't you think?'

The two of them strode around the yard, assessing tasks and narrowing them down by priority and time requirements. By the time Doug emerged, his hair strewn across his face, Ned and Willow had a detailed to-do list for the next weekend.

After collecting the eggs, they headed inside to get ready for school. Ned scanned his emails as he ate his breakfast, He was halfway through making Vegemite sandwiches for school lunches when his laptop started chiming.

'Uncle Jonno,' cried Willow, abandoning her battle with the hairbrush to answer the Zoom call. Ned listened with one ear as he added fruit and snacks to the school lunch boxes.

'Ask your dad if he can hunt out my old knitting bag. I've got a bet I want to settle with one of the other scientists.' Whatever bet it was, Ned figured it involved a female member of staff, because somehow Jonno managed to commandeer Doug into making lunches so Ned could find the required bag. He searched the floor-to-ceiling cupboards, pushing aside Colin's stamp collections and thirty years' worth of *Grass Roots* magazines before finding the soft corduroy knitting bag Jonno had once treasured.

The handmade bag, embroidered with 'Jonathon' and filled with chunky knitting needles and wool, had been a gift from their grandmother, Mam, who'd been responsible for Colin's brown jumpers. Ned tugged on a strand of wool, finding out too late it was tangled somewhere in the cupboard. Maeve's old sewing basket crashed to the ground, followed by a loosely folded wad of fabric. Bobbins scattered in all directions. He yanked the troublesome orange wool and returned to the kitchen with a frown on his face.

'Hope your bet's worth the mess I just made,' said Ned, waving the knitting bag in front of the laptop screen.

'Oh, trust me, bro, sure is.'

The smitten expression on Jonno's face said it all. *Knew it.*

Ned returned to the hallway cupboard. The fabric he'd wedged into the shelves above the towels refused to stack nicely, and it wasn't until Ned shook it out, planning to refold it, that he saw why.

A type of hoop was clamped over several layers of fabric. A patchwork top, with intricate purple flowers, then a thin layer that looked like wool and finally a floral back. In the blink of an eye, he was reminded of the brighter days before Jessie got sick. Purple sneakers, purple ribbons, purple bedspread. There was no doubting who the quilt had been intended for.

He could hear Willow and Doug in the kitchen, incredulous that Uncle Jonno had once knitted scarves and slippers, but his mind was on the woman across the paddock, who'd once taught them to sew and encouraged them to knit. The tiny hand stitches were the work of someone with patience, precision and perseverance, three qualities he thought Maeve had buried alongside Jessie.

He pushed the quilt back into the cupboard and started making room for the sewing basket. Willow skipped down the hallway with a hairbrush in hand. She paused at his side.

'Oh, that's so pretty. Whose stuff is it, Dad?'

'Your grandmother used to sew.'

'Gigi was a sewer?'

Gigi? He'd overheard Doug and Willow debating the right name for their grandmother the other day but somehow missed the outcome. *It suits better than Granny or Nanna*, he thought.

She picked up a patchwork pin cushion, studded with needles and pins, made from the same print as the unfinished quilt he'd tucked away moments earlier.

'I love this purple material,' Willow said. 'Do you think I can make something for my room while we're staying?' She peered into the cupboard, her expression hopeful as she discovered the colourful stacks of fabric.

'I'm not very crafty, and Flopsy would have a field day with all those spools of cotton.'

Willow cradled the sewing basket like it was her new favourite thing.

'I could try. Or Gigi could teach me when she's better.'

Taking the hairbrush, he began working on Willow's knots.

'Maybe,' he said carefully, recalling his decision to take things slowly. How long had it been since Maeve had picked up a needle and thread? And was it crazy to think she was well enough to consider doing so again?

He plaited Willow's dark hair, secured it with a scrunchy and reached for the sewing supplies.

'I'm going to ask Gigi about it when we see her next,' said Willow, watching closely as he returned the basket to a lower shelf, beside an old Singer sewing machine.

A month ago, Ned would have laughed at the idea. There's no way he could've believed they'd have that type of relationship with Maeve, but the sight of Willow's optimistic expression and the quiet success of their dinner with her, indicated it mightn't be so far-fetched.

He closed the cupboard and ushered Willow towards the kitchen.

'Let's not rush into anything yet,' he said. 'You've got a bus to catch, and I've got gardens to groom. Get your skates on, my girl,' he said, tickling her until she picked up her pace. It certainly wasn't the time to dwell on whether or not they'd be sitting at his mother's knee and learning to sew, or bake, or crochet.

If any of the boys were upset about Reg's sudden change of accommodation, they didn't mention it. In fact, it struck Diana a few days later as she waited with the three younger ones at the bus stop that they mightn't even have noticed his absence if she hadn't mentioned it.

'Did you pack me yo-yos, Mum?' Leo said, twisting in an attempt to open his lunch box while his backpack was still strapped firmly to his back.

'Course I did, honey. Two for each of you. And remember your homework. I'll be calling Miss Kenna if you don't,' she said, straightening his collar.

Leo stood up a little straighter and Diana bit back a smile. The new teacher might have been fresh out of uni at the start of the year, but by term four had the devoted pupils wrapped around her little finger.

The sound of the bus engine floated up the hill. Harry and Elliot jumped down from the low limbs of the paperbark trees and gave her a quick farewell kiss before the bus came into sight, while Leo was happy to hold her hand right until the bus arrived. Diana spotted the Gardiner kids sitting directly behind the bus driver and waved when she caught their eye.

'Make sure you look out for Willow and Doug.' Pride swelled in her heart as Leo sat with Ned's kids. She waved them off and retraced her steps down the driveway, heading straight to the garden.

Ned met her in the yard, pulling on his gardening gloves, and they fell into a comfortable pace. After harvesting and watering, they moved on to pruning the leggy shoots and suckers of the roses, making each bush picture perfect for the photo shoot. It felt like they'd added a hundred wheelbarrows of clippings to the bonfire pile in the space of two hours, but the rose patch looked infinitely better.

'It seemed like a smart idea to leave the roses until this week,' said Diana, glancing at the scratches running up and down their arms and rethinking the short-sleeved dress she'd planned to wear on Friday, 'but there's no way these will be healed by the time the photographer arrives.'

'Nothing like a touch of authenticity,' Ned said. 'And the roses look top-notch. Want me to keep going with the mulch while you make the bouquets?'

He'd listened carefully when she'd explained her plans for the week, and she liked how he methodically worked through the day's jobs without hesitation. She beamed at him, not missing the way the fabric strained across his broad shoulders, then headed to the packing shed. Pulling her phone from her back pocket, Diana selected a Roxette playlist and sang along as she transformed the buckets of flowers into bouquets. Sun streamed through the packing shed windows, heating up the room and making Diana work faster. A cool-room was on her flower farm wish list, along with domed poly-tunnels so she could grow more seedlings and start them earlier.

All part of the five-year plan, she reminded herself. Or perhaps, if the magazine spread and Sadie's launch boosted their business like Bron predicted, they might have enough profit to invest earlier. The possibility made her even more determined to capitalise on the opportunity.

The door creaked open, and Cameron stepped in carrying one of his Geelong training shirts. She called out a cheery hello, but kept working, her hands weaving the long lupin stems and foliage together.

'Almost packed for your weekend away, mate?'

He nodded, holding up the shirt. 'This one's got a hole, though. Can you please mend it for me?'

She looked at the stitching along the side seam. 'With my eyes closed. Give me a hand finishing this up and I'll fix it when we head in for smoko.'

He assessed the workbench and started sweeping the excess leaves and stems into a waste bucket.

'Gramps called. He's still sooking about you chucking him out.'

'I didn't chuck him out! He stormed out.'

She saw Cameron's eye twitch, the same telltale sign Pete used to show when there was something on his mind.

'Go on, spit it out.'

'He thinks you're clearing the way for a new bloke.'

Diana hoped her face wasn't as flushed as it felt, and she glanced out the window to where Ned was dressing the garden beds with bark mulch.

'That's the last thing on my mind. Between you four boys, the flowers, the cricket, this launch event and every other ball I'm juggling, I can tell you right now there's *nothing* going on in my love life!'

Diana finished the bouquet she was making, eased it into a bucket of water and put a hand on each of her son's shoulders, turning him to face her.

'I promise you, Cam, there's no romance on my radar. Speaking of relationships, your phone's been running hot and we've seen Georgie five days this week. Perhaps I should be interrogating you? How are things going?'

Cameron's mouth snapped shut. The tips of his ears glowed pink and he picked up his shirt.

'Go on . . .' Diana encouraged him, starting on another bunch. The tried-and-true tactic of working side by side for important conversations hadn't failed her yet.

'Georgie's awesome. And she's not afraid to bring me back down to earth when I start getting too far ahead of myself with the cricket dream,' he said, the pile of leaves in front of him growing as he picked up speed. 'She makes me laugh; she makes me feel good.'

'As long as you're both responsible. I went to school with a girl who fell pregnant at sixteen and, while we were stressing about pimples, she was dealing with a newborn. I know Dad used to talk to you about guy stuff, but if you have any questions, I understand a few of the ins and outs, too—' Diana grinned at her inadvertent pun and Cameron's horri-fied splutter.

'Ewwwww. Seriously, stop now.' He covered his ears with his hands and squeezed his eyes shut.

'That's all I'm going to say.' She gently removed his hands from his ears. 'Just remember, consent is king. And don't forget you're sharing a house with little—and very impressionable—brothers.'

Much to her surprise, he pulled her into an impromptu hug. His bear-like embrace reminded her so much of Pete, especially when he rested his chin on top of her head.

'Thanks, Mum, I won't. Georgie's going to come to Geelong and watch the game. And then when I make nationals, Georgie'll be able to come to all the fancy dinners and stuff. We've got it all worked out.'

His words resonated with confidence.

Ah, young love, anticipation, easily made plans and the whole world to explore. Diana squeezed him back tightly, remembering that heady stage well, aware she'd probably had her last ride on that particular roller-coaster.

'Of course you do, Cam,' she said heartily, 'of course you do.' Diana thought back to her last conversation with Lara. Hers and Pete's *had* been the perfect marriage, even with a few minor squabbles here and there. They'd rarely gone to bed with an argument between them, they'd never temporarily separated like some of her friends. That type of love only came around once in a lifetime and she was lucky to have found it.

16

'Cracker of a morning,' Ned said, hugging the kids before they hopped on the bus.

He didn't miss donning his white pharmacy uniform on days like this, with the sun warming his skin and the breeze carrying the scent of blossoms and lush pastures. He strode down the driveway, glancing towards the shearers' hut. Why hadn't Colin bothered to fix it up, and how come Maeve seemed content to live in such a hovel? Was she so destitute she couldn't afford a small rental?

Before he knew it, Ned found himself veering off the gravel track and across the paddock. Sheets and towels flapped on the clothesline, a weed had started sprouting in the gutter and a family of swallow hatchlings chirped from a clay nest in the gables. He spotted Maeve around the side of the hut, going slowly through a series of movements, pausing every now and then to reference a book propped on an outdoor table.

Tai chi? Yoga? He hesitated.

Nothing good comes from yoga, a voice in his head whispered.

He felt suddenly foolish. He'd been happily estranged from Maeve for years, and now he was waltzing over to her place to discuss renovations? He was about to walk away when Maeve twisted in his direction, arms spread wide. Their eyes met. Looking pleased to see him, she dropped her pose.

'Nice sunshine,' she said, dodging a fallen branch as she walked over to him. He nodded, noticing how three of the four windows on the front of the shed were open. The fourth, which remained shut, had a torn flyscreen.

Aware that Diana would be expecting him, Ned got right to the point. 'Did Colin ever talk about renovating the shearers' hut? I'd have thought looking at it, it would have annoyed the hell out of him.'

She shrugged. 'He was so busy with his chickens and his flowers, he probably didn't even notice.' She glanced at the house. 'I was grateful enough that he offered it, I certainly wasn't going to ask him to upgrade it for me, too. Plenty of people have lived in worse.'

Ned recalled the wording of the will.

'Did the lawyers call you, about the will? I'm not sure how much was in his super, but the acre with this shed is yours.'

She nodded. 'He was a good man, your father, especially after everything . . .' Maeve trailed off, looking back again at the small building. 'There won't be enough for a grand renovation, but next autumn, when the paperwork's all gone through, I'll be installing a heater and fixing a few urgent things.'

Ned eyeballed the rusty roof, crumbling chimney and holes. Looked like more than a 'few' urgent things to him. Not to mention that hay shed on their side of the boundary, leaning at a precarious angle, and the stringybark tree that swayed like a drunken B&S ball-goer. He and Jonno had a responsibility to fix them, he decided.

The photo crew were scheduled to arrive at midday and the morning of last-minute deadheading and pruning passed quickly.

Ned glanced across at Diana. *Quickly for him perhaps.* She'd been restless all morning, her gaze darting to the road every five minutes, and he noticed her grimace when she checked her phone after lunch.

'Are they lost?'

She shook her head, tapping out a quick text. 'Just running late. What's another hour of watching the driveway and worrying about putting my foot in my mouth, right?'

'You'll be great,' he said. 'This place is as neat as a pin.' And although he hadn't worked with Diana long enough to know if she harboured any deep, dark secrets, he couldn't imagine they were travelling all the way from Melbourne to write an unflattering, exposé-style article.

When they arrived, the photographer, Carlotta, and Sadie's assistant, Ellen, quickly put Diana at ease.

'This place is gorgeous,' said Ellen, admiring the property.

Carlotta set up quickly, assuring Diana they would have plenty of angles to work with. In the middle of harvesting the ranunculus and trying to stay out of the way of the tripods, reflector lights and bossy photographer, Ned overheard his name.

'Don't move a muscle, Ned. Stay right where you are, that's perfect.'

He looked down at his armload of pale flowers as the camera lens snapped. 'You've got the wrong bloke,' he said with a smile. 'I've only just started here.' Ned searched for Diana, who seemed to have disappeared into thin air. He could have understood if the roles were reversed, and Colin was being asked to pose alongside his protégé, but there was no way he deserved any credit for Diana's hard work.

'Just pretend we're not here,' said Carlotta, switching camera lenses and re-angling the fancy umbrella flash.

Diana emerged from the garden shed, her linen field apron gone, her hair loose and the sleeves rolled up on her fitted shirt.

'A little help here?' he called to her.

She held up a finger and mouthed 'one minute' as she strode across to Ellen. Ned put the flowers into water, looped the buckets over his arm and started towards the packing shed.

'Ned . . .' He paused, hearing a question in the way Diana said his name. 'I know this is a really big ask, but is there any chance you could bear to be in one or two shots? The photographer sent Sadie a few raw images with you in the background, and Sadie loves the idea of having the teensiest bit of variation.'

Her face creased in apology, but he could tell she wanted him to say yes. And against his better judgement, he wanted to be the one to help her out. Not for Sadie Woodford, whoever she was, but for Diana.

What's the harm in one or two photos?

'A little to the left. Lean in a little closer there, Ned. Chin up, Diana. Can you boost those flowers a little higher and twist them so that floaty foliage drapes over your arm a little?'

Diana felt Ned's shoulder nudge her ear.

'Sorry,' he murmured, his breath warm on her forehead. The sun was high overhead, casting dark shadows that frustrated the photographer, but Diana had a feeling the heat running through her body was more to do with the crisp scent of Ned's shaving cream—or was it cologne?—than the late-spring temperature. He smelled amazing, like salt water and sage.

As she shifted position, she saw something she hadn't expected. A flash of colour through the buttons of Ned's shirt. He has a tattoo? She was intrigued by the discovery. What else didn't she know about her new employee?

She smiled at the camera, but instead of thinking about dahlias and magazine spreads, she found herself thinking about Ned's ink work. Was it a novelty character or a phrase? Chinese symbols, a footy mascot or one of those intricate skulls?

'Okey-dokey, look alive, folks. Big smiles!' said Carlotta, switching cameras. Diana cringed. She could feel Ned's body shaking with laughter.

'This is worse than wedding photos,' he whispered.

'If she makes us lean any closer together, it'll *look* like a wedding album, too,' she said, regretting that the magazine hadn't hired Toby for the job. Lara's partner had been a newspaper man before managing the Bridgefield General Store, and his growing photography business was testament to his skill and relaxed manner behind the lens. She was also quite certain he wouldn't have made her pose so close to Ned.

They moved to the rose garden and waited while the photographer set up. Diana looked across to Ellen, who had spent most of the afternoon on her phone. For a minute she was envious, wishing she'd had a moment to touch base with Angus.

Don't fuss, Dad and Cam will be too busy with cricket to talk anyway. She pushed the thought aside and looked at Ned.

'I'm dying to quiz Sadie's PA about the launch event.'

Ned laughed. 'If only that phone wasn't surgically attached to her ear, right?'

Apart from confirming the date and gushing about how lucky Diana was to have caught Sadie's eye, the only information Ellen had offered between photos was that the launch event was being sponsored by a boutique winery and the publishers were going all out.

Diana tried again while Carlotta switched camera lenses.

'What else can I do to help with the launch? Obviously, we'll be focused on getting the flower farm into shape, but do you need local recommendations? Florists, caterers, musicians?'

Ellen gave her a dazzling smile.

'You're doing enough already, babes, and we're already super organised. I've engaged the local CWA ladies to cater the launch, the rest will fall into place closer to the event. Honestly, you should see the wine labels we've printed. They've got the book cover, the date, and even the name of your flower farm on them.'

Diana was thrilled.

Ned seemed suitably impressed too. 'What have her other launch events been like?'

'My friend, Bron, who handles all the PR, said this was the first time Sadie's done a rural launch, but usually it's a no-expenses-spared type of thing.'

Overhearing them, Carlotta chimed in with her agreement. 'Sadie's a dream to work with, too. The exposure will be worth its weight in gold.' Seeing Diana's nervous glance at her watch, the photographer smiled apologetically and added, 'Sorry, we're almost done. Now stand by those roses and pretend you're having a light conversation, discussing the latest floral trends or something.'

'Like the lifespan of aphids?' Ned said, not trying at all to hide the glint in his eyes.

He was being such a good sport. As he ran a hand through his hair, Diana's eyes went to his chest again, curious to see if there was a hint of ink, or if it was just her imagination.

'Or maybe the push for "country of origin" labelling on flowers, just like fruit and veg, or the evils of floral foam?' Diana suggested, working hard to keep a straight face.

When the photographer was finally satisfied with their 'candid' conversation shot, and photographed them making posies, she started scouting out the final photo location.

'I'm so sorry, Ned. I didn't know they were going to rope you into this as well.'

'Would've worn my good gardening shirt if I'd known,' he said with a wry grin. Diana assessed the faded blue denim shirt, rolled up to his elbows, and the tan trousers with green grass stains on the knees. He looked ruggedly handsome, something Sadie, Carlotta and Ellen had evidently been quick to spot. In fact, if she had to place her hand on her heart and swear on it, she'd probably admit that Ned Gardiner was hot with a capital H.

The cheerful photographer kept nudging them together, and as much as Ned tried to keep out of Diana's personal space, he found himself cataloguing new discoveries he hadn't noticed before. From up close, he could see a light dusting of freckles on her skin, two abandoned ear piercings, and a peach-like downy hair on her neck. She smelled good too, and when her long locks tickled his neck, Ned's mind bolted in a direction that had nothing to do with flowers or photos. He leaned back a fraction, painfully aware of her proximity, and worked hard to take his mind off the warmth of Diana's body, just millimetres from his.

'Sorry,' she grimaced, sweeping her golden hair over her shoulder with an apologetic smile.

'It's all good.' Ned forced a smile in return. Was he imagining the crackle of energy between them? Normally when he was this close to a woman, there were a lot less clothes, no spectators, and he was in no doubt that the attraction was mutual.

Ned's mouth felt like sawdust. *Think of the aphids*. He swallowed, glad Diana couldn't read his mind and grateful when the photographer piped up from behind the tripod.

'We'll be done in two minutes, pinky promise. Right, one foot on the shovel there, Diana. Like you're digging up some bulbs. And Ned, can you crouch down, as if you're about to scoop them up and load them in the bucket,' said the photographer. 'That's it. Now look up at Diana. Cheesy grin.'

Like I'm about to propose, he thought, kneeling on the dirt.

'C'mon, Ned, you can do better than that,' crooned Carlotta from behind the camera.

Diana lifted an eyebrow. He tried a little harder but it wasn't much of an improvement. Using the last fragments of his acting skills, Ned mustered up a half-hearted smile.

'Oh, are you guys still coming for dinner after we're done here?' Diana whispered out of the corner of her mouth. Ned started to object, but the sudden growl of his stomach gave him away. He hadn't realised he was hungry until she mentioned it. They both laughed, real smiles this time. The camera shutter went rapid-fire.

'Perfect! That's a wrap,' said Carlotta, lifting the camera strap from around her neck. Ellen ended her phone call and hurried across.

'Gosh, that phone hasn't stopped ringing all day. Everyone wants a piece of Sadie Woodford, and I've been telling them what a gorgeous flower farm you have here. Our journo, Tori, will have so much to write about when she comes tomorrow morning. Everything went smoothly from our end, you've got all you need, Carlotta?'

The photographer nodded.

'Pretty sure she's got enough pictures for about ten magazine features,' Diana added. 'I'm so thrilled to finally get the ball rolling. I get the tingles when I think about Darling Dahlias being part of the launch event.'

Carlotta looked up from her camera. 'Not to blow my own trumpet, but these photos are divine. You looked amazing together.' She rushed on. 'My editor's going to be chuffed.'

'Sadie's super pleased, too,' Ellen said. 'I sent her a sample of the photos from earlier. She's wild about this backdrop.'

Ned watched Diana swell with pride. He helped carry the tripods, lights and camera gear to the photographer's car, then loaded the buckets of bouquets into Diana's car.

'They aren't my finest work,' he said, closing the tailgate behind him.

'Can't imagine why,' Diana joked. 'It's not easy to make a posy with a camera trained on your every move. Dinner tonight is the least I can do.'

17

A stiff breeze had picked up by the time Diana drove into town. She parked in front of the Bridgefield General Store, her hair swirling around her as she unloaded the bouquets, and tried to open the shop door, a task made harder with her delicate cargo.

'Here, I'll grab it,' came a voice from behind. She turned to see Sarah Squires hurrying out of a shiny Hilux, great clods of dirt falling from her boots with each step.

'Thanks. The wind's whipped up, hasn't it?'

Sarah nodded as she held the shop door to stop it slamming shut.

'I'm helping a friend with his Appaloosa gelding, goes like stink. Perfect for pentathlons,' she responded cheerfully.

Diana hadn't the foggiest what Sarah was talking about but judging from the loose pieces of hay clinging to her shirt, Sarah's broad smile and flushed face, it was horse related. *Either that, or something to do with rolling in the hay . . .*

Diana set down the buckets of blooms. When she looked up, she saw Sarah was examining her closely.

'You're all dressed up for a day in the paddock,' Sarah said, an incredulous note in her voice.

'Photoshoot glam,' called out Lara from across the counter.

'The usual, Diana?' Toby added. 'Or should we call you Miss *Country Home* magazine?'

'Magazine photo shoot? That's a bit fancy. I miss all the goss when I skip sewing group. Mind you, the upside of all those dates has been pretty good.' Sarah winked, selected one of the bouquets Diana had stacked into the flower stand, then rested it on the counter with her newspapers. 'These are divine, Diana. It must be so nice to sit around all day having your photo taken and playing with flowers.'

Diana managed a weak laugh. She'd heard a few variations of this line since starting Darling Dahlias. Never intentionally nasty but they trivialised the hours and hard labour she invested in her business, and it hurt coming from a friend. She bit her tongue.

'See you at the next crafternoon,' Sarah said.

Diana and Lara nodded, confirmed the date, and watched her leave with the large bouquet.

'Playing with flowers? Pffft,' said Lara, making Diana's coffee.

'You thought it was a bit harsh, too? Thank God, I thought I was just being sensitive.'

'Way harsh,' said Lara. 'All that sex is short-circuiting her brain. I was tempted to tell her so, too, but we don't want sewing circle to get awkward. Or lose you valuable customers.'

Toby emerged from the store kitchen, restocking the pie warmer with their specialty house-made pies and bagging one up for Diana.

'How was the photo shoot? Front page billing?'

'Not likely. But surely, they'll have a few good ones from the millions they took,' Diana replied.

'Did Angus and Reg get Cameron to cricket training in time?'

Diana pulled out her phone, pleased to see a reply to her voicemail.

'Speak of the devil. Hopefully they're sitting in the spectators' section, quiet as mice.'

Lara leaned across the counter as Diana opened the photos they sent and laughed when she saw them.

'Look at that! While you've been posing for photos, Reg's been a poster child for fans-r-us.' Angus had snapped him hanging over the cricket fence so one of the cricketers could sign his shirt.

'Cameron would have been so embarrassed,' Diana groaned.

'What was it Pete used to say? You can pick your nose, but you can't pick your family?' Toby grinned.

U2 came on the radio on the drive home, taking Diana's thoughts to Pete and last night's loneliness, then the guilt she'd felt for checking out another man just an hour earlier. A man that she'd insisted come for dinner, even though she could sense his hesitation.

Diana shook off the notion, along with the multitude of flaky pastry crumbs from her pie, as she parked her car. *I've got the boys, the flower farm and this beautiful home,* she told herself sternly. *What more could I want?* And although she'd assured Cameron and Reg and Lara that she wasn't looking for a lover, the idea didn't terrify her as much as it once had.

Ned couldn't shake the feeling that something was off when he drove down Colin's driveway. It wasn't the clunky noise the Land Rover made each time he changed into second gear, or the fact that Diana McIntyre was taking up more brain space than he could afford at the moment. He looked around the yard, trying to define it.

The wind had doubled in strength somewhere between Darling Downs and Colin's place. The shrubby daisies flanking the verandah shuddered as the gusts funnelled between the house and the sheds. Doug and Willow were red-faced and sweating by the time they'd walked back from the bus stop, moaning about the wind.

'Give us a quick hand, guys, it's going to be even windier tomorrow,' he said, turning his thoughts to Diana's flower farm. *She'll be pleased the photographer made it today, not tomorrow. If this front continues as predicted, there'll be lots of snapped stems and wind-burned petals.*

Tree branches lashed back and forth, and the school uniforms danced along the length of the clothesline as the children helped bring the washing in.

'Feels hotter than Darwin,' said Doug.

Ned nodded. He remembered these northerlies—hot, dry and almost hungry in their intensity, as if they were just waiting to gleefully throw a trampoline across the paddock or fan a fire. He was glad for the work they'd put in earlier that week, whipper snipping the long grass around the piles of tin and scrap metal.

After dumping the laundry on the kitchen table, he headed back outside, switching on sprinklers and tapping the side of the water tank. A hollow thud echoed back. He wasn't sure when Colin normally topped up the water tanks, but he knew he'd need to shandy the last of the winter rainwater with bore water soon. *Do these tanks supply the shearers' hut, too?*

Willow gasped.

'There's tin flying across the paddock, Dad.' They hurried after it. Maeve emerged from the shearers' hut as Ned was heaving the old cast-iron bathtub towards the loose sheets of reclaimed roofing iron. Her hair whipped around her face and wrapped her black shirt against her slim frame.

'I've already rounded up a few lengths of guttering since the wind picked up,' she yelled, tossing a stray drench drum back into a large bin.

Ned upended the bathtub and dragged one end onto the pile of tin while Doug helped gather the rest of the errant plastic drums.

'Why did Colin even keep all this junk?' Maeve asked.

'Never know when you'll need a spare pair of tractor forks or a new roll of fencing wire,' Ned said.

'New?' Ned snorted with laughter. 'That tin is almost translucent,' he said, making the mistake of facing straight into a gust of loose topsoil.

'Arghh!' He clawed at his eyes and felt the top sheet of tin scrape past him. A yelp came from Maeve. When he prised open his eyes, blinking furiously against the gritty wind, he felt his blood chill. Maeve was on the ground, clutching her ankle. Doug was standing dead-still, his face ashen. The loose sheet of corrugated iron cartwheeled across the paddock.

'The roofing tin was coming straight for Doug,' Willow said, dropping to her grandmother's side. 'Gigi pushed him out of the way just in time.'

'You okay?' Ned asked, quickly securing the remaining tin. 'Dougie? Maeve?'

'Fine,' said Maeve, the grimace on her face telling another story.

'I thought it was going to slice my head off,' Doug spluttered, promptly bursting into tears.

A crack rang out, followed by an almighty creak. Ned turned to see what the noise was. *As if a photo shoot, a bung ankle and a near decapitation weren't enough . . .* A gum tree branch had just slammed onto the shearers' hut.

Diana stretched out on the cane lounge and pressed the glass of cool water against her neck, listening to the ice cubes clink as the standard roses swayed in the wind and the boys took turns on the slip and slide. *Thank God that breeze held off until now,* she thought, shuffling her seat across the verandah so the wind pushed the sprinkler mist in her direction. *Better than any air conditioner.*

She was programming an early alarm into her phone, planning to get a good watering in before the sun came out, when a call came through.

'That'll be Cameron with an update on the training day,' she said to Bonzer, who wagged his tail from his basket. But when she looked at the screen, she saw it was Ned.

'I have to ask a favour,' he said. 'Do you mind if I drop the children at yours while I take Maeve to the doctors?'

Doctors? Diana sat up straighter at his urgent tone.

'Of course, or I can come collect them if that speeds up the process. What's happened?' she said, shoving her feet back into the sandals she'd kicked off.

'I think Maeve's sprained her ankle, but it could be broken.'

'You'll be waiting all night at Hamilton's A&E. Hold tight. I'll call Lara on the way to your house. If she's around, she'll open up the Bush Nursing Centre.'

Diana was relieved when Lara picked up her mobile almost immediately.

Once a plan was in place, she hurried through the back streets of Bridgefield to Colin's property. Ned had Maeve loaded into the car when she arrived.

'Lara will meet you there in five,' Diana said, casting Maeve a sympathetic look. 'Keep me posted.'

Willow and Doug were happy enough to jump into her car and filled her in on the story as they drove back to Darling Downs.

'Then the roofing tin nearly cut my head off,' said Doug, making a slicing motion across his neck.

'And a ginormous branch fell on Gigi's house. It's lucky she wasn't inside at the time, she could have been squashed to death,' Willow added.

The children joined the slip and slide fun when they arrived. Confiscating the bottle of dishwashing detergent, Diana went inside, checked the roast chicken and made a start on the sides, chopping raw broccoli, cranberries and bacon for one salad, then hard-boiling eggs for a potato salad. *Ned's eggs*, she realised, lowering them into the saucepan of water. Once the potatoes were diced and simmering away next to the eggs, she opened a packet of chips and called the children. The deck was soon covered in damp footprints, wet children and excited dogs.

Cameron called right in the middle of it all. He didn't sound pleased. 'Are you having a party?'

'No, it's just Willow and Doug and your rowdy brothers. How was cricket? I'm so sorry I have to miss tomorrow's game, but there'll be plenty more to come . . .' It was everything she'd already explained. *But a good mother always puts her children first.*

'I wish you could have come with me instead of Gramps. He's driving me nuts,' Cam said. Diana recalled the photo Angus had sent Lara. 'The minute we got to the club, he was at the gate with a Texta, getting Aaron Finch's signature twice, in case the laundry-safe marker wasn't really laundry safe. And he talks non-stop about cricket stats, as if Georgie needs to know how many games and test matches each of the coaches have played. Don't even get me started about the special guests that are coming tonight. He'll bust an artery at this rate.'

Diana bit her lip to stop the smile that threatened.

'Don't let it worry you, they'll be used to fans.' She twisted in her chair at the sound of an approaching car. 'Ned's just arrived, I've got to go, mate, but I'll have a word with Grandpa and he'll rein Reg in.'

Diana used her reflection in the window to smooth her hair, then checked the button that kept popping on her shirt dress.

'Ned?' Cam said the name like it was something he'd stepped in.

'Yeah, he's had a shocker of a day. Getting roped into the magazine shoot was bad enough, then there was drama with some loose tin—'

Cameron interrupted with a snort of contempt. 'Did he now?'

'Hey,' Diana chided gently. *Someone woke up on the wrong side of the bed.*

A knock at the door came as she gave Cameron a bright farewell. There was nothing more she could do for him from 300 kilometres away, not tonight anyway, and she knew there was no chance of talking him round when he was in a mood.

Ned came through the door, smelling like soap and looking a whole lot less stressed than he had an hour ago. The children thundered through the house.

'Dad! Come and see the box we've made, ready for the kittens,' said Willow, enveloping him in a hug.

Diana watched Doug race to his side, gushing about the fun they'd had on the slip and slide. She opened the fridge, caught his eye, and raised the wine bottle in one hand, and a beer in the other.

He shot her a weary smile and nodded to the beer with a 'thank you' before turning his attention back to his children and dutifully following them into the laundry.

'The kitties will be happy in there, won't they Dad?'

Ned agreed, admiring the box Willow and Elliot had decorated with drawings of cats and lined with towels in readiness for the new arrivals. His gaze shifted to the perfectly labelled canisters of cleaning supplies, baskets brimming with neatly folded cloths and matching washing hampers, with hand-written labels for whites, mixed and darks. After the chaotic few hours he'd just had, the sense of order was distinctly calming.

'Do you think Gigi would like a kitten as a get-well present?'

Ned crouched down so he was at eye level with his daughter.

'They're not even born yet. I'm not sure she needs the extra stress of looking after something at the moment.' Plus, he still wasn't a hundred per cent sure she could look after herself. He rubbed his stomach dramatically. 'And if I don't get some food soon, I'm going to think about eating the arms off little girls with big hearts,' he said, lifting her milky-white arm to his mouth and pretending to gnaw on it.

Willow shot out of the laundry, giggling.

'What about boys made from slugs and snails and puppy dog tails? Wouldya eat them?' Leo and Doug peered at him with cheeky looks.

'Even better,' he said, gnashing his teeth together as the boys hooted with laughter.

Diana slid a beer across the bench when he returned to the kitchen, then filled the table with food that smelled every bit as good as it looked.

'That's the best thing I've seen all day,' he said, beaming at her. It was almost true—if he didn't count the sight of Diana in that cotton dress—and he paused as the strange but tasty salad hit his tastebuds. The children were hoeing into the food enthusiastically.

'Is that . . . broccoli?' He whispered between mouthfuls, liking the way she smiled back at him, conspiratorially.

'The boys hate the sound of it, but it always disappears in a flash. I just don't use the B-word too loudly when I'm dishing up,' she murmured.

He washed down the last of his meal with the beer. The McIntyre house, with their flowers, much-anticipated kittens and warmth, was a parallel universe.

'How's your mum?'

'Lara doesn't think her ankle's broken, just badly sprained. Hopefully the ice and painkillers will help, and we'll take her for X-rays tomorrow,' Ned said. Maeve hadn't wanted a fuss, and even though she hadn't been able to put any weight on her foot, she wouldn't have gone to the clinic if he hadn't insisted.

'Did you get the branch off the roof, Dad?'

Setting his knife and fork together on the plate, Ned shook his head.

'That's another problem for tomorrow, Dougie, after the wind dies down.' Just like the lucky miss with Doug and the corrugated iron, the damage to Maeve's home could have been much worse.

'What a day, right? Thanks so much again for stepping in with the photoshoot,' Diana said.

He waved it off. In the scheme of things, the hour or two in front of the lens to make Diana happy had been one of the easiest, and most enjoyable, parts of the day. He gathered up the dinner plates and turned to see her taking a passionfruit sponge from the fridge. He pretended to swoon, earning him another of Diana's bright smiles.

'If that's the reward, then it was well worth it,' he replied, knowing that if she asked him to do it all again tomorrow, he'd probably say yes.

18

Diana savoured the last mouthful of sponge cake, enjoying the kick of the passionfruit topping.

'Best sponge cake I've had in years,' said Ned, reaching for her dessert plate and stacking it on top of his. 'It's also the first sponge, but definitely still the best.'

She liked the way he pushed the chairs under the table and didn't hesitate to start filling the sink. *Reg could learn a bit here.* As he rolled his sleeves up, she found herself scanning his skin for more tattoos, seeing nothing but bubbles clinging to his hairy forearms as he did the washing up.

After the children raced outside for a twilight game of hide and seek, Diana summoned up the courage to ask the question that'd been on her mind all week.

'Colin never spoke about your mum. Did they separate long ago?'

Ned's hands stilled in the soapy water and a silence followed as he resumed scrubbing the dishes.

Great one, sticky beak, she thought, but when he continued he sounded hesitant rather than annoyed.

'They separated after I went to uni, but Colin helped her out from time to time. I didn't realise she was living back here until recently.'

That took her aback. *We've had our ups and downs*, she thought, *but I've never been in the dark about something so important* . . . then her cheeks burned as she thought of the extended McIntyre family. *You hypocrite!* Not that long ago, she'd been oblivious to Lara's abusive ex-husband, and completely in the dark about the rift between Angie's husband Jonesy and his twin brother, Max.

'Every family's got its skeletons,' she conceded. Though from the scuttlebutt she'd heard around town, Maeve's alcoholism had been the nail in the coffin for the Gardiner family.

He was quiet a moment, his hands busy with the dishes.

'Maeve didn't used to drink. She used to cook and sew and make jokes about Colin's floral obsession. Always nagging us about tucking in our T-shirts and pronouncing words correctly. Then when Jessie got sick . . .' From the rawness in his voice, and the way he trailed off, Diana sensed Ned didn't speak about it often. 'I know everybody processes loss differently, and every second person's got advice on how you should and shouldn't handle these things, but she never got help. Not proper help, anyway. We tried. Colin, Jonno, me.' He gave a wry laugh. 'I even had my university lecturer recommend a rehab centre after Maeve disgraced herself at my graduation.'

Diana could only imagine the shame and humiliation he'd felt.

'That's a pretty big burden to shoulder, on top of your own grief,' she said gently. 'I'm sorry you had to go through all that.'

With a shrug, he washed and rinsed another glass.

'She was never violent or cruel, which is more than you can say for a lot of alcoholics. After Doug was born, I gave up trying. It's easier to forget when we're far removed.'

Her heart ached for him; for everything he'd been through and all he'd missed out on since.

'But you're speaking to each other now?'

'More this month than the last decade. Apparently, she's been sober for years now, but Colin's accident . . .' Another shrug. 'She's the only grandparent the kids have.'

A plate slipped from the draining board, clattering into the sink, breaking the spell.

Ned gave her a wry look, his lips pressed together, and kept scrubbing a bowl that was already clean. He reminded her of Colin, months ago, when he'd confided that neither of his sons seemed interested in taking over the egg farm.

'Your dad would be proud,' she said softly. How often had she said those same words to her boys? She slung the tea towel over her shoulder and went to the corner of the bench where her iPad was charging. With a few quick taps, she paired the music with the speakers in the lounge room. A Bon Jovi hit cut through the tension in the room.

'Got a little heavy there, didn't it?' She pulled a box of chocolates from the fridge, relieved to see his back had lost a little of that ramrod straightness.

'Sure did.' He pulled the plug. 'We're going to be working together for a few months. Bit of sharing's required, I guess. And in the interests of full disclosure, my ex-wife is completely out of the picture. She's too busy reinventing herself as a yoga guru. The one-way ticket to India was a bit of a deal-breaker.'

India? Diana was floored. *What mother could abandon those beautiful children? An absent ex-wife, a dead father, a recovering alcoholic for a mother. Nobody could say he'd sailed through life. No wonder he was making an effort to reconnect with Maeve.* Diana thrust the box towards him. Chocolate was a great balm for most things—heartache, grief, boredom, and she was confident it'd work perfectly as a mood lightener too.

Ned reached for a mini Cherry Ripe.

'Thanks. Now's the part where you make me feel better by telling me you've got a cat-hoarding problem.'

She lifted her hands in surrender at his gentle teasing. 'Game's up. You've caught me out.'

They walked together to the sofas, both laughing. Ned took the large captain's chair by the window and Diana nestled herself into the corner of the lounge, folding her knees up under herself.

'Nope, a houseful of cats is not my forte, despite the pending kitten situation. Squeaky clean, I'm afraid.'

His face creased with mock disappointment.

'Well . . .' she craned her neck to check for children, 'there's one thing . . .'

He raised an eyebrow.

'. . . there's chocolate hidden all over the house. Inside old handbags, behind pot plants, in the bottom of my sock drawer and inside an old bread maker that hasn't been used since Toby started selling sourdough at the general store.'

She liked the rumble of his laughter and realised how much she enjoyed his company. Her gaze went to the family portrait again. *Whatever would Pete make of it all?*

The hot wind blew well into the evening, and Ned was relieved to see the shearers' hut was still standing and the sheets of scrappy tin were secure when his headlights shone across the paddocks. He'd manoeuvred the cast-iron bathtub on top of the tin before heading to Diana's for dinner. It had been heavy as hell, and he'd known it would do the trick once it was in place, it was just the execution that had let him down in the gusty winds.

Too many years dealing with scripts, Webster packs and customers, and not enough time outdoors, working with my hands.

He slowed in front of the dark hut. The hay shed creaked and groaned in the wind, adding to the racket of the gum tree limbs striking the tin. *How on earth did Maeve ever sleep?*

Pulling up at Colin's, he carried Willow inside. She stirred but settled under the light cotton sheet. Doug murmured about kittens as Ned tucked him in, but he fell back to sleep when Ned turned on the ceiling fan, worn out after a big night.

Soft light spilled out from under the spare bedroom door. He wondered how his mother was coping with Panadol, or whether he should offer something stronger from his medicine kit. Lifting a hand to knock, Ned paused, deciding against it. *It's odd enough sleeping under the same roof—she doesn't need me babying her.*

He quietly closed the door between the hallway and the kitchen and was rescuing a teabag from a mug when a clack, clack, clack came from the hallway. *Crutches.*

He opened the kitchen door for Maeve, and from the grimace on her face, it was clear she was both sore and tired.

Ned pulled out a chair for her. 'Cuppa?'

'Thanks,' she said, easing herself off the crutches.

'Diana fixed you a plate,' he said, gesturing to the foil-covered dish as he reached for the milk. 'Bit fancier than my pasta.'

'She didn't have to do that,' said Maeve, sipping the milky brew.

'Try telling Diana that,' he said with a smile, taking the empty seat beside her. 'She's also volunteered her brother-in-law Jonesy to look at your roof.'

Maeve frowned into her tea. 'It's nearly summer,' she said, shaking her head. 'We can fix a tarp over it until the will is settled. Shouldn't get too much rain between now and then. I was saving for a new heater, but it'll have to wait until the roof's fixed.'

It pained Ned to think she didn't even have the savings for essentials.

'Insurance?'

Maeve shook her head.

'Colin had enough outlays. I didn't want him wasting any more money on me.'

It didn't sit well, but just as Maeve refused the Panadeine Forte he offered, he gathered she had been adamant about maintaining as much independence as possible.

As he stood under the shower later that night Ned came to a decision. *I'll get the shearers' hut up to scratch. And then, when Jonno takes over the farm, he won't have to worry about the eyesore next door.* But as he stepped out of the shower and caught a glimpse of the colourful ink crisscrossing his chest and torso, he knew that was a lie. Just like the flowers he wore on his skin for Jessie, he would be renovating the shearers' hut for his mother, not for the aesthetics of it.

Ned returned to the kitchen to switch off the lights and found Maeve on the sofa, her fingers stroking the cover of the story book Leo was so fond of. *Jessie's book.*

The sorrow in his mother's eyes was the most emotion he'd seen since returning home. More than when he'd broken the news about Colin, and even more than when she'd seen her grandchildren for the first time. He could almost hear the sadness in her unspoken words, sense it in the set of her stooped shoulders but, for the life of him, he couldn't think of a single thing to say.

Diana surveyed the garden the next morning, keen to see how many blooms she'd lost to the hot northerlies. The anemones under the shade cloth had fared better than the ranunculus. *Must get more shade cloth,* she frowned, moving onto the next row. The poppies and stocks looked a little limp, and the strong wind had bent the tops of the foxgloves, giving them a curve, but she was confident they'd still be saleable.

Switching on the sprinklers, she could almost hear the sigh of relief as the flowers drank up the water, each droplet glistening like a diamond. A magpie edged in closer, flapping his wings as if he were showering.

'Get it while you can, buddy,' she said. 'Going to be another hot one today.'

Noise erupted from the house, and before long the boys ran into the yard, followed by Bonzer and Paddy. Harry and Elliot were barefoot and in board shorts, their skin tanned from the recent sunshine.

'Ready for a swim, Mum?'

Diana lifted her secateurs and bucket.

'Flowers first, guys. You know the drill. I'll be in shortly. How about you tidy your rooms before the journalist gets here?' She ignored the grumbling that erupted as they trudged back inside.

Diana's ring tone cut through the wind.

'Dad, how're things?'

Angus sounded out of breath, as if he were jogging. 'Just a minute, love . . .'

She twisted against the wind, trying to hear better. Over the honking and rumble of city traffic, she heard him call for Cameron. He was puffing even louder when he came back on the line.

'I've nearly caught Cam. He just needs calming down.'

Calming down?

The hot northerly winds and soil moisture levels quickly felt like the least of her problems. Her hand flew to her mouth as she realised that in the drama of last night, she'd forgotten to give Angus a heads-up about Reg.

'Oh, Dad, I meant to call you last night, tell you he was a bit stressed about Reg. What's happened?'

'Hold up.'

She heard his hand muffling the phone.

'Hey Cam, your mum's on the line.' The muffled sound disappeared and his voice was clear again. 'He stormed out at brekky. Emotions are running high. I thought a quick word from you might be the ticket.'

Diana jammed the phone between her ear and her shoulder, a sense of dread in every step as she hurried out of the wind. 'Mate, what's up? Didn't you sleep well?'

'I did *not* sleep well,' Cameron shot back. 'Nobody, and I mean, *nobody*, should have to share a room with their grandfather, especially when I'd planned to share it with Georgie.'

Diana moved the phone away from her ear a little, easily imagining Reg instilling his values. He'd stepped up on a similar soapbox years ago, never allowing her and Pete to sleep in the same room when they visited, even when they were sharing a house at uni. She should have thought to brief him beforehand.

'Then he had the nerve to lecture us,' continued Cam, evidently hitting his stride.

'He means well, mate, he's just old fashioned. Your dad and I received the same sermon when we were first dating.'

'It was horrific, Mum. I've never been so embarrassed in my life. Georgie was mortified, too. I can't deal with having him around, I just can't. Not after everyone at the hotel breakfast buffet heard him banging on about contraceptives and shotgun weddings. How am I even supposed to play today?'

'You can, mate, and you will,' she said in her best soothing voice.

The shed door opened and Leo bounded in with a towel around his neck. His ears pricked up when he heard Cam's voice.

'Hey, Cam, how'd you go at the function? Did you meet Ian from the Coodabeen Champions? Gramps said he was Geelong's number one ticket holder. Have they asked you to play seconds yet? Miss Kenna told everyone in class that you're a dead cert, and I heard Barry from cricket saying he's sure you'll make the Big Bash league soon.'

Diana shooed Leo out of the packing shed and went into damage control.

'Cam,' she cautioned, 'you've got bigger fish to fry this weekend, this is your big debut. Take a big breath.' She felt a small sense of relief when she heard him take a ragged breath. 'And another, mate.'

An ambulance or fire truck zoomed past in the background, but she could tell from his long, slow sigh, that between the venting and the breathing, he was slightly calmer.

Diana hung up a few minutes later, when she'd secured a promise that he'd go back to the cricket ground. She made another phone call before she started on the posies.

Reg sounded upbeat when he answered.

'Ah, Annie-girl, you wouldn't believe who I've just been having coffee with,' he said, delight in every word as he told her about the retired chairman of Cricket Australia who just happened to be at the same cafe as him. Her father-in-law didn't seem to have an inkling of Cameron's anguish. She longed for Pete's patience, and for him to gently remind his father to pull his head in, like he'd done in the past.

'Reg, do you have any idea how Cameron's feeling today? I've just had to convince him not to pack it all in, because of some badly timed lecture on your part. You need to back off.'

She could picture Reg's mouth opening and shutting like a Murray cod but he finally agreed.

Diana went back to making more bouquets, and finished them quickly, her annoyance compounding when the magazine journalist still wasn't there by morning tea time, as promised.

'Google Maps must have sent her from Melbourne via Brissie,' Diana grumbled, swiping her windblown hair from her eyes and opening her Facebook page. Her irritation evaporated when she saw Sadie Woodford had not only liked and commented on her post about yesterday's photo shoot, but she'd shared it on her account and given Darling Dahlias a generous plug.

> Want the inside scoop on the hottest new flower farm in the country? Nestled at the foot of the Grampians, this glorious farm is managed by former graduate and boss-mum superstar, Diana McIntyre.

Diana's hand flew to her chest. *Hottest new flower farm? Boss-mum superstar?* Delighted, she kept reading.

> Here's a little behind the scenes teaser. Can't wait to see it splashed across the pages of *Country Home* mag next year! If you like what you see, join us next March at the *Blooming Marvellous* launch.

Sadie had also added the book launch details and pre-order links to her book, in order to whip her fans into a frenzy. Breathlessly, Diana took a screenshot and forwarded it to Angus, Lara, Angie and Penny. She debated whether to message it to Ned, too. Recalling the depth of their conversation last night, she hit send.

Holy moly! That's 1500 likes in an hour! She was still scrolling through the Facebook comments, replying to compliments, and marvelling over the flurry of new followers on the Darling Dahlias page when the boys stormed into the flower shed.

'We're starving, Mum. Do we have to wait any longer for lunch?' Harry carried the containers of yo-yos and muffins she had restocked specially for their city visitor.

'Can we go swimming now?' added Elliot.

Diana wavered. She was getting sick of saying no. No to Cameron's cricket. No to Reg. No to this morning's swim. *Sadie's launch will be worth it*, she reminded herself, stuffing her phone into her back pocket. She doled out biscuits and a text arrived from Tori, the journalist, to say she was running a few hours late. The boys cheered when she went inside to don her bathers.

'Quick dip, so we're back in time for the interview,' she said.

They piled into the four-wheel drive, towels around their necks and smiles on their faces, and headed to the dam. Diana sank her feet into the mud, not deep enough to where the yabbies burrowed but far enough that the silky earth squished between her toes. *Bliss.* The water was deliciously icy, shaded by the trees on the northern end, and by the time she breast-stroked her way back to the boys, she felt refreshed.

Ned drove carefully into town that morning with the children, watching out for felled branches and sticks from last night's violent winds. There were several piles of freshly cut wood on the roadside. He waved to a family working with chainsaws on the outskirts of Bridgefield, evidently used to cleaning up after gusty winds.

'Do you think Gigi will stay with us a few nights, Dad?'

Ned lifted a finger from the steering wheel, returning the greeting from a passing car. 'Not sure, Dougie. If she wants to, she's more than welcome.' He'd voiced the offer to Maeve the night before, and while she'd thanked him, she hadn't committed either way.

Their first stop in town was at Imogen's house. Oscar and Doug had hatched a plan for the catch-up earlier that week.

'Hi Imogen, bye Dad,' said Doug, scrambling out of the car as Oscar appeared on the porch.

Imogen strolled across the yard, an elderly greyhound by her side. She greeted Ned and Willow with a breezy hello.

'He's not shy, is he?' She laughed as the flyscreen door banged in Doug and Oscar's wake. 'Fancy a coffee?'

Ned shook his head. 'Thanks for the offer but I need to see Lara before her morning class starts.' He hesitated, looking back at Imogen's home. Through the windows he could see the boys duelling with plastic swords. He hoped it wouldn't end in tears. As if sensing his hesitation, Imogen waved him off with a reassuring smile.

'They'll be fine,' she said. 'See you this arvo.'

Lara was waiting for them when they arrived at the Bush Nursing Centre.

'Sorry I didn't have these handy last night,' she said, handing over a pair of crutches that looked about two decades newer than the backup pair she'd fished out of the storeroom the previous night. 'They'll be a much better fit for your mum.'

'Thanks, Lara, and thanks again for seeing us out of hours last night.'

She lifted a shoulder and gave an easy shrug. 'I do it all the time,' she said, walking him to the door. 'Emergencies rarely stick to a nine-to-five schedule. And we'll drop by tomorrow to help get that branch off the roof.'

Her thoughtful offer took Ned by surprise. *First Diana, now Lara helping them.*

'I don't want to put you out.'

'Wouldn't offer if I didn't mean it,' she said matter-of-factly.

Willow swung on his hand, then craned her neck to look at the sandwich board across the road.

'Dad! It's cheese-and-bacon pies today. Doug is going to be spewing he went to Oscar's house.'

Lara laughed. 'You're a lady of good taste. They're my favourite, too.'

'You head over and order one for me as well,' Ned said, digging his wallet out and handing it to his daughter. 'Check for cars before you cross, though.'

'Okey dokey,' Willow called, as she skipped down the footpath.

Ned turned to Lara. 'While I've got you, can you suggest any social groups for Maeve?' he said, recalling how the brochures on grief had encouraged community connectivity.

'Absolutely. We run Pilates at the centre twice a week, and a Move It or Lose It class, although they'll be tricky with a bung ankle. Toby's started a board game afternoon at the shop. The show society's always looking for helpers for the annual shindig in May . . . Would any of those work?'

Ned tilted his head. None of them sounded like a perfect fit but he didn't want to discount them outright.

'They're food for thought,' he said, thanking her. He left and quickly caught up with Willow at the general store.

An older customer, sporting rainbow overalls and a lilac perm, complimented Willow on her manners. 'Always good to see the young ones opening doors and saying good morning. You must be Colin's family,' she said, bestowing them with a warm smile. 'I'm Pearl Patterson, but everyone calls me Nanna Pearl. Willow's been telling me all about her new friends.'

Willow's chest puffed up a little.

Ned nodded, feeling another rush of gratitude for this close-knit community. They'd been shown more kindness in Bridgefield in the last month than they had in their last three city postings.

'Nice to meet you, Pearl, I'm Colin's son, Ned. And it seems Willow's already introduced herself.'

Willow passed him the warm pies and turned to admire the woman's handbag, which was every bit as flamboyant as her clothes, with appliqué flowers and ladybird buttons.

'I made it myself,' said Pearl. 'You can achieve lots in a sewing crafternoon.'

'A crafternoon?' Willow was impressed with this new word, while Ned immediately thought of Maeve. *Might be a better fit for her than Lara's Pilates or Toby's board games.*

Knowing Willow would invite herself to these crafternoons if they lingered much longer, Ned looped an arm around her shoulders and tapped his watch. 'We really do have to get to Hamilton, missy. Nice to meet you, Pearl.'

They collected Maeve and continued to the rural hospital, where an X-ray showed it was a bad sprain, not a break.

'The swelling makes it look worse than it is, and you'll have some impressive bruising to show for it in the next few days,' the radiologist told them. 'Rest up, make sure you keep using those crutches and you'll be running marathons in no time.'

A quick detour to the supermarket for supplies, then they were back on the road again. Willow chatted the whole drive home, telling Maeve all about Flopsy, the McIntyre's pregnant cat Jinx, the names of her teachers and best friends from the last two schools and even their crotchety neighbour from the Darwin apartment block. Her grandmother absorbed the information with an occasional nod and amused comment.

They made it back to Bridgefield by early afternoon.

'Come back to our place, Gigi. I didn't get to show you my room last night.'

'Hold on, Willow, help me get the groceries unpacked first,' Ned said, rounding the car and handing Maeve the crutches. They were more ergonomic than the pair she'd used last night, but from the way she winced in the short walk from the car to the house, Ned could tell the sprain was painful.

Once Maeve was settled on the couch with an icepack, and pillows elevating her foot, Ned fetched the last of the shopping from the ute.

'Where does this go, Dad?' Willow reached for the big pack of toilet paper. 'It won't fit in the bathroom cupboard.'

Ned looked up from the groceries, amused to see Willow balancing the 24-pack on her head. *Harry and Elliot's influence, no doubt.*

'Try the linen press.'

A moment later, Willow ran into the room clutching the purple quilt.

'Look what I found, Dad. It's amazing,' she said, fizzing with excitement as she spread the handmade blanket across the table for a closer inspection.

Ned heard Maeve inhale sharply. He looked from his daughter to his mother; Maeve's distraught expression was worlds away from Willow's delight.

'That was for Jessie.' The words were little more than a whisper, as if the wind had been knocked out of her.

Willow froze, catching her bottom lip between her teeth, a worried expression crossing her face. And as Ned opened his mouth to reassure his little girl, he realised he couldn't promise anything on Maeve's behalf. He'd seen his mother unravel before, just like the raw edges of the fabric on the unfinished quilt. Was this a step too far, too soon?

19

Diana rushed through a shower that afternoon, rinsing out the dam water. She blasted her hair with the blow drier and sat the boys down in front of a movie just before the journalist, Tori, arrived. After a quick tour of the gardens and packing shed, they settled on the deck. Tori bit into a yo-yo, brushing crumbs from her notepad as she wrote.

'So tell me, Diana, would it be fair to assume Sadie Woodford's your biggest influence in the Australian flower game?'

'Definitely,' said Diana, pouring them both a glass of icy lemon cordial. 'She's a self-made woman, and there's a lot to be said about learning what to do from someone who's out there doing it successfully. Her workshops helped me turn my dream into a reality, and that's something I'm incredibly grateful for.' Diana paused. 'Of course, my friends and family helped, too. I inherited my green thumb from my mum, Annabel, learned so much from my mentor, Colin Gardiner, and my late husband, Pete, supported me every step of the way.'

Diana pointed to a rose at the centre of her garden, brimming with deeply cupped coral flowers. 'See that Abraham Darby rose?'

The journalist moaned with pleasure as she bit into a muffin, then gestured for her to continue.

'My husband Pete bought it for me twenty years ago. It spent the first few years in a terracotta pot, and I moved it from one uni share house to another while I studied teaching. It was the first thing I planted in the garden when we purchased Darling Downs.'

Diana smiled at the memory. Pete had given her four more to mark the arrival of each of their boys.

'I've since planted hundreds of other roses in a riot of colours and scents, but Abraham will always be my favourite because it reminds me of Pete and everything I'm working towards,' she explained.

'The oldest and most treasured rose in the garden. That's perfect,' Tori said. 'You've given me oodles to work with here. I'll slip in a few comments from Sadie's team and we'll be tickety-boo.'

Tori doubled-checked the spelling of names, apologised again for running so late, and packed away her notebook with a promise to send an advance copy of the magazine. She then started to drive down the driveway but paused at the hedged roundabout. Leaned out the window she said, 'I'm an idiot. I forgot to ask about Mr Tall, Dark and Handsome from the photo shoot. He's a farmhand or something more?'

Diana stumbled mid-stride. 'Oh, Ned? He's—'

While she felt she knew him well from Colin's conversations, she'd only recently met him in person. How could he possibly be anything more? She mustered up a casual smile.

'As my mentor's son, he's a very handy person to have around. He's just a friend,' she said, leaning on the car door, surprised to find that the answer didn't seem to encapsulate the fast friendship and camaraderie they shared. Not to mention the fizz of attraction when they worked together, or the curiosity that stirred when she tried to picture what was under his shirt.

Willow put Jessie's quilt away the moment she realised it had upset her grandmother, but Ned could tell she felt bad for inadvertently stirring up memories. To her credit, Maeve hadn't yelled or burst into tears, but she had been noticeably quiet since.

Keen to give his mother some space, and his daughter a distraction, Ned commandeered Willow into action. They found an old ladder in the shed and carried it across to the shearers' hut.

He propped it against the northern wall.

'You'll have no nails left to chew if you keep that up,' he said, gently taking Willow's hand from her mouth. 'Stop stewing, missy.'

She sighed, her shoulders slumping, and peered at the branch overhanging the roof.

'You're never going to move that by yourself, Dad.'

He followed her gaze. She was probably right, but if he could, it'd save him asking the McIntyre family for favours. 'No harm trying. Hold the ladder here,' he said, tapping the sides. 'Two hands, yeah?'

Willow nodded, a cheeky look spreading across her features. 'Remember last time we used a ladder?' She mimed raking her fingernails down her face.

Ned nodded, happy to see her smiling, even if it was at his expense. So much had changed since they'd beaten a hasty path through the red centre, and he was glad to be dealing with fallen branches today, rather than falling cats.

From roof height, he quickly realised he'd underestimated the damage to the hut, and the size of the branch.

'Hate to say it, but you're right,' he said, descending the ladder. 'We're going to need help.'

Bron called just as Diana was mixing a gin and tonic.

'How did the interview go? Did she throw you any curve balls?'

'Tori was lovely. I talked up Sadie's new book, said I was thrilled to learn from the best in the business. A three-page spread, apparently, depending on how the photos come up. And did you hear about the wine labels they made, for the launch?' Diana was giddy as she described them to her friend.

'See, I told you it would be worth it. Sadie Woodford chose *you* out of all the emerging flower farmers in Australia. You're taking the bull by the horns, Diana, just like you planned.'

Diana signed off and, feeling quietly pleased with how the interview and photoshoot had gone, enjoyed a final moment of peace before the boys finished their movie.

She floated around the house on cloud nine, right up until Angus phoned shortly after dinner. Her father's usual upbeat tone was distinctly missing. In fact, Diana thought as she quizzed him on the game, he sounded downright exhausted.

'Cameron got out for a duck.'

'Not even one run?' She sighed and tried to remember a time when he'd got out without adding a run to his team's tally. 'Oh God, you don't think it's because of the tiff with Reg?' She winced, remorse cutting sharply through her excitement.

'The exact same thing could have happened if you'd driven him down yourself,' Angus reasoned, but still she felt a pang of guilt. 'We're leaving the city now, see you in three hours or so.'

The slamming of a car door startled Diana out of her restless sleep. She dragged herself off the couch, feeling a crick in her neck, and groggily made her way across the lounge room. Moths swarmed around the ute's headlights. The car smelled of fast food when Angus rolled his window down. Cameron got out and marched past with a mumbled 'thank you' to his grandfathers.

'I'm sure he'll be more grateful for being driven to Geelong after a good night's sleep,' she said. 'You sure you're okay at the hotel, Reg?'

Reg gave her a weary smile. Or was it sheepish?

'I'm flying out in a few days anyway, and it's not a bad spot to stay, love.'

It wasn't exactly an apology, but still relief flooded through Diana's body. Angus had obviously worked his magic on Reg's ruffled feathers. And, as she looked a little closer, she saw he was wearing one of Colin's striped shirts. She smiled and invited him for a farewell dinner before he went.

Cameron's lights were off when she paused outside his bedroom door, but she knocked lightly anyway.

'Can I come in, Cam?'

Silence. She tried again.

This time he replied. 'I don't want to talk about it, okay?'

She folded her hands together and paused a moment before walking away. Knowing she wouldn't be able to get back to sleep anytime soon, she made a cup of tea and sat on the couch with the back issues of *Country Home* Tori had given her. Penny had been right. Neither the journalist nor the photographers had been out to trip her up and, as she turned the glossy pages, she saw the articles and photographs were very flattering. She rearranged the magazine on her lap, so the lamplight fell gently over the front cover and her delicate pink cup and saucer were in the frame. A few snaps on her phone and she had a nice enough photo to upload to her Instagram feed. She tapped out a caption and infused it with more enthusiasm than she actually felt.

> Saturday night done right. A great magazine, a quiet household and a hot cuppa. Bliss! Hope your evening's as relaxing as mine x

Diana tagged Sadie Woodford, plus Bron's marketing agency, GeelongPop, and the magazine's social media account. She shared the same picture across to the Micro Flower Farm's Facebook page, getting a little boost with each and every like and comment, and tamping down the niggling feeling that the publicity might have been at Cameron's expense.

In bed, after an hour of tossing and turning, she reached for her phone and edited her caption to remove the last sentence. Authenticity had always been a cornerstone of her business plan and, just as she'd declined the make-up artist and hair-dresser for yesterday's shoot, she didn't want to go down the slippery slope of falsifying her life, or portraying herself as someone she wasn't.

Much to Ned's surprise, the entire McIntyre clan descended on the property the next day, even Diana's sister who lived by the coast. Before he knew it, the paddocks were a hive of activity.

The sound of the chainsaw cut through the still air and, before long, the branch that had speared through Maeve's roof was a pile of firewood. Ned watched Tim back the trailer in close, reversing as easily as if he were driving forward.

'He makes it look simple, doesn't he?' Diana said as she reached for a round of firewood, tossing it into the trailer. 'I won't even mention how well Tim backs my caravan; it'd make you sick.'

Ned laughed, gathering an armful of wood.

'I'm more impressed by the way he felled that gum tree. You'll have firewood for a year when we get all that cut up.'

Diana surveyed the heap. 'You sure you don't want it, Ned? Or your mum?'

'No way, it's the least I can do. Colin's been stockpiling firewood for years—no chance of going cold around here. You rounded up all the workers,' he said, gesturing to the multitude of helpers at various positions around the shearers' hut.

Lara was on the smaller chainsaw, cutting the limbs into rounds, Jonesy and his friend Brett had already removed the damaged sheets of tin and were now assessing the repairs needed to the roof trusses, Angus was turning snags on the barbecue for lunch, and Willow was giving Angie a tour of Colin's garden.

'Things better with Reg, then?'

Diana looked across to the backyard, to where Reg was umpiring the kids' game of cricket. Maeve watched on with an icepack on her ankle.

'Yeah, Dad must have got through to him while they were away,' she said. 'I think he wants to make the most of these last few days before he returns to WA.' She seemed pleased that they were parting on a better note. 'He even offered to babysit the boys tonight when I'm at sewing group, which is great because Cam's patience seems threadbare today. I'm better off paying him to take his girlfriend to the movies or out for dinner, just so he's out of the house.'

'The game didn't go well?'

'That's an understatement.' Diana brushed a baby huntsman spider off the bark with a sigh. 'He's angry at me for missing it, he's angry at Reg for being Reg, he's angry at himself for playing badly . . .'

'Angry at the world?' Ned offered, gathering more wood.

Diana nodded, giving him a weary smile. 'Something like that.'

Remembering the potent cocktail of hurt, hormones and an almighty sense of injustice from his teenage years, Ned felt a stirring of empathy for the teenager and then for Diana, who was probably bearing the brunt of it all. Most of the time he'd been sad about Jessie or angry about his parents separating, Maeve had been too drunk to realise and Colin too busy keeping everything afloat to gauge how serious it was. He pushed away the memories and turned his focus back to the task at hand. So used to the background roar of the chainsaw, he didn't even notice it had stopped until a sharp whistle pierced the air. They turned towards the barbecue.

'Grub's up,' called Angus. Everyone gravitated towards the deck chairs and picnic rugs arranged on the southern side of the shearers' hut.

Ned was glad he'd whipped through the shops the previous day and had ample supplies for a lunch spread, although the store-bought burgers and snags didn't look half as good as the ones the McIntyre's had brought with them.

When they all sat down to eat, with paper plates on their knees, Ned discovered there was an enormous difference in the taste too.

'These sausages are sensational. Which butcher do you use?' he asked, picturing the main street of Hamilton but drawing a blank on a butcher's shop. *Horsham maybe?*

'You're looking at him,' Angus grinned, then turned to point at Diana. 'And her, and her, and him.' His smile widened as he pointed to most of the adults present. Maeve, sitting in the comfiest camping chair, with her leg elevated on a stump, looked as surprised as Ned.

Toby laughed at Ned's expression. 'Don't worry, mate, you'll get roped into meat-packing day if you stand still long enough.'

Angie's little girl Claudia piped up.

'And when you look in the coolroom, when the meat's hanging on the hooks, the ribs are striped like candy canes. Well, if candy canes were actually made of bones and meat and covered in blood.'

Harry and Leo chipped in, trying to outgross one another with stories of exploding entrails. Reg started looking a little green around the gills, and Diana sent the boys off to play. Willow's ears pricked up when Lara mentioned sewing. 'Do you go to the crafternoons? Gigi used to be a good sewer, but she said she can't teach me to sew because she's probably forgotten how to do it. Can she come, so that she can remember again?'

All eyes turned to Maeve, who looked like a deer in the headlights.

'Everyone done with the tucker then?' Angus said loudly, easing himself out of his deckchair and lifting the barbecue hood.

Ned caught Lara's eye. *Would this be a good 'community connector' activity?* Lara gave a quick nod and, while the others began packing up their plates or fetching a final sausage in bread, she moved her chair next to Maeve's.

Willow perched on Ned's knee and rested her head against his shoulder.

'Why doesn't Gigi want to sew with me?' Her quiet voice was sad and she leaned into Ned as he ran a hand over her silky hair.

'I'm not sure, pipsqueak, but that's more about your grand-mother than you.'

Diana looked across, fixing Ned with a look of motherly concern.

'Everything okay?' she mouthed.

He nodded and spoke gently to his daughter.

'She's not been well, remember? And I'm not sure how she'd go sewing with a sprained ankle.' The answer seemed to appease Willow, who sat back up and frowned as she looked at Ned's glasses.

'Dad, these have got more fingerprints on the lenses than mine. They're covered in dust, too,' she said crossly, promptly sliding them off his nose and polishing them on her T-shirt. When she was satisfied with the job, she handed them to Ned, then loped across the lawn to join the rest of the kids in the machinery shed.

'Is that a Champion 9G? What a beauty,' said Jonesy, squinting across the paddock to the orange tractor.

Ned, slipping his specs on, nodded towards it.

'Take a closer look if you like.'

Leaving Maeve with Lara and Diana, Ned took Jonesy across to the machinery shed.

'My old man would give his right arm for an old girl like that,' said Jonesy. 'He's had an eye out for one of these tractors ever since they did the round-Australia rally in them.'

'Colin's had it for yonks,' Ned admitted. 'It's more useful as a jungle gym in its current state. I don't know the first thing about machinery.'

Angie came across to the shed, her niece Lucy on her hip. 'No, no, no, no, no,' she said sternly. 'There're enough vintage motorbikes in our shed, we're not collecting tractors, too.'

'But it's still got the original canvas hood,' Jonesy said, awe in his voice.

Angie gave an indulgent eye roll. 'Rob talks about old stuff the same way Diana talks about her flowers. It's an addiction,' she laughed.

Ned swallowed hard. As someone who'd lived with an alcoholic, he cringed every time the term was used jokingly. Too caught up in their banter, neither Angie nor Jonesy seemed to notice his introspection.

'Let me know if you want to sell it,' said Jonesy. 'For Dad, not me,' he added, getting an elbow in the ribs from his wife.

'*Don't* let him know if you want to sell it,' countered Angie. Ned wasn't sure if she was joking or not, and for a split second he found himself missing that type of relationship, with inside jokes and conversations that were as much about gestures and things unsaid as words.

Classical music floated through the house, courtesy of Sarah's home entertainment unit with its hidden speakers, soundbars and whole-house connectivity. Diana, who had been to the Squires' home on numerous occasions, barely noticed the flash accessories, but Nanna Pearl spent the first half of sewing circle admiring the plethora of digital integrations.

'Whatever his faults, it must have been good having a nerdy husband,' Pearl said, peering at the touch-screen displays in the hallway, which showed live footage from the security cameras. Sarah lifted her glass of prosecco and clinked it against Lara's with a smile.

'Ex-husband. He might have been tech savvy, but he wasn't smart enough to remember those cameras captured more than just burglars,' she laughed. 'His loss, my gain. Speaking of exes, I hear you've been in touch with your high-school sweetheart, Imogen? Do tell.'

Imogen happily set aside the project she'd been working on all year. Sewing wasn't her strength, but she loved the social aspect, even when it included a cross-examination from Sarah Squires.

'Bit fancy getting a Zoom call from Antarctica,' Imogen said. 'Though next time I'm hoping to see penguins, or at least a killer whale. Jonno could be pulling my leg and calling from an office in Melbourne for all I know.'

Diana paused, glass raised to her lips. *Jonno Gardiner?* How come she hadn't heard about this at the school gate?

She finished her bubbles and pulled some fabric from her basket. Ned had spoken about Jonno's polar expeditions over the last few weeks, sounding every bit the proud brother as he updated her with little snippets each time they were in touch. Judging by Leo's sudden interest in all things Antarctic, Doug and Willow kept in close touch with their uncle, too.

Imogen smiled, then nudged Diana. 'If only those Gardiner boys didn't have such itchy feet, right? Ned's not hard on the eye, is he?'

What is she implying? Diana wondered. Reg had got the wrong end of the stick about Ned, and suddenly she was now worried about how often she'd dropped his name into casual conversations with her friends and family. She fed the fabric into the sewing machine and pressed the pedal hard, but her plan to drown out the conversation with machine noise backfired when the thread snapped. *Darn it.* She wrestled the fabric out from under the foot and re-threaded the needle, feeling everyone's eyes on her.

'What?'

She especially didn't like the mischievous smile creeping over Sarah's face. 'I was chatting to the hunky Mr Gardiner at the school assembly last week. There's something about the combo of brains and brawn, isn't there? Imagine: a pharmacist *and* a gardener.' She put on a husky southern drawl that belonged to a TV soapie star. 'Pass me those Xanax, sweetheart . . . Now bend down and pick up that shovel, sugar.'

Sarah and Imogen fell about laughing, and even Nanna Pearl and Lara had a giggle.

'Ha ha,' Diana said sarcastically. 'I'm sure he'd be thrilled to know you think so highly of him.'

Lara changed the subject. 'I've invited Maeve Gardiner to join us—she might take a little encouragement, though.'

Pearl clasped her hands together.

'Oh, good. I'm after extra helpers for—' But Penny, who'd been quiet all evening—still recovering from her weekend away with her city girlfriends—jumped in.

'Nanna Pearl, give the poor woman a break. Let Maeve dip her toes back into society before you lump her with committee roles,' she scolded.

Couldn't have said it better myself.

Sarah poured another glass of bubbly and leaned forward, ready to hear a dissection of Maeve's reclusive tendencies, but Nanna Pearl swiftly moved the conversation to Bridgefield's Christmas concert. Diana felt like landing a kiss on top of her purple perm.

'Now, I'm about to sign off on the stall layout and I need your thoughts, ladies.'

Diana grabbed the platter of sweets she'd brought with her and handed them around, knowing the machines would be still for a while yet as the octogenarian held court.

20

Bridgefield turned on the late-spring charm through November and into early December, with a string of blue skies and crisp mornings offering enough sunshine and rain to make the grass grow at a rapid rate. There was no sign of the wind that had torn branches from trees a few weeks before. In fact, Ned decided with a smile, they couldn't have asked for better conditions to reroof the shearers' hut.

Ned lifted the sheet of shiny corrugated iron and waited for Toby to get a grip on the other end before walking across to Maeve's home.

'Toss us up another box of screws, mate,' the plumber, Brett, called.

Ned located the screws, gave them to Doug, and watched his son jog to the ladder, where Lara was waiting. She passed it to her brother-in-law, Jonesy.

'Nice work, buddy, we'll make a chippie outta you yet.' Doug's smile stretched from ear to ear at Jonesy's comment and he ran off to tell Willow and Maeve, who had wandered across for a look.

Ned and Toby grabbed another sheet of roofing iron.

'They'll be done in no time,' Toby called over his shoulder cheerfully. Toby was easy company and Ned found they worked well together. 'The farmers in the district are all pleased with the rain. Is it doing the trick with the dahlias, too?'

'Yep,' Ned said, offloading the sheet to Lara. 'Everything seems to grow an inch overnight. Diana's got new flowers coming into bloom each week.'

'That's great, she's worked pretty hard for it.'

Ned agreed. 'That Sadie author has struck gold there.'

A strange look passed over Toby's face.

'Yeah, I'm not sure she's as perfect as Diana imagines.'

Toby's comment caught Ned by surprise. From everything he'd heard, Sadie Woodford's only crime was an all-consuming passion for flower farming and dedicating her life to promoting the industry.

'What do you mean?' he asked.

'An old journo friend in Ballarat was talking about her. Usually, I give pub talk as much credence as the gossip in the general store.' From the way he shrugged, Ned got the sense Toby heard all manner of stories in his line of work. *Probably plenty about Maeve, too.*

Toby glanced at Lara and continued. 'There was something with one of her employees. My mate said an ex-staffer approached their mag about a tell-all,' said Toby, mentioning the publication's name.

Ned knew the magazine he was talking about immediately, and also what kind of headlines they ran. Lovers' tiffs, secret children, bankrupt superstars. Surely Diana would have heard something if there *was* anything to hear?

'And are they running it?'

'Nah, it was a few years back when I was still working in the city, not recent. The publisher who prints her books is a major advertiser and the bloke eventually gave up.'

Ned exhaled with relief at Toby's words.

'You're not dwelling on that again, are you?' Lara asked. 'I've read that magazine and, if the story was legit, they'd run it without hesitation. Disgruntled employees and ex-lovers of B-list celebrities are their bread and butter.'

Toby lifted an eyebrow and adjusted his grip on the corrugated iron. 'Can't argue with that type of logic,' he said.

As they worked, the conversation turned to Ned's travels.

'I told my daughter about your adventures,' Toby said. 'Holly's planning a trip around Australia in her gap year. She's infinitely jealous that your kids have already ticked off half the places on her itinerary.'

Ned laughed. 'Yeah, they don't know how good they've got it,' he said. 'New faces, new cities, different climates, different schools.'

'Where are you off to next, when you've finished here?'

Ned thought of Jessie's map, pinned to a cork board in Colin's house, and couldn't help his eyes drifting to the deckchairs Willow was setting up in the shade for her and Maeve. Their next destination was normally a hot discussion topic between him and the children, with the anticipation of their upcoming adventure every bit as exciting as arriving in a new town. But as he carried the iron sheet across the paddock, he realised they hadn't discussed their next trip yet.

The sky changed from pink to red, with streaks of silver and gold reflected in Lake Bridgefield below. After seven kilometres of speed walking, Diana felt like the windmill at the top of the track, full of creaks and groans.

'Let's pause here a minute, Pen.'

'No arguments from me,' Penny said, stretching against the base of the windmill.

Lara jogged up the side of the hill, barely sweating, despite having run twice as far as they'd walked. 'How's the view this morning?'

Unlike their feelings about exercise, that was one thing they could all agree on.

'Amazing,' Penny said, taking out her phone and snapping a photo of the three of them with the sunrise in the background.

'You should use this on your socials,' Penny said as she showed Diana the photo.

'Pfft, fine for you young 'uns. I look like a beetroot in active wear,' said Diana. 'I don't know if anyone else needs to see that. Remember, I'm an ambassador for—'

'Sadie Woodford,' Penny and Lara chorused.

'As if we'd forget. You've only mentioned her name about a hundred times this week,' Lara said. 'Poor, Ned, he'd hear it even more than us.'

Diana gave them a withering look but couldn't hide her smile for long. The last month had flown past and she was getting more excited about the event as the spring flowers made way for the summer blooms. The dahlias were shooting up and she had regular emails from Bron, Sadie's PA Ellen, and even a few from Sadie herself.

'Seriously, though, from a marketing perspective, your followers will love a few candid snaps that have nothing to do with flowers. They're buying into Darling Dahlias as a package and you, my love, are the main part of that brand.'

'Sweaty, no make-up, with a cheesy smile is a branding angle?' Diana was doubtful.

'Authentic, living your best life,' Penny corrected. 'It's one of your marketing pillars, remember?'

She was right. Diana begrudgingly uploaded the picture to Instagram and the farm's Facebook page.

'Oh, you should see the bottles of wine that arrived yesterday.'

Penny peered at Diana's phone screen. 'The labels are gorgeous!'

'Is that gold foil on them?' Lara asked as she squeezed in for a look. 'I hate to think how much this type of launch costs.'

'Doesn't seem to be an issue. Nanna Pearl said they've already pre-paid for the catering,' Penny said. 'Love how Bridgefield gets a mention, too. Did you ever imagine seeing your business splashed across the side of a wine bottle, sis?'

Diana grinned. 'All thanks to my good friend, Sadie.'

They headed for home at a more conversational pace, Penny talking about the upcoming harvest and Lara telling them about the Bunbury marathon she'd booked for Toby's Christmas present.

'Isn't that the worst Christmas surprise ever? A marathon ticket . . .' Diana couldn't think of anything worse.

Lara laughed. 'We've never been to Western Australia before, so it'll be a holiday as well. It's not until April, so we've got plenty of time to train.'

'Definitely not *my* type of holiday,' Diana shuddered. 'Maybe you can stay with Reg, throw a few wet towels on his floor and complain about the room service?'

They arrived back at McIntyre Park to find Angie bustling around the farmhouse kitchen they'd grown up in, scones in the oven, and Claudia setting the table with pots of jam and cream. The men were nowhere to be seen.

'I'm under strict instructions to keep you here until I hear from Rob,' Angie said sternly. 'There's a certain Christmas gift that needs some finishing touches at Darling Downs.'

What could they be working on so early in the morning? No matter how much she quizzed them, they wouldn't say another word about the surprise. Angie's sky-high scones tasted as good as they smelled.

'Well, this completely counteracts all the calories I burned up on Windmill Track,' Diana said, loading her scone with homemade jam and looking at her sisters. They'd stood beside her every step of the way, as friends as well as siblings. *Definitely did something right in a past life to deserve these three.*

Angie buttered a scone for Claudia and asked, 'How many flower subscriptions are you up to each week, Diana?'

Diana delighted in telling them about the growing number of repeat customers.

'You'll be giving Sadie tips at this rate,' Penny said with a wink.

'And how's Ned settling in?' Angie passed Claudia her scone. 'For someone who hadn't done much with plants since high school, he certainly seems to know what he's talking about.'

Diana nodded, loading her next scone with apricot jam.

'I think he's enjoying the sabbatical. It's different to his regular work in pharmacies.'

Angie fixed her with a curious look.

'And are *you* enjoying his company?'

Diana weighed up the best response to her little sister's not-so-subtle digging. He *had* been welcome company. And after working alongside him for two months, she knew he was not just a hard worker and a quick learner, but kind and funny. Mindful of the teasing she'd received at the sewing night, and the way all three sisters had leaned in closer, she kept her answer flippant, deliberately omitting the above facts. There was no way she'd be mentioning the little zing she felt each time they worked closely together, either.

'The flower farm would never be ready for the launch without him, he's been invaluable. Speaking of which,' she pushed her chair away from the table and carried the dishes to the sink. 'I've got a million things to do today. Do you think I'm allowed home yet?'

Angie checked her phone and gave a nod.

'Good to go, sis.'

Diana's own phone had a flurry of notifications too, she noticed. Opening her social media, she was floored by the response to the sunrise photo. Penny was right, there wasn't a single criticism among the comments. If anything, the unfussy, unfiltered photo seemed to be more of a hit than the carefully staged one a month earlier, when she'd taken the time to blow-dry her hair and even pull out the lippie and mascara. One comment from Bec, a florist with a podcast on the flower-growing industry, really touched her.

'Can't beat natural beauty, Diana. Our future is bright with ridgy-didge women like you at the forefront.'

By early December, Ned felt like they'd eased into a rhythm. Early mornings were for the chooks and eggs, weekdays were spent at the flower farm, and weekends were for exploring and tidying up the property. A new roof had improved the shearers' hut no end, and Ned had commissioned Jonesy to return for several more jobs, slowly making Maeve's home more comfortable.

'What colour are you going to paint the kitchen, Gigi? Orange would look awesome,' suggested Doug.

'It really doesn't need paint,' said Maeve crossly, getting up from the table and walking across the small kitchen with only a hint of a limp. She'd moved back into the hut in November, once the roof was replaced, and her ankle seemed to have healed well since then.

'If it's the cost that's worrying you, Maeve, then don't let it,' Ned said softly. 'I said this was on me and I meant it.'

She returned to the table with a tray of tea and biscuits. Doug pushed the Dulux sample chart towards her.

'Okay, so maybe not orange, but this blue could be cool?' Doug selected a colour that matched the blue of the nearby mountain range.

'How about purple?' Willow added quietly.

A discreet prompt for Maeve to consider sewing and the patchwork quilt, perhaps? Ned wondered. Neither Willow nor Maeve had mentioned the sewing again, but Lara had repeated her invitation when they'd returned the crutches the previous week.

Maeve looked at the chart, and then at Willow.

'What do you think of this one?' she asked as she pointed out a soft colour that was a cross between purple and grey.

Willow nominated a slightly lighter shade.

'Or this one? It's called Mauve Garden. That's only a few letters different to your name, Gigi.'

Ned had watched the bond strengthening between his mother and children in the last month, but the look that passed between grandmother and granddaughter in that moment was something else.

Doug slipped a hand into his as they walked back to Colin's house.

'We never have a rancho relax weekend anymore, like we used to do in Darwin and Perth.'

Ned tickled him under the chin.

'That's because none of our rentals had a backyard, let alone a farm attached. There's always something that needs doing around here.'

'I like it here, Dad.'

'Me too,' Willow said, still smiling because Maeve had agreed on her paint choice and said they could have a shot on the rollers and brushes.

'It's not a bad spot to be,' he said, surprised that after so many years of avoiding the place, he was able to view the property with fresh eyes and was a step closer to understanding why his dad had loved it. They lingered outside, soaking up the fragrance of Colin's garden. Diana's concept of working with nature had been bang on. It didn't seem to matter whether it was Colin's or Diana's patch, he'd come to find a measure of peace when he sank his hands into the earth.

Bees darted in and out of the plants, doing daily fly-bys to check the progress. Just like the dahlias that had started to bud up at Darling Downs, Colin's garden was on the cusp of bursting into bloom. The seedlings they'd planted not long after arriving had turned out to be cosmos, and the delicate flowers were a cheerful sight.

'Look, Dad, I made a Christmas posy,' Willow declared, bounding up to him with a handful of red geraniums, white-scented stocks and glossy green lilly-pilly leaves. She carefully placed her posy in a vase and took it into the lounge room, sitting it beside the Christmas cards that seemed to be multiplying on the mantlepiece. From the number of cards being exchanged, it seemed the small school was bursting with festive cheer.

Willow looked up at him, a question on her lips. 'Do you think Gigi will come to the concert?'

Ned pondered this as he made sandwiches with thick wedges of Toby's sourdough.

'Not sure, missy. We can invite her.'

'She seems better now though, Dad.'

Again, he found himself agreeing with his daughter. There had been no sign of the dark depression or relapse he'd feared. He wasn't sure if that was due to their company or the counselling sessions, or a combination of both, but he was buoyed by her progress.

Doug perched himself on a stool by the bench. 'Do you think Santa will come on a fire truck? Gigi said you and Jonno got to ride in the front of a fire truck with Santa once, back when you lived in Gippsland?'

Ned blinked. *We did?*

Doug added lettuce to the bread. Willow spooned on the curried egg, put the sandwiches together and handed out the plates. 'She said you were planning on being a fireman for ages after that.' Willow studied him, baffled by his blank expression. 'Don't you remember?'

Ned racked his brain for a memory. It seemed like something he'd recall. *What else have I forgotten over the years?*

After lunch, they headed back to the shearers' hut and found Maeve watering her sweetcorn. While Doug extended the invitation to the carols, Willow inched closer.

'Can I have a go?' she asked.

Maeve handed the hose to her granddaughter. Ned didn't miss Maeve's small smile as Willow held the hose with one hand, then slipped her other into Maeve's.

Diana could see Angus, Tim and Jonesy's utes as she crested Paperbark Hill, but it wasn't until she pulled up that she saw what they'd been working on. A tall timber stand with steel wagon wheels stood in pride of place beside the front gate.

'Merry Christmas, love,' Angus said, striding forward. She looked from her father to her two brothers-in-law and her four sons.

'You guys,' she said, giving them all a big hug. 'This is gorgeous.'

She ran her hands along the rustic timber that had been fashioned into a flower stall. Dark-green shade cloth wrapped around the back and sides of the upper half and, although the timber had been sanded and oiled—with linseed from the smell of it—she could see the years of history etched into each piece, and loved that they'd come together to create something so special just for her. It was perfect.

'It's not even Christmas yet.' Her tone was gruff to hide the welling emotion.

'Pffft, it's December, isn't it? And we figured you may as well have it now and get some use out of it,' Angus said.

'Recognise the timber?' Tim lifted the long handles on the side of the structure—moving it the same way you'd shift a wheelbarrow—and she saw the outline of an old wool stencil.

'From Mac Park?' she asked as she passed a hand over the faded black letters. The same stencil they'd used to mark the merino wool bales before they left the family farm.

'Sure is. That bit's from the old wall in the shearing shed, and those smaller pieces are from old floor grates,' Tim said.

'Uncle Jonesy's the brains behind the operation,' Cameron added. 'We were just the lackeys, weren't we guys?'

Harry, Elliot and Leo nodded.

Jonesy swatted away the praise. 'I just built the thing, they did all the fiddly finishing stuff,' he said.

Diana walked around the flower stand. She felt like rushing to the garden to pick dozens of bunches, so she could fill it, and then admire it in its official capacity.

'I *love* it.'

After they'd left, Diana did another lap around the stall, moving it closer to the gate, so it was right beside the signage for Darling Dahlias. *Not that there'd be any mistaking what its purpose is when it's brimming with flowers*, she thought with a smile. Diana was so tickled pink that she got up even earlier than normal to make bouquets for her new roadside stall the next morning.

'Picture perfect indeed,' Ned said when he pulled up, just as she was standing back, taking a photo of the finished product.

'Isn't it divine? The boys all pitched in to make it as an early Chrissie present,' she beamed.

'There's even a spot for the tall flowers,' he said, going in for a closer look. 'Must admit, those foxgloves are my favourite thing in the garden right now.'

Diana looked at him, surprised. 'Mine too. I always think it's the sweet peas with their glorious scent, or the roses with their classic beauty, but right now I'm crushing on those polka-dot speckles.'

She thought about his comment as they worked together that day. Perhaps it was just natural that their tastes would synchronise as they spent so much time together? The day passed easily, as they all seemed to do lately.

They divided up the tasks, with Ned harvesting the commercial flowers and Diana planting in seedlings. By the time they'd made the day's bouquets and shared lunch on the deck, there was time for another check of the dahlias and then deliveries.

'Won't be long until we need to get that string support underway,' said Ned, working alongside Diana to pinch out the buds. While they didn't tie individual plants—there were too many for that—they had recently hammered stakes around each dahlia patch. The rows of the twine 'fence' would increase as the plants grew, so by the time the dahlias were waist high and blooming, they'd have adequate wind protection. It was a method Colin had taught her and she wondered if Ned thought of him, as she did, as they worked with the flowers, following his techniques.

'Twine's in the shed, ready to go. How're things with your mum? Ankle all healed?'

Maeve's name came up in conversation occasionally, and judging from the way he spoke about her, the counselling had revived their relationship. She was pleased for them both, even if had taken Colin's death to make them realise it was worth another attempt.

'She said it still hurts if she pivots suddenly, but apart from that it's pretty good. She doesn't miss the crutches.'

'I'll bet. And Jonesy said the house is coming along in leaps and bounds.'

He nodded, and from the way he smiled, she could tell he was pleased.

'I mean, it's never going to be the Hilton,' he offered, 'but she's happy there.'

Diana was tempted to ask if he was happy there, too, but something stopped her. He seemed to have adapted well to the change of pace, but what if he said he couldn't wait to pack up his van and leave? And what would it mean if she didn't like his answer?

21

The roadside stall continued to bring Diana joy every time she drove along the driveway, and, when she bumped into Mrs Beggs later that week, it seemed like it was also quite a conversation topic among locals.

'That little stall is the darlingest thing,' Mrs Beggs said, waving from the leather couch Toby had nestled in the general store window. 'I've heard it mentioned twice since I arrived for my coffee. Did you ask the boys to make it for you, or did they come up with the idea themselves?'

Diana set down the buckets of bouquets and began freshening up the display by the front counter.

'It was Cameron's idea,' Toby said, delivering a cappuccino and hot pie to Mrs Beggs. 'He heard Diana talking about one she saw online. Jonesy found a set of plans on the internet and, once Tim and Angus had scrounged up a bit of wood, they got started.'

Diana felt another swell of pride. Mrs Beggs pressed a hand to her chest.

'Oh, what sweethearts they are, love. They must make you proud.' The conversation veered to cricket and, after assuring

Mrs Beggs that Cameron would be back on the premier side before long, Diana headed to Hamilton. Irene, the elderly lady behind the counter at the little op shop, was just as delighted with the bag of donations as she was with the posy Diana had brought her.

'Cornflowers! And look at those roses,' she said, putting the flowers in a vase. The joy of giving flowers would never fade, Diana smiled, watching the old lady fuss over the blooms.

'This will add some festive cheer,' she said. 'You're an angel, Diana. And if I don't see you before, have a wonderful Christmas, won't you?'

Diana returned the wishes and headed to the flower shop next door. The florist, who was up to her elbows in greenery, greeted her with a cheerful wave.

'These look amazing, Kate,' Diana said, eyeing off the two flower arrangements in the centre of the workshop. Both had the same ruffly David Austin roses, sweet peas and fluffy grey filler, but the way they'd been arranged gave them a completely different feel.

'You're just in time,' Kate said, 'I'm running short on poppies and foxgloves!'

'Then these should keep you going a little longer,' Diana said, setting her brimming buckets beside the large workbench. 'What floral magic have you woven to make these two so different? I can't put my finger on it, but they're poles apart. My bouquets always look like carbon copies of one another.'

Kate picked up one of the arrangements.

'This one's for a lady who's had a baby.' Then she picked up the second one. 'And this one's for a lady who lost a baby. I'll be delivering them both up to the hospital this afternoon.'

Understanding flooded through Diana. It was in the arranging and the little extras. One had joy and promise in the accent flowers, while the other was understated, no tightly shut rosebuds that would wither before blooming, the flowers placed together with touching tenderness. In the joy of growing and picking beautifully blousy bunches, it was easy to forget their important role in marking not just the happier but also the sadder aspects of life.

'They're both beautiful,' Diana said. 'I'm sure they'll be appreciated.'

Normally Diana bounced out of the florist, inspired by Kate's gorgeous arrangements, but on days like this she felt grateful to be mostly on the growing side of the floral business, with a few bunches of flowers here and there, not the made-to-order bouquet side of things. She thought of the families who would be receiving those bouquets today, one brimming with joy, the other in the throes of the most painful grief. Her thoughts then turned to Maeve. No wonder Ned's mum had had trouble picking herself up and moving on.

Diana browsed in the sewing store next, leaving with a bag full of fabrics for their next sewing group session. She coasted home with a sense of accomplishment. Her phone rang when she was almost in Bridgefield.

Imogen's voice came through the car stereo. 'Hey, mate! We still on for the sewing circle?'

'You betcha,' Diana replied, looking at the pile of fabric on the front seat. 'We'll whip up these pressies in no time.'

'You're the master craftswoman. Just teach me how to ruffle, tell me what bit to sew where, and I'll be right. Your sisters all coming?'

'Yep, and a couple of the other school mums. It'll be a blast,' she said. She slowed as Colin's mailbox came into view, with her thoughts on Maeve again. Was Christmas not the season for giving? She decided to drop in and extend a personal invitation.

Ned was just shutting the side of the mobile chook tractor closest to the house when he spotted dust floating down the driveway. Visitors? Imogen had already been and gone that morning with the load of eggs, and he wasn't expecting anyone.

Shielding his eyes against the afternoon sun, he smiled as he recognised the flash of a white four-wheel drive. He quickly lifted an armpit and took a cautionary sniff. Yep, smelled like he'd been out working in the sun all day too. What was it about Diana McIntyre that made him conscious of his personal hygiene, or in this case, lack of?

She emerged from the car with her hair all floaty and loose. He cleared his throat, more to distract himself from perving than the need to announce his presence. It wasn't like he didn't see her most days now, but there was something about the sight of her with her hair falling around her shoulders . . . *business and pleasure. Oil and water. Same, same,* Ned reminded himself.

'Flower emergency?' he asked

She shook her head, making her dangly earrings jangle like wind chimes. 'Nope, I just had a random idea as I was driving past. Your mum home?'

'Should be.'

'Wow, it looks a million times better,' she said as they walked to the shearers' hut.

'Your brother-in-law sealed up all the holes, put a new wood burner in before finishing the roof, and insulated the ceiling.' *New ceiling fans and paint also helped,* he thought, looking down the hallway when Maeve opened the door. He left Diana with Maeve and headed back to the house, setting the shower a little colder than normal. Maybe Jonno was right. Maybe he should think about dating again. Ned shook his head as he towelled off. What would Jonno know? He was the single, childless 39-year-old who got more excited about Antarctic krill and killer whales than women.

After getting dressed and skulling a glass of icy water, Ned opened his laptop. Jonno was online, as promised, and the Zoom call connected with no difficulties.

'How's everything at Colin's?'

'Chickens can't compete with leopard seals and killer whales,' Ned grinned.

'Least it's more interesting than the corporate jargon you normally try and offer up.' They both laughed.

'True,' Ned conceded.

'And better than the daily grind in a suit and tie, right?' asked Jonno.

Even though the connection was a little hazy at times, Ned could see his brother was watching him carefully, and would recognise a glib answer a mile away. He considered it before replying. Had he even missed his old job since settling in Bridgefield? He hadn't missed the flurry of babysitters, or dropping the children at before-school care each morning before work. The camaraderie of a bustling pharmacy team maybe, and the satisfaction of a full day's work but apart from that . . .

'It's been all right,' he said cautiously. 'Good, even.'

'Geez, don't go all gushy on me. What about the lady you're working with? The flower farmer? Are you scratching for customers?'

'Quite the opposite. Diana sells to local florists and the Bridgefield shops. Plus, she has a flower subscription service and a roadside stall. I had no idea flowers were such serious business. There's even a market for events,' he said, telling Jonno about the upcoming book launch.

'And the eggs?'

'The hens are laying like there's no tomorrow, and Colin's suppliers will take as many as we can give them. Productive little business.'

'Thanks for keeping it running for me, I bet you're itching to leave?'

'Not at the moment, but we will once you're home. Doug and Willow like travelling around, making new friends, seeing the country,' he said, knowing he sounded defensive. 'You should see how well they've fitted in at the school—you don't get that from staying in the one place all your life.' He glanced at his watch. The kids would be waltzing down the drive soon.

'You should think about staying. The kids might like living in one spot for a year or two,' Jonno suggested.

'Bit rich coming from a bloke who's just as nomadic.'

Jonno laughed. It wasn't the first time he'd thrown his oar in about putting down roots, and Ned knew it wouldn't be his last.

'Can't blame a man for trying to drum some sense into his hard-headed brother, can you? I'm planning on packing away the suitcase when I get back, maybe you should too. How's Maeve?'

'Better than I thought. She's stuck with the counselling, and I think it's helping,' Ned admitted.

Willow and Doug's chatter carried down the driveway. He couldn't help but smile. 'Here come those poor neglected, badly adjusted kids now.'

They flung their backpacks down in the middle of the doorway and launched themselves at Ned.

'Dad! Harry and Elliot said Jinx is going to have her kittens any day now. Can we get one? Puh-leeeease!'

Ned barely held back a snort. 'One cat's bad enough,' he said. 'Say g'day to Uncle Jonno.'

They both waved hello.

Doug thrust a badly crafted snowman in front of the camera. 'Look at the Mawson snowman I made in art class today, Uncle Jonno! It's like the one you made at the research station.'

'Dead ringer, mate.'

'You should see how many friends I've got,' said Willow, rattling off a list of names, their ages and where they sat in the classroom.

Doug carried Flopsy into the kitchen, made him wave to Jonno, and then asked about the research project Jonno was working on.

Badly adjusted, my arse, grinned Ned.

Maeve knocked on the glass sliding door a moment later.

'Would you mind taking me to Diana's house this evening?' she asked.

Ned sent up a silent prayer for the determined McIntyre sisters and their kind hearts.

'Happily,' he replied, opening the door wider. 'You should come in, there's someone you might like to see.'

And even though he had a sceptical view of religion, he found himself sending further thanks skywards as he watched Maeve clap eyes on her youngest son for the first time in years.

22

The last morning of school was complete chaos in the McIntyre household, and Diana was glad when 8 a.m. rolled around. The overnight arrival of kittens had added an extra dimension of excitement to the morning, too, and it proved quite a challenge dragging the boys away from the laundry.

'How about I ferry your backpacks up the driveway?' she offered, luring the trio outside. Elliot tossed his school bag into the back of the four-wheel drive, narrowly missing the buckets intended for the flower stall.

'Careful!' *It's like they've eaten sugar instead of Weet-Bix.*

She sent them ahead on their bicycles to burn off the excess energy and followed in the car. Diana filled the flower stall with bouquets in all colours of the rainbow as they waited for the bus.

'Grandpa said this is the Rolls Royce of flower stalls,' said Harry, reaching for the handles. 'But I think it's more like a Ferrari with these big wheels.'

Seeing he was about to give a demonstration, Diana dashed to stop him.

'You have to wait until all the vases are empty before shifting it,' she reminded him, breathlessly. If the last few weeks were any indication, the stall would be empty well before the bus brought them home.

The school bus ambled into view, and she was amused to see the bus driver wearing a Santa costume. Waving them off, she collected her empty flower buckets and returned Imogen's call on the short drive back to the house.

'Hey, stranger, when are we doing this movie night?' Diana asked.

'We've got Christmas carols tomorrow, and these monsters are going to their dad's house afterwards so we'll be able to watch *Bridget Jones's Diary* or *The Holiday* in peace. Does this Sunday suit, or shall we wait till the week before Christmas? I've already got the champers chilling.'

Diana laughed at the longing in her friend's voice. Everyone was frazzled by the end of term, especially at this time of year. Even Ned had taken a day off.

'If it involves Cameron Diaz and Jude Law, I'm in. This weekend's perfect—Cam's got cricket Saturday but I'm as free as a bird on Sunday. I'll bring the nibbles. See you tomorrow at the concert.'

'I'll be there with bells on,' Imogen said with a laugh.

Diana let the dogs off the chain. They followed her as she strode into the shed, gathering the tools she needed for her day's work. A sense of peace descended as she walked along the drip lines, checking the plants growing either side of the irrigation hoses. After a keen sniff around the perimeter, scouting for evidence of rogue rabbits and kangaroos, the dogs returned to her side. It felt quiet without Ned, and she was glad of their company.

Sadie's launch was creeping closer every day, as was St Valentine's Day, one of the biggest days on the floral calendar, and she thought about the jobs lined up between now and then. Ned's help had been exactly what she needed to get everything in place; now all she had to do was maintain the fertiliser, keep the water up to all the plants, stay on top of the weeds and hope there was no extraordinary interference from weather, pests or wildlife in the meantime. Only last night, she'd seen a video on Facebook of a Yarra Valley friend's sunflower crop being decimated by a flock of sulphur-crested cockatoos. And as she'd typed her condolences, sending virtual hugs to Eliza, she had breathed a sigh of relief that it wasn't her flowers.

Bonzer trotted across with a Christmas decoration in his mouth. Diana rescued the plastic bauble, which had been attached to Elliot's school bag earlier that morning, and then stroked the dog's soft ears.

'You're trouble, aren't you? At least it's not Cam's cricket gear this time.'

She looked towards the house. Cameron's year eleven exams had finished weeks ago, and if she'd thought he'd be at a loose end, she'd been mistaken. Even the offer of an extra bit of pocket money to help her and Ned with the flowers hadn't been enough to tempt him away from his weights training and backyard cricket drills. And if the previous week was anything to go by, he'd top it off with a long run and training tonight. She found him on the deck by the laundry, doing sit-ups.

'I've got no idea where you get your stamina from, mate. I'm still sore from hiking Wildflower Ridge with your aunties the other weekend.'

He barely paused, his brow sweaty and jaw gritted in concentration as he continued exercising.

Too busy training to chat . . . now that's dedication.

'I'll make us morning tea,' she said brightly, hoping he'd be chattier once he'd finished. She wanted to check whether he had presents sorted for his brothers, and if he needed anything in town before Christmas. But when he came through the kitchen, sweat darkening his shirt, he paused only briefly to skull a glass of cold water.

'Thanks, but no thanks.' Cam said, glancing at the muffins she had set out for him.

She quizzed him about the gifts.

'Don't worry Mum, I'm on to it.' He strode out as quickly as he came in.

'Hey, have you invited Georgie to the concert tomorrow?' Diana called after him at the same time as the laundry door clicked shut. When had the sudden aloofness arisen, making him feel like a housemate, not a son? Was it after his last game with the local A Grade side, when someone quizzed him on his lack of match time in Geelong? They hadn't seen much of Georgie either. *Now what's going on there?*

Her phone rang in her pocket, and Diana smiled at the sight of her little sister's name on the screen.

'Hi, Angie, how're things?'

'I'm run off my feet, but I promised Claudia I'd call and see if your kittens have arrived yet? She's desperate to get first pick of the colours.'

Diana walked into the laundry with the phone still cupped to her ear. Jinx was lying in the colourful cardboard box, snuggled up in soft towels. Five shiny little lumps of fur glistened under the downlights. 'Clever mumma cat has three gingers, one grey and a little black and white runt.'

She listened as Angie consulted with her daughter and promised to save the black-and-white one for her niece.

'You're a gem, Diana. Hopefully it grows up to be a good mouse-catcher. How are your boys?'

Diana groaned. 'It was a madhouse this morning, everyone hyped up about Christmas and kittens. I bet their teacher will be cracking out the champagne as soon as the school bell rings this afternoon. And Cam's in a funny mood, too. Hopefully that blows over quickly.'

'He'll come good, it's just a crazy time of year for everyone,' Angie reassured her.

Diana walked out the laundry door, blinking in the sunshine. She wasn't sure why anyone would voluntarily incorporate old tyres into an exercise drill, but Cameron seemed focused on the task at hand, sweating as he carted them from one side of the yard to the other. She clung to Angie's words. *He'll come good.*

'Wow! There's an angel in this one,' said Willow, rummaging through the dusty plastic tub.

'And look! It's a Christmas cat,' Doug said, fishing out a photo-frame ornament with a photo of a kitten wearing a red hat. The sight brought back a slew of memories as Ned turned the decoration in Doug's hand. Yep, just as he'd remembered.

'That's Santa Claws,' he said softly. 'He was a little feral your Uncle Jono found at the old rubbish tip.'

'Flyblown and stinking to high hell,' said Maeve, shuffling across the couch for a closer look. Doug passed her the decoration. Her gaze became distant as she studied the faded picture. 'He was all black, apart from this tail, and the blowflies had had a field day with a big cut on his leg. Your uncle brought him home in his school backpack, took two times through the washing machine to get the stink out,' she said.

'You put a cat in the washing machine!?' Willow was so horrified she nearly dropped the ornate angel.

'The school bag,' Maeve said. 'Though I was tempted to put the kitten in there, too. He wasn't as bad when they'd picked all the maggots out of his leg though, some as big as your fingernail.'

'Ewww, that's so gross,' Doug said.

Ned shook his head, remembering the carry-on as Jonno and Jessie argued over who would hold the kitten and who work hold the tweezers. From memory, Jessie won, and Jonno had been the one plucking maggots from the oozing wound.

'He paid us back ten-fold though. Best snake hunter we ever had,' Ned said.

Maeve hung an embroidered ornament on the tree and nodded. 'He was Jessie's favourite. Colin had a soft spot for him, too. Buried him under his favourite rose. Probably why it grew so well,' she said, standing up and walking to the window.

Doug and Willow abandoned the Christmas decorations and joined her.

'Which rose, Gigi? That big pink one?'

Maeve shook her head with a small sigh. 'The rose was at the Gippsland house, where we lived before Bridgefield. Before . . .' She paused and Ned knew she was thinking about Jessie's final months in hospital. 'Long ago now,' she said. 'C'mon, enough crying into our teacups. Santa will have been and gone if we sit around reminiscing about each and every one of these decorations. Let's get them on the tree,' she said, grabbing a handful of Jessie's crafty mementos.

Ned studied the box of decorations, still not sure if it had been a good decision to resurrect the past. Each and every handcrafted piece told a story, from the glitter-covered pine cones he'd proudly created in kindergarten to the intricate hand-stitched items his sister had crafted before she died.

He smiled as the children fished the last of the decorations out of the boxes and pulled his phone out of his pocket. 'Jump in front of the tree. I'll get a picture for Uncle Jonno,' he said.

Quick as a flash, Willow flung a piece of tinsel around her neck, feather boa-style, and pulled a cheesy grin. Amused by his little poser, he almost didn't notice Doug dragging Maeve into the frame.

'No, no just you two,' she said, shaking her head.

'But Gigi, you helped,' Doug said, tugging on her hand insistently. Maeve looked at Ned briefly. He gave a small shrug.

'Go on.' It was only then he realised he didn't have a single photo of his mother and his children together. 'Squeeze in.' He snapped a couple of photos and, even on the phone screen, he could see her awkwardness.

'Now take a silly one, Dad,' Willow said.

Doug went for his default 'crazy' look, with his finger stretching his mouth wide, tongue poking out. Willow scrunched up her face and pushed the tip of her nose upwards, so it looked like a pig's snout, their expressions so ridiculous that Maeve burst into laughter. Ned found himself smiling as he captured it on the phone camera. It was infinitely better than any of the other shots.

'C'mon, Gigi, that's not very crazy,' Willow said.

Maeve crouched down between them, bared her teeth and crossed her eyes, sending the two kids into fits of giggles. Ned kept photographing, snapping away so the old memories were now tempered with some new, lighter ones.

All four boys were in the backyard when Diana paused for a drink the following day, and as she looked across over the rows of flowers to see Cam adjusting Leo's grip on the bat, she felt better about things. If Cameron was worried about sport or depressed, he'd be lazing on the couch like a misery guts, not exercising flat out or throwing the ball to his brothers.

Setting the water bottle down, she checked her messages, smiling at the sight of Ned's name on her screen: 'Appointment in Hamilton running late, sorry. Will you be okay if I don't make today?' She wrote back, assuring him she'd be fine, her fingers typing so fast that she didn't realise she'd automatically added 'xx' at the end of the message, just as she did in messages to her close friends and family.

Diana groaned, embarrassed as she wondered whether he'd notice. Mentioning it would just draw unnecessary attention to it if he hadn't. *Get over yourself, Diana. He's an employee, not a love object.* She prayed he skim read most messages and emails like she did and went back to work. But as she harvested armloads of zinnias, she found herself contemplating his reaction when he saw it.

Surprise? A smile? Or God forbid, a grimace? When a car turned down the driveway, she was almost grateful for the interruption, distracting her from such a ridiculous train of thought. The rumbling V8 engine was as much a giveaway as the halo of purple curls behind the steering wheel. At five-foot nothing, Nanna Pearl wasn't exactly the driver you'd expect for an old Monaro, but according to Penny's husband, Tim, there was no talking her around to a modern car, not when the Monaro was still ticking along.

The dogs bounded after Diana as she downed her tools and walked across to the driveway. Even Jinx the cat came out to greet their visitor, as did the three younger boys, who ditched their game. The older lady hefted the heavy door open and stepped out of the car, patting each of the dogs in turn. Tim's brother, Eddie, jumped out the other side and scooped Jinx into his arms.

'Beautiful morning for it, Pearl,' she said. 'Hi, Eddie.'

'Certainly is, Diana. I ordered this weather specially for tonight's Christmas concert. Got a direct line to the man upstairs,' she said, tilting her chin up to heavens.

They laughed. Diana could almost believe it. Still, she felt the tiniest bit on edge. Pearl Patterson didn't just roll up unannounced to shoot the breeze.

'I've picked everything for the wreath-making stall, you didn't have to collect it, though, I was planning on delivering everything this afternoon. Or did you want me to set up earlier?' She knew the flowers would fare better in the cool, dark shed throughout the day and, although the Monaro boot probably had just as much room as her Cruiser, she'd feel terrible if water slopped around in the back of Pearl's beloved car.

Pearl waved a hand. 'No, no, I'm not here to hurry you along. Penny mentioned you had kittens, and Eddie and I wanted to choose one before they're all snapped up.'

Diana felt her shoulders ease a little. *Jumping to conclusions again, Diana.*

'Perfect, though they won't be ready to go for a while yet,' she said, leading them towards the house.

'Pretty kitties,' said Eddie, stroking Jinx's soft fur. The mother cat jumped from his arms as soon as they walked inside, circling the cane basket as if counting all the kittens. It reminded her of the way she'd felt when Leo was little: escaping for an hour or two was pure bliss, but the time spent away from her babies was often fraught with mother's guilt.

As Eddie deliberated between the ginger and grey kittens Diana poured Pearl a cup of tea. Pearl chatted on as they sat down, updating Diana on the last-minute concert details.

'Hard to imagine, but in just a few hours the town green will be alive with picnic blankets, stalls and families.'

'Relocating the concert from the school to the town hall was a master stroke, Pearl. Everyone's looking forward to it.'

With a bit of luck Diana hoped she'd finish up early, so she could sneak in a little shopping before the carols began.

'Now, Diana—' Nanna Pearl smiled over the rim of her teacup after a sip.

Diana's stomach sank. *Here it comes . . .*

'I had a last-minute cancellation for another little errand. Sarah Squires had some horse emergency today, so she's heading to the equine vet specialist in Ballarat. Tonight, of all nights.' Pearl threw her hands in the air. 'It won't take more than fifteen minutes, you'll be a darl and step in, won't you?'

'Selling raffle tickets again?' Diana asked warily. She'd landed that task the year before last, a tough gig on a forty-degree night. At least the weather would be milder tonight, she conceded.

Pearl finished off her tea and leaned across and patted Diana's shoulder. 'I knew I could count on you.'

With a wave of talcum powder, she was up from the table and striding into the laundry, enthusiastically endorsing Eddie's kitten of choice.

As Diana rinsed the teacups, she was unable to shift the feeling that she'd just walked right into another of Nanna Pearl's lifelong volunteer roles.

'Got everything guys?' Ned buckled his seatbelt.

Willow nodded, the pom pom on her red-and-white hat bobbing with every move, as she flashed a toothy grin. He still hadn't got used to the missing front tooth, which had come out courtesy of an extra-hard candy cane the previous day. Doug's reindeer antlers lolled to one side as he nodded with excitement.

'Do you think Santa will be there for the concert, like he was in Darwin?'

'Not sure, mate. Maybe he won't come at all,' Ned teased, tweaking the bright red nose his son had claimed from the box of Christmas stuff. 'They didn't have flash concerts like this in Gippsland when I was a kid,' Ned said, taking the drive slowly to ensure the picnic supplies in the ute tray didn't rattle their way loose.

'Can we stay till it's dark, Dad?'

'Do you think Harry and Elliot will be there already?'

'Can we spend $10 each, or do we have to share it?'

Most of the street parking was already taken, and Ned had a job answering their questions as he searched for a park and watched for pedestrians.

'Wow! Check out all the white tents!'

'Look at the jumping castle!'

The normally quiet street was alive, with families all heading for the large grassy spot beside the town hall. Even with the windows wound up, Ned could hear the tinny carols pumping from a set of speakers. He'd never seen Bridgefield so busy. Pine saplings were affixed to light poles, and there was tinsel hanging off every available surface. *Jessie would have loved this,* he thought, recalling the colourful decorations they'd found.

Hordes of children were gathered around a novelty stall, throwing wet sponges at a primary school teacher. Ned hoped that wasn't the task Pearl needed his help with after the barbecue. Finding Diana's stall, the children unloaded their buckets of greenery.

'Hi, Diana,' they called before disappearing with Leo.

'You're a lifesaver,' said Diana, when she turned and saw Ned's bucket of extra foliage. 'The stall's been going gang busters.'

'So I see. They look great,' he said, admiring the wreaths being made by a trio of women around Maeve's age. Diana moved between them effortlessly, quick with a smile and a suggestion when needed.

'Can't half tell you were a teacher in a past life.'

Diana seemed pleased he'd remembered.

'And a darn good one at that,' added one of the ladies. 'The town was sad to lose her to motherhood, and now she's chosen flowers over teaching. Such a shame.'

A shorter lady chuckled as she said, 'You've got a fortnightly flower subscription. I'd say you get more direct benefit out of Diana's current line of work.'

The first woman grinned sheepishly. 'It's true, but as soon as my grandkids start school, I'll be wishing she was back in the classroom, pulling them into line.'

The ladies returned to their wreaths, ribbing one another in what was obviously a well-worn friendship. He couldn't remember Maeve ever having friendships like that.

'I'd better find Pearl and see what she needs me for,' he said. He weaved through the crowd, keeping his eyes peeled for Willow and Doug, and before he knew it, he was introduced to the other barbecue helpers and given a pair of tongs.

'And you're just the right size, too,' said Pearl Patterson, looking him up and down as she handed him an apron. He slipped it over his head.

'I'll grab you in an hour,' she said with a wink, slipping away.

Aren't all aprons the same size? Ned shook his head and began loading sausages onto the hotplate.

23

The wreath workshop was every bit as popular as Pearl had predicted, and at the end of the allocated time, Diana was proud of the results.

Diana left the pruners and buckets in the marquee, along with the wreaths to be collected, and went to find her family.

As promised, Cameron had staked out a prime piece of lawn, directly in front of the concert stage, although from the number of teenagers already sitting on their rug, she suspected there might not be much room for her or the younger boys when the carols started.

Cameron spotted her. Evie, Lara's teenage daughter, waved too, fitting back into her Bridgefield social circle as if she'd never left for boarding school. Diana picked her way across the jigsaw puzzle of rugs and deckchairs.

'Hey, Mum,' Cameron said, stretching his long limbs.

Where's Georgie? Diana wondered.

Evie stood up, handing her a plate.

'We saved you some tucker, Aunty Diana. And Nanna Pearl's looking for you,' she said. Diana bit into a fruit mince pie Evie had made, savouring the buttery pastry and rich fruit filling. She saw Evie was watching for her reaction and lifted two thumbs up.

'Best yet, Evie-girl,' she said. Her niece beamed proudly. After her quick snack, Diana did a hot lap around the stalls. Books, crafts, handmade trinkets and tiny little skirts and tutus that would be perfect for Claudia and Lucy. Her shopping bag was bulging by the time she reached Angie's bake stall.

'Have you seen Nanna Pearl?'

Angie handed her a piece of jelly slice and pointed towards the hall. 'She just headed in there.'

Diana found Pearl in the hall kitchen. Ned was there too, smelling like fried onions and sausages. It wasn't a bad smell, but she bet he was wishing he'd packed a spare set of clothes.

'You'll have every dog in the district running after you,' she chortled. He agreed with a good-natured smile. Pearl pushed a red velvet bag into Ned's hands and a green one into Diana's.

'And you'll have all the kids in Bridgefield running after you when you slip these on. I'm not sure which'll be better,' she said, clasping her hands. 'I'll set up the special chair and bags of candy canes while you two get changed.'

Ned pulled a white curly beard from his bag.

'Just a wild guess, but I'm assuming we're officially Mr and Mrs Claus?' Ned asked.

Diana groaned. 'No, no, no, Nanna Pearl, this isn't going to work. I'm not a petite little thing like Sarah.' *And she's a million times fitter than me, thanks to all that horse riding and rolling around in the hay . . .*

But the older woman wasn't having a bar of it. 'I'm in a pinch, darling Diana, and you were the first person who popped into my mind. You'll look great.'

'I really don't think—'

Pearl whipped out of the hall kitchen with remarkable speed for an eighty-something-year-old, calling over her shoulder, 'You'll be fine, trust me.'

Darn Sarah and her injured horse. Diana untangled a green sparkly dress from a pair of black-and-white leggings. A pair of elf ears fell to the ground.

'Nope, we're Santa and his elf,' she corrected, holding up a lime-green tutu that looked like a larger version of the ones she'd just bought for her nieces. *No wonder Nanna Pearl had been light on the details.* Diana stripped off in the bathroom and reluctantly wriggled her way into the costume. It felt like she'd been poured into a sausage skin. She tugged the dress down as a knock came at the door, followed by Ned's deep voice.

'Everything okay in there? I hate to rush you, but the crowd has started chanting.'

Diana looked in the mirror. *Why hadn't Pearl roped Penny and Tim into this, or Cameron and Evie?*

Ned was right. The sounds of 'Santa', 'Santa', 'Santa' were ringing through the hall windows. *It's for the greater good . . .*

'Coming.' She stepped into the tutu, took a deep breath and opened the bathroom door. She felt instantly better when she spotted Ned. His tanned ankles stuck out from the too-short pants. Even with the white beard and wig, plus what looked like a pillow shoved under his top, he looked as ridiculous as she felt.

'Ho, ho, ho,' he said, his eyes sparkling without his glasses.

Diana felt her face flush as he glanced over her costume. She dropped into an awkward curtsy just as he stepped in closer. She felt her head connect with his padded belly and sprang back, almost tripping over her sandals. Ned reached out a hand to steady her and she felt a zing as their hands touched.

'Sorry!'

'Sorry,' Ned said at the same time.

They both cracked up.

'I was just going to put these on your head,' he said, holding up the set of elf ears. She stepped in closer and took the ears from him, sliding them over her loose braid, conscious of just how much she wanted his hand to glide over her hair, cup the back of her head and draw her closer . . .

The realisation shocked her.

Oh God, I like him. I properly like him.

She stepped back quickly and cleared her throat as if it would erase the shiver of attraction. The noise outside was growing louder and, from the sounds of it, the crowd had also started clapping and ringing bells.

Pearl burst into the storeroom, clapping her hands.

'Fabulous news, Sarah just called. You're off the hook, Diana, she'll be here any moment.'

Diana didn't need to be told twice, and retreated to the bathroom to peel off the costume.

Sarah flew through the door, simultaneously applying lipstick and unbuttoning her shirt, revealing a soft lilac bra with intricate straps, satin and lace. 'I almost didn't make it, but now that I've spotted this year's Father Christmas, I'm glad I got back in time,' she chuckled, stripping down to matching bikini bottoms and shimmying into the tight outfit. Diana's stomach flipped, as she dressed in a daze, jealousy running white-hot through her veins. As much as she hadn't wanted to walk out of the hall dressed as an elf, she sure as hell didn't want Sarah doing it with Ned. She didn't want Sarah Squires doing *anything* with Ned, full stop. But there wasn't a darn thing she could do about it now.

'Thanks for offering to step in—wish me luck,' said Sarah, humming a few bars of the sexy tune 'Santa, baby'.

Diana's 'good luck' came out like a squeak. *Sarah will love
every moment in the spotlight. With Ned. In a ridiculously
cute outfit that flatters every perfect centimetre of her perfect
bloody figure.*

Pearl handed them a bulging sack of sweets and ushered
Sarah out the bathroom door. Ned, waiting outside, looked
over his shoulder, catching Diana's eye with a 'what have I
got myself into?' expression.

'You look perfect! Come, come,' Pearl said to Ned. 'Rob
Jones is waiting for you.'

The chanting was reaching fever pitch. Diana spotted Jonesy
with his Harley Davidson motorcycle and sidecar. Tinsel was
wound around the handlebars and her brother-in-law had
gaffer-taped a set of reindeer antlers to his motorbike helmet.

'*That's* Santa's sleigh this year?'

'Isn't it a beauty? The kids will love it,' Pearl said, her
eyes bright with excitement. Swallowing a sense of dread and
inevitability, Diana watched Ned help Sarah into the sidecar,
then climb onto the back of the Harley. Diana and Nanna
Pearl followed them around the side of the hall in time to see
the delight on the children's faces as they arrived. Ned looked
every bit the gentleman as he helped his elf from the sidecar.

Maybe I should have forewarned him about Sarah, Diana
thought mournfully, watching her friend hold Ned's hand
a beat longer than necessary. Even in a ridiculous synthetic
Christmas outfit, Ned Gardiner was downright sexy. *Why is
it only now when he's in someone else's crosshairs that I've
realised this?*

'And what would you like for Christmas?' Ned asked, his voice
slightly hoarse by the time they reached the end of the long
line. Sarah caught his eye and winked, then fished around

in the fabric sack. The little boy sped up at the sight of the lollies. He relayed his Christmas wish list, jumped off Ned's knee and happily trotted off with the sweets.

'We done?' He looked left and right. *Where had Diana gone to?* He'd been just as surprised by Pearl's last-minute task as her, but pleased they'd been paired up. And then, before he could even catch his breath at the sight of Diana in the elf get-up, she'd been demoted. Not that Sarah wasn't friendly. She just wasn't Diana.

The band had started warming up when the line had dwindled to the last dozen.

'Holy cow, these high heels are killing me,' said Sarah, her elf ears dipping forwards as she rubbed at a blister on her foot.

She grabbed Ned's shoulder for balance, and he knew if he looked to his left, he'd see right down the front of her top. He craned his neck in the opposite direction, scanning the crowd again for Diana, but it was useless without his specs.

Pearl Patterson strolled over, tinsel draped over her shoulders, with Eddie right behind her. 'Hold on, one very special guy would love a quick word with the man in red. He didn't want to push in,' Pearl said.

Ned hadn't had much to do with Tim's disabled brother, but it was the first time he'd seen Eddie act shyly. Normally when he went to buy milk and collect his mail, Eddie greeted him like a long-lost friend.

'Always time for a word with Eddie,' he said, readjusting the synthetic beard. Sarah prepped the lollies as the young man stammered out the most thoughtful Christmas list he'd heard all night.

'A hat for Tim, new oven for Nanna Pearl, a kitten for Penny and a new little brother for Lucy,' he said.

Ned heard Nanna Pearl's breath catch, and when he looked across at her she was dabbing her eyes. Through the crowd, he caught sight of Tim reclining on a picnic rug next to theirs, with Penny leaning back against him, watching little Lucy as she played with her cousins. Had they been trying for another? He wasn't sure, but it felt like a fitting note to end the night on. The magic of Christmas felt well and truly alive when he received a bear hug from Eddie.

They were sent off with much applauding and whistling.

'Ho, ho, ho,' Ned called over the roar of the Harley engine.

'And Merry Christmas,' called Sarah, waving like a royal. Much to the delight of the adults, she threw the spare lolly bags into the crowd as they rode away.

The suit had grown hot and itchy, even in the short space of an hour, and if Ned thought he smelled bad after the sausage sizzle, he smelled even worse now. He wished he'd packed some deodorant.

'You want to get changed first?' Sarah gestured to the small bathrooms. 'Or we could save water . . . ?' she suggested with a smirk.

Even without his glasses he could read the subtext. *Christ, she's only half-joking. How do I get myself out of this one?*

'Ladies before gentlemen,' he said quickly, aware that his answer may have been different if Diana had extended the same invitation.

Ned marched into the kitchen. Pearl twisted the cap off a beer and handed it to him. 'Mighty fine job there, Ned. You should have heard the praise for our mystery Santa.'

He tugged the beard down, pulled off the matching wig and cap and slipped his glasses back on. Aside from a few awkwardly placed elbows, and Sarah's flirting, he'd actually quite enjoyed the experience. Some of the little wish lists had warmed his heart, although, if he had a dollar for every electronic device requested, he'd be a wealthy man. And if Willow and Doug had suspected his true identity, even with his best attempt at a disguised voice, they didn't spoil it for the other children.

The icy-cold beer was exactly what he felt like, second only to the towel, soap and deodorant Pearl fished out of her basket, Mary Poppins-style.

'Your dad donated this "North Pole Freshen Up Kit" set after his first stint volunteering as Santa. It's been very well appreciated by the Santas thereafter,' she said.

'What?' *Colin had been the Bridgefield Santa?* 'He didn't ever mention it.'

'Doesn't surprise me, he was a quiet achiever in that respect. Never asked for anything in return for all the things he donated over the years. Like all those eggs for the Australia Day breakfast and flowers for church functions. They were just the tip of the iceberg.'

Ned studied his fingernails. *Maybe if I'd come home more, I would have known.*

'Enjoy that beer, you've earned it,' Pearl said, giving him an encouraging nod. 'I'll hurry Sarah out of the shower.'

The beer went down a treat and he lit up when Diana peeked around the kitchen door. One side of her face was covered in swirls of face paint, a butterfly design identical to one Willow had when she told Santa her wish list.

'How was it?'

'Let's just say, I'm glad it's over,' he said, running a hand through his hair. 'Here, I'll get you a drink.' He went to the fridge Pearl had opened earlier and fished out a cider, handing it to Diana.

Pearl returned and pushed a bunch of keys into Diana's free hand. 'The choir will be waiting for me. Can you lock the kitchen door when you're finished here, love? We don't want a repeat of last year's supper sabotage.'

Supper sabotage?

Diana spotted Ned's raised eyebrow as Pearl bustled out of the kitchen.

'Bunch of ratbags snuck in and helped themselves to the shared supper,' she explained as she sipped her drink. 'Harry and Elliot swore they weren't involved, but I don't want to tempt fate.'

Ned could just imagine. He opened his mouth to reply but the sight of glitter shimmering on her skin had him clamping it shut again. *Blimey.* He wasn't sure what was more appealing; wholesome gardening Diana, sexy elf Diana or the fairy princess Diana. And for the first time he couldn't find a single reason why he shouldn't mix business with pleasure.

His fingers longed to reach out and trace a line from her collarbone to her earlobes, followed closely by his lips, all possibilities that had no place at a family Christmas event. *Back the truck up, Gardiner.*

He tried to think of a good reason to walk away, but his eyes kept returning to the errant glitter, nestled so sweetly at the base of her neck. *Think of something else. The smell of the garden, scattered with dynamic lifter. Think of the forgotten eggs Doug found underneath the chook tractor.* But even the stinky smell of fertiliser and rotten eggs wasn't enough to quell the effect Diana had on him. He had to leave before he did something deliciously foolish.

Sarah's heels clip-clopped along the floorboards, and he almost collided with her on his way out of the kitchen.

'Sorry,' Ned called over his shoulder, making a beeline for the bathroom.

Diana caught sight of her reflection in the hall window, not surprised that Ned had been looking at her strangely. Her hair was all over the place, the braid mussed up by the face painter's headband and the hastily removed elf ears. The glittery face paint sparkled, illuminating the freckles on her forehead, and she felt less sure about the fairy princess design. *Cute on Willow, Lucy and Claudia, but maybe a bit ridiculous on me . . .*

She whirled around as Sarah walked in.

'Snazzy face paint. And did you see how hot your new flower man is without those glasses?' Sarah said, pretending to fan herself. 'I can barely even remember my ex-husband's name when he's in the room, you know what I mean?'

Diana silently fumed as she sipped her cider, glad that Sarah didn't seem to require an answer. *She's already having it off with half the men around here, now she's set her sights on Ned, too?*

Diana took another swig, washing away an unwanted image of Sarah and Ned entwined in a moonlit paddock.

Where on earth had that *come from?* She shook her head, trying to rationalise the dynamic between her and Ned instead. Working so closely with him and being forced together for the photo shoot would have the same impact on any living and breathing woman over the age of thirty. *It'd be weird if I didn't feel some kind of connection,* she told herself. *Sarah's spent half an hour in his company and she's already lusting after him.*

The sound of a neighing horse interrupted her train of thought. Confused, Diana looked for a wayward pony just as Sarah pulled a phone from her handbag. *A horse ringtone?*

'Hey, you,' Sarah said, her voice a few octaves lower than normal. Her smile grew as she nodded, wandering out of the kitchen into the main part of the hall to continue the conversation.

Sarah returned with a smug look on her face. 'When it rains, it pours. I mightn't make the next sewing circle. Mr Friday Night is keen for another date and as much as I love catching up with you gals . . .' She headed to the door. 'Put in a good word with Ned, yeah? No sense keeping all my eggs in one basket.'

I bloody well will not. Diana felt a wrench of injustice as she said goodbye to Sarah. Feeling both frumpy and frustrated, she swung her bag over her shoulder and locked the kitchen door as the sounds of the choir came through. She stopped at the bathroom door, her hand hovering to knock, but something made her hesitate.

Don't be silly. It's not like you're barging in there for a perve. It's just polite to let him know.

She rapped twice and cleared her throat. 'Carols have started,' she called. 'I'll see you out—'

The door opened and she found herself nose to nose with Ned Gardiner.

'there . . .' she trailed off, aware of every inch of the man standing before her. Steam wafted from the room, shrouding them in mist and, for a moment, the world shrank to just the two of them in a bubble and . . . Diana slowly met his gaze.

It felt like she'd been razed by a blowtorch. *Oh my goodness!*

What would happen if she lifted herself up on her tiptoes and pressed her lips to that dewy hollow at the base of his throat? Without further prompting, she felt her heels rising off the ground, as if she were about to do that very thing.

Diana pursed her lips and put a hand on the doorframe to steady herself. Ned moved a little closer, brushing her colourfully painted cheek with his fingertips. His touch was soft, but the trail he traced on her skin felt electric.

How long since I've been touched like this?

She leaned into his hand and when his fingers reached her chin, she tipped her head back until there was nowhere else to look except in his eyes.

The Christmas music ramped up a notch in the background.

She should walk away now. Join her family before it gets dark.

But in that moment, she knew she wanted more. Needed more.

Diana searched his eyes, seeing her own desire reflected in Ned's.

Oh damn.

Her mouth sought his and in the moment her lips met his, she knew she didn't want to be anywhere else. Her brow brushed up against the frame of his glasses, and although his smooth skin felt so different to Pete's goatee, Ned's mouth was every bit as kissable as she'd imagined. She felt herself smiling into him, giddy with desire. Mariah Carey's 'All I want for Christmas is You' filtered through from outside. *Fitting.*

She looped a hand around his neck, pulling him closer. This was exactly what she wanted.

Ned and Diana sprang apart when a shuffling noise came from outside, followed by loud whispering.

Every fibre in Ned's body wanted to ignore the noise and continue what they'd started, but instead he stepped back, nearly banging his elbow on the bathroom door, and ran a hand through his damp hair. *Christ almighty, why didn't we do that earlier?*

Diana smoothed the front of her dress—*were her hands suddenly sweaty too?*—but the smile dropped from her lips as Christmas tunes flooded into the Bridgefield Hall and a small group of mischievous-looking boys skulked in through the back door.

'Harry, Elliot!' Diana fixed them with a glare that would have made grown men retreat. 'I hope Santa's watching,' she warned.

The boys took a step back, and Ned spotted Doug and Leo standing in their wake. *Little buggers.*

The twins had evidently recruited more supper saboteurs this year. The only good thing about the situation was that they'd heard the children before they snuck into the hallway.

The boys raced out of sight as Diana strode to the door. Ned followed her, grappling with the proper etiquette. Did he acknowledge what just eventuated between them, or were they going to pretend it never happened?

'Little terrors,' she said, pulling the door shut behind them, still shaking her head.

Ned nodded. It was easier to focus on misbehaving children than what had just transpired. 'I'll have a stern word with Doug,' he said gruffly.

Diana pulled the keys from the lock and looked up at him. She looked ethereal with the twinkling fairy lights behind her and wisps of golden hair settling around her face.

'Sorry for my boys leading your kids astray, they're not normally such trouble,' she said.

Ned wanted to smooth out the line that had appeared on her forehead. Christ, he wanted to do more than that, but as they walked around the back of the hall, and the sea of picnic rugs came into sight, he knew it wasn't an option.

'No harm done,' he said. 'It's kinda fun to be led astray every now and then.'

Her conspiratorial smile made his heart gallop in his chest. He'd wanted to kiss her, but was he ready for all that came with it? She was only two years widowed with not one but four sons. And she was too good for the type of relationships he'd favoured in Fleur's wake, hook-ups with ladies like Sarah who knew exactly what they wanted and weren't afraid to ask for it. Diana McIntyre was the complete opposite of no-strings attached. What if she didn't want what he wanted?

What if she did?

He looked at her, almost shyly, to gauge her reaction. Her smile was all the answer he needed.

The carollers on the stage finished their song, and in the gap between songs, he heard a voice calling out.

'Diana! Ned! Over here.' Penny waved at them from near the front of the stage. They made their way across to her and settled on the last spare rug. Willow clambered onto his lap, scrunched up her nose and sniffed.

'You smell funny, Dad. Where have you been? You missed the best bit!'

'You should've seen Santa Claus, he came on a motorbike and everything,' Leo said.

'It was so cool,' added Doug brightly, striving to look like the picture of innocence.

I'll have a word with him later.

The music started up again, and Ned couldn't help the little smile that crossed his face as the chorus veered towards kissing and mistletoe. Diana's eyes met his and she smiled too.

'I need to go to the loo, Mum,' Leo said, jumping up and holding the front of his shorts.

Diana nodded to the trees behind the hall. 'Just go behind the bush, mate.' But no amount of encouragement would convince him. 'Back in a minute,' she said, leading him through the crowd.

Willow wriggled, her elbow clanging into Ned's ribs. He shifted slightly, shuffling backwards to give her more space, but jerked as the hard edge of a boot came down on his fingers.

Ouch!

Ned's hands had toughened up over the last three months of working in the field, so it was surprise rather than pain that made him jerk upright. He looked behind to see who'd inadvertently trodden on his fingers and found Cameron glaring at him.

Righto . . . Obviously not in the Christmas spirit tonight.

'Mind if I steal a corner of your mat?' Ned said mildly, sliding his hand back.

The teenager's eyes narrowed and he made a show of stretching his legs out to full length, sliding them along the edge of the red-chequered rug. 'You've got your own, might be easiest if we all stick to our own patch.'

Ned raised an eyebrow and looked around, but no one else seemed to have heard the low tone. Was that a growl in Cameron's voice? The boy had previously been polite, maybe he was having a growth spurt and all the testosterone had gone to his head?

'O-kaaay,' Ned said, turning back to the Christmas performers and accepting one of Willow's candy canes. *Maybe I imagined it,* he told himself, catching Diana's warm smile as she returned to the rug. Not touching, but close enough that he could smell her soapy scent over the fairy floss and the food stalls.

24

Diana was still seeing bits of glitter in her peripheral vision as she ferried sav blanc into Imogen's lounge room and topped up their glasses a night later. They'd eaten their fill of dip and crackers, made a solid dent in the platter of meringues Diana had brought and somehow polished off a bottle of wine already.

'All I want for Christmas is a Jack Black lookalike,' Imogen said, gesturing to the television screen. She'd chosen *The Holiday*, and it was lucky they'd both seen the film, because their chatting outweighed their watching. 'He's cuddly and funny, like a sexy teddy bear.'

Diana laughed. 'I'm more a Jude Law fan myself. He knows how to rock a scarf and tweed jacket. I'll take him.'

'Righto, Jude Law for you.'

'What else's on your list?' Diana asked. 'An exotic holiday? An Audi convertible?'

They'd been playing this game for quite a few years now and it was always more fun with a few drinks under their belt. The last two years Diana's dream Christmas had involved getting through the holiday season without breaking into tears every ten minutes. The year before then, when Pete was perfectly healthy, her wish list had been a kitchen renovation and a paddock full of established peonies. She hadn't known that only a few short weeks later she'd be regretting that she hadn't wished for her family's good health. *Stupid, stupid me for taking my beautifully perfect family for granted.*

'Nope, no holiday or car this Christmas,' Imogen replied. 'I definitely need a cleaner or a servant . . .' Imogen's elaborate Christmas list faded into the background as Diana watched Jude Law on screen. If she squinted her eyes a little, he looked a bit like Ned, with that slight wave in his hair, especially when he wore those horn-rimmed glasses. She smiled, absent-mindedly twisting hair around her fingertips, as she remembered their kiss the night before.

Imogen tapped her leg, jolting her out of her daydream.

'You look like you're having a little Jude Law perve-party there,' Imogen said. 'More meringue?'

Diana glanced at the plate that had somehow emptied itself as she'd been thinking.

'You caught me,' she fibbed, accepting the platter for a refill. 'Have fun at the concert last night?'

Imogen tipped her head to the side, considering the question before answering. 'Yes and no. I got a heap of stocking stuffers at the markets, and a certain fabulous friend helped me make a stunning wreath.'

Diana admired the willow and gumnut wreath hanging on the wall.

'But Oscar ate so much fairy floss he spewed on the way home,' Imogen added, 'and the sight of Sarah in that elf outfit made me wish I'd exercised instead of binge-watching Netflix over winter. Or do you think it's all those men keeping her fit?'

A meringue crumb chose that moment to lodge itself in the back of Diana's throat. She coughed. Imogen clapped her on the back, then handed her a glass of water, which Diana gulped down gratefully.

'Maybe,' Diana spluttered.

'It'd be easier to hate her if she wasn't so nice,' Imogen continued.

Nearly always nice . . . Diana recalled Sarah's comment about flower farming at the general store and then the way she'd looked at Ned like he was a fun challenge. Diana retrieved a stray strawberry from Imogen's floor, wondering what her friend would say if she knew she'd kissed Ned last night. Keeping her lips firmly clamped, so the secret didn't accidentally tumble out, Diana nodded instead.

'Sickening,' declared Imogen. 'There should be a punishment for people who look gorgeous in Christmas colours.' Her faux grouchy tone softened. 'How are you feeling about the actual day though?' She rested a hand on Diana's arm. 'It can't be easy, your third Christmas without Pete . . .'

Diana carefully bit into another cream-topped meringue, feeling sugary crumbs tumble down her chin, aware of Imogen's eyes on her. *Am I a terrible person for thinking of yesterday's kiss instead of my late husband?* She chewed slowly, savouring the cold cream and the sharp sweetness.

'I'm fine,' she admitted. 'Things are looking brighter than last year. And the launch event is a worthy distraction.'

Imogen sat up straighter

'Oh my goodness, how about Sadie's gorgeous Christmas post? I wanted to jump on Etsy and order every single thing in her living room. That tree alone would cost an arm and a leg.'

Diana nodded, knowing exactly which Instagram photo Imogen was talking about—a magnificent Christmas tree styled to perfection in the gardening guru's holiday home, and Sadie looked gorgeous, as usual, as she added a star to the top, her cream knit dress and towering stone chimney giving off a Swiss chalet-vibe.

'You know she grew it herself?' Diana said.

'What? Get outta town.'

Diana nodded gleefully. 'She told me all about it when we spoke last week. She's been growing it for three years.'

Imogen sighed into her wine glass. 'I hope you still remember us simple folk when you're sitting around the table at Sadie's fancy holiday house, comparing homegrown Christmas trees, book contracts and TV shows.'

Diana swatted her friend's leg. 'That'll never happen.'

But as she drove home later that night, Diana couldn't help imagining what it would be like to be part of Sadie's inner circle. Even more reason to make sure the event was as perfect as possible.

Her tribe was curled up on the couch, three-quarters of them fast asleep, when Diana let herself into the house later that night. The blue glare of the television screen lit up the room, illuminating her four boys all lined up on the sofa. For a moment there, she thought Cameron was also asleep. But as she peeled down the blanket, ready to scoop Leo up first, Cam spoke softly. 'I'll get Harry,' he said, pushing aside a knitted rug.

'Thanks, mate,' she said, gathering Leo into her arms. He barely stirred, and soon she was back in the lounge room, reaching for Elliot.

'I'll carry him, Mum,' said Cameron.

'I can do it,' she insisted, her voice still hushed.

'But you don't need to,' he said, his voice stern as he gently nudged her aside. 'Dad would have wanted me to be the man of the house and I reckon it's time I took that role a little more seriously.'

She found herself tearing up as he cradled Elliot to his chest.

'You're a treasure,' she said, following him down the hallway and resting a hand on his shoulder. The dim hallway light flickered and a meow came from the laundry.

'Oops, better let Jinx out before bed, she'll be ready for a break.' She gave his shoulder a squeeze. 'Night, Cam. And thanks for watching the boys tonight. Don't know what I'd do without you. Not like Georgie to leave early. Is everything okay with Georgie? Didn't she like the movie?'

Cameron opened his mouth, then closed it, and as hard as she tried, Diana couldn't quite pick the fleeting expression that crossed his face. *Maybe he's tired?* It *was* after 11 p.m.

'You look knackered,' she said. 'Get yourself to bed, we've got a few big days ahead.'

Jinx meowed again, more plaintively this time, and her phone pinged as she turned towards the kitchen.

'Night, Mum,' he mumbled.

The phone pinged again with another message and despite the yawn she'd stifled while walking into the kitchen, Diana felt more awake than ever when she saw Ned's name on the phone screen.

The weekend was filled with Christmas preparations and the children busily making last-minute gifts for their teachers. Inspired by a craft idea Leo had shared, Doug had painted smiling faces on not one but three garden rocks and glued them each to a block of wood.

'I think Miss Kenna would like a bookmark better than a bunch of door stops,' Willow said, looking up from her collection of colourful paper and glue.

Ned intervened, knowing it would quickly escalate as they were still tired from Friday's concert and hyped up about starting school holidays in just a few days.

'I think she'll like them both,' he said, watching Doug frown with concentration as he wrote 'My teacher rocks' on the timber.

Once the crafts were finished, Ned sent them outside to play and pulled out his phone. Diana had sent a photo of her first yellow decorative dahlia bloom, and a silly grin spread across his face as he spotted the 'xx' at the end of the message. He hadn't been sure whether she'd meant to send them the week before, but this time he was convinced they were intentional. He'd found himself recalling the stolen moment throughout the weekend, and wondering if Diana was too, and whether it also brought a smile to her lips.

After doing the eggs in the first strains of daylight, and loading the children onto the school bus, Ned was out the gate early on Monday morning. The rational part of his brain was still floundering in the dark, unsure if kissing Diana McIntyre had been a good idea or a terrible one, and he was curious to see how things would play out between them from now on. Would it be awkward? Cringingly polite? Had she regretted the moment?

And what about Cameron's possessive attitude? he thought, glancing towards the farmhouse when he pulled up. But there was no sign of Cameron and, although Diana's initial greeting was shy and her cheeks slightly pink, she didn't mention the kiss. The question that had run through his mind all weekend resurfaced: *Was it a one-off?*

It wasn't what he'd pictured when he'd decided to stay for six-months. *But, man, that kiss . . .*

Ned savoured the memory as he tied off the twine, then checked that the new rung around the temporary dahlia fence was tight enough. Too tight and they'd pull the steel dropper posts inwards, too loose and they wouldn't be any use in supporting the leggy green shoots.

'That should do them,' he said, turning to find the lady hijacking most of his thoughts was just inches away.

'They look great. Thanks for coming in this morning.'

Even though Diana's face was shaded by the wide-brimmed hat she wore every day, he could hear the smile in her words. 'What's on this arvo?'

They walked back to the garden shed, their steps in unison.

'Off to Hamilton shortly,' he replied, 'and then back in time for the school assembly. Are the end-of-year ones long and waffly or quick, painless affairs?'

Diana's smirk was answer enough.

'Let's just say the principal starts planning in February. It's a little faster now the carols are combined with the town concert, but you'll still have school captain speeches, awards, parent committee updates and the like. The individual class skits are pretty cute, but nobody will notice if your Christmas shopping spree goes a little over schedule.'

Shopping spree? Momentarily confused, Ned frowned, then laughed.

'Not shopping. It's Maeve's last counselling appointment until mid-January. She's doing well, though, better than I'd expected. Thanks for talking to her at the sewing circle, you made a real impression.' He met her eyes, finding kindness and understanding.

'Anytime. Has she started sewing with Willow yet?'

Ned shook his head.

'Willow hasn't asked again, but it'd be nice if they had something to work on together in the summer holidays. Maeve's offered to watch them for a few days when I'm here, so we'll see how that goes. How about you guys? You've probably got a quieter fortnight ahead, without any cricket?'

She nodded. 'Though that brings its own problems. The boys go a bit stir crazy when the sports take a break. Driving to Geelong and back is one thing, but Cam especially gets cranky when he's not playing.'

Can't argue there, Ned thought and, when Cameron jogged down the driveway a few minutes later, he wondered if the guy had supersonic hearing. *Or had the place bugged.*

They both called out a hello, receiving a grunt from Cameron in reply. He stayed on the deck, swiftly transitioning from running to push-ups, with one eye on the garden as Diana and Ned packed away the tools and loaded bouquets into the Land Cruiser.

Least I don't have to overthink the farewell we'll have, thought Ned, climbing into his ute. The next time they kissed—and he hoped there would be a next time—there wouldn't be an audience.

'See you at the assembly,' he said. When he looked in the rear-view mirror halfway along her driveway he saw she was smiling in his direction, with her hand touching her lips.

Ned was still thinking about the unexpected situation they'd found themselves in as he turned into Colin's driveway. Neither of them was actively searching for a relationship, but after Friday night it was evident there was something there.

The ute did its usual shudder as he took it down through the gears, and he thought of autumn and life beyond the immediate future. When Diana's peak dahlia season was over, and Sadie's launch was done, he'd planned to return to his career and pick up their travels where they'd left off, with a clean slate and the knowledge that he'd sorted Colin's affairs and helped Maeve handle her grief without relapsing.

He paused by the pin-up board in Willow and Doug's room, looking at their special map and all the locations with two stickers—Jessie's dream destinations that they'd already ticked off the list—and then all the single stickers they hadn't got to yet. He touched them with a finger—Rainbow Beach,

Monkey Mia, Carnarvon, Cape York, Bruny Island, Streaky Bay—thinking of all the places he'd promised Jessie that he'd travel to, when she couldn't. Six months earlier, the sight of all those single stickers had inspired him, and the adventures they were yet to have fuelled dinner-table conversations with Willow and Doug. But as Ned looked back at the map of Australia, for the first time he could remember, it didn't hold quite the same appeal.

Tuckered out after the excitement of Christmas Eve cooking, wrapping and kid wrangling, Diana sank into the couch and started on the chips and cider the boys had left out for Father Christmas. *Or Mother Christmas, as the case may be.*

It felt like an eternity ago that she had collapsed on the couch with Pete after a late-night wrapping and stocking-stuffing session, predicting which presents would go down the best, which purchases they would regret, and a shared gratitude for having a roof over their heads, bellies full of food and good health. But tonight, as the twinkling tree lights glinted off the presents below, she felt a sense of achievement instead of the heart-wrenching nostalgia of the previous two years.

She'd managed the morning's flowers on her own, finished the salads and ice-cream sandwiches for tomorrow's lunch at Mac Park, and had the three younger boys fast asleep before 9 p.m. Even Cameron had turned in earlier than usual, and she'd caught the tail end of *Love Actually* as she ironed everyone's outfits for tomorrow.

'Definitely a win,' she declared as she sat down, smiling as Jinx strolled into the lounge room and jumped up onto her lap. Diana stroked her soft fur.

'Thank God we don't have to trek halfway across the country tomorrow, hey puss?' She nestled back against the comfy couch, thinking of Imogen and Sarah, who were travelling to their families in Canberra and Adelaide, and then, as the clock approached midnight, her thoughts strayed to the Gardiner household. From Ned's description, she could almost picture the tree they'd made, the special decorations they'd used for the first time in two decades and the cheesy carols Willow had playing on repeat. Was he sitting on the couch right now thinking of her, or feeling nostalgic for the people who were absent this Christmas?

After finishing the snacks, she climbed into bed, switched off the bedside lamp and mapped out the jobs for the week between Christmas and New Year's. As well as the flower side of things, there was packing for a few nights in Port Fairview. It had been a couple of years since she'd towed the caravan herself, but New Year's at Angie's property was too good to resist. With a bit of luck, she'd even manage the 400-kilometre roundtrip without putting another dent in the van.

Diana dozed off, dreaming of beach days, sandy picnics and sunshine ahead.

Ned lifted the lid of the Weber, deftly stepping aside to avoid a dousing of steamy, smoky meaty aromas, and gave a quick nod. It was ready, and not a moment too soon. Any more Christmas lollies, dips and chips and he wouldn't have room for the main course. 'Tongs, Dougie?'

His son proffered the utensils with the gravity of a surgeon's assistant. 'How do they get the duck and the chicken inside there? Does the turkey eat them?'

Maeve, Willow and Ned all laughed as Ned set the Christmas lunch on the outdoor table. Covering the meat with alfoil and a wire cloche, Ned gave his son a wink. 'That's the magic of a turducken, buddy. It's best not to question the hows and whys, just enjoy the end result.' He relaxed into his deckchair, whistling.

'I thought you were sick of Christmas music, Dad,' said Willow, nudging him so that the new bracelets he'd bought her for Christmas jingled against one another.

'If you can't beat 'em, join 'em.'

Maeve raised her can of soft drink. 'Hear, hear.'

Flopsy emerged from the lilly-pilly bushes, his tail twitching at the imposition of people in his garden. As well as humming the maddening Mariah Carey song, Ned also found himself patting the tabby cat. It had been a good morning; better than any Christmas he'd shared with Maeve in his adult years. There had been no issues, no alcohol, and the gifts had been given and received with a tenderness he hadn't thought possible.

Maeve asked the children to help her serve the salads. If Colin had told him a year earlier, when they were speaking to him from Perth, that they'd be sitting in the garden at Bridgefield this Christmas, Ned would have told him he was dreaming.

We've come a long way.

'It's a shame your father's missing this,' Maeve said, quietly passing him a platter.

Ned nodded.

'Jessie and Jonno, too.' He unwrapped the meat and began carving. Their eyes met as he heaped pieces of turkey, duck and chicken onto the large dish. She smiled, reminding him again of the mother she'd once been, and he smiled back.

They ate Christmas lunch in the dappled shade of Colin's Manchurian pear tree, in the company of birds and blowflies, who seemed equally entranced by the mouth-watering aromas. When Ned carried the last of the dishes inside, he remembered the final present he was yet to give.

His mother turned at the sound of her name and stared at the small wooden box he held out to her.

'You already got me the painting of the lake,' she said with a firm shake of her head. 'That was more than enough.'

The oil painting had caught his eye at the Bridgefield General Store, the muted pink-and-grey landscape perfectly suited the new soft-mauve walls inside the shearers' hut. Ned's gaze dropped to his hands.

'This is something I should have given you months ago,' he said, remembering how close he'd been to scattering all the ashes that day at the creek.

Wordlessly, Maeve took the box. He heard her breath catch as she looked inside at the small canister of Colin's ashes, before cradling the box to her chest.

Her soft voice was thick with emotion when she finally spoke. 'There're things we all wish we'd done a little differently in retrospect, aren't there?'

Diana woke on Christmas morning to the sound of the boys racing through the house.

'Awesome! Santa put water pistols in our stockings.'

Leo rushed in and showered her with hugs and Merry Christmasses. 'Can we open our other presents yet, Mum?'

She snuggled Leo into her, rubbing her nose against his. 'You know the rules, buddy, not until everyone's up.'

Harry and Elliot appeared in the door and all three groaned in unison. She winked at them as she climbed out of bed. 'How about I get the coffee machine going and make some fruit toast?'

She knew the smells and sounds of breakfast would lure Cameron out. Sure enough, he wandered into the kitchen as the little boys wolfed down breakfast.

'Merry Christmas, honey. OJ or coffee?'

Cameron mussed up the twins' fair hair and swung Leo up onto his shoulders, a tired contentment creasing his face. Even though he towered over a head above her, he would always be one of her little boys.

'I'll make it, Mum, you take a load off.' Cameron gestured to the stools but she shook her head with a smile.

'I'm on to it. You should see if Santa left you anything,' she said.

'I'll get it,' Leo yelled, scrambling to the floor. When Leo rushed across to the fireplace, Diana noticed Pete's stocking was hanging next to hers. *I didn't put that up* . . . It hadn't been there last night when she went to bed either. And from the look of it, there was something in it.

'You must have been really good this year, Mum,' Leo said. 'Santa Claus left you something heavy.' He carried her stocking over to her. The twins abandoned their breakfast to look.

A small grin twitched at the corners of Cam's mouth. 'Don't drop it, squirt. Might be fragile.'

What is it? She wondered. Delighted, Diana fished out a box of her favourite strawberry and cream Lindt balls, a pair of earrings she'd seen at the Christmas concert the week before, and a water bottle covered in pictures of pink gum flowers.

'Oh,' she breathed, her eyes heavy with happy tears. Her vision shimmered as she looked at her sons, then down at the gifts. 'They're beautiful. Santa Claus knows me well,' she said, opening her arms and drawing them to her.

'What's in Dad's stocking?' Harry bounced across the room, barely waiting for Diana's approval before pulling five chocolate marshmallow Santas from the large stocking. *Pete's festive chocolate of choice.*

Diana's heart did a strange dance between sorrow and gratitude as she caught Cam's eye. He gave a nonchalant 'don't ask me' shrug before looking away.

'It's got a note!' Elliot said, clearing his throat. 'It says "Ho, ho, ho! A little magic from the North Pole to remind you of your dad. Love, Father Christmas."'

'Beautiful, Cam,' she said quietly, handing him a coffee after they'd eaten the marshmallow treats. 'That was very sweet.'

'Dunno what you're on about,' Cameron insisted, the grin contradicting his words.

They moved on to the other gifts, and before long the living room was a mess of discarded paper and happy boys.

'Right, gather it all up and we'll get a photo,' Diana said, snapping several pictures on her phone. She uploaded the best picture to her social media and typed out a quick caption:

Looks like a wrapping paper factory exploded in my lounge but how about those smiles! Merry Christmas from our home to yours x Diana

It was only after she'd posted the photo that she realised there was still a gift hidden at the back of the tree.

'Oh, Cam, you've got one left.'

He unwrapped the cricket bag she'd bought at Reg's sugges-tion, and while she hadn't expected him to gush like Elliot when he opened the new JK Rowling novel or Leo finding a Lego set under the tree, she expected a little more enthusiasm from her eldest.

Wrong colour? Wrong brand? She was about to tell Cam he could exchange it for a different one when her phone rang. *Speak of the devil.*

'Happy Christmas, Reg.'

'Merry Christmas, Annie-girl! Where're my favourite grandsons, then?'

'Kids, come say hi to Gramps.' Diana put the phone on loud-speaker, handed it to the twins and started on the breakfast dishes. Cameron cleared the wrapping paper as Leo spoke to Reg, then took the call off loudspeaker when it was handed to him.

Odd, thought Diana, watching him walk out of the room.

The younger boys bounded outside to test their new water pistols. She found a Christmas music mix and when Mariah Carey came on was immediately transported to the concert and the magnetic lure of Ned Gardiner. She'd sent him a message before breakfast, wishing him a Merry Christmas. And unlike last week, when she'd fretted over accidentally putting 'xx' on the end of her message, she signed off with not one but two love hearts—red and green. *Will he reply with the same?*

She quickly reined in her thoughts when Cameron emerged from the hallway, irritation in his stiff gait. What had Reg said now? Drying the last of the dishes, she set the tea towel down and gave him a sympathetic look.

'Did Gramps give you a hard time about cricket again?'

Reg had taken to calling each weekend, quizzing Cam on batting stats, training techniques, and game time. He'd obviously overstepped the mark today.

But when Cameron set her phone down on the bench, his words were clipped. 'So, he was right?'

Diana blinked, bewildered by his hurt tone, until she looked at her phone and saw a message from Ned. An *open* message from Ned:

Happy Christmas to you, too, hope it's a blooming marvellous day. Want me to come early tomorrow and help harvest before it heats up? 💚🎄🖤

Seeing his name on her phone screen usually set butterflies loose in her belly, especially with those love hearts on the end, but now, with Cameron standing right there, Diana felt awful.

'Why are you opening my messages?' She regretted the defensive comment the moment it came out but was baffled as to what else to say.

We've only kissed once.

Your grandfather's wrong—of course I'm not replacing your father.

I'm not sure if it's something yet . . . but I want it to be.

Diana swallowed. *None* of those lines would make the situation any better. Before she could explain, he turned and walked out.

'Ca-am . . .' she called, drawing his name out into two syllables. Exasperated, she reread the text.

It wasn't even flirty or suggestive. But just like the love heart emojis that had seemed such a good idea this morning, Diana knew the message showed there was more than just friendship on the table.

25

Ned carried the basket of washing to the laundry, wondering how on earth the children had worn so many clothes in only two days. Turning the machine on, he detoured past their bedrooms, pleased to find them fast asleep. *Christmas wore 'em out*, he mused.

He carefully slipped Willow's glasses into their case and removed the book from her sleepy grip. Doug had already flung off his quilt. After straightening his sheets, Ned unpinned the map from their wall and carried it into the living room. Quickly moving the fruit bowl to one side of the dining table, Ned had plenty of room to spread out the map.

It was ragged around the edges, with little creases, marks and the odd rip along the folds. *Really must get this thing laminated.* He ran a hand over the stickers, reading them as though braille: the gold stars where Jessie had wanted to visit, accompanied by little sticky dots he'd bought decades ago to track his progress. Doug and Willow had proudly taken over by adding their own stickers beside the locations they'd visited.

He looked over to the mantlepiece. Nestled among the Christmas decorations were two photo frames. A new one that Maeve had given him earlier that day. It was empty, but intended for the photo they'd taken by the tree. The other was a frame he'd found in Colin's cupboard, their last family photo with Jessie. *So many double stickers, Jessie. We've covered some ground.*

Ned turned at the sound of three quiet taps on the glass door and was surprised to find his mother there, lit up by the floodlight being dive-bombed by moths and bugs. 'Come in.'

The evening was still warm and a light breeze followed Maeve inside, ruffling the map on the table. 'I know I thanked you earlier, Edward,' she said, standing just inside the entrance, 'but I meant for everything. Not just today. For giving me another chance. For making me see the counsellor. For fixing up the hut. For letting me be a grandmother.'

He looked away, not wanting Maeve to know part of him was still wary of a future relapse. Perhaps there was no such thing as a guarantee, though, and if seven years of sobriety wasn't enough, then what *was* the magic number he was waiting for? Ten? Fifteen?

'They're good kids, and they're happy getting to know you, too,' he said.

Maeve fiddled with the Christmas wreath Willow had made at Diana's stall. 'I know I let you all down, Edward. You and Jonathon and Colin seemed to be coping so well without Jessica. I tried moving on but unless I was drinking, it felt like the grief would swallow me whole. And then I gave up trying . . .' Maeve shook her head and cleared her throat. 'I hope you know it wasn't your fault. You boys didn't deserve to get caught up in my mess and I'm so sorry it's taken me so long to get through to the other side. I don't blame you for walking away but I'm glad you gave it one more shot.'

Flopsy meowed and weaved his way between Ned's legs. Ned stooped down to pat him, then for the first time, gathered the cat into his arms. The resulting purr sounded like a two-stroke chainsaw, and he took comfort in the cat's warmth.

He studied the cat, who was sliding its whiskers back and forth across his shoulder, a slither of tinsel stuck in his fur, then looked back at his mother.

'So am I.' Ned met her eye, and then looked towards the mantlepiece where the two family photos would soon sit, side by side. The mum she'd once been and the grandmother she was trying her hardest to become.

Maeve moved to the table. 'Looks like a treasure map.'

Ned glanced down. It *was* a treasure map of sorts, he supposed, though he suddenly felt shy about showing Maeve.

'Is that . . .' Maeve's voice dropped to a whisper. 'Jessica's map?'

Just like he'd done, she traced her fingers over the surface. 'I'd forgotten all about this.' Her voice caught. 'You added all these stickers?'

Ned nodded. All the years he'd been travelling, all the holidays he'd factored into his adult life, had revolved around the map spread out before them, and although he'd never done it for the kudos, it was nice to see Maeve understood. She turned and he softened as she wrapped her arms around him in a hug.

'That's some legacy,' she murmured, her voice muffled against his chest. 'I just thought you were . . .'

Ned gave a wry smile as the cat squirmed, forcing them to draw apart. 'Cursed with itchy feet? It's okay,' he said. 'I didn't broadcast the fact.' It was easier to let everyone believe he was fickle than explain the special meaning behind the travel. He'd done that once, and Fleur's scorn had been enough to ensure he didn't tell anyone again.

She carefully refolded the map and handed it to Ned.

'No, I thought you were running away from everyone who'd let you down. And with good reason, too. I really am sorry, Edward.'

He reached down and gently squeezed her hand. 'I know you are.'

'Teenagers, right?' sighed Diana, allowing Penny to refill her glass.

'Teenagers,' agreed Lara, one eye on the cousins squabbling over the water bombs. The last few years Evie, Cameron and Toby's daughter Holly had entertained the younger children after Christmas lunch while the adults kicked back on the deck. But this year, they'd snuck out to the machinery shed and roared across the paddock on the motorbikes before anyone could say 'dishes'. It wasn't until Jonesy and Tim confiscated the water bombs and corralled the kids into a game of badminton that Diana finally told her sisters about the mid-morning 'hiccup' with Cam and kissing Ned.

'I knew it,' said Angie, clapping her hands. 'Didn't I say Ned would be perfect for her?' She looked to Penny and Lara for backup. From the way all three grinned, Diana knew the subject had been thoroughly dissected.

Diana groaned. 'I haven't even let myself think that far ahead, but after Cameron's reaction today, I feel like it's doomed before its even started.'

Lara shook her head and made a 'tsk' noise.

'Cameron's *overreaction*, you mean. I love that boy to death but he's not your keeper.'

Penny leaned in, not even noticing the champagne spilling over her glass.

'Tell us all the details, then—was it a swoon-worthy kiss?'

Diana felt another flash of annoyance at Cameron for forcing her hand. Ideally, she would have waited at least a few weeks to see if this thing with Ned was a one-off, but she knew Cameron would have told Evie about the love hearts on the text message, who would have told Lara, who would have told Penny and Angie. *If only I hadn't fanned the flames by jumping straight on the defensive this morning.* She arched an eyebrow.

'Unlike Sarah Squires, I don't kiss and tell.'

'But . . . ?'

Diana couldn't help the tiny smile that snuck through her stern façade. Her sisters didn't miss it either.

'Ha! You don't even need to say a thing,' said Lara, sinking back into her chair with a knowing smile. 'I'm happy for you, sis. We all are.'

The situation didn't feel as dire after hashing it out with her sisters and, instead of batting away their comments and questions, Diana found herself opening up.

'It won't do you or the boys any good to wallow in misery and swear off happiness to suit some preconceived mourning period,' said Penny.

'And Ned seems nice,' said Angie.

'Really nice,' added Lara.

Angus and Toby found them laughing when they walked outside with the cheese platters.

'You look like the cat that's got the cream, Angie,' said Angus, topping up their glasses with cold bubbly.

'Let's just say I'm not often wrong, Dad,' Angie giggled, before steering the conversation to their New Year's plans in Port Fairview.

Sleep had come easily after the air was cleared with Maeve. Ned rose early on Boxing Day, collecting the eggs and moving the chook tractors as the sun crested the eastern horizon. He whistled as he refilled their feed and water, and was showered, shaved and dressed before the children even stirred.

Ned whisked an egg with milk for the cat, then prepped larger batches for scrambled eggs when Doug and Willow walked in, both yawning.

Any initial hesitation at the early start evaporated when they arrived at Diana's at 8 a.m. and spotted the shiny new scooters with Christmas tinsel trailing from the handlebars.

The boys were out the door, greeting them before Doug and Willow had undone their seatbelts. Soon all five children raced up and down an improvised obstacle course between the house and the sheds.

Diana greeted Ned with a wry grin. 'Santa needs to work on risk analysis. I've already had the icepacks out this morning. How did your guys fare?'

Ned told her about the books and microscope Willow had been delighted with, and the jigsaw puzzles and toolkit Doug had received. They chatted as they walked towards the flower paddock. Bees buzzed from plant to plant, busy pollinating, and birds called out from the towering gums, their cries echoing in the trees across the yard.

'The day panned out better than I'd expected,' he admitted. 'Nothing fancy, just Maeve and the kids and lunch in the garden.' Even as he said it, he knew that was an understatement. 'The nicest Christmas in years,' he added with a smile.

She nodded, and he could tell she was genuinely pleased to hear it had gone smoothly. Ned shoved his hands in his pockets to stop himself from reaching across and pulling her close. Whatever they'd started last week at the Christmas concert hadn't dwindled over the days apart. If anything, it felt supercharged, and he worked hard to keep his mind on the job at hand.

After a productive morning harvesting flowers, they carted the buckets of blooms from the paddock to the packing shed.

'You should charge extra for the critters that come with the posies,' Ned said, watching a tiny green spider run across the petals.

'Ladybugs maybe, not sure if people would pay extra for spiders, caterpillars or praying mantises. Least it proves it's locally grown and not flown in. And it shows they aren't doused in chemicals or pesticides,' she said.

Ned liked that perspective. He'd never questioned the origin of flowers he'd seen in florist windows or at supermarket checkouts, but there was something about Diana McIntyre that made him see things—hell, she made him *feel* things—he hadn't expected.

Watching her with the flowers, he realised how keenly he wanted to see her do well. He thought of the conversation with Toby, and the industry gossip he'd heard about Sadie Woodford's disgruntled ex-staffer. *Where there's smoke, there's fire, right?*

Lara hadn't thought it worth worrying about, so why did it still niggle him? Was it because Sadie Woodford always seemed mighty quick to capitalise on Diana's best photos? Just this morning, she'd reposted Diana's picture of the roses bathed in morning light, along with a reminder about ticket bookings for their upcoming event.

'Any more news from your celebrity friend? I see she gave you another shout-out on socials.' He stripped foliage from the stems, watching Diana light up beside him.

'Did you see how many likes it got when Sadie reposted it, compared to the numbers on my original Facebook post? I told you she had the golden touch, didn't I?'

Ned gave a non-committal shrug. He wouldn't be signing up to the Woodford fan club until after he'd met the woman and made his own judgement.

'A few thousand likes is the least she can do for all the effort you're putting in. It reminds me of how the drug reps send extra perfume and make-up samples for the staff to try. It's a small price for them to pay for the word-of-mouth marketing they get in return. Sadie's using your place as a backdrop, and I bet you've mentioned her name in many more conversations than she has yours.'

Diana rolled her eyes. 'It's a great deal,' she laughed. 'The best thing that's happened to Darling Dahlias since I dreamed the crazy idea up. Just you wait until you see the magazine spread, and then the paparazzi lining up at the gate, all trying to get a shot of the famous Sadie Woodford. It'll be worth every single minute of hard work.'

Ned wondered what it would be like to have such optimism and passion. *Ask her if she knows about the tabloid story being pulled.*

'Did you hear—?' But his question was drowned out by a toot from the driveway.

'Perfect timing,' Diana said, wrapping the final bouquet, and almost doing a double take at the sight of Imogen's van. A flourish of signwriting covered the bonnet, and the side was decorated with images of flowers and ladybirds.

'Snazzy new logo,' Ned said, as they followed Imogen to the back of her van.

'Well, New Year is the perfect time for a fresh start,' she said, her gaze moving between the two of them. It wasn't until Diana looked at her watch, then he did the same, that he realised he'd been unconsciously mirroring her body language. He straightened and crossed his arms for good measure but, when he looked up, Imogen fixed him with an amused expression.

She'd noticed it too. *Had Diana told Imogen about their kiss?* He knew they were close.

They both waved as the van rumbled down the driveway. Ned turned to Diana.

'Does she—?'

'What were—?'

Their sentences came out at the same time and when a giggle spilled over Diana's lips, he wanted to brush his fingers along them and do away with the words.

'You go first,' Diana said, a rosy flush creeping up her neck and cheeks.

Ned struggled to remember his train of thought. 'Does she know about . . . ?'

She bit back a laugh before covering her face with her hands and cringing, more like a teenager than a forty-something mother of four. He was glad he wasn't the only one who felt awkward, hot and unsettled all in the same breath when it was just the two of them.

Her cheeks were pink and her eyes shone when she grinned back up at him. 'Nope, Imogen doesn't know about the Christmas concert . . .' she said. From the way she trailed off, he got the feeling it wasn't their secret anymore. 'But my sisters do.'

Ned wasn't sure if that was a good thing or a bad thing. Either way, it explained Toby's extra-warm smile when he'd collected the newspaper on his way through town that morning.

Diana's eyes met his and if it hadn't been the middle of the day with six children a few hundred metres away, he would have dipped his head to see if her lips felt every bit as good as he remembered. And from her wistful sigh, he was pretty sure she was thinking something similar.

'Right,' she said brightly, clamping her hands on her hips and swivelling towards the farmhouse. 'Let's put the jug on.'

Ned closed the garden gate behind them and stepped around the abandoned scooters, ramps and jumps. The children were sprawled out in the lounge room, the twins glued to the Boxing Day test, while the other three played a determined game of Uno. Ned roughed Doug's hair and scored a thumbs-up from Willow. Diana bustled around the kitchen, pulling out bowls and ingredients.

'Anything I can do to help?'

'You already helped a heap this morning,' she replied, sifting flour. 'We're a good team, imagine how fast we'll be by the end of summer.'

Ned washed up in the laundry, then took a seat at the island bench, spotting Cameron at the kitchen door, towel around his neck, wearing only footy shorts. *He's a fit bugger,* Ned couldn't help but think.

'Hey, we can help out with the flowers, too,' Cameron said, pulling a shirt on as he walked across the kitchen.

'Would've been more help if you hadn't been out till all hours last night,' Diana responded, returning to her baking. 'A herd of cattle could have stampeded through the hallway and you wouldn't have woken this morning. Were Georgie, Evie and Holly out as late as you? Aunty Lara and Toby won't be thrilled.'

Cameron frowned, giving Ned a look that was darker than the bags under his eyes. 'Just Telf and Knowlesy. Marty piked out,' he said. 'He's all wrapped up with his new girlfriend, trying to woo her. She'll probably fall for it too, hook, line and sinker, before realising she's way too good for him.'

Diana laughed, oblivious to the daggers her son was sending Ned over the top of her head. Ned didn't have to search too hard to find Cameron's double meaning. *This is going to be interesting,* Ned thought, recalling Cameron's 'back off' message at the picnic. He finished his coffee. *If Cameron needs a bit more time to get used to my presence here, then I'll give him a wide berth.*

He stood, tucked his chair under the bench and thanked Diana. 'We might duck off and leave you guys to it.'

Diana wiped her hands on her apron, looking bewildered. 'But aren't you staying for scones? There's no salt in them, I promise.'

'I'd love to, but . . .' Ned felt Cameron's cool glare. 'I don't want to barge in. These kiddos have been here all morning, we'd probably better head back and get stuck into a few jobs at our place. I'll see you tomorrow.'

Diana had figured the moment with Ned would evaporate as soon as they stepped into the house—six children in earshot and eyesight had that kind of effect—but she hadn't expected to go from simmering sexual tension to ice cold in the space of five short minutes. Something—or someone—had changed the dynamic. She narrowed her eyes at Cameron's back as he sank into the recliner. *Was he causing trouble? Surely not.*

'He's like a cranky bear without much sleep. You should stay,' she said to Ned. She fluttered the apron, feeling flustered all of a sudden. 'For brekky,' she added quickly. 'I'm making a double batch.' *Why did she feel like a teenager today?*

'I don't want to overstep the mark,' Ned said gently. 'And really, I should take a squiz at the watering system at Colin's. It needs a good checking over before we head off.'

Heading off? For one sickening moment, Diana thought he meant heading off for good.

'Big adventure on the cards?'

'We're off to Byaduk for a few nights. My uncle had a bush block there,' Ned paused, then elaborated. 'Colin inherited it from him a few years back, and now it's mine and Jonno's. The property's right on the river, so we'll set up camp and roll out the swags. Maeve will look after the chooks over New Year's,' he said.

Diana picked up the butter knife and cut cream into the flour mix, trying to picture the tiny inland town. She'd been to Byaduk for a Rural Women's Day luncheon, then the odd cricket match with Cam, but never ventured further afield.

Ned gathered up his children and shuffled them onto the deck, his voice animated as he described how the isolated, scrubby block was the perfect campground. She followed him outside, unable to muster up the same enthusiasm for camping.

'Willow and Doug are hanging out to sleep under the stars, aren't you, ratbags?' The two children nodded eagerly as they climbed into the ute.

'You're not a camper?' He raised an eyebrow, evidently noticing Diana's shudder. 'Crickets and frogs lulling you to sleep . . . Bird song at dawn . . . ?'

'Mosquitoes all through the night and no block-out curtains,' she countered, shaking her head firmly. 'I'm more of a caravan type of camper,' she added. 'And there has to be a toilet.' After four natural births, her bladder didn't appreciate the challenge of midnight treks to a shared toilet, or even worse, a hastily dug hole.

'You don't know what you're missing.'

'Pretty sure I do,' she said, returning Ned's grin as she waved him off.

She had the scones in the oven less than ten minutes later. The three younger boys made light work of the fluffy treats, asking for seconds, and then thirds before they were full.

'Doug and Willow are going camping. Can we go camping too, Mum?'

Diana heaped homemade plum jam onto her scone. 'Nope, we're taking the van to Port Fairview for New Year's to watch the fireworks with Claudia and Aunty Angie.'

'Awesome!' Harry said. 'Can I take my fishing rod?'

Handling stinky bait was about as appealing as a makeshift camping toilet, but Harry flung his chair back and raced from the table before she could say 'maybe'.

'I'm packing my rod too,' Elliot said, joining his twin.

'We're only going for a couple of nights, though,' she called after him.

'Me too. And my squid jig,' Leo said, not wanting to be left out.

Diana finished her scone in peace, smiling at the sight of the boys rushing between the garage and the shed where the van was parked with goggles, flippers, fishing rods, tackle boxes and scooters under their arms. Buoyed by their energy, Diana pulled a suitcase from her wardrobe. She wouldn't start packing for their trip yet, but just the thought of a seaside getaway made her happy. *Things are pretty darn perfect right now.*

26

The Land Rover rumbled to a stop in an overgrown driveway. In fact, if it hadn't been for his phone's GPS announcing their arrival, Ned would have driven straight past the bush block that had once been his uncle's, then his father's and now his.

Wrangling the three-bar gate open, he took a deep breath of the warm, dry eucalyptus-scented air and paused to take in the view. Low scrubby bushes dotted the paddocks, and a handful of kangaroos looked up as they drove onto the property. Ned pulled up by the small river.

The children scrambled from the ute and Ned started unpacking, hauling the deckchairs off the tray first. The eskies were next. He spotted a large Tupperware container hidden between two of the swags. That hadn't been there when he'd packed for their New Year's Eve adventure. He dragged it across the tray.

'Hey, what's this?'

'Doug!' Willow turned on her little brother, hands on hips. 'You were supposed to remind me to get it out before Dad saw,' she said crossly.

'Oops,' said Doug with a shrug. He looked up at Ned. 'It's your birthday cake. Strawberry and choc chip.' The pride on his face turned to pain as Willow landed an elbow in his ribs.

'Doug! Now you've really ruined the surprise,' she grumbled. Ned pulled them into a hug, one under each arm.

'When did you two ferrets sneak that in?'

Willow wriggled out from his arm and whisked the container away. 'No peeking, Dad,' she said.

'Gigi helped us when you got the groceries,' said Doug. 'We got you presents too, but you have to wait until tomorrow to open them. And there's another surprise as well.'

Willow's groan made Ned laugh.

'You're such a blabbermouth, Doug,' she said.

'Lucky me,' Ned said. 'C'mon, kiddos, get your bathers on and we'll see if this river's still good for swimming.'

Tugging off his shirt, Ned slathered sunscreen over his chest and shoulders. The flowers and vines across his torso disappeared for a moment, then reappeared milky white under the sheen of thick sunscreen. When the kids were suitably ghost-like with a heavy slathering of the same, they eased their way down the rocky embankment. Ned strode in. The cool water lapped at his calves, then his knees and waist. *Magic.*

The swimming pools of the Top End couldn't compete with fresh running water and, unlike the springs at Mataranka, he could relax knowing there were no reptiles lurking below the surface. He floated, watching the children tiptoeing into the water.

'Are you *sure* there're no crocodiles,' said Doug, his eyes darting around.

'A hundred per cent sure,' said Ned. 'An eel or two perhaps, and some freshwater yabbies, but they won't eat much.'

They floated and swam, paddled and talked, and for the first time in a long time, Ned didn't feel the familiar itch to hurry on to the next adventure or new landscape. And with a jolt of surprise, he realised that the six months he'd promised Diana was now halfway through. It hadn't been the grind he'd expected it to be. If anything, that time had passed in the blink of an eye, and he had a strong suspicion the next three months would go even faster. Something told him it wasn't just the chickens and flowers that he was reluctant to walk away from.

'C'mon, Mum, we could be swimming by now,' Cameron said, his voice carrying from the front of the car. 'You've checked the brake lights and indicators twice, there's nothing hanging loose. Can't we go?'

Diana tucked her hair behind her ear.

'Keep your hair on, we'll be on our way in a minute.' She did another lap of the caravan, checked the van door was latched, rattled the windows to make sure they were shut tight and peered at the car hitch one last time. Satisfied, she hopped into the driver's seat and buckled her seatbelt.

'Righto, crew, who's ready for holidays?' The joyous back-seat response contrasted with Cameron's pointed glance at his watch. She gingerly eased the van out of the shed, blinking at the sunlight, when movement in the dahlia patch caught her eye.

'Harry!' She turned. 'You were in charge of the sprinklers. Quick! Go switch them off.' What else had they forgotten? 'Elliot? Did you make sure Jinx has enough food and water? And Leo? Did you chain the dogs up like you promised?' The boys nodded insistently as Harry jumped out of the car. He then dashed back and they were halfway down the driveway when Leo piped up from the back seat.

'Mum, I forgot Big Ted.'

Cameron looked up from his phone, groaning. 'We're never going to get there.'

'I'm not reversing this van down the driveway,' said Diana, pulling on the handbrake. 'Run and get it.' Leo bolted down the driveway. 'Keep your hair on, Cam,' she said, patting her eldest son's leg. 'We'll be there before you know it. Fireworks don't start till midnight anyway. A quick detour to Byaduk and we'll be in Port Fairview mid arvo.'

Cameron's face fell.

'Byaduk? What are we doing at Byaduk?' His shoulders sank. 'I knew I should have accepted a lift from Aunty Lara.'

'We're going to see Willow,' said Elliot. 'I promised her we'd call in.'

'There'll be cake,' added Harry. 'It's their dad's birthday today.'

Cam's head snapped around.

'We see them too much already. Why are we mucking up our one and only trip away in . . .' He jabbed at his seatbelt clasp, spluttering as if she'd suggested they were detouring via the Nullarbor. Diana could almost see the steam pouring out of Cameron's ears. '. . . our only trip away in *forever*.'

'Don't be so dramatic, Cam. Your cricket is one of the main reasons we don't go anywhere apart from Geelong,' Diana said, rolling her eyes. 'It's New Year's Eve, we're in no rush.'

'You mightn't be,' he huffed, opening the door. 'I'm catching a ride to Port Fairview with Evie.' He threw open the car door, and stormed up the driveway, where the phone reception was better.

Does he really have a problem with Ned or is he just going through some growth stage, where his hormones are multiplying faster than his shoe size?

'What's wrong with Cam?' asked Elliot. 'Birthday cake's always a good idea.'

Once Leo was buckled in, Diana eased the four-wheel drive forward again, feeling the weight of the van behind her. She stopped at the mailbox and wound down the window.

'Jump in,' she said.

Cameron shook his head and fussed with a loose piece of weatherboard on the farmhouse replica mailbox. Another job for the list in the new year, one that Pete would've fixed the second he saw it was loose. *Is that what this is really about?* Was he concerned that Diana was replacing his father?

'It'll only be a quick stop, Cam,' she promised, gently. 'Come on, the boys promised Doug and Willow.'

Cameron lowered his voice so only she could hear it. 'I can't believe you're celebrating *his* birthday when we haven't even talked about what we're doing for Dad's birthday yet.'

Diana recoiled in her seat, stinging from the accusation. Pete's birthday was over a month away and, although she hadn't given it much thought yet, she'd meant it when she'd told the boys they'd always mark the occasion with a cake and candles.

Cameron cleared his throat, avoiding her hurt gaze as he spoke again, louder this time. 'I've already texted Aunty Lars, she'll be here in a minute. I'll see you at the beach.'

Diana weighed up her options. Maybe he *did* need time to cool off. After the Boxing Day brush-off, and now this outburst, she knew he wasn't likely to join in singing Ned 'Happy Birthday'.

'Okay,' she conceded. 'We'll see you there this arvo.'

His accusation stayed on her mind for most of the drive. It wasn't until they passed the turn off for Mount Napier State Park an hour later that she felt the melancholy lift. Houses appeared in the distance and before long they were travelling past a cricket oval enclosed by an ornate white picket fence. Following the road out of Byaduk, they finally located the lane leading to the Gardiner's bush block. Ned hadn't mentioned his birthday, but thoughtful little Willow had cooked up the idea of a surprise birthday lunch, recruiting Maeve to help bake a cake.

She pulled up at the address Maeve had given her. The road was freshly graded, but the track through the property looked more rugged than she'd expected. Colin's battered Land Rover was parked in the paddock and she could hear their cheerful chatter on the breeze.

Parking the van and the car, Diana slipped on her sunnies to combat the bright sunshine.

'We'll walk from here,' she said. The boys dashed ahead, intent on the tall trees shading the river. When Doug and Willow came into view, Diana was surprised to find she was a little nervous. *Will Ned be okay with us gate-crashing his birthday?*

How many times had her family teased her for putting the cart before the horse and inviting herself to things? The memory of Cameron's dummy spit slowed her steps. Was she mad for rushing in? *Bit late for that now.*

She switched her cane basket to her other arm and wished she'd packed popcorn and lamingtons instead of mini quiches, a fruit platter and yo-yo biscuits.

'Happy birthday, Ned,' chorused the twins. Leo launched into enthusiastic song and Diana arrived at the edge of the river just in time to join in the 'hip, hip, hoorays'. She peered into the water, glad she wore sunglasses as she gaped at the sight before her. She'd expected strong, broad shoulders and perhaps one or two tattoos, but she hadn't imagined the mass of artwork covering Ned's chest.

She had a tiny daisy tattooed on her shoulder blade, a university dare she forgot about most of the time, while Pete had been ink-free, and vehemently opposed to piercings, tattoos and the multicoloured hair trends that were now as popular

with teenagers as with grandmothers. Ned's body, on the other
hand, was more like an artist's canvas.

Her gaze followed the intricate ink to the dark hair that
trailed from his belly button to his swimming trunks. *It was
worth dropping in just for that!*

Ned abandoned his leisurely floating and swam to the edge
of the river, following Willow and Doug up the banks. He
hadn't shared his birthday with anyone other than Doug and
Willow in years, and yet here Diana McIntyre was, appearing
from the middle of nowhere, bearing gifts.

Ned reached the grassy paddock and shaded his eyes against
the sunshine as a wicked thought popped into his mind. *That
flowery dress looks like the very best kind of gift wrapping.*

Diana tossed him the towel he'd draped on the Land Rover's
bull bar and, as he took it, he noticed she was having trouble
dragging her eyes away from his tattoos.

'Would've spruced the place up a bit if I'd known we were
expecting guests,' he joked, hoping the artwork wasn't a deal
breaker. He towelled his hair roughly, used it to swipe the
water off his torso and wrapped it around his waist.

Willow issued instructions like a drill sergeant, and by
the time Ned had located his shirt, commandeered a hat and
hung his towel over a branch to dry, there was a feast spread
across their picnic rug.

'See, Dad, didn't I tell you we had a good surprise planned?'
Doug said, proud as punch.

'Sure did, kiddo,' he replied, touched by their gesture. 'You
guys have outdone yourselves.'

Willow beamed at his praise, then carefully uncovered the
birthday cake. The ring-shaped cake was even more colourful

than last year's attempt, something he hadn't thought possible, with the word 'Dad' written in chocolate Smarties.

'Best birthday cake ever,' he said, lips twitching as he caught Diana's eye.

'It's like it got caught in the middle of a paintball fight and a colour run,' Harry said, receiving a sharp pinch from his twin.

Willow's smile wavered and he saw Doug trying to work out if the assessment was a criticism or compliment.

'I mean, it's totally awesome,' Harry said hastily. 'Really cool.'

'I love it,' Leo said.

'Me too,' Diana added, producing napkins and a knife. Willow arranged candles around the circular edge.

'Make a wish!' Doug said as Ned leaned over to blow out the candles. Ned closed his eyes, grateful for his children, who were more thoughtful and perceptive than he ever remembered being at that age, and the twist of fate that had delivered Diana McIntyre into his life.

And when he blinked them open, Diana's bright smile made him wish a little harder for the future he hadn't even imagined until now.

'Forty-two, huh?' Diana said as she rested against the river bank, finishing a can of soft drink. She looked at him, leaning back with one arm draped over a bent knee, the other leg stretched out long. With the warm sunshine on her back and the anticipation of a new year, with new beginnings on the horizon, she had almost forgotten Cameron's harsh words.

'Don't tell me you're going to spout some bulldust about being over the hill? We're hardly ancient.'

She shuffled down a little so that her feet dangled in the river. Imogen would have made a wisecrack about only being as old as the man you're feeling, but the confidence Diana had harnessed at the Christmas carols seemed to have deserted her. It had been so long since she'd flirted that everything sounded corny in her head.

'If the magazines and blogs are true, we're in our prime, apparently,' she said with a smile.

'Reckon they're on to something.'

The appreciative tone in his voice made her wish they were alone. Just as well the children were skimming rocks, fifty metres upstream. There was something magical about sitting by the water, no traffic, no chores, no animals and no flowers to pick, but she had a sneaking suspicion that the magic was as dangerous as it was alluring.

She plucked blades of grass, tossed them into the river and watched the gentle current carry them downstream. The familiar stirrings of guilt returned. *Am I betraying Pete?* Diana gave a small sigh and toyed with her dress's floral fabric.

'We'd better make tracks before the roos and the drink drivers are all out.'

Ned eased himself up and stretched a hand towards her. She took it, feeling the warmth switch between them, and allowed herself to be pulled to her feet.

'Happy birthday,' she said, tipping her head back to look at him. *That smile . . . temptation in a nutshell.* It took a lot of willpower to brush past him and round up the troops.

'Come on, you lot,' she called. 'Let's hit the frog and toad.' *Before your mum ravishes the birthday boy.*

There was grumbling as the boys ditched their rocks into the water. They trudged along the bank with Willow and Doug in tow and reluctantly carried the picnic platters back to the roadside.

'Thanks for the pressies, too, guys. I needed a new beach towel,' Ned said. The big orange-and-blue towel had been part of an initiative of the town's new progress association, one of Pearl Patterson's ideas. This Bridgefield memorabilia felt less intimate than the town's polo shirt or hoody, but more useful than a mug or tea towel.

'Our pleasure,' Diana said, buckling her seatbelt and checking her mirrors. She'd stayed longer than planned and Angie would be wondering what was keeping them. With a bit of luck, Cam would have cooled down a little in the meantime. *Or*, she thought as she looked at her watch and realised their quick detour had stretched to two hours with Ned, *maybe he'll be even surlier?*

Diana pulled out gently, waving as she went. The Gardiner's were only just out of sight when a patch on the side of the road caught Diana's eye. The bleached fur and cream bones looked like they'd once belonged to a kangaroo. She gently veered into the middle of the road, glad there was no oncoming traffic, but she'd barely gotten up to speed when the van started to vibrate. It felt as if she was driving on rumble strips.

She gripped the wheel tighter, then gasped at the sight in the rear-view mirror. It looked like dust coming from the wheel. Strange for a sealed road. She glanced at the road in front of her, then back at the van, which was now listing to one side.

'Shit!' The sight sent her heart into a gallop. Diana pressed the brakes, resisting the urge to slam them on. 'Hold on.'

Despite her best efforts, they jerked forward in their seats, Elliot bracing himself against the dashboard as they came to a quick stop. Alarm rang out from the backseat.

'Sorry, guys,' she said, tugging on the handbrake. Diana jumped out and jogged around to the passenger side. Flat as a tack. *Gah!*

'That doesn't look good,' Elliot said, appearing by her side. 'Where's the spare tyre?'

Diana gave an exasperated laugh. 'No idea, mate. Your dad . . .' she trailed off, finishing the sentence in her head . . . *always took care of that type of stuff.* And while Pete had taken care of plenty of those tasks, like servicing the vehicles, keeping an eye on the property fences, since he'd gone, she'd slowly gotten used to checking the oil on the lawn mower, occasionally whacking a bit of air in the car tyres and cleaning out the gutters every spring. But she hadn't even thought about checking the caravan backups. Making it to Port Fairview without denting the van or losing it off the back of the tow ball, had been a higher priority.

Harry and Leo joined them, their grimaces mirroring her own.

'Yeesh! It's exploded,' said Leo. She was none the wiser after a thorough search of the caravan. *Where on earth did they keep the spare tyre?* She looked back down the road towards Ned's. Elliot followed her gaze.

'Ned will help us,' he said simply.

Diana took a deep breath. She didn't like asking for help or playing the 'damsel in distress' card, but it wasn't like she could magic up a tyre. And Elliot was right. Ned would help them without batting an eyelid.

27

Diana helped Ned wriggle the wheel until it shuffled free of the axle, bringing dust and small stones with it.

'You don't do things by halves, do you?' he grinned, rolling the half-shredded tyre towards her.

Diana groaned. 'If I'd known how sharp those kangaroo bones were, I would've given them a wider berth. Bloody roos. Even when they're long dead, they're still a traffic hazard.'

Sighing, he brushed his hands on his shorts. 'Want to unhook your car and try your luck finding a tyre repair place in Hamilton?'

Diana shook her head.

'At 4 p.m. on New Year's Eve? Fat chance finding anyone open besides the pubs and restaurants,' she said. 'I'll try roadside assistance.'

Casting another glance at the roadside, where the children were scaling a gum tree, she pulled her phone from her pocket. Angie had messaged back, promising to pass on news of their delay to Cameron. Diana texted a quick thanks and then dialled the RACV, where she was transferred to the local mechanic on call.

'Don't see many of those tyres on the road these days,' said the bloke after she gave the model number. His long 'hmmmm' was followed by a sigh that didn't sound promising. 'Nope, none in the workshop. I can order it in, but with New Year's it's not likely to arrive until January second. Byaduk, you say? There's a little tyre joint near Macarthur. I can try him if you like? Worst-case scenario, you might need to leave the van overnight.'

'You're welcome to camp here,' said Ned after Diana had finished the call. She turned to him, the flippant reply she was contemplating vanishing as she imagined the possibilities.

'Can't promise fireworks, but the night sky will put on a pretty good show. Nothing like spotting a shooting star when you're tucked up in a swag.'

Diana bit her lip to stop a chain reaction of internal fireworks. Her ringing phone brought her back to her senses. *You're a mum. With children to think of.* Ned put the tyre in the back of her car as she answered the call.

'You're in luck,' said the RACV bloke. 'Old Kev from the Macarthur Mechanics reckons he ordered one of those tyres for a customer that did the Harold Holt.'

Diana let out a breath. 'Thank goodness,' she said. 'What time will he be here?'

The man sounded sympathetic. 'That's the only problem. He's hit the sauce a little early. The coppers are out in full force on New Year's. Can you sit tight and wait until tomorrow? No other buggers will be delivering any earlier.'

Diana looked at the children swinging from branch to branch like chimpanzees and then over to Ned, who was shoring up the timber he'd slid underneath the van, to take the weight of the missing tyre. Magpies and corellas were starting their late-afternoon chorus, and the sun was about as far west as it would go before it started sliding towards the horizon. *Would it kill us to skip the fireworks just once?* On such a quiet country lane, the van wasn't likely to be a traffic hazard overnight. Maybe this was an opportunity to get to the bottom of things between her and Ned?

'Of course, there's always the option of getting the van towed,' said the RACV bloke on the end of the phone. 'I can see how far away the nearest tow truck is that'd take a caravan.'

Diana made a quick decision.

'No, that's fine. We've got enough supplies to rough it here for a night.' *And she'd find out one way or another whether there was anything between her and Ned Gardiner.*

Ned hefted the swag over his shoulder, trying to focus on the smell of old canvas as he strode back to the camp site. It was safer than letting his brain skip ahead to tonight, when Diana would be tucked up in her pyjamas. *Does she even wear pyjamas?*

He watched her carry Leo's single swag, while the twins battled with the big double swag that Cameron had planned on using at Port Fairview. *Cameron won't be thrilled about it,* Ned thought, *but what choice does she have? It's not like she can pull a tyre out of a magic hat.*

The younger kids had been excited about the change of plans, especially Ned's two.

'Can you round up a few more branches for the fire?' Ned asked Doug. 'We'll probably stay up a little later now we've got guests.'

'Watch out for snakes,' Diana added automatically. The twins dropped the swag perilously close to the edge of the river bank, seemingly invigorated by the reminder about snakes, and raced off to help. Leo and Willow weren't far behind.

'Don't know about you, but I'm ready for a drink,' Diana said. She leaned the small swag alongside the Land Rover. 'I've got Moët chilling in the Engel fridge.'

'Not sure I'm classy enough for Moët,' he said, watching for her smile as he played up the pronunciation of the 't'.

'Even on your birthday?'

'Not even on my birthday,' he said, reaching into his esky. 'I thought you might have sampled a bottle of those fancy launch bottles?'

'I wouldn't dream of it,' she said indignantly. 'They're for the big event in March. I don't want Sadie to think I'm pilfering supplies beforehand.'

Ned twisted the top off a cider and slid it into a stubby holder before passing it to her.

She accepted it with a grin. 'Anyway, it's best I don't drink a whole bottle of bubbly on my own.'

He was glad to hear it. If, by some stroke of magic, he was lucky enough to kiss her again, he wanted it to happen because she wanted it too, not because she was three sheets to the wind.

Ned shook his head, looking at the posse of swags lined up at their feet. What was he thinking? *Romance in the midst of five children? Fat chance.* But as his eyes slid up to meet Diana's, he recognised the mixture of nerves, anticipation and longing, headier than any glass of imported fizz.

With the kids to gather kindling and scrunch up newspaper, the small campfire was underway in no time. Before long, they were heaping their plates with sausages. The coals burned down to embers and eventually yawns spread around the campfire like a Mexican wave.

'Time to roll out the swags?' Diana said, glancing across the fire for Ned's nod of approval.

'Definitely. Grab your toothbrushes, guys.' His T-shirt crept up to his belly button as he raised his arms to the sky and stretched. She wasn't sure how, but he managed to make even a simple move like that look sexy. Her theory that the Christmas concert kiss was a one-off was getting weaker by the minute.

Willow caught her looking at Ned. 'Are you just going to talk about boring grown-up stuff?'

Ned walked around the campfire towards his daughter. 'Nah, we'll probably just eat all those birthday chocolates and polish off the rest of that scrummy birthday cake you made.'

'Da-addd!' she said, grinning as she poked a finger into his chest. Ned pretended to flail, as if he was about to fall over backwards, then straightened up.

As hard as she tried not to stare, the tender relationship between Ned and his children was beautiful to watch. She noticed the way he lovingly brushed the knots from Willow's long hair, then divided and weaved the strands together into a braid.

'There you go, missy,' he said, twisting an elastic around the end and taking her glasses. Diana dragged her attention back to her sons. Harry was reluctantly sharing the double swag with Elliot and Leo was in one of the singles.

'Quick photo, you lot,' she said, pulling out her phone and snapping a picture of the children tucked into their beds. The orange coals and campfire smoke added a warm glow to the image, and she smiled when she checked the screen.

'Are you going to put it on your Insta, Mum?' Harry asked.

Diana glanced at Ned, then Willow and Doug. 'It's a pretty cool shot,' she said. 'Maybe. Would you mind if I did?'

Ned gave a 'fine by me' smile and his children nodded eagerly.

Through the rustling of the swags and sleeping bags, Diana heard Leo's voice. 'Now you'll be famous, too,' he said. 'My mum has thousands and thousands of followers. They might want you to be in magazines, as well.'

And while she didn't catch Doug's reply, the comment got her thinking. As Sadie had explained in the very first workshop, an online presence *was* a crucial part of modern business. But as Diana looked at the five little heads poking out the top of the swags, she closed the apps and switched off the phone. Regardless of the chemistry between her and Ned, this unexpected camping trip felt like something she wanted to hold tight to her chest, just for them.

Diana checked her watch and was surprised to see it was nearly midnight. There hadn't been a peep from the swags for more than an hour, and the time had passed quickly with Ned and her discussing next week's workload.

'Only a few more minutes left of your birthday,' she said, closing the lid on Ned's box of chocolates before she was tempted to eat another. 'Hope you didn't mind us gate-crashing?'

'I'm glad you did.'

She was too. The calm evening was so different to the excitement and carnival-like atmosphere of Port Fairview's foreshore on New Year's Eve. The gentle rustling of leaves, water rushing in the river, calling birds and . . .

Diana tilted her head, trying to identify the pop, pop, pop noise. 'Fireworks?'

Ned scanned the dark horizon with her. 'Let's see.'

He stood up and stretched a hand in her direction. She kept holding it as they walked to the small rise halfway across the paddock.

'Your neighbours must've known it was your birthday.'

They stood shoulder to shoulder, hands still entwined, until the fireworks fizzled out.

Ned pulled her closer. She rose up onto her tiptoes and pressed her lips against Ned's before she lost her nerve. Her hand went to his jaw, and she felt his fingers thread through her hair as he gently pulled her closer. Although she knew the children could wake any minute, she couldn't stop herself stealing one more kiss, then another. He smelled like sunscreen, tasted like chocolate and, judging from the warmth pressing against her, he was every bit as interested as her.

Yep, definitely something there.

She sighed against his lips and pulled away before lust stole her senses. Things would be so much easier if there was no spark, and she didn't need a degree in pharmacy to read the desire in his dark eyes.

'Been wanting to do that again since the Christmas carols,' Ned said, running a finger along her bottom lip.

'Same.' She glanced back at the camp, let out a reluctant groan and rested her forehead on Ned's collarbone.

'I know, right? As much as I'd like to explore this further, I reckon a rain check's the sensible option.'

'Definitely the smart idea,' she said, leading the way back to the campfire. *Sensible sucked, big time.*

'Another drink?'

She nodded and watched him pour more glasses of the port he'd brought out after the kids were in bed. Bats screeched in the gum trees overhanging the water and the moon momentarily disappeared behind a cloud, the darkness almost enticing her to slip her hand into his again. It took a monumental amount of willpower not to, and she was glad when the sky cleared.

'This means we're officially old, you know,' she said, following him towards the water.

'The port or the self-control to stop when every centimetre of my body's crying out for more?'

They laughed at the same time.

'Both.'

She settled next to him on the rocky slope, stretching out her legs. 'Do you ever think of settling down in one spot?' she asked, keeping her eyes on the moonlit river.

She'd asked him the same question when he'd first arrived in Bridgefield. He'd deflected the query then, but the answer was so much more important to her now that she could imagine him as a lover, rather than a labourer.

The silence grew. His arm brushed against hers, sending fissions of warmth through her.

'Sometimes.'

She wanted to probe, and push, and make a joke about prescribing himself some medicine for his perpetually itchy feet, but the camaraderie they'd developed working among the flowers had disappeared. More serious undertones had appeared in its place, and she injected lightness into her voice to try to return to familiar ground.

'I mean, this is obviously a horrifically barren and uninviting landscape. Who'd want to live here, right?' She spread her arms, gesturing to the sheep sleeping on the opposite banks, the moonlight that bathed the landscape in an otherworldly glow, the undulating hills.

'Tough gig,' he agreed. 'Though not many people have the freedom to travel Australia as a family, or the luxury to chase their dreams. Even if we keep doing this for another decade, we still won't have seen everything there is to offer.'

The explanation had rolled off his tongue so easily. *Perhaps it's the line he uses when friends challenge his nomadic lifestyle*, Diana thought. *What use is a spark if there's no*

future? Swallowing a twinge of disappointment, Diana turned
to face him.

'So, you can't see yourself putting down roots anytime soon?'

'Up until now, I've never found a compelling reason to stay
in the one spot.'

Her heart did a little hop, skip and jump. 'Until now . . . ?'
She bit her lip and lifted her eyes to meet his. 'Look, Ned,
I'm going to lay my cards out on the table. I'm not looking to
rush into another relationship, but if this is going to go any
further—' She paused. *If I'm going to put my heart on the line.*
'Then I need to know if you think that future could include
a widow in her mid-forties with four children, a flower farm
and more family ties than you can poke a stick at?'

There. I've said it. She felt a little lighter for getting it off
her chest, but the vulnerability was almost as weighty.

She knew her heart wasn't strong enough to handle another
unexpected loss.

And yet—she licked her lips as she looked at him—she still
found herself drawn to him in a way that shocked her. Was
she already too invested to avoid getting hurt?

Ned admired the courage it had taken Diana to address the
elephant in the room. Her question deserved a bloody good
answer, but could he give her what she needed? Was it brave
or foolish to think he could take on someone else's children—
four of them at that? It would be a complete 180-degree turn
to go from locum work, and being on the road, to staying put
in the one spot.

Colin would be pleased with Ned's decision to press pause
on the constant travelling, but if he were still alive, he'd probably also be giving him a word or two about treading carefully
so he didn't mess things up. Jonno's advice to set down roots,

and his pledge to Maeve that they'd put the past behind him, rang in his ears. *Take the flying leap. Do it.*

He thought of Jessie, and all the joys, triumphs and decisions she never got to experience in her ten years. He'd crossed so many places off her list, but there were still so many more they hadn't got to yet. Would he be failing her if he decided to stay in the one spot? Or would he be failing himself, and Doug and Willow, if he kept moving?

He felt rather than saw Diana shift uneasily beside him and knew this was a decision that needed to be made here and now.

Ned reached for her hand and traced over the soft freckles. 'It's looking that way.'

Even in the moonlight, he could see Diana's smile was brighter than the sunflowers lining her garden fence and he kissed her again, confident he'd made the right call.

28

Diana woke to see the sun creeping over the horizon. She rolled onto her side. The children were still dead to the world, tuckered out after a big night. She turned the other way, spotting Ned's dark hair sticking out the top of his swag. Just thinking about last night sent a thrill through her.

They started the morning slowly, with bacon and eggs on the barbecue. Diana switched her phone on, and in the peaceful paddock by the river, with kangaroos and vocal birdlife, the phone call from the tyre man felt almost like an intrusion.

'Guess we'd better get this show on the road,' she said, prompting an immediate chorus of 'can we stay longer?' from her boys. She started to pack up the fishing rods they'd insisted on bringing.

'Do we have to come while you get the tyre fixed? Can't we go fishing with Doug and Willow instead?'

'Fine by me,' said Ned.

Diana looked at him uncertainly. It was true, her boys didn't *need* to collect the tyre with her. But she still didn't want to presume anything.

'Sure you don't mind, Ned?'

'Course not,' he said. 'Reckon we can catch dinner for your mum while she's gone?'

Ned knows what he's getting himself in for, she told herself as she drove to the mechanic shop. Watching your partner's kids is part and parcel of the deal with blended families.

'Partner.' The word out loud sounded as foreign on her lips as it had in her head. They were too old to use the term 'boyfriend and girlfriend'. And 'de facto' sounded way too impersonal. A new thought occurred to her. What if she slipped up and referred to him as her 'husband'? Or, even worse, what if she called him 'Pete'? She groaned as she found the work-shop. *So much to get my head around.*

Kev at Macarthur Mechanics looked a little worse for wear, but despite his bloodshot eyes and slightly grey complexion, he made light work of fitting the new tyre to the old rim.

'That should get you out of trouble, love,' he said. 'You going to manage bolting it back onto the caravan yourself? I can mosey down and give you a hand?'

Diana gave a grateful smile as she shook her head. 'I'm all good, thanks. I've got a friend who knows his way around a tyre jack.'

A 'friend'? That was the term her mother had always used when a neighbour or relative had found love later in life— 'Aunty Eleanor has a new friend'—usually followed by raised eyebrows or a meaningful pause before the word 'friend'.

Maybe she'd ask Ned if he had a preference. The thought had her smiling all the way back to Byaduk.

The shower was Ned's first stop when they arrived home a few days later, and the razor was almost blunt by the time he'd whipped off the scruffy stubble.

'Righto, grommets,' he said, tossing fresh towels towards Willow and Doug. 'Get in the tub and wash off all the camping grot.'

He left them to their bath and wandered across to the shearers' hut, where he found Maeve in her kitchen, pulling a dish from the oven. The new cabinets were only basic, but combined with fresh paint, patched plaster and Willow's colourful artwork on the fridge, it looked infinitely more cheerful than it had months earlier.

'Thanks for holding the fort. Any dramas while we were away?'

Maeve sliced the pie into large wedges and loaded a plate with the lion's share. Quiche? Zucchini slice? Whatever it was, it made his mouth water.

'Nothing apart from the zucchinis quadrupling overnight and nobody here to eat them. Will the kids eat zucchini pie for dinner?'

'A few veggies won't go astray after three nights of barbecues. Thanks.' He swapped the savoury dish for the cooler bag he'd brought with him. 'As long as you'll accept a few yabbies in return?'

Maeve thanked him softly, and as she stowed them in her fridge, he saw it was well stocked compared to previous visits.

'A baking spree?'

She hesitated, then opened it wider, so he could see a platter with a cake and what looked like cream cheese icing, plus jars of tomatoes, cling-wrapped plates of muffins and . . . *are those pickles?*

'That'll be the last time I plant six zucchini seedlings,' she said, not quite managing to hide her smile. 'I've put a few things in Colin's fridge for you, too. Send them back if you don't like the zucchini pickles or savoury muffins. At least if nobody eats the zucchini and walnut cake at sewing circle, I can feed it to the chooks.'

Ned headed back across the paddock with a plate of warm pie and the feeling that his mother's life was well and truly back on track.

Diana criss-crossed the lawn, flicking on the taps that fed the drip irrigation system. The plants were thirsty, and she could almost hear them give a collective sigh of relief as the water trickled into the soil.

A deep V8 engine rumbled down the driveway, and she turned to see Pearl Patterson hunched over the Monaro's steering wheel. The boys rushed outside to greet Eddie, while the lilac-haired Pearl ambled across to admire the flowers. Just as Diana was trying to work out what job she was about to be lumped with, she noticed that Pearl's hands were as colourful as her magenta slacks.

'I'm rounding up some mulberry pickers, thought your lads might be happy to earn a few dollars these next few mornings?'

Diana listened as Nanna Pearl outlined the ambitious project she'd proposed for the upcoming launch.

'It's another feather in the bow of our CWA crown,' said Pearl. 'You know how everyone loves our mulberry jam?'

Diana nodded. The branch members held the recipe close to their chests, and according to Toby, the jam sold twice as fast as any of the other varieties on the general store's produce stall.

'Well, Penny helped me pitch the idea to the bigwigs that are paying for the catering of your event, and your fancy friend Sadie adored it, too. We'll provide all the food for the event, at an excellent price, and we'll also make one hundred and fifty pots of locally sourced mulberry jam, so each of the guests can take a little piece of Bridgefield with them when they leave. Extra fruit pickers would be a big help.' Pearl cast a shrewd eye over the scooter obstacle course cluttering Diana's driveway. 'If you can spare them, that is?'

Diana didn't need to be asked twice, after explaining that Cameron had stayed on in Port Fairview with Angie and Lara, she put the offer to the younger boys, who jumped at the chance to earn some pocket money.

'I wouldn't mind some more helpers, reckon Ned Gardiner's kids would be keen, too?'

Diana promised to ask on Pearl's behalf. After texting Ned with the offer and directions to the Patterson's orchard, Diana pulled her pruning shears from her pocket, and set to work. When Ned's car pulled into the driveway, she had a trolley-load full of beautiful, bloom-filled buckets. Diana felt a shiver of nervous excitement as he beamed at her. Even though they'd spent months working alone when the children had been at school, there was something decadent about the idea of just the two of them, all alone, after their New Year's adventure.

'Hey,' he said, tugging gardening gloves on. Bonzer roused himself from his official supervisor's perch, tail wagging, as he lumbered over to greet Ned. Paddy the pup gave him an enthusiastic welcome, too.

'Morning.' Even though she knew they were alone, Diana glanced around to double-check before landing a kiss on his cheek. He leaned into it, turning his head to brush his lips against hers.

'Never had that type of welcome at any of the pharmacies,' he murmured against her lips.

'That's because they can afford to pay you a fortune.' Diana grinned and pressed a spare set of pruners into his hands. 'I've got to sweeten your crummy wages somehow.'

'Imagine getting that concept through legislation. Everyone would be fighting over minimum wage jobs.'

She turned her smile to the dahlias before things went any further.

Their banter and flirting made the morning pass quickly, and she enjoyed working her way down the wide aisles of flowers, almost back-to-back with Ned as he cut from the parallel row until the new wire trolley was full. Ned pulled the trolley back to the shed, stacked the brimming buckets in the coolroom and returned with the empties. A searing heat ran through her each time he brushed past, and it was an effort to concentrate on the job. *Get a handle on it, you're not a love-sick teenager.*

'Gosh, these are luscious,' said Diana, inspecting the next row of blooms. She tried not to choose favourites, but the coral, apricot and soft pink dahlias always took her breath away. Diana reached the middle of the row, where the dinner plate varieties were grouped together, and arrived at the eternally popular Café au Lait, with its creamy pink petals.

'If only we could get these beauties to grow all year round,' she said. She'd planted more of these tubers than any other variety this season, to account for their popularity. Studying the bush, Ned considered her question with such seriousness that she ached for his eyes to rest on her like that. Before she could stop herself, Diana strode through the flowers. She pulled him to her with a kiss so hot that when they broke apart, gasping for breath, she was surprised to see the flowers weren't wilted.

'For the love of God,' Ned said, a gravelly edge to his voice. 'Never mind the torture you're putting me through, spare a thought for those poor, innocent flowers.'

Diana stepped away giddily, the lush green leaves and heavy blooms regrouping.

'I'll be on my best behaviour from now onwards,' she grinned, liking the way he snorted with laughter, as if he would find it equally difficult.

Somehow, she managed to make it through the working day without trampling any more of the flowers. When Imogen arrived, Diana was confident their friend was none the wiser.

'You've gone quiet on socials,' Imogen scolded as she swung the van door open. 'I thought you'd be ramping up, ready for Valentine's Day, not winding down? Sadie's out-posting you three to one at the moment.'

Diana realised in the hubbub of New Year's, she'd not only avoided posting her own pictures, but she hadn't been religiously scrolling through her newsfeed or sharing Sadie's photos to her story either. She still kept tabs on her mentor's posts, but her screen time was a lot less than normal.

'I've had my hands full,' Diana said brightly, not daring to glance in Ned's direction.

'I'm a convert, Sadie's pretty amazing,' Imogen said, frowning at Ned's sudden coughing fit.

'Absolutely,' agreed Diana. 'Anyone else would come across as preachy, but Sadie's video about the evils of floral foam was pretty funny. Educating people and changing perceptions isn't for the faint-hearted, but she's leading the pack.'

Keen to make up lost ground, Diana snapped several photos in the patch after Imogen had left. Ned's phone rang, and while he walked off to take the call, she uploaded her dahlia photos with a garden update and reminder of where locals could purchase the bouquets.

Fresh photos flooded into her newsfeed and she beamed at the sight of Cameron and his cousin Evie, plus Toby's daughter Holly, at the beach. *He looks happy enough,* she thought, hoping the sea air and salt water would wash away all traces of the argument they'd had, and he'd return tomorrow with a better attitude.

Diana felt Ned's shadow fall across her as she scrolled through Sadie Woodford's page.

'She's younger than I expected,' Ned said, his breath tickling her ear as he peered over her shoulder.

Diana resisted the urge to lean back against his body.

'What age did you say she started flower farming? She must have hit the ground running straight out of high school to build such an empire from the ground up.'

Nodding, Diana shared what she knew. 'Started with a few acres, then bootstrapped her way through a few seasons until she was earning enough to quit her corporate job and expand the business. The rest is history. Knowing that she started out with just her personal savings and a whole lot of determination was a huge inspiration.'

Diana tapped the phone screen, enlarging the testimonials page on Sadie's website.

'That's the photo from your brochure,' he said, smiling at the picture of Diana.

'Yep. I mean, I don't plan to run workshops and become a media darling like Sadie, but it's pretty cool to be in her orbit.'

There was an almost shy look on Ned's face when he handed back the phone and shifted to stand in front of her.

'Speaking of orbits, a locum's job has just cropped up in Horsham.'

It took a while for Diana to compose her thoughts. Delight, alarm, surprise, guilt and anticipation all jumbled together. *He wouldn't mention it if he wasn't considering it.* She bit her lip, waiting for him to continue.

'I've just had an email from the agency. There's a hospital contract on the horizon in May. A maternity leave position.'

'And you're considering it?' She couldn't hide the note of hope in her voice. Was he really about to put down roots?

The summer holidays went by in a blur of farm work. Not only were Diana's dahlias in full bloom, but Ned found himself starting earlier each morning to keep up with peak egg production at Colin's farm.

'Why are there so many eggs, Dad? We didn't get more chickens, did we?'

Ned finished refilling the water tank in the chook tractor and turned to Doug. 'No mate, it's the longer days. More sunlight means more eggs.'

Once the feed was refilled, and the eggs collected, they drove into the next paddock and did it all again with the final chook tractor.

'You're getting good at this,' Ned told Willow as they waited for Doug to open the gate. 'I could nick off on holidays and leave you in charge, no worries.'

She preened at the praise, before logic prevailed. 'But how would we collect the eggs? I can't even reach the ute's foot pedals yet.'

'Harry said him and Elliot already know how to drive their paddock bomb. Cameron taught them. Do you think he'd teach us?' Doug asked.

Ned chuckled wryly as he leaned an elbow on the ute window. *Not bloody likely.* Ever since Cameron had returned from Port Fairview, he'd made it clear he had his eye on Ned. As well as the deck workouts that ensured he had a bird's-eye view of the flower paddocks for a couple of hours each day, the teenager had shifted an outdoor table and chairs into the cutting garden.

'Such a great idea,' said Diana earlier in the month, gesturing to the children perched under the colourful umbrella with paints and crafts, their cheerful chatter carrying over the rows of flowers. A few days later, the slip and slide that had previously been in the backyard was set up along the fence line too, along with a set of cricket wickets. And while Ned liked the idea of having the children in eyesight instead of running around Diana's property or holed up inside watching television, he suspected Cameron's 'help' was more to do with policing him and Diana.

Doug repeated the question about driving lessons, bringing him back to the present. 'Not sure you need to worry about driving just yet, buddy. Cameron's got enough on his plate with cricket and starting year twelve,' he told Doug. Like Diana's youngest three, Doug and Willow seemed to worship Cameron. To his credit, the teenager tolerated the two tag-alongs, but driving lessons would definitely be stretching it.

The children rushed inside to start on breakfast as Ned finished with the eggs. After grading and boxing, he strode across to the house, wolfing down a quick brekky and hanging washing out before heading to Darling Downs. It was hard to believe all the shorts, bathers and play clothes would be replaced with school uniforms in just a few short days.

'Look, that's Miss Kenna's car,' Doug shrieked, spotting a white Volkswagen as they drove through town. The school's noticeboard was decorated with 'welcome back' details, the grounds had been freshly mowed ahead of Monday's start, and from the line-up of teachers' cars, the classrooms were almost ready for the new term.

He found Diana in the trial seedling patch on the far side of the yard, her bright pink shirt standing out among the rainbow of flowers. Ned rolled up the sleeves of his favourite working shirt—a light blue check from Colin's wardrobe—and joined her.

'Look at this one, Ned, it's gorgeous,' she said, pointing out the new flower among the lush green leaves. While the decorative form wasn't too different from the other new varieties that had emerged in the last month, the colour was a unique mix of latte and lilac.

'It's pretty enough to give Café au Lait a run for its money,' he said, checking the stem. Unlike half of the new seedlings that would be composted at the end of the season, this one had the trifecta breeders looked for—striking colour, strong stem and an upright form.

'Colin's right, there's something special about breeding the new varieties. Should we name it after him? Colin's Pride? Or what about Sadie's Success?'

He loved how excited she was, and that he was part of this journey with her, but this was Diana's success. At a stretch he could call it *their* success, not anyone else's. 'What about something that encompasses this season and your farm. Darling Summer Romance?'

She grinned, shaking her head. 'That's already a rose. Maybe New Beginnings?'

Ned winced. 'Sounds like a motivational meme. Bright Start? Fresh Start?'

Even though the seedlings needed several seasons before they could be released to the public, Diana's happiness was contagious. Ned found himself beaming as they worked side-by-side, brainstorming names. 'How about Darling Delight?'

Diana clasped his hand. 'That's perfect, Ned. Lock it in.' She dropped his hand quickly as the children migrated to the outdoor table and chairs with a jar of tadpoles and Doug's microscope. Cameron jogged past in just his footy shorts. Ned and Diana both waved, as they did each day, and Cameron responded with a nod for his mum and a scowl that seemed reserved just for Ned. Diana rolled her eyes, a cheeky glint as she turned to him.

'It's going to be such a shame when everyone's back at school next week,' she said, her fingertips brushing his leg.

While Cameron's round-the-clock surveillance had put a stop to any overt contact between them, the chemistry had subsequently skyrocketed. A sharp breath escaped from Ned's lips.

'It's lucky you've got all those orders to fill, phone calls flooding in and a mega celebrity launch event to prepare for.' *Or there's a chance we wouldn't get any work done.*

And from the amused look on her face, Diana knew exactly how hard it would be to keep on track.

29

Ned slid the last bucket of flowers into the back of the delivery van later that afternoon and latched the heavy door.

'That'll keep the florist happy,' Imogen said, tearing off the delivery docket and handing it to him.

'Thanks, Imogen, I'll just take this call,' Diana said, lifting the trilling phone to her ear. 'Ned, I've got smoko sorted in the pantry. Don't wait for me.' She walked away as she answered the call.

'Speaking of happy . . .' Imogen said, eyeing him keenly. 'You two have been making cow eyes at one another all January. Everything's come up roses then?'

'Something like that,' Ned replied. As scary as it felt to be committing this early in a relationship, it had all the hallmarks of a new beginning. For them both.

They looked across at Diana, who was still on the phone.

'More advance orders for Valentine's Day, most likely,' Imogen said. 'Speaking of which, I've seen the quilt your mum's working on. That's a love letter and a half if ever I saw one.'

Ned nodded. He'd driven Maeve to several sewing circle catch-ups since the first one, each at a different home and, although he didn't know much about sewing, the purple quilt looked close to being finished.

'She was making it for . . .' He trailed off. They'd been using Jessie's name more often, but it still didn't roll off the tongue. 'For Jessie.'

'Sounds like the perfect project for healing. Maeve had better keep her head down though, or Pearl Patterson will have her hosting the group before too long.'

'I don't doubt it for a moment,' he said, remembering the way Pearl had coerced him into Santa service at the Christmas concert. Imogen left with a promise to arrange another playdate for Doug and her son Oscar soon.

Ned packed away the afternoon's tools and caught Diana's attention, miming 'cup of tea'? She nodded eagerly and gave him a 'be there in five' signal. Striding across to the farmhouse, Ned left his work boots by the door and went inside. He'd just opened the pantry and was reaching for the strawberry muffins Diana said she'd made, when the screen door opened.

'These smell as good as they look,' he said over his shoulder, peeling the lid off the plastic container. He swiped a finger along a smudge of icing on the lid. *Mmm*. 'And they taste even better,' he said, turning around. But instead of Diana in the kitchen, he met the disapproving glare of Cameron.

Sweat trickled down his tanned chest and, even from where he was standing, Ned could hear rock music pumping from Cameron's headphones.

'You right there?' Cameron said, eyes flashing as he grabbed the container of muffins. 'Maybe you want to help yourself to a biscuit while you're at it? Put your feet up on the sofa and wait for Mum to cook you dinner, too?'

Ned let the container go but stayed where he was, wary of getting into a game of tug of war with a territorial teenager.

'Take it easy, mate. It'd be a shame to see them hit the deck.' He lifted the corner of the Tupperware container from where it was tilting precariously towards the floor. Cameron frowned as he pulled the Tupperware towards him. *Right-o.*

'Coffee?'

'This isn't your house.'

Ned filled the kettle. Dealing with aggrieved customers at the pharmacy was different to a hostile teenager, but he figured the same cautious, yet conversational tone was a safe bet.

'I'm just trying to help out. Diana's been working her butt off, least I can do is make her a cuppa.'

'Coming in here like you own the place, thinking you can just barge into our lives,' Cameron said. 'I don't like you sniffing around.'

Ned made three strong coffees and handed one to Cameron. 'I'm not trying to replace anyone. I like your mum,' he said. 'A lot.'

Cameron thumped the mug down. Coffee puddled on the benchtop.

Ned resisted the urge to wipe it up. 'Don't you think she deserves to be happy, too?'

Cameron glowered at him, took his coffee and stomped out of the kitchen before pausing in the doorway. He tilted his head to the window, where Diana was crossing the lawn.

'We need her more than you. And just so you know—' Cameron's eyes narrowed, 'she will always choose us. Always.'

The challenge would have held much more gravity if coffee wasn't trickling over the edge of his cup. Ned held his tongue and waited until the teen was gone before he mopped up the mess. Had he bitten off more than he could chew? Would Cameron eventually thaw, or would he keep pushing until Diana was forced to choose between them? Had he been that myopic and self-centred as a teenager? He knew grief manifested differently for everyone. At least when he'd been in the depths of despair after Jessie's loss, he hadn't had to contend with a replacement sister being shunted into their lives. *Is that what it's like for Cam?*

The back door shut and he heard Diana softly humming a Madonna tune. He knew without looking she'd be folding her gloves together like a pair of socks and putting them into the little basket she kept by the back door with her pruning shears and a tube of sunblock. He ran the cloth over the floor as she walked in.

'Oh, I like the look of this,' she said cheerfully. 'Don't stop on my account, the bathroom floors could do with a once over as well. In fact, I could happily drive to Geelong and leave you in charge of tidying up the whole house.'

Ned straightened up and rinsed the wet cloth in her sink. *Should I mention Cameron?* It might be a conversation better raised when Diana wasn't about to embark on her weekly 600-kilometre-round trip to Geelong for Cameron's cricket game tomorrow.

He glanced towards the hallway. 'Is it a big match tomorrow?'

She swept through the kitchen, filling up water bottles and pulling Gatorade from the fridge.

'Yep, the coach is giving him a run in the premier match again. Fingers crossed.'

While it didn't excuse Cameron's behaviour, Ned knew he was likely bearing the brunt of the boy's pre-game nerves. A lock of hair had escaped from Diana's ponytail.

Resisting the urge to tuck it behind her ear, Ned sipped his coffee, then asked a question that had been on his mind all week. 'Can I take you out for dinner soon?'

She looked so pleased with the invitation that he was glad he hadn't mentioned Cameron's attitude.

'An official date? For all the world to see?' Her voice was playful.

'Maybe not the Bridgefield Pub,' he said. 'Well, unless you wanted to?'

Diana shook her head. 'God no, I'm not quite ready for that. You could bring your guys over here and Cam could look after them for the night?'

Ned shook his head, drained his mug and gathered his keys. A strong coffee and shower might help Cameron's mood, but babysitting was in the same fantasy land as driving lessons.

'Maeve's happy to watch them,' he said, and suggested a nearby restaurant.

'I can't remember the last time I was wined and dined. I'm looking forward to it already.'

'Me too.'

Ned heard the bathroom door open as he slipped on his boots. Cameron's footsteps echoed down the hallway and his angry words from earlier ran through Ned's mind. *She will always choose us. Always.*

Diana chanced another subtle look at Cam as they drove through Geelong the next morning. Cameron looked so handsome in his team uniform, even with his pensive frown. He'd been quiet on the drive here last night and had turned in early at their hotel.

'It's okay to be nervous,' she said lightly, keeping her eyes on the road. 'Just like Sadie says, being nervous means you care and you're taking some kind of risk.' She thought of the cricket clinics, the local under-15s, under-17s and A-grade matches they'd driven him to, training camps and squad try-outs she and Pete had attended over the years.

'Easy for you to say, Mum. You don't have everything riding on today,' he said softly.

Diana's heart ached for him and she wished he understood that she would pad up and stride onto the pitch in his place if she could. *We've worked long and hard for this, too. It's such a shame Pete's not here to watch.* And then, just as soon as the thought occurred, it was replaced by a searing sense of disloyalty.

This is crazy. Just thirty minutes ago you were thinking about the date with Ned, now you're wishing Pete was here. Make your mind up . . .

She tucked the conflicting emotions away, needing all her focus to navigate the city traffic, relieved as always when the cricket oval came into view. Pulling into the parking lot, she gave her son an encouraging look.

'You've got this, honey. Play your cards right and you'll cruise through the ranks.'

A deep sigh was the only reply she received. Hadn't he wanted this all along? Wasn't she just supporting his dream, the one he'd been talking about since he could hold a bat? After parking, she opened the boot, surprised to find Pete's old cricket bag.

'Where's your new one?'

Cameron looked everywhere but at his mother. 'I like this bag,' he said, pulling it out of the car.

Was today the first time he'd reverted to Pete's old cricket bag, or hadn't he used the new bag at all? *You might have noticed if you weren't wrapped up in your bubble of happiness with Ned.*

'But the other bag's heaps nicer. It doesn't have any tears or scuffs. And it's bigger,' she added, struggling to keep her voice hushed.

'I didn't *want* a new one,' he said, drawing the attention of the woman parking beside them. Cameron swung the bag over his shoulder. 'Just because you've forgotten about Dad, doesn't mean I have to.'

His words landed with a thud in the pit of her stomach, and it was only the steady stream of spectators and players converging on the car park that kept Diana from gasping out loud.

Ned was amused by the sight awaiting him when he pulled up by Colin's machinery shed the next afternoon. Three piglets, two children and one grandmother in the old pig pen. From the squeals and smiles, it was hard to tell who was the most delighted.

'Surprise, Dad,' said Willow, bounding across to the Land Rover with a black-and-white piglet under her arm.

'When did you arrange all this?' Before he knew it, he was holding a wriggling pig called Baconballs and being introduced to her siblings—a runty little piglet called Chops and a chunky baby boar called Porky.

'Porky's your one, Dad,' Doug said, marvelling at the way their tails curled and uncurled as they trotted around the pen.

'Butch called around last week, while you were at the flower farm,' said Maeve. 'You've done such a good job fixing the old pig pen, it seemed a waste to leave it empty, didn't it, kids?'

Willow and Doug nodded eagerly. *Little schemers.*

'They arrived this morning. Gigi says you can't beat homegrown pork.'

Homegrown pork? Ned couldn't hide his astonishment. *Not only had these three kept their piglet plan a secret, but the children were calm about the idea of eventually serving them for dinner?*

'Don't worry, Dad. Gigi says they'll be big and mean and ugly by the time we eat them,' Doug added, running off with his new friends at his heels, more like puppies than future meals. Willow joined in and the birdsong was quickly drowned out again by peals of laughter.

Shaking his head, Ned looked at his mother.

'I wouldn't have thought four months was enough prep for the stark realities of farm life.'

'They're more astute than you give them credit for,' Maeve said, filling an empty bucket with dry grain and topping it up with water. 'I told them straight up that the pigs would be strictly for meat purposes, and they agreed to the terms and conditions. They also know there's more to you and Diana than just business.'

Maeve's comment stopped Ned in his tracks.

'They do?' Neither had mentioned it to him.

'Course they do. They're bright kids, Edward. They would have been blind to miss the sappy smiles you've been exchanging. If I could see it in the five minutes before and after sewing circle, they've had ample opportunity to see it for themselves over the summer.'

Ned grimaced. It wasn't the only thing he'd neglected to tell them recently. He'd been meaning to sit down and share the news about their extended stay in Bridgefield, but between the whirlwind of school holidays, the eggs, the flowers, Cameron's attitude and Jonno's pending arrival . . . He kicked at the dirt. It was the first time Doug and Willow hadn't been actively involved in planning their next move.

He left Maeve with the children and the piglets and started on the house chores. With one load of laundry pegged out, another load underway and the kitchen straightened up, he checked his watch. Right on time.

Jonno was already online when Ned connected the Zoom call.

'Hey, bro, how're the new piglets?'

Leaning back into his chair, Ned raised an eyebrow. 'You knew too?'

'I might be thousands of miles away in the middle of the ocean, but don't you worry, I've got my finger on the pulse. Your kids were pretty stoked, they FaceTimed me with Maeve this morning. Sounds like we'll be having a spit-roast for my welcome home dinner?'

The thought was too much for Ned and he shook his head, much to his brother's amusement.

'I can't even go there,' he said, looking out the sliding door to where the children played.

'You've spent way too long buying supermarket meat, bro. How's everything else going?'

Ned updated him on the new chickens that were due not long after Jonno's return, and the emails he'd received from regulars who normally bought Colin's retired hens.

'You sure you won't miss seals and whales when you take this on?'

Jonno chuckled as he considered the question and pointed a finger at the computer screen. 'You sure *you* won't miss the hens and eggs when you return to your travels?'

Ned shrugged lightly, thinking of the days spent in the sunshine and open air. He filled Jonno in on the locum contract he'd signed with the Horsham Hospital.

'The travels are on hold for a few more months, but I'll probably miss the flowers more than the chickens,' he admitted.

'The flowers or the flower *farmer*?'

Ned didn't bother hiding his smile. Jonno was no fool. 'I'll be knee-deep in medicine and Webster packs at the hospital pharmacy most days, but I'll still see plenty of Diana.' He thought of Cameron's parting shot yesterday. 'Least, I hope so.'

A few prompts from his brother, and the whole story came tumbling out. Jonno let out a low whistle afterwards.

'She must be special if you're thinking of putting down roots. I haven't seen you keen on anyone since Fleur.'

'And look how well that turned out.' Ned groaned then shook his head. 'They're poles apart, and with another decade and a half under my sleeve, I'd like to think I'm a better judge of character.'

There was a knock on the sliding door and Ned turned to see the children grinning through the glass, a piglet under each arm. *Next thing they'd be bringing them inside.*

'No pigs in the house,' he called. Jonno erupted into laughter and Maeve walked up the path, steering them back to the yard, shooting him an indulgent 'kids, hey?' look. After finishing the Zoom call, Ned printed off the Horsham contract and put it next to the fruit bowl. Tonight's mission: to share the news about their change of plans.

For the first time ever, Diana walked out of the cricket ground with her eyes glued to the footpath, unable to meet the gaze of the other parents or players. Even though she couldn't see their curious glances, she could still hear their whispers.

'Did you see the boy chunder all over the pitch?'

'What about his hissy fit when the coach pulled him up?'

'What's he aiming for, to be the Nick Kyrgios of cricket?'

City driving tested her patience at the best of times, but it was made even worse by reliving the moment her son tossed his cricket bat—and his chances with the premier side—away. Had it been the thing with the new bag that tipped him over the edge or the pressure of it all? Either way, it took a Herculean effort to keep her mouth shut until she hit the highway.

'I've never been so mortified in my life, Cameron. What happened back there?'

Diana took her eyes briefly off the road to look at him. Where was the youngster who whacked on the zinc cream, delighted to spend all weekend on the cricket oval? Had she not done enough? Or had she pushed him too hard? And how the hell were they going to fix it? All those years of training, all the hours in the backyard with Pete, and she'd never seen him play as poorly as he had today. Or vomit on the cricket oval. Or throw a whopping great tantrum.

Cameron stared straight ahead, his mouth clamped shut.

'It's nearly February. You can't just give up three-quarters of the way through the season. All that training . . .' *All that promise. All those years of dreaming.*

She snuck another look at him, trailing off when she saw him swiping at his eyes.

'Just leave it, Mum.'

Leave it? She spent the next 100 kilometres trying to unravel the last few days, weeks, months to work out where things had started to go pear-shaped. It couldn't be based on Ned's presence, surely?

Diana's mobile ring tone blasted over the car stereo system with an incoming call from Penny. They reached for the stereo touchscreen at the same time. Cameron hit the 'decline' button first.

'Cam,' she said slowly. 'You know we'll have to update the family at some stage.'

He kept his gaze firmly out the window. Lara tried calling an hour later, and then Angus, when they were nearer to home but no closer to talking about his dismissal from the team.

'Have you spoken to Georgie yet?'

Cameron mumbled under his breath, his words hard to hear over the road noise. 'She wouldn't care anyway. She dumped me before Christmas.'

'Oh, Cam.' She shook her head in disbelief, hating that her son hadn't confided in her. The turn-off for Bridgefield came into sight. Diana shifted in her seat. 'You didn't say anything.'

'You're always too busy. If you're not doing the flowers, you're thinking about the flowers, and if you're not thinking about the flowers, then dickhead Ned's hovering. Not to mention Sadie Bloody Woodford. When was I supposed to tell you?'

Dickhead Ned? Diana was glad she'd slowed the car down to sixty or she'd have veered off the road. She pulled over.

'I'm your mum, Cam. I'll *always* have time for you. I had an inkling, but I can't help you if you don't talk to me,' she said.

'Dad would've noticed,' he shot back.

Diana sucked in a quick breath, her frustration and disappointment morphing into anger. 'I didn't ask him to die, Cam. Not once in our whole marriage did I ever wish him dead. Not then, not now. And you might not have noticed, but I'm trying my best.' Knowing she should calm down didn't stop the words spilling from her lips. 'I get that it's been hard for you guys to lose your dad, but it's been hard for me, too.' Her eyes burned. She reached for his hand. 'I know you're upset about the cricket, and breaking up with Georgie must have been really tough, but don't make this my fault, Cameron.'

Diana searched his face, desperate for some understanding, something other than his stony silence.

'Can we at least talk about it?'

'Talking's not going to bring Dad back. It's not going to get me in front of those selectors again. And Georgie's made herself clear.' He tugged the car door open, his feet crunching on the long grass as he stepped out.

'Don't be crazy, Cam. It's nearly dark.'

'I can walk.'

How many times had she pulled over and threatened the boys with the punishment of walking the last kilometre home when they were bickering or kicking seats? She'd come close to enforcing it on several occasions, with Harry especially, but never had she begged them *not* to walk. Diana felt a headache coming on. This wasn't at all how she'd expected today to pan out.

She wound down the window and drove at walking pace alongside him, fighting to keep her voice steady. 'Get back in the car, Cam.'

He marched on ahead.

30

Diana's hope that Cameron would walk through the door with an apology and hug was dashed when he arrived home an hour after her, stalked through the house with his shoes still on and slammed his bedroom door behind him.

If it weren't almost 11 p.m., she would have called her sisters, but given the unholy hour Lara and Toby started their early-morning runs, and the trouble Penny had sleeping with Lucy's back molars coming through, she opted for texting Angie instead.

You awake?

After a quick shower, she saw the message remained unread. Angus would be fast asleep too. Although she suspected Ned would be awake, Cam's accusations were too fresh in her mind. With a sigh, Diana crawled into bed, where she tossed and turned for an hour, unable to wind down. She pulled the spare pillow to her chest. *Pete's pillow. What would he say about today? Would he have noticed what I'd missed?*

Regardless of where the blame lay, Cam's loss of faith in her hurt more than she'd imagined. Her phone buzzed on the side table, illuminating the room. If only it were Pete, messaging her support via some magical telephone. Diana looked at the phone.

Ned.

She took a moment before opening it, knowing his message wouldn't bring the same joy as usual.

> How was the match? I've booked a table at the Royal Mail
> next weekend if that suits? Or we could have dinner in Halls
> Gap if you like? 🖤

Diana closed her eyes and sank back onto the pillow. Last night she'd fallen asleep in Geelong with Ned on her mind and a smile on her lips. Tonight, just the thought of him evoked longing and guilt. Had she become one of those mothers so focused on her own happiness that she'd neglected her children's needs and wants? Despite the late hour, she crawled out of bed.

Jinx jumped up from her basket, sparking a chorus of meows from the kittens. She slipped out the laundry door the moment Diana stepped outside. Together they meandered through the rose garden, ending up beside the first Abraham Darby rose Pete had given her all those years ago.

My God, look at all those deadheads and rosehips . . .

For all her hours of pruning and cutting in the commercial garden, she hadn't got to the house yard. *Neglecting my social media over New Year's, my house garden in January and now evidently Cameron.* The list of her failings kept growing.

With a sigh, Diana reached across and snapped the orange rosehips off with her fingers. Her dressing gown caught on a branch, and when Diana yanked her sleeve, a sharp thorn jabbed into her knuckle.

'Ouch!'

She wasn't much for omens, and scratches from rose thorns were par for the course in her occupation, but she couldn't help wondering if the extra-sharp jab was a message from above.

Sinking down on the timber bench, Diana sucked on her sore thumb. Jinx jumped onto her lap.

'Oh Jinxy, what a mess.' Taking comfort in the cat's gentle head butts, Diana rubbed the spot under Jinx's chin that sent her into seventh heaven. If there was something that had to be bumped off her to-do list, it wouldn't be the children or the flower farm and, as much as she'd wanted Ned's company— craved his gentle touch—she suspected a lover was the only optional extra in this scenario.

Pfft. A few stolen kisses and a whole lot of chemistry didn't amount to a lover.

'But that's where it was heading,' Diana sighed, already hurting at the idea of farewelling her bright future with Ned.

Not just yet, though, she decided, drawing the cat closer. *I'll tell Ned in person.* Until then, she could pretend all three things were still within her reach—her family, her flower farm and dinner dates with her almost-lover.

Taking one last breath of the rose garden's rich fragrance, Diana carried the cat back to her basket. The kittens ambushed Jinx the moment she lay down. Diana looked on as the furry babies latched on with little decorum, all needing something from her. It was a feeling Diana recognised and had never resented until that moment.

Colin's dusty Land Rover looked out of place next to the polished and waxed cars in the hospital car park, and it wasn't until Ned was getting directions from the receptionist that he noticed long tufts of cat hair on his navy shirt. *Flopsy. Way to make a good impression at a future workplace.* Normally Ned's locum contracts were interstate, and he didn't have the luxury of in-person handovers, so it was a novelty to be offered a tour of the Horsham Hospital.

The pharmacy was tucked in the bowels of the building, all artificial lighting and recycled air. A vase of flowers added a colourful touch to the otherwise clinical space. On closer inspection, they looked very familiar. He grinned.

'You like those?' Polly Stringer, the pharmacist, he'd agreed to replace after Easter, picked up a business card from beside the vase. 'Grown down the road in Bridgefield. Take the card, they're the best flowers in town.'

Ned lifted a hand.

'Keep the card, I've got a few already. I've been helping Diana these last few months.' The pharmacist was astonished. 'In fact,' Ned added, leaning over to admire the posy. 'I made that bouquet myself.'

'Now I know why your name sounded so familiar,' Polly said, pausing to introduce Ned to each staff member as they continued to a common room. 'Diana did the flowers for my sister's wedding. It was her first time supplying for an event, and she had an older gentleman there showing her the ropes. Gorgeous flowers.'

Ned felt strangely wistful. His father would have been in his element, working alongside Diana, but it wasn't until now that he fully appreciated how Colin had inadvertently played such a pivotal role in bringing them together.

'That was my dad,' he said, briefly explaining the circumstances that had brought him back to Bridgefield.

'I'm so sorry about your dad,' said Polly, leading him into a staff room. 'Take a seat, let's get down to business.'

Ned took in their surroundings as she pulled up his resume. From the slow cooker bubbling on the staffroom bench and the well-stocked biscuit jar, it looked to be a cosy, communal work environment.

'Your bona fides check out, and if you've got the McIntyre family seal of approval, then you must be a good worker. You're in good health?' Ned nodded. 'Apart from moonlighting as a florist and helping damsels in distress, are there any other bad habits I should know about? Drugs? Alcohol? Gambling?'

'Not unless you count child-wrangling and a soft spot for Aussie Rules.'

'As long as it's not Collingwood, I won't hold it against you. And you're right to start after Easter?'

Ned confirmed he wasn't a one-eyed Magpies supporter and was free to begin on the suggested date that would work with her forthcoming maternity leave.

'The next ten weeks will fly past,' he assured her, noticing how her hand kept returning to the small of her back when they stood.

Polly farewelled him with a handshake, pleased with his offer to call in for a handover day later that month.

Contentment flooded through him as he followed the south side of the mountain range towards Bridgefield. As well as being happy with the news about his next contract, the children had climbed onto the school bus this morning without a backwards glance. Even Maeve, who wasn't one for fuss, had thawed a leg of lamb to celebrate the announcement. *I think we'll end up staying more than six months.* Diana's golden hair, floral dresses and flowers ran through his mind.

Between the Geelong trip and the back-to-school rush, he wasn't surprised she'd forgotten to reply to his message about their date. He smiled as he approached Darling Downs. As tempting as it was to call in and surprise her on his day off, he was due to meet Butch at the egg farm for a chook tractor repair job. *Just have to look forward to seeing her tomorrow.*

Diana was washing up for lunch when she saw Ned's name flash up on her phone screen, bringing with it that now-familiar combination of guilt and longing.

Answer it! The quicker you call it off, the easier it will be for both of you.

Diana looked into the mirror. With bags under her eyes from two restless nights and a stress pimple erupting on her forehead, she looked every bit as mournful as she felt.

'Maybe I should let Sarah Squires at him after all,' she told Jinx, who was eyeing a moth in the ensuite window. The idea made her even more miserable. *Tomorrow I'll tell him,* she promised herself, sending the call through to voicemail. Cameron was nowhere to be seen, although evidence of his back-to-school prep was spread across the kitchen bench.

She moved the folders, textbooks and stationery aside and made sandwiches, leaving one on the bench for Cameron to eat whenever he got back from his run.

He'll be in for a shock when the schoolwork starts ramping up. The phone rang again, Lara this time.

'Hey Lars, how're things?'

'Forget about me, how are you? Evie just called in her recess break to tell me Cam's quit the premier league!'

Diana sighed. *Had he now?* Cameron had been tight-lipped ever since Saturday night.

'I can't believe he's throwing it all away,' she said, frustrated he'd made the decision and hadn't told her. 'Am I really that bad a mum that he didn't think he could tell me?'

Lara was quick to leap to her defence. 'This sounds like his problem, not yours. On the upside, you'll have more time for romance without all the driving to Geelong and back.'

Diana picked at the bandaid on her sore thumb, not wanting to admit her fledgling romance was over before it had begun.

'Can you ask Toby to bring his camera to Sadie's launch? There'll be a handful of press photographers at the event, but I'd love some pictures to use on my website. Ones I don't have to remortgage the house to afford,' she added with a weak laugh.

'He's already arranged a day off, there'll be no keeping him away,' Lara said brightly. 'I've swapped shifts at the Bush Nursing Centre and Angie's mother-in-law Rosa is coming over to watch Claudia and Lucy, so we'll all be there to revel in your success.'

Lara's enthusiasm for the event lifted Diana's spirits, but the excitement gave way to nerves as she logged onto Facebook. Sadie's page was flooded with entries to win a double pass to the launch, and as Diana read the comments, she saw the day was tipped to be the floral industry event of the year. *Just a little bit of pressure . . . You wanted this, remember?*

But when she thought of Cameron quitting cricket, and the conversation she needed to have with Ned, she wondered how things would have panned out if she hadn't chased Sadie Woodford's endorsement.

Diana found herself dragging her heels the next morning. Had it really been only a week ago that she'd been eagerly awaiting school's return, and the opportunity to be alone with Ned? She waved off the school bus and trudged down the driveway with a heavy heart.

She'd brainstormed many scenarios for today, but nothing prepared her for the rush of joy, then sorrow, when Ned's ancient Land Rover pulled up outside the flower shed. *Get it over and done with,* she told herself, carefully easing off her gardening gloves to avoid jarring her sore thumb. Unlike the weeks before, when she'd downed tools and rushed across to greet him, Diana lingered in the paddock, a lump in her throat.

Ned slipped off his glasses, polishing them on a corner of his shirt as he walked towards her. A note would have been easier but, as Diana had to remind herself, she'd never been a coward. She bit her lip, finding it hard to voice the words she didn't want to say. *Spit it out.*

'Sorry, Ned, I can't go on the date.'

He blinked behind his freshly polished glasses, his eyes locked onto hers. A hesitant smile crossed his face. 'We can make it another time? Or do a picnic instead of a restaurant?'

He stepped closer. The warmth of him, that intoxicating scent of the ocean, were nearly her undoing.

'I'm sorry, I just . . . I just can't do this,' she said, avoiding his gaze as she gestured between the two of them miserably, but instead of seeing the hurt, she heard it in his reply.

'Right. Um . . . that's not where I thought this was going, but . . .' He cleared his throat, rammed his hands into his pockets and took a step back. In the blink of an eye, it felt like they were strangers again. 'I'll start on the dahlias then?'

Diana managed a quick nod. *A new relationship is the only negotiable in the equation,* she reminded herself. Still, she couldn't help stealing a look at him as he marched to the opposite side of the cutting garden, a stiffness to his gait that hadn't been there when he'd arrived. They worked in silence and, while she'd expected questions, Diana was equally glad and disappointed Ned didn't probe.

That's what you wanted, wasn't it? Maybe it wasn't as special to him as you thought, a voice in her head whispered as she carried her buckets to the packing shed. As forlorn as she'd felt after brushing Ned off, the awkwardness ramped up a level when lunchtime rolled around. She gestured to the house at half past twelve.

'Can I get you—?'

'I'm good,' said Ned, tightly, washing his hands and striding to his ute.

She peered through the sheer lounge room curtains, then back at the cheese and corn muffins she'd made on Sunday, in a back-to-school baking frenzy. Knowing he wouldn't have packed lunch, she ate quickly and chased the lunch down with a Panadol to ease the persistent pain in her hand. She loaded two muffins onto a plate and delivered them to his car, hoping they might soften the next blow coming his way.

31

All sorts of things had been running through Ned's mind when he'd driven to Darling Downs that morning, and while every scenario had involved the golden-haired woman standing in front of him, not one of them had involved her reneging on their relationship. Diana's about-turn had stunned him into silence as he worked through the rows of flowers. *How had I misread the signals so badly?* It wasn't like he'd planned to permanently abandon his pharmacy career in favour of farming, but he'd thought Diana was just as keen to see where the chemistry would lead.

A snapshot of their fledgling relationship had played on a loop as he'd cut flowers and pulled weeds that morning; Diana's salty scones, face paint that had glittered when he kissed her at the Christmas concert, and the way her eyes lit up when she talked about her flowers and her family. Had Cameron played his trump card? And after a tense morning, she was now walking towards him looking about as morose as he felt, and carrying a plate of muffins. *Pity muffins. Please-go-back-to-being-an-employee muffins.*

'Thanks, but I'm not hungry,' he said, and just like the time when they were roped into the magazine shoot, his stomach growled, making a liar out of him.

'No, I insist,' she said, and when she passed him the plate, leaving him with no alternative but to accept the 'it's not you, it's me' offering, he saw sadness etched into her beautiful face.

He tried for a lighter tone. 'Am I completely clueless or did I miss something?' he asked.

'I thought I could do this, but it's too soon,' Diana replied.

'Too soon? Does that mean we're pressing pause or . . . ?'

She shook her head sadly, and he wanted to ask her if there was a chance for them, tell her it felt he'd known her for years and not months, but then the phone started ringing and she was fumbling in the pocket of her field apron. She mustered up a shaky breath and walked away to answer.

'Hey, Bron. Yeah, absolutely, that's great to hear.'

Would her friend spot the forced enthusiasm, see what an effort it was for Diana to smile when he was sure she was every bit as hurt as he was? Ned closed the ute door and polished off a muffin as he headed to the flower shed. Diana joined him shortly after, another of those mixed expressions on her face.

'The magazine is out today. Apparently, we made front page.' She paused, then looked up at him. 'And I wanted to talk about doing split shifts or changing up the workload. It might be easier if we focus on different tasks.'

Split shifts? That answers my earlier question then.

He thought back to the photo shoot, and the poses that had felt so forced at the time, but in retrospect had been an unexpected icebreaker. Damned if it didn't feel bittersweet to have their magazine-perfect pictures hitting the newsstands today of all days. *Just in time for Valentine's . . .*

'He did *what*?'

The phone call from Cameron's high school came through just as Diana was pulling into the primary school car park. She yanked on the handbrake and cringed as the glossy magazine version of her and Ned flew off the seat and into the passenger footwell.

Perfect, just bloody perfect.

She switched the call from the car speakers to her phone, embarrassed at the thought of being overheard as the principal outlined Cameron's classroom meltdown, which was eerily similar to his cricket tantrum.

'But Cam's never been in a fight. He's not that type of kid.'

The car park slowly filled with four-wheel drives, utes and mini-vans. Parents strolled to the playground and students filed out of classrooms and lined up in neat rows for assembly, and here she was, sinking in her seat as Cameron's principal made reassuring noises down the phone line.

'Nobody landed any punches, but who knows how it might have escalated if the relief teacher hadn't intervened? Can you think of a reason he'd act out?'

As Diana scanned her mind for anything out of the ordinary, besides her relationship with Ned, her gaze landed on the school's digital noticeboard.

All students back Feb 1 . . .

Lunch orders Feb 11 . . .

February birthdays . . .

Diana closed her eyes and leaned her head against the steering wheel. She'd nearly forgotten Pete's birthday, one of the very things Cameron had mentioned during his hissy-fit on New Year's Eve. Through the car window, Diana heard the primary school bell ringing. The principal wound up the call, reassuring her they'd be in touch if anything more happened.

God, I'm dropping balls left, right and centre, she thought, jogging past the swings. *No wonder Cam's hurting.* Every other year she'd planned a cake well in advance and they'd marked the occasion with something fun. Nobody had said a word about it at breakfast, and it had completely slipped her mind to remind them.

Diana stole into the stuffy hall, feeling dreadful. The students sat cross-legged in their assembly rows, while the parents were squeezed into the tiny plastic chairs, knees almost up to their armpits. Diana took a seat at the back. The sun still had some bite when they headed outside, ears ringing from the students' enthusiastic rendition of the national anthem. Imogen caught up with her at the gate and laid a concerned hand on Diana's arm.

'You were as quiet as a mouse this morning. You holding up okay, hon?'

Diana studied the dirt on her bandaid. She'd hoped Imogen hadn't noticed the strained silence between her and Ned at this morning's pick-up. *Obviously, she had . . .*

She gave a quick recap of Cameron's cricket fiasco.

'This sounds like a conversation to be continued over a glass of wine,' Imogen said, drawing her into a fierce hug.

Diana gritted her teeth as her tender hand was squashed between them. *It's a tiny scratch, stop being such a sook,* she berated herself.

'A bottle, more like it,' Diana said, her laugh coming out more like a splutter. 'It's been a shit week,' she admitted. 'As you saw from this morning's delivery, the flower orders are going gangbusters, which is great. Event RSVPs are through the roof, and I'm booked for more Valentine's Day bouquets than I could have imagined. But now Cam's been dropped from the cricket side, I'm getting calls from his principal and I forgot it was Pete's birthday today.'

Imogen winced, shading her eyes from the sun. 'We need a vat of wine,' she said, face creasing with sympathy. 'And it's not midnight yet, so you haven't forgotten. There's plenty of time to get the party hats out. What happened with Cam?'

'Something in English class today. The students had to grade each other's creative writing task. Apparently, Cameron didn't take the constructive criticism very well and nearly decked someone.'

'He punched someone?'

'He would've if the teacher hadn't pulled them apart.'

Just then, a trio of prep students piled onto the slide, one of them bursting into tears when he became the battering ram at the bottom. *Little kids had little problems, big kids had big problems*, Diana mused.

'Holy moley, I thought he was a lover, not a fighter.'

'Me too,' Diana said grimly.

Imogen lowered her voice and leaned in closer.

'Speaking of lovers, what's happening with you and Ned? Last week he couldn't stop smiling, today he looked like I'd run over his dog. Tell me I'm wrong, Diana.' Imogen's voice became stern. 'Tell me you and that gorgeous hunk of a man had a tiff over pruning techniques, nothing more.'

Diana hoisted one of the boy's backpacks over her shoulder. Even though she hadn't heard Cameron's side of the story, the call from the principal validated her decision to break things off with Ned. She'd been too distracted, too focused on herself. What else would crumble if she didn't draw a line in the sand now?

'I wish that were all it was,' she said, as Sarah Squires joined them.

'Hello, lovelies, we missed you at the sewing circle last week, Diana. That's a turn up for the books, me finally making it and you bunking off,' she said, giving Diana a cheerful smile.

'Or were you in the flower fields, recreating that romantic magazine spread with Ned Gardiner? My jaw nearly hit the ground when I saw the cover in the newsagents today. You're a dark horse, aren't you? Off the shelf again when you've barely dipped your toes into the singles scene.'

The throbbing in Diana's hand was joined by a dull ache in her temples.

'You know what they're like with magazines, all airbrushing and photoshopping until everyone looks loved-up and gorgeous.' Somehow, Diana managed a nonchalant shrug, then added, 'Nothing romantic to report around here, not with this lot.'

She gestured to the playground, where Harry had Sarah's son Ryder in a headlock. Leo dangled upside down on the monkey bars, his tanned belly on display for all the world to see, and Elliot sat under a gum tree, lost in a book. She glanced back at Sarah and Imogen, the latter's furrowed brow contrasting with Sarah's blatant curiosity.

'So, there's nothing at all between you and Ned?'

Diana slowly shook her head. 'He's free as a bird,' she said, each word burning as it left her lips.

Sarah made a puzzled face. 'That's what I thought! Then someone said something at sewing group last week, and I saw that magazine cover today . . .' She shook her head. 'I knew you weren't the type to rush things, Diana, with Pete being your childhood sweetheart and all. Don't worry, I'll be sure to extend a warm, Bridgefield welcome when I see him next.'

Diana was pretty sure her day couldn't get any worse.

As much as Ned felt like packing the children into Stan the Van and driving until it didn't hurt anymore, he made an effort to stick with their usual routine that afternoon.

The children bounced off the school bus and skipped down the driveway, devouring a quarter of a watermelon in record speed before setting up the sprinkler in the yard. Clad in bathers and haphazardly applied sunscreen, Willow and Doug ran back and forth through the water.

Maeve arrived with a bucket of tomatoes.

'Would you believe there're so many ways to preserve tomatoes online? Canning, freezing, sauce, passata . . .' Ned was trying his best to feign interest but his attention was diverted by the sight of the piglets entering the yard, his cheeky children trailing behind them. Maeve laughed, while Ned groaned.

'Hunting down missing pigs is the last thing I need today.'

She assessed him with a shrewd look. 'Three pigs, two kids and a sprinkler? That's the best thing I've seen all week. This heat must be getting to you. What's wrong?'

Ned shrugged. Reconciling with Maeve was one thing, talking to her about his love life was a different kettle of fish.

'Nothing,' he said quietly, sinking back into the outdoor chair. *Everything.*

'I could do with extra hands for today's haul of tomatoes. Can I steal Doug and Willow for an hour? Maybe when you next check in with Jonno, see if he'd prefer sauce or passata?'

Ned agreed to both of Maeve's queries and, once the piglets were returned to the pen, she ushered her dripping wet grandchildren across the paddock.

After half an hour of brooding, Ned grabbed the keys. They needed milk for tomorrow's breakfast, and now that he'd processed the news, he was keen to try to talk it over with Diana.

He called into the Bridgefield General Store first. The old-fashioned doorbell clanged its usual welcome and voices spilled out from the storeroom.

'Be with you in a minute,' called Toby. The conversation continued at lower volume, yet Ned couldn't help overhearing as he eased two bottles of milk from the fridge.

Sounds like Lara and Toby.

'But it doesn't look good, does it? Dropped from the Geelong team, then a punch-up at school.'

A punch-up? Were they talking about Cameron?

'I'd be reading the riot act if it were Evie. Sounded like she took it hard,' replied Lara.

Who else could it be, Ned thought, his feelings swirling. *And I thought I was having a shitty day . . .*

He studied his phone, concern about Diana building, when Toby emerged from the storeroom. From the sympathetic look Toby gave him, he had a feeling they knew about Diana and him too. The sisters were tight, had they known the axe was falling before he had?

Ned paid for the milk, stowed it in the esky he'd attached to the Land Rover tray with ockey-straps and headed to Darling Downs.

He wasn't sure what he could say to change Diana's mind about their relationship, but he was confident he'd come up with something when they were face to face, or at least offer some comfort for whatever had gone down with Cameron. He slowed as Diana's floral stall came into view at the top of Paperbark Hill. The vases were all empty. *She'll be pleased with that.* Then a flash of orange caught his eye.

A Subaru Brumby ute hooned across the paddock, turning so sharply at the fence that rocks and dust sprayed across the road, obscuring Ned's vision. *Didn't the kids say Cam's paddock bomb was orange? What the . . . ?*

Ned pulled over onto the side of the road, rethinking his decision. Letting the teenager say his piece was one thing, but he hadn't been prepared for this level of hostility. *Thank Christ there isn't any oncoming traffic.*

The tiny Brumby ute was halfway back across the paddock by the time the dust had cleared, but the arm sticking out the driver's window, middle finger extended to the sky, sent a clear message. *What's next?*

Ned wondered if he could live with himself if the hot-headed teenager was injured trying to make a point.

Don't poke the bear. With a weary sigh, Ned eased the Land Rover into gear and moved away.

He returned to Colin's and, at a loss for a better option than cracking into the port in the back of the pantry, he set up the Zoom call under the shade of the grape-covered pergola. Jonno's video camera connected, and just the sight of his brother in a beanie and multiple layers lifted Ned's mood a fraction.

'How's the homeward voyage? Looks icy.'

'We're still a few days off Macquarie Island, it won't get much warmer for a while yet,' Jonno said, updating him on the icebreaker's anticipated arrival time. After an update on egg production, Maeve's steady progress and checking his brother's tomato preference, as promised, Ned filled him in on Diana's bombshell.

'No wonder you look ropeable. It's got to be her teenage son's doing, right?'

'He's not a happy camper. You should've seen the warm welcome he gave me.'

Even Jonno, who had perfected the art of circle-work as a teenager, winced when he heard about the hoon driving.

'I'd be mentioning it to his mum, if I were you. Regardless of whatever's going on between the two of you, she'd want to know about that, surely?'

'And risk alienating Diana even further? Cameron's right. Even if he's being a pain, she'll always put them first.'

'Singing from a completely different songbook from Fleur, isn't she?'

Ned gave a terse nod. His ex-wife had put her children first for all of two years, then loped off with just a note and a forwarding address.

'So, you're just going to walk away?'

It sounded like a cop-out when Jonno put it like that. Diana's commitment to her family was one of the traits he admired most about her, right up there with her work ethic and sunny disposition.

'Claudia Schiffer look-alikes don't waltz into your life every day,' Jonno said with a laugh. 'Not around here, anyway. For what it's worth, I wouldn't be letting a moody teenager with a chip on his shoulder have the final say.'

Ned stayed out on the verandah afterwards, digesting his brother's comments. The thought of going in to bat against a grief-stricken teenager felt like a recipe for disaster, with a hefty side serving of hurt. His swirling thoughts weren't any clearer after he'd upended a bucket of grain for the piglets, collected the afternoon's eggs and restocked the chook tractors with food and water. He'd thought Diana was on the same page about a shared future. And after years without wanting anyone or any ties, he felt gutted to have the option taken away from him. Even worse, he didn't have a clue how to fix it.

Diana wasn't sure who she was angrier with that night, Cameron for getting straight off the school bus and giving the paddock bomb a thrashing, or herself for letting everything slip. Grabbing a wooden spoon from the kitchen drawer, she took her fury out on a bowl of sugar and butter. Round and round the spoon went, forcing the ingredients together. By the time Cameron walked in the back door, she had the bowl clamped between her torso and her left arm, regretting the decision to cream the cake mix manually, but too determined to give in to the pain in her hand.

Cam eyed her warily, trying to gauge whether she was about to burst into tears or bite his head off. He certainly wasn't expecting an order to change into good clothes.

'Where are we going?'

Let him stew on it . . . she thought as she measured out the flour and milk.

'Out!'

Cameron looked puzzled, but after watching her crack eggs with so much force that the first one exploded over the benchtop, he had enough sense not to ask again.

After racing through the shower in record speed, Elliot rounded the corner with a 'tada'. Diana softened her stance when she saw the effort he'd made. As well as the denim shirt she'd suggested, he'd added a bowtie and suspenders.

'Aren't you a handsome chap?' she said, kneeling down to his level. Elliot's navy-blue irises were the same shade as Pete's and she couldn't believe that she'd nearly forgotten this special day. *Almost a betrayal of Pete . . .*

With the cake in the oven, Diana tried to scrub away the awful day in the shower. Estee Lauder's fanciest body wash proved a poor match for the way she was feeling and she stayed under the water until there were no more tears left to cry. A quick towel off, eye drops, and make up, then she studied her swollen thumb. Scratches were as common as freckles at this time of year, but they weren't normally so painful.

Loosened by the warm water, the bandaid came off easily to reveal an angry, inflamed wound. *Nasty.* Adding a swipe of Dettol, she covered it with a bigger bandaid, and hoped a dose of Panadeine Forte would take the edge off. She pulled on her linen dress with the peplum waist, and entered the kitchen to find Cam easing the cake from its tin.

'Want me to make icing?' he said. His offer felt like an olive branch.

'It's too warm to ice. We'll dust it with icing sugar,' she replied.

The boys debated over the restaurant on the drive to Horsham, settling on the old pub on Dimboola Road. Seeing her sons dressed in their finest, toasting Pete and blowing out candles on the hastily made cake further cemented her resolve. *Breaking it off with Ned was the right thing to do,* she told herself. Romance would just have to wait until the boys were older, when the flower farm was less intense, and when she didn't feel a sting of disloyalty every time she looked at the family portraits.

'One more game of pool, Cam?' Harry asked, rushing up to the table with a cue and chalk.

Cameron shook his head. 'I'm out. Nearly lost an eye last game.'

Diana pounced on the opportunity, pushing a two-dollar coin into Harry's hand. Cameron couldn't storm off or slam the door in here. When he'd gone, she turned to Cameron.

'You ready to explain what happened at school, yet?'

His Adam's apple bobbed as he stared at his hands.

'It was nothing, Mum,' he mumbled, downing the last of his soft drink. 'Don't worry about it.'

The memory of her stomach sinking as she spoke to the principal returned, and Diana folded her arms across her chest.

'I *am* worried, Cameron. *Very* worried. And I'm planning on sitting right here until you tell me what on earth happened today. And last weekend at cricket.'

Cameron took a deep breath. She let the silence stretch between them and when he spoke, his voice was more vulnerable than she'd expected. 'Higgo said my poem made him want to hurl himself off a bridge.'

'Scotty Higgins?' Diana's eyes narrowed as she pictured the short boy with a smart-arse attitude. 'The kid with the buzz cut? Don't waste your time worrying about him. Bit heavy to be writing poetry on your first day back, though, isn't it?'

'There's a new English teacher, full of brilliant ideas.' Cameron's tone was steadier now. 'What does he expect if he chose grief as the topic? Sappy romantic stanzas? Peppy narratives on dead pets?'

Diana cringed. A creative writing task on grief? Of course, that would have struck a nerve, and on Pete's birthday, of all days.

'Oh sweetie, you should have told the teacher why it was so raw instead of taking it out on another student.'

'I don't *want* anyone's pity. And it doesn't matter if I'm the best cricketer in the whole country, or if I chuck my guts up on the pitch. It's not going to bring Dad back, is it?'

Diana shuffled across the vinyl bench seat and leaned into him. A lot had happened since Pete died, and just when she thought they'd gotten over the worst of missing him, reminders like this bought it back to the fore. She looked around the busy tavern, the wait staff bustling between tables, the couples at the bar and the young families clustered close to the indoor playground. Not that long ago they'd been one of the families in those corner booths, within shouting distance of the ball pit, with Pete eagerly awaiting the day he could play 8-ball with the boys instead of rescuing them from the top of the climbing equipment. No matter how much it hurt to move on, they would have to, eventually.

'It's not going to bring him back,' she agreed wistfully. 'But we'll always remember your dad. And at least we've still got each other, right?'

'Unless you hook up with a nomad. Then Dad will just be someone you used to know, and I'll be at uni in Ballarat, struggling to keep up with your forwarding address, with no home to come back to on weekends.'

Diana felt pain, both physical and emotional, as Cameron bowed his head. She drew him to her, rubbing his shoulder. 'Is that what you thought, Cam? Oh, sweetheart, I'd never pack up and leave Darling Downs. Not for all the chocolate in the world.'

'I'm sorry, Mum.' There was a rawness to Cameron's apology. No bluff, no sarcasm, no attitude, just remorse. 'I'm so sorry for being such a shit.'

And in the middle of the busy restaurant, with a half-eaten cake on the table in front of them, they resolved to put the arguments, accusations and broken trust behind them.

32

The next week felt like an exercise in self-control for Ned. Diana was within earshot and eyesight, but further out of reach than ever. Orders kept flooding in from the magazine coverage, making split shifts completely unfeasible. He'd stringently avoided entanglements with fellow pharmacists, or dispensary staff, for this very reason. *Oil and water,* Ned thought ruefully, taking special care to maintain his distance when he passed Diana between the rows of flowers.

He'd be lying if he said he didn't miss the jokes, her company and the shared lunches. While the regime of harvesting, weeding, watering and planting was the same as it had been the month before, there was a stilted manner to it all.

'I'm away tomorrow afternoon, if that's still okay,' he said, loading her brimming buckets onto the big-wheeled wire trolley.

'No problems,' Diana said with a polite smile as she added more flowers to the bucket by her feet.

The Diana he'd known a few weeks ago would have asked if it were another of Maeve's appointments, or something chicken related. She would have known Jonno's icebreaker was docking in Hobart tonight, but this new, distant Diana quickly returned her attention to the blooms.

He tugged the trolley towards the shed. She joined him in the packing room soon after, and when he carefully handed her the first bouquet, ready to wrap, like they'd done a hundred times before, pain flashed across her face.

What was that? It wasn't sadness or tiredness; it was physical pain. She took in a sharp breath, and he realised she'd favoured her right hand throughout the week.

'Everything all right?'

As she peeled off the glove, he noticed a red-rimmed bandaid on her left hand.

'I'm fine.'

Stepping closer, he gently reached for her hand. 'It looks angry,' he said, suspecting it was worse under the large plaster. Panadol, Nurofen, rest and elevation were what he'd order if he were standing behind a pharmacy counter. Hell, it's the advice he would have given days ago and, although it didn't really feel like his place to give advice, a lifetime devoted to helping and healing was hard to shake. Touching her hand and remembering the way her fingers felt in his hair, on his jaw, tracing a lazy line along his neck as they kissed, felt like a fresh form of torture.

'A cut?'

Shaking her head, Diana took her hand back. 'Just a scratch.'

But he didn't miss the way she gritted her teeth every time she transferred the bunch to her opposite hand, the inflamed injury obviously troubling her.

'You should get it checked out,' he said softly. 'Before it gets worse.'

'I've got it under control, but thanks,' she said, flashing a tight smile that didn't reach her eyes.

Ned nodded. Message received loud and clear. *It's not your place, it's not your problem, butt out.*

As much as Diana felt like skipping assembly the next day, she forced herself to Bridgefield Primary and clapped as gingerly as she could when Leo accepted an award for student of the week. It was more likely to do with the posy of roses he'd given his teacher that morning than any academic milestones, but he looked as proud as punch.

'It was the sweetest thing,' said Miss Kenna, beaming at her afterwards. 'And his Valentine's Day card with pressed flowers—gosh, you've taught him well, Diana.'

Diana rounded up the children and was almost in the car park when Sarah ambushed her at the school gate.

'Hey, glad I caught you. What type of date do you reckon Ned might like? Horse riding, or is he more of a dinner and movie kinda guy?'

Finding it hard to be flippant, Diana managed a casual shrug. 'I wouldn't know, horses and movies have never come up when we're working together.' *Just flowers . . . and music . . . and dreams . . . and lost loved ones.*

Diana left the boys to their own devices when they got home, rushing to finish filling the endless list of orders. She stretched an elastic band around the final bunch of flowers, wincing as a sharp stem grazed her thumb.

Luckily, it's just my left hand. She waited for the throbbing to abate before sliding the bouquet into a bucket. Two days until Valentine's, and it seemed like every loved-up couple in the Western District wanted dahlias. After finishing the posies, she opened her laptop. Another three flower subscriptions, a dozen extra bouquet orders and seven emails all needing attention. *God, it's hot in here.*

Diana untied her field apron and tossed it aside before seeing what requests Sadie's assistant Ellen had today. Yesterday she'd urgently needed a dot-point summary of Darling Dahlia's history, today she was after a contact at the local council.

Doesn't matter whether it's the mayor or an economic development officer, babes, we just need a few officials so we can tick the 'working collaboratively with local government' box, IYKWIM?

Her shoulders sagged. She barely had enough time to have her sore thumb checked out, let alone try and work out the acronyms Ellen was so fond of. How did Sadie fit everything in? Or did Ellen take care of all the fretting, leaving Sadie to do the important stuff? She thought of the boxes of specially labelled wine in the cupboard, the individual pots of lovingly made mulberry jam that Nanna Pearl and her CWA friends had made, and the advance copy of the hardcover book that a courier had dropped off an hour earlier. There seemed to be a lot of running around required from everyone in Sadie's orbit. *I could do with an assistant but I'd still be run off my feet.*

It felt ridiculous to wish away this purple patch of paying customers, but Diana was hanging out for Valentine's Day to be over. At least then she'd have a chance to catch her breath before Sadie's big launch event. And then there was Ned . . .

She reached for the packet of Panadeine Forte on the packing room table. The tablets wouldn't ease the ache in her heart or make her feel any better about brushing off his concern, but they might take the edge off the pain in her hand. She washed them down with a glass of water and went to close the box.

Seriously? They're the last ones? Diana groaned, realising her thumb would be unbearable without the tablets. Reluctantly, she called Lara.

'Fancy poking around in my thumb? I think there's a tiny bit of rose thorn in there.'

'Is that still bothering you?' Lara asked crossly. 'I told you to see the doctor about that.' She heard Lara gathering up her keys. 'I'm all booked up at the clinic, but I'm just about to do a home visit. I'll dash in on my way past.'

Diana looked at her watch as she strode into the house yard, wondering what Ned was up to on his unexpected afternoon off. The timing couldn't be worse, on the cusp of Valentine's, but he'd known how busy they were, so it must have been important. Canoodling with Sarah Squires? Booking himself and the kids a one-way ticket to Western Australia? Nobody would blame him for changing his plans, when she'd made it clear there was nothing to stay for. *It's my only option,* she told herself sternly, glancing at the family portrait as she walked inside.

The boys were in the middle of a movie marathon and paid her no attention as she rummaged through the freezer, sighing with relief as the bag of frozen peas moulded around her left hand. The phone blinked with new notifications. Another email from Ellen, plus one from Bron. Lara still wasn't there by the time she'd replied to the emails.

Maybe just a little look . . .

Settling on the couch to wait for Lara, Diana opened the Micro Flower Farm Facebook Page and scrolled down to her photo from mid-January. She'd captured Ned mid-stride, carrying multiple flower buckets in each hand. The perfect juxtaposition of strength and beauty. She'd been proud of the shot, but now it felt like a painful reminder of all that she'd lost, and how well she and Ned had worked together.

She jumped, hiding the phone and the peas when Lara came through the door. With her hair tied back in a tight bun, and wearing her grey nursing uniform, Lara looked every bit the professional, but the furious scolding that followed was something Diana knew she would only inflict on family, not patients.

'This is a bloody dog's breakfast,' Lara said, assessing the wound. 'There'll be no fishing about for a rose thorn, I'm sending you off to Dr Sinclair,' Lara said, spying the semi-thawed bag of peas. 'It's a wonder you can even button up your jeans with this hand, let alone make bouquets.' Narrowing her eyes at Diana, Lara pressed the back of her hand to Diana's forehead.

'Hot as Hades,' she said, tsking even louder this time. 'Maybe this is karma punishing you. Where is Ned anyway? Don't tell me you've thrown the baby out with the bathwater.'

It was Diana's turn to muster up the evil eye. They'd already had this conversation a few times, firstly when Diana had told them she'd broken things off with Ned. Considering they were her sisters, they'd seemed mighty quick to jump to Ned's defence. Lara obviously hadn't let it go, Penny had called earlier in the week, offering to babysit if she had any Valentine's dinner plans, and even Angie had checked in with her mid-week, reminding her how much she and Ned had in common.

'I'm not mad, you know,' Diana said crossly. 'We're working just fine together. He's been the perfect gentleman about it all. He just had something on this afternoon.'

'Maybe he's buying a new outfit and getting ready for his date with Sarah,' Lara said, raising an eyebrow. 'Did you know she's asking him out?'

Diana nodded weakly, pressing her lips together.

'At least Sarah's got a clear idea of what she wants, and isn't afraid to ask for it,' Lara said, watching Diana carefully.

She's right, Diana thought as her sister pulled out her phone. *Why would Ned want to hitch his cart to someone with so much baggage when he could have a no-strings, good time with Sarah?*

'Garry, it's Lara from the Bush Nursing Centre. I need an immediate appointment with Dr Sinclair, please. I have a pain-in-the-butt patient who needs antibiotics at the very least.'

Lara covered the phone with her hand and lowered her voice to a fierce whisper. 'Quite possibly amputation.' And at the same time as she fixed her sister with a furious glare, Lara reached out, squeezing Diana's good hand with tenderness and concern, then put the call on loudspeaker.

'She's fully booked but happy to see you when the official appointments are finished. Could be five o'clock, could be six. Come now though,' the receptionist offered.

'You'll head in as soon as I leave, then?' Lara asked, checking her watch.

Diana nodded and gestured to the kettle. 'As soon as I've had a coffee and changed out of this grotty work gear.' She flicked the jug on to prove her point and Lara left for her next appointment.

The phone buzzed on the benchtop while Diana changed into clean clothes. She set down the coffee, goggling at the flurry of emails flooding in.

I can't knock off early today, she decided. Not when it involved an hour or two of waiting. Sadie Woodford wouldn't let a little pain get in the way of business. Another website notification popped up—*another order*—and before she could change her mind, Diana rescheduled the doctor's appointment for the following morning. At least Dr Sinclair wouldn't have a backlog of patients at 9 a.m. Striding into the en suite, she upended the travel toiletry bag on the bench, triumphantly locating strong anti-inflammatories from Pete's cricketing days. *Only a little out of date.*

She swallowed them down without water and returned to work.

Ned watched a handful of passengers disembark from the small aircraft and stride across the tarmac at the Mount Gambier airport, but his mind drifted again to Diana. How had she managed the afternoon without him? Had she seen a doctor, or at least sought advice from her sister Lara? He hoped so.

'There he is!' Willow yelled, nearly slipping off Ned's shoulders, her whole body wobbling as she waved madly. 'We're over here, Uncle Jonno.'

Even though they were the only people waiting on the tiny arrival platform, Jonno hammed it up for his niece, doing a double-take when he spotted her.

'How's my favourite niece?'

Ned waited until she'd had her fill of hugs before he joined the reunion, clapping his brother on the shoulder and hugging him tight.

'No razors in Antarctica?'

Jonno snorted, running a hand down a whiskered cheek. 'Needed all the extra warmth I could get out there, bro.' He looked around the small regional airport. 'Aren't we missing someone?'

'Doug's at a sleepover party. They've got pony rides,' Willow said matter-of-factly. She patted his arm, as if softening the blow.

The brothers both laughed.

'Replaced by a flea-bitten nag, eh? Nothing like kids to keep my ego in check.'

The wheeled suitcase was quickly commandeered by Willow, who drove it like a rally car towards the exit, narrowly avoiding several travellers. *Maybe Cameron's been giving her driving lessons already?*

They piled into Colin's Land Rover, Willow firing off a million questions, barely letting her uncle answer before launching into the next one. Ned did a quick lap around the dazzling Blue Lake, which was every bit as sapphire as the name suggested, and treated them to a counter meal dinner before pointing the ute east. They'd barely reached the Victorian border when he heard Willow snoring.

'I could get used to airport pick-ups. Beats the hell outta the train,' said Jonno.

Ned stroked the steering wheel affectionately. 'The old Rover's been good. Poor old Stan the Van's not used to staying in the same parking spot for quite so long.'

'Yet you've signed a contract for another six months. How's that feeling now the shine's gone off the relationship with Darling Diana?'

Ned knew the working conditions were a pale substitute for the friendship and intimacy that had blossomed along with the dahlias. He wondered if she ached to go back to the way they were too, or if she'd done her best to shove it out of her mind, like him? Shaking his head, Ned stared at the strip of road ahead, aware of the rising moon and the stars in the dark sky and thinking of the magazine on his bedside table. The glossy pages were a reminder of what they'd had, yet were also the reason they'd had to give it up. He'd reread the line about her Abraham Darby rose so many times he knew it off by heart.

It will always be my favourite because it reminds me of Pete.

'Just a summer fling,' he said.

'Yeah, and I'm a monkey's uncle. You wouldn't have mentioned Diana's name in all those Zoom calls if she was just a passing fancy.'

Ned sensed rather than saw his brother's shrewd look. He hadn't done a very good job convincing himself of that, what made him think he could pull the wool over his brother's eyes?

'It's complicated. She's still grieving, the kids are too. A small town like Bridgefield isn't the smartest choice for one-night stands and the last thing she needs is somebody waltzing in for a few months and making her the hottest topic on the bush telegraph.'

'Have you actually *asked* her what she wants? A wise man once said . . . ?' Jonno assumed a deeper voice, similar to their father's, 'Assumption is the mother of all fuck ups.'

Ned's eyes flicked between the highway and the pine plantations that flanked the road, mindful of log trucks and the kamikaze emus living in the forests.

'I think she's made it pretty clear.' Glancing at him, Ned tried to change the subject. 'Sure you're ready for egg farming? It'll be a change from research expeditions.'

But Jonno wasn't having a bar of it. 'Don't worry about me. These sea-faring legs are ready for a spell on dry land.' He flicked on his phone torch and pulled something from his backpack. 'You'll never guess what I found at the airport.'

Ned looked across to see the magazine featuring Diana's flower farm.

'They obviously had nothing else for this edition, did they?' Jonno laughed and turned to the main spread. 'Who's this schmuck then? Did you drop a diamond ring in the long grass or something?'

'I didn't have much say in the matter.'

'You don't look like you're hating it though. And I can see why. Is she a stunner in real life, too, or have they photoshopped the bejeezus out of her?'

'Even prettier,' Ned said quietly.

Jonno let out a low laugh. 'I rest my case. You're totally into her mate.'

Ned sighed. 'She's almost finished the dahlia season, I start work at the pharmacy as soon as this event's over, and Cameron's like a guard dog, baring his teeth every time I come near the house. Not much room for romance with those odds.'

'If Cameron's the main thing standing between you two getting together, then smooth the way. You've got to have something in common. You know what it's like to lose someone.

Even if Cameron doesn't like you much right now, he's got to be smart enough to realise you at least understand what he's going through.'

'Losing a sister's different to losing a father,' Ned said quietly.

'Correct, though you've lost one of each, so you're kinda qualified to talk on both subjects.'

Ned thought on that as they drove into Colin's. The outside light was on at Maeve's and as they drew closer, they saw she was sitting on her verandah.

'That old hut's had quite the spit and polish,' Jonno said, impressed. 'Vast improvement.'

Ned hung back, watching his brother gently embrace Maeve. Even though his love life was a shambles, Ned felt grateful that his family was knitting back together, a little tighter each day.

The morning before Valentine's Day arrived with a stunning pink-and-gold sunrise, the streaks of red a worryingly similar shade to those running up Diana's arm. If she'd thought making bouquets one handed was difficult yesterday, her attempts to wash her hair were near impossible.

Diana dried her damp, knotty locks, then pulled them into a messy ponytail, wincing each time she moved her thumb. As soon as she'd dropped the boys at cricket with Angus, got antibiotics and stronger pain killers from the doctor, she'd get back to her flowers. *Thank heavens Ned is working today.*

'Here's my busy girl,' her father said, drawing her into a hug when she arrived at the cricket oval. 'How's tricks at the flower farm? You look like you've been run off your feet.'

She grimaced, noticing her shirt was misbuttoned. 'Oh, Dad, you have no idea. It's like harvesting on steroids,' she said, giving him a quick kiss on the cheek. 'Thanks for taking the boys today, I'll grab them tonight. Have a good game, guys,' she called, blowing her sons a kiss as they dragged their bags to the cricket clubrooms.

Even with the air conditioner cranked up a few notches, Diana felt as limp as a hydrangea in a heatwave when she arrived at the doctor's surgery thirty minutes later. Her thumb was throbbing like it had come between a dahlia stake and a sledgehammer. Her arm was now aching, too.

One more day, then I can put my feet up. One more day. It was a mantra she'd been relying on for the last week, counting down the days as Valentine's got closer.

Dr Sinclair wheeled into the foyer and fixed Diana with a quizzical look. 'Diana, I thought Garry said you were coming yesterday?'

Diana stood, the sudden movement making her feel dizzy, and followed the doctor's wheelchair into the small room.

'Now, what can I do for you?'

'It's my hand,' Diana said, sinking into the spare chair. There was such a splitting pain, she couldn't move without wincing. *Was it hot in here?* She fanned her face as Dr Sinclair gloved up. 'I think it needs penicillin, but can you make it strong? I've got a million things to do for Valentine's Day and—'

Dr Sinclair shook her head, examining the wound. 'Armageddon could be coming for all I care, it's off to hospital for you. *Now.*'

Diana waved her good hand in the air, but from the stern look on the kind doctor's face, it didn't look as airy as she'd hoped.

'I'm fine. *Fine.* Great even. I'll rest the minute the flower orders are filled tomorrow, I promise.'

'As much as I admire your work ethic—' Dr Sinclair punched a number into the phone, 'it seems to be quite the McIntyre way—but you won't be picking many flowers if they amputate your arm for blood poisoning.'

Diana let out a gasp. *Lara had only been joking, hadn't she?*

Dr Sinclair spoke calmly into the phone, arranging an ambulance to take Diana to the hospital.

Ambulance? Hospital?

'It's not that bad,' she protested, shocked as Dr Sinclair explained about the infection she suspected had resulted from the rose prick.

'Best-case scenario, it's just sporotrichosis, rose gardener's disease, a fungal infection,' she said gently. 'But extreme cases involve blood poisoning, recurrent infections and flesh-eating bacteria that have to be surgically removed. And, of course, if the rose thorn penetrated your knuckle, the bacteria can push in further. I'm not taking any chances.'

33

Ned left Jonno to catch up on sleep, picked up Doug from his sleepover and dropped both the children off at Maeve's place for a baking day, before heading to Darling Downs. He noticed the empty flower stall beside the mailbox. Normally it was overflowing with bouquets this time of the morning, but the vases were empty and the chalkboard had been washed clean by the overnight showers. It was even more curious when he went to the packing shed and found the day's orders still pinned to the corkboard. No note from Diana, no sign of life at the house either.

Cricket, perhaps? The oval had been humming with activity when he drove past yesterday, but he thought she'd be here today of all days. He harvested the flowers as quickly as possible, conscious of the workload in front of them. After filling the flower stall, Ned moved onto the bouquets for the general store.

He thought of the McIntyres as he crossed the stems, angled the blooms and secured the posies with elastic bands. Was it pathetic to miss them already? The tightknit family had warmly welcomed them to Bridgefield, he'd even pictured sitting down to Sunday roasts at McIntyre Park.

Diana's cat wandered into the packing shed and he paused for a glass of water, pouring a bowl for the cat too.

'You probably need it more than me, kitty.'

From the sight of the tortoiseshell's saggy underbelly, she was still feeding the clutch of kittens. He could understand why she liked escaping briefly to the packing shed. He thought of Diana again, and the sacrifices she instinctively made for her children. Her four boys were lucky to have such a devoted mother, he couldn't fault her for that.

Setting aside the buckets for Imogen to collect, Ned crammed the local blooms into the ute cab. Diana's large four-wheel-drive was better suited to deliveries, and he looked at his phone again before turning the engine over. Surely, he'd be told if something was amiss. Ned tried Diana's number, but the phone rang out.

You're just the lackey, remember? Hopefully she'll be back soon. They had a mountain more work to do this afternoon and he'd be there until midnight if he was doing it alone.

Diana felt her eyelids drifting closer and closer together, and the effort it took to keep them open became harder and harder.

'I've got to get back, Pete,' she mumbled, willing her legs to swing themselves off the side of the hospital bed. 'Sadie will be there any minute, Bron doesn't know where all the buckets of flowers are for the stage, I haven't turned the sprinklers off.'

Penny loomed into view, patting her good hand and Diana noticed a drip had somehow appeared in her arm since she'd closed her eyes a few moments ago.

'Hey, hey, calm down. It's only February, not March. The surgeon's coming soon, there'll be plenty of time to recover before Sadie's launch. Just rest.'

Diana heard Lara's voice from the other side of the room. 'She's confused, I knew I should have driven her to the doctor's myself yesterday. She's as stubborn as a mule.'

'Ned doesn't even know—' Diana tried with all her might to sit up, but the attempt was useless. Why was she floppy like a rag doll? And what about the flowers?

'What about Valentine's Day?' Her voice came out like a croak as she sank back onto the pillow, hating how helpless she felt. All the hard yards had been for nothing. The magazine spread, the massive demand for Valentine's Day flowers would be useless if she couldn't fulfil the orders. Giving up Ned had been the hardest thing she'd done in a long time, perhaps this was her penance for getting her hopes up—and his too—and imagining she could have it all.

I've really done it now, she thought as the doctor came into the room. *I've ruined everything.*

'It's okay, Diana,' said Penny. 'Nanna Pearl's calling Ned. He'll take care of the flowers.'

She tried to listen as the doctor calmly outlined the action plan, hearing the words 'surgery', 'thorn,' 'abscess' and 'thumb', but all she could think of was Ned's colourful ink work all over his torso and the cat scratches running from eyebrow to chin on the first day they'd met. She'd never imagined an angel would take the form of a tattooed pharmacist who saved falling cats, but maybe she'd been wrong all along.

Ned could see his phone vibrating on the seat when he reached in for the last buckets of flowers. Pearl Patterson's name danced on the screen.

Probably chasing Maeve about the sewing circle tomorrow night. Either that or she wants me to don an Easter Bunny costume for the town fair Willow and Doug have been talking about. Planning to call her after he'd unloaded the flowers, he continued into the general store.

'You work well under pressure,' said Toby, helping him with the buckets. Ned shot him a bewildered look. The Valentine's Day orders *had* exceeded their expectations, but there were more than enough flowers in bloom, it was just manpower they were lacking today.

'You haven't seen Diana, have you?'

Toby's eyes widened and for the first time since they'd met, he seemed lost for words. 'Mate, I thought you knew. Diana's just been admitted to hospital. She's about to have surgery.'

Ned swallowed down an image of the clinical room Colin had never walked out of, then Jessie in the palliative unit. *Jesus.*

'Didn't Nanna Pearl call you?'

Ned felt his hands clench as he fought against the memories. The panic was easier to quell than the guilt. Was it yesterday he examined her hand, or the day before? Why hadn't he insisted she see a doctor, taken her temperature, pressed her for symptoms? Ned could barely look at himself in the rear-view mirror as he threw the car into reverse and gunned it for Darling Downs. He tucked the phone in his chest pocket and returned Pearl Patterson's call.

'Lovey, we need your help.'

'I know,' he said, lifting a distracted hand off the steering wheel to wave to one of Diana's neighbours. 'Toby just told me. I'm on to it.' Pearl signed off with a promise to rally the troops from her end for tomorrow, and he pulled up at Colin's with a plan to enlist his own army of helpers—his family.

34

The back streets and golden paddocks of Bridgefield flew past as Ned drove Stan the Van to the flower farm with Maeve, running his mother through everything they needed to do in readiness for the big day tomorrow. Jonno followed behind in Colin's Land Rover, Willow and Doug strapped in beside him.

He gave them a brief rundown of the flowers he needed and where to find them. The bouquet subscriptions Diana had been so proud of still needed to be filled today, and then there was the prep for Valentine's Day tomorrow.

'You really know this flower business inside and out,' Maeve said, a note of pride in her voice as she slipped on her gardening gloves. 'And she's obviously still special to you, if you're planning on pulling this all together in her absence.'

Ned shook off the praise. He didn't deserve it—not until they'd delivered what they'd promised to the customers Diana had worked so hard to attract.

Toby arrived a few hours later, still in his shop uniform.

'Can't have you all going hungry,' he said, placing a platter of warm pies and pasties down on the bench.

'Any word on Diana?' Ned asked.

'Out of surgery and doing well,' Toby said, loading the subscription bouquets into the back of his old Subaru station wagon. Thanking them for the dinner and update, Ned sent him off with the list of drop-off addresses.

'What's next, Dad?'

Ned stretched, giving Willow a tired smile as she finished her pie.

'Next I need a hug,' he said, folding her into his arms. Giggling, she set aside her makeshift dinner and wrapped her arms around him.

'Then I need to find Diana's laptop and check for new orders. After that it's home to bed, we've got a big day tomorrow.'

An afternoon breeze had kicked in, making the plants dance as Ned strode through the commercial garden to the house garden. He couldn't help but admire the massive rose in the middle of the yard, even though it was clearly a link to the man who still held Diana's heart.

Nobody was home, but he could smell her every step of the way. The aroma of sugary baked goods in the kitchen, then the floral perfume she wore as he neared the bedroom. Ned hesitated at the door. It felt weird entering her house uninvited, let alone her bedroom when she so clearly didn't want anything more than a professional relationship.

Then be professional, he told himself, spotting the laptop plugged into the desk near her wardrobe. *Get the laptop, check the orders, and go home.*

The scent of Diana intensified as he crossed the plush carpet, skirted the pale pink bedspread, and collected the laptop. Ned paused as he passed the old-fashioned dressing table with its oval-shaped mirror. There, between her perfumes, earrings and a framed wedding photo with her husband, was the magazine with them on the cover. He smiled softly, noticing how dog-eared the copy was.

Ned shut the door behind him and took the deck steps two at a time. He was just climbing into the van when headlights crested Paperbark Hill and turned into Darling Downs. Angus pulled up, Cameron in the passenger seat. The twins and Leo waved as they emerged from the back of the dual cab.

'How is she?'

'Still groggy,' Angus said, 'but at least she's not off with the fairies like when they admitted her.'

Ned nodded, his worry for Diana compounding. He'd never seen her anything less than level-headed.

'I should have noticed earlier,' he said tersely. 'Should have made sure she saw someone.'

Angus shook his head and gave a wry smile.

'You're not a magician, mate. She said you tried to, Lara as well. Unlike these buggers.' He patted Cameron's leg, an affectionate note in his scolding. Cameron shrank a little in his seat, and despite the ute's dim interior light, Ned could see the teenager's eyes were red. 'They live with her. If anything, *they* should have noticed something was up. How's everything here?'

'It's cool,' Ned said. 'I'll do my best with the flowers, you guys just work on looking after Diana, yeah?'

'You're a good bloke,' Angus said with a smile. 'She'd have been lost without you these last few months.'

'Don't know about that,' Ned said with a shrug. 'Just trying to help.'

'I know you are, lad, I know you are.'

Ned felt a swell of emotion. It was the type of thing Colin would have said. He turned towards Stan the Van, then paused, remembering something. 'Hey, do you know the password to her laptop? I've got to access everything for tomorrow.'

Cam leaned across, his voice quiet as he said, 'She changes it every few months, but there's a notepad she writes her passwords in. I'll get it.'

Now that's a turn out for the books, Ned thought, as Cameron disappeared into the house like a man on a mission. He returned, flashing Ned an abashed look as he handed over the booklet. It wasn't an apology, but it felt almost like a truce.

Finally home, and with the children in bed, he poured himself a strong coffee, sat down with the laptop and opened Diana's notebook. *This would be a hacker's dream find*, he thought, skipping past banking logins, government website passcodes and credit card numbers. Finding the right section, he ran a finger down her swirling handwriting.

The last dozen passwords were crossed out, but he could see they were a variation of her husband's name.

PeteAutumn123

PeteWinter123

PeteSpring123

Ned sighed softly as he read the final entry.

DarlingDelight123

Their new dahlia seedling, the one they'd named together.

Diana stirred at the soft knock on her door. It felt like she'd spent most of the night awake, stressing about the flower farm, and dozing on and off for much of the morning. It was better than dwelling on the social media posts she'd planned, the mountain of orders that would surely come in during the day, all the people who were depending on her to make February the fourteenth special. Ned couldn't possibly manage on his own. It would be a disaster.

The knocking came again, then Bron appeared by her side, a bouquet of lilac and cream dahlias under her arm. *Darling Delight dahlias.*

'You poor thing,' Bron said, her hushed voice full of sympathy. 'What terrible timing.'

Diana nodded, blinking as her eyes welled. Even though Angus and her sisters had been in touch this morning, assuring her they'd be helping fill her shoes, and Ned had everything under control, Diana knew there'd be mess-ups, missed opportunities and all-round mayhem without her overseeing the day.

'It couldn't be worse. I've been using the online ordering system for months now and even I miss things with that website software. I can't bear to think how many customers we'll lose.'

'It'll be fine,' Bron said, taking a seat by her bed. 'I called in on my way here, they've got quite the production line happening. I took a few action shots for Sadie to use on her social media.'

Diana brightened a little, until she remembered that the two weeks until the launch event would fly past, and with a bung hand, she'd be five-fifths of useless. Luckily, the flower farm was almost book-launch ready.

'Is that why you've driven all this way on a Sunday morning? Did Sadie's publisher send you to confirm we were ready? The hard yards are all done, honestly.'

Bron shook her head, smiling, and waved a hand. 'No, nothing like that. I had a quick squiz myself and it's divine. Absolutely blooming marvellous.' Bron plucked a ladybird off the posy's foliage and watched it run up and down her fingers. The painkillers made Diana's head feel a little cotton-woolly but she sensed there was something her friend wasn't mentioning.

'Oh, God, don't tell me Sadie wants to cancel the launch?' Diana couldn't help jumping to conclusions. As soon as she'd woken up this morning, she'd known there'd be disgruntled customers today, but she hadn't thought about them kicking up a scene. What if they complained on Sadie's social media about missing orders or imperfect bouquets that were cobbled together by Penny or Lara? All promises but no delivery. *It was one of the traps Sadie warned against in her masterclass.*

Diana assessed the IV drip and the bandage on her hand. Or was Sadie embarrassed to be associated with someone stupid enough to be hospitalised for a garden injury? Both options were equally damning, and completely, utterly her own fault.

Bron cleared her throat and glanced around the hospital room, uncertainty marking her movements. 'There's been a slight hiccup with Sadie's assistant, Ellen.'

Ned and Jonno arrived at the flower farm before sunrise, starting the morning harvest with head torches to beat the predicted hot spell. As the sun rose, they were joined by Lara and Toby, then Angie and Jonesy, who'd come all the way from Port Fairview. And right on 8 a.m., when they were ferrying the final buckets to the packing shed, the temperature spiked and a breeze kicked up.

By the time the CWA ladies rolled in with an impressive brunch platter, they were all ravenous and the fans were working overtime in the warm packing shed. But they didn't pause for long, working steadily throughout the day, with Angus, Tim and Imogen tag-teaming on deliveries.

Penny had sent Diana several photos throughout the day, simultaneously uploading them to the Darling Dahlias socials, and Ned, frowning, overheard Lara as she called Horsham, concerned about her sister's sluggish replies.

You don't have time to stress about Diana, he thought. *Make her proud today, then you can see her tomorrow.* It wasn't until the last bouquet was wrapped and loaded into the back of Imogen's van that Ned allowed himself to lift his foot off the pedal.

It felt like 10 p.m., not 5 p.m. Although Ned was used to delegating during long shifts, staff at the pharmacies knew exactly what roles they needed to play. Today's team were enthusiastic, but completely unskilled, and it had been an epic day.

'We've done it, lad,' Angus said, scraping the leaves and stems from the packing room workbench. 'That's the end of it. Let's load the van up, Jonno, and finish this fine day.'

'Wait a sec,' Ned said, his weary voice revealing just how spent he was. Ned looked at Cameron, who had been perched at the camping table and folding chair in the corner of the packing room all day.

'Are we done?'

The teenager navigated the website software, checking the back end, front end and emails to ensure he hadn't missed anything. He'd been sheepish around Ned at first, but happy to put his tech skills to good use, quickly realising there was more at stake than pride and grudges. *Perhaps he's thawed a little . . .*

'Yep, all done,' Cameron said.

A cheer went up around the warm room. Ned exhaled slowly and peeled his damp shirt away from his sweaty body.

'This deserves a knock off drink or three,' Jonesy said, landing a kiss on Imogen's cheek and leading the way across the yard.

'I'll be there in a minute,' Ned said, letting everyone file out ahead of him. He knew he should eat and find out how Maeve had fared with all five children, but he needed a moment.

As he put everything back the way Diana liked it, Ned contemplated her road to recovery. He'd googled rose gardener's disease late last night, after printing out the orders and conceding defeat with Diana's website software. The gnarly images were the stuff of nightmares and the infected skin around the wound would be tender for weeks at best.

A shuffling noise broke through the silence, and he saw Cameron in the doorway. *Surely, he's not going to have another crack at me? He's done a pretty good job of putting our differences aside today, in front of everyone else, but still . . .*

'I don't have the energy for an argument, mate,' Ned said. 'You made it clear you don't want me and your mum together, and we're not anymore. Case closed.'

But there was none of the teenager's confident swagger. If anything, the boy looked as knackered as he felt. Forlorn even. *Diana?*

'Has something happened?'

Confused, Cameron quickly shook his head. 'No, Mum's fine,' he said. 'Well, as good as you can expect.'

Ned's pulse steadied and he let out a relieved breath. The boy's gaze fell to the floor, and when he looked up, Ned saw shame and guilt written on his face.

'I was . . . I . . .' He cleared his throat. 'I was so mad at you. Furious at her. Pissed off at everyone, really.' Giving a dry laugh, Cameron swiped at his eyes. 'I didn't think about what it would be like to lose her properly, not until I heard she'd been taken to hospital.'

For all his muscles and his confidence, Ned recognised a boy who had been through the wringer and come out swinging. Tears brimmed in his red-rimmed eyes, but the sincerity was heartening.

'I'm sorry, Ned. Sorry for being a prick and trying to scare you off. I'd rather Mum was alive and happy than miserable or dead, because she worked her guts out.' Cameron held out a hand.

Ned gave a nod, discovering Cameron's handshake was every bit as strong as he'd imagined. 'Apology accepted. Thanks for your help today, too. We would've been stuffed without your tech skills.'

He knew Diana would have been proud to see her son owning up to his mistake, but the gesture was too little, too late.

Diana wasn't sure whether it was Bron's inside information or the morphine that made her head swim, but she was still trying to work out the implications of Bron's news later that night. Sadie Woodford—*her* Sadie Woodford—had tens of thousands of followers, surely a few cranks were to be expected . . .

And despite Bron's assurance that Sadie's disgruntled assistant was stirring up trouble out of spite, Diana could tell her friend was rattled.

The phone rang, and Diana couldn't help the massive yawn that came out when she answered.

'Sorry, sis. Were you dozing?'

Diana gave a wan laugh. 'Thank God it's just you, Lara. Imagine if I'd answered a customer's call like that. Who knew all this lazing around would be so exhausting?'

Another wave of tiredness rolled through her and she couldn't suppress a second yawn.

Lara laughed. 'We were coming to visit, but it sounds like you need to rest.'

Stifling yet another yawn, Diana convinced her sisters to come. By the time Penny, Angie and Lara arrived, she'd commandeered a face washer, a strong cup of tea and was ready for whatever news they were bearing.

'Hit me with it!' she said, before they'd even settled in the plastic chairs. 'What went wrong?'

Penny elbowed Lara in the ribs. 'And I thought you were the pessimistic one, Lars? Nothing went wrong. Your lovely Ned Gardiner was a superstar. A slave driver, but a superstar nevertheless.'

'You should have seen him in action,' Lara nodded in agreement. 'Nothing if not determined.'

'And even a happily married woman like myself can appreciate him for the fine specimen he is. That chiselled jaw!' Angie blew out an exaggerated breath.

Diana sank back against the pillows, bracing for the blow that was surely coming. 'But how did you handle the website gremlins? How many orders did we turn away?'

'Ye of little faith,' Lara scolded with faux indignation. 'It went seamlessly.'

'Did you see that photo I popped on Insta?' Penny asked. 'It's going gangbusters and I'm pretty sure it ain't just the pretty flowers stopping them scrolling.'

Diana knew which picture Penny meant. She'd spent plenty of time that afternoon studying the shot of Ned, backlit by the packing shed window, his face creased in concentration as he worked. Sadie had reposted it an hour after Penny had uploaded it. *Sadie!*

'Which reminds me, what do you make of this?' Diana relayed Bron's news to her sisters.

'It doesn't make sense to me,' Angie said. 'Why would Bron drive from Melbourne to Horsham on a weekend just to give you a heads-up about one of Sadie's troublesome ex-colleagues?'

'Is this the same one Toby's journo friend mentioned? The jilted lover?' Lara asked. 'I thought that was just gossip.'

Diana shook her head. 'That was a beat-up, Lars, Sadie told me herself. No, this is her ex-PA, Ellen. She'd been working around the clock to arrange this launch event then, *boom*, Friday morning she walked off the job. Bron said there're whispers of legal action.'

'Sounds nasty,' Penny said. 'Maybe it's a publicity stunt?'

Diana shook her head, tired again. 'If anyone's orchestrating a PR stunt, it'd be Bron, but she was none the wiser. Poor

Sadie's got enough to worry about with her book coming out and new workshops launching in a fortnight.'

Lara got up and straightened Diana's sheets. 'Either way, it's not your dogfight. You can get max value from her influencer status and, come the second of March, you'll probably never hear from her again.'

Diana smiled as they trailed out the door. 'You don't know Sadie like I do, she's not like that.'

35

Puddles flicked up slush as Ned and Jonno drove through the paddocks and by the time the brothers finished collecting the eggs, Jonno's new Ranger ute wasn't so shiny.

'It doesn't look like the duck's guts anymore, Uncle Jonno,' said Doug, climbing out of the back seat and frowning at the mud-splattered paintwork.

Jonno chuckled at the boy's worried expression. 'Nothing stays new forever, buddy. Wait until the middle of winter, then we'll really put it through its paces.'

It had been a rainy fortnight in Bridgefield, the last days of summer ending on a soggy note.

'Won't be long till we're pulling out the beanies and thermal underwear,' Ned murmured, scraping his muddy boots on the doormat outside Colin's front door.

'You need a hand with the flowers again this week?' asked Jonno. 'Or do you want me to make myself scarce now that Darling Diana is back on deck?'

Ned shook his head. With only one day before the big launch, the flower farm was as neat as a pin.

'No thanks! Diana's got Lara and Penny coming this arvo, the famous Ms Woodford is due to roll up this evening, and Cameron's got a curriculum day. He's helping harvest this morning.'

Jonno raised an eyebrow, impressed. 'Good to see the kid's pulled his head in. About bloody time.'

But while Cameron's behaviour had improved, the distance between Ned and Diana had widened while she was in hospital. She'd been grateful for his help with the Valentine's Day rush and for holding the fort in her absence, but the text messages she sent had been achingly formal. Similar to the type of 'thank you' emails he got after his locum pharmacy gigs.

'Can we help today, Dad?'

Ned ran an eye over Willow's messy ponytail, proud of her for attempting to style her own hair yet sad that she no longer needed him to do it. Another reminder of how much had changed in the last few months.

'Not a chance. But if you pull your finger out, I'll drop you at school on my way to Diana's.'

After school drop off, Ned continued towards Paperbark Hill and paused at Diana's flower stall, already brimming with bouquets. He'd miss working with them, though not quite as much as he missed working with Diana. Feeling a little nostalgic, he tried to assess the property with detachment. The flowers and the dry paddocks had responded well to the recent downpours. Under Diana's watchful eye and with a hand from Jonno, he had mulched, fertilised and pruned the place to perfection ahead of the big launch event tomorrow. A marquee had appeared overnight, and he parked beside a delivery truck in the driveway, as a team of strangers efficiently unloaded seats and tables.

From the steady stream of gift bags, wine and table decorations that had taken over the packing shed in the past week, he was sure the event would be talked about for months, if not years, to come. Diana spotted him as he strode into the cutting garden.

'Isn't it amazing?' she said, her excitement about setting up momentarily overriding the walls she'd erected between them. 'It's like the midnight circus has come to town. I wouldn't be surprised if Sadie's arranged juggling waitresses and roving performers for tomorrow.'

Her eyes sparkled as she turned to him, and he couldn't help but return her smile. She deserved every bit of happiness, even if it didn't include him.

'They wouldn't dare mess with Pearl's army of CWA helpers,' he grinned and they shared another smile, because only yesterday they'd sat through a detailed run-through of Pearl's catering schedule.

'Weather's playing the game, too,' he responded, pulling out his phone. Although he knew tomorrow's forecast inside out, for a split second he'd felt that old zing between them. *One more day. Surely you can get through one more day pretending you feel nothing, smell nothing, want nothing.*

'Twenty-five degrees and clear skies,' he said, looking over her shoulder. 'Marquee might be surplus to needs after all.'

Exactly like me, he thought, turning to join Cameron in the flower patch.

'I could get used to this,' Diana said as Cameron carried a tray of cold drinks out to the garden. She sucked at one-handed gardening, but there was still plenty she could do. Cam had really stepped up his game these last two weeks, and Ned had been worth his weight in gold. *How will I manage without him?*

Diana sipped the ice-cold water, not allowing herself to dwell on the things outside her control. Isn't that what Sadie had said, when she'd called to double-check the final event arrangements the week before? Diana hadn't expected the call, nor had she planned to confide in her mentor, but when Sadie had raved about the magazine cover, and asked if there was a romantic back story, Diana had been quick to assure her their relationship was strictly professional.

'Probably just as well,' Sadie said. 'You're like me, your flowers are your life.'

It wasn't until after the call Diana realised she should have corrected her. *Family* and flowers were her life.

'Righto, what else do we need to do before tonight's *intimate* supper,' Lara said, waggling eyebrows and interrupting Diana's train of thought.

'As intimate as you can get with a handful of journalists and Sadie's entourage, right?' Penny grinned, striding across the yard and checking her watch. 'I can't believe we didn't get an invite.'

The pre-launch event had been the idea of Sadie's new PA, Cassandra, who had half the charisma of Ellen but twice as many last-minute ideas. Diana was a little starstruck by the idea of sipping wine with Sadie, her publisher and Bron and her city media mates in five short hours. Ned downed his glass of water in one long gulp and she couldn't stop her eyes following him all the way back to the flower patch.

All the hard work will pay dividends, Diana told herself, determined to focus on the insulated coolroom and hoop house on her wish list instead of the ache in her chest. *If Sadie can bootstrap her way to success, then I can too.*

Ned couldn't help but mellow at the sight awaiting him when he got home that afternoon. Jonno, who'd promised to make pizzas for dinner, was flipping dough like a pizzeria pro. Flour dusted nearly every surface of the kitchen, from the benches to the slate tiles.

'Hey, Dad!' Doug yelped as he jumped off the dentist chair and met him at the door with a hug, before tugging his hand towards the dining table.

'We're doing a project on states and territories in class, and I told Miss Kenna about our map. Can I take it into class, Dad? Pretty please?'

After a moment's consideration, Ned fetched the map and tucked it into the side pocket of Doug's school bag. 'You'll look after our special map?'

Doug nodded eagerly.

'I'll make sure he's super careful with it,' Willow promised, ferrying the pizza toppings from the fridge to the bench.

'Pizzas will be ready in halfa,' Jonno said, nodding to the window, where Maeve was making her way across the paddock. 'Maeve's bringing the garlic bread.'

Judging by the bulging bag on one arm and basket on the other, she was bringing more than just that. Ned opened the door and relieved her of the bags, recognising the familiar purple fabric. Jessie's quilt.

'You finished it, Gigi? It's beautiful,' Willow breathed, washing her hands like a surgeon before touching the patch-work blanket.

'It's yours. I stitched the binding on at our crafternoon—' Maeve's response was cut off as Willow flung her arms around her, the quilt sandwiched between them. They then went to spread it on Willow's bed and Ned tasked Doug with setting the table while he topped the pizza bases.

Ned put the Hawaiian pizza in the oven and was starting on the meat-lovers when Doug shrieked and slipped on the fine dusting of flour on the slate. The two glasses of creaming soda he'd been carrying tumbled through the air. To Ned's relief, they hadn't shattered on impact but then he saw what had broken their fall: Doug's school bag!

Doug gasped. 'Aunty Jessie's treasure map!'

A curse slipped from Ned's lips. He unrolled the map, trying to blot the bright pink stain with a tea towel.

'It's ruined,' Willow cried, racing into the room and skidding on the tiles. Although Ned tried to move the sodden map out of the way, Willow careened into it and him. They all watched in horror as the map ripped in two.

'I didn't ruin it, *you* ruined it,' Doug cried, gaping at the torn, soggy map.

'Oh my!' Maeve said, wincing when she walked into the kitchen. After so many years of guarding Jessie's map like a talisman, Ned couldn't speak.

'Shit, Ned, I'm so sorry, bro.'

But when Ned turned to Jonno, intending to roar at him for getting flour everywhere in the first place, his brother's expression was so horrified it was comical. And, for the first time in weeks, Ned felt laughter bubbling out of him. Then Jonno was laughing, and Maeve, too.

Willow and Doug looked between them. Flopsy strutted in through the cat flap Ned had recently installed, surveyed the scene and scurried out quickly, setting Ned off again.

'Why are you laughing? That's our special map,' Doug wailed. Willow looked on the cusp of tears, too.

Ned caught his breath, kneeled down, and pulled his children into his arms. 'It's okay, guys, we'll get another map.'

'But that one's got all of Aunty Jessie's special places on them, and ours, too,' said Willow.

Ned squeezed them tight, then shuffled back, so they were at arm's length. He touched their chests. 'Aunty Jessie's in there, kiddos.'

Willow reached out, snaking a hand through the buttons of his shirt. 'And her stories are written on you too,' she said, touching the roses and violets and daisies and forget-me-nots that were inked onto his skin in her honour.

He nodded and hugged them close again.

'And she's in the quilt Gigi made,' Ned said, then turning to Doug, 'and the books you like to read at night. We'll get a new map, and after we've plotted out some fresh places to visit, we'll fill it with stickers from our adventures. How about that?'

From the bedroom window, Diana could see the CWA ladies ferrying platters and jugs and cutlery to the mobile coolroom, the packing shed and the marquee ahead of the invite-only soiree. Even with kid's birthday parties and Pete's annual stock agency Christmas do, she'd never seen the place so busy.

'Mum, Bron's pulling up,' Cameron said, leaning in the bedroom doorway.

'Already?' Diana sprang back from the window. 'Help me with this zip, mate?' As he walked in, she could see he'd gelled his hair. *And ironed his shirt.*

'You look snazzy for someone who's babysitting his brothers tonight ...'

With the back of her dress zipped up, she followed him into the kitchen to see Georgie. Smiling, Diana gave the young woman a hug.

'Great to see you, Georgie,' she said, noticing the girl had taken just as much care with her appearance as Cam. Was this a fresh start for them both?

Bron burst through the door. One look at her friend's wide eyes, and Diana knew something was very wrong.

'What's happened?'

'Oh my God, I just found out. Have you seen Twitter?' Bron staggered into the kitchen, not removing her shoes, and sank into a stool. 'It's over, Sadie's done for! All this work.'

The breath went out of Diana in a whoosh and, feeling nauseous, she gripped the kitchen bench for support. Losing two special people in the last three years had been more than awful and, after everything with Ned, she wasn't sure she could handle losing Sadie too.

'An accident?' she managed to say.

'Oh, Diana, no, no, no. Sorry, how insensitive of me.' Bron jumped to her feet, shaking her head, and pulled out her phone. 'She's been done for fraud, plagiarism. The publishers have pulled the book.'

Diana could barely keep up, going from devastation to disbelief in a split second. 'You've got to be joking.'

'I wish I were, Diana, but my phone started going crazy when I pulled up in your driveway. It's just hit *The Sydney Morning Herald* website, and Twitter is erupting into a shitstorm.'

Diana looked out the window at the marquee, then down at her bandaged hand, and finally the paddocks of flowers that were her life.

'Sadie wouldn't do that, she's not . . .'

Diana pulled out her phone, dialling Sadie's mobile with trembling hands. Straight to message-bank. Diana picked up and cradled the advance copy like a baby, listening as Bron read the online article aloud.

On the eve of publication, Australian publisher Prevett & Curran have pulled widely praised Sadie Woodford's third book from shelves, after the bestselling author was accused of plagiarising many of its how-to sections and anecdotes. According to unnamed sources from within Woodford's team, the comprehensive guide to flower farming had striking similarities to a previous staff member's personal blog and another's unpublished manuscript.

Bron groaned. 'Sadie promised me it was a storm in a teacup. I need to draft a crisis management plan.'

Diana scrolled through social media as Bron jogged to her car, returning with her laptop.

'It's Ellen Merton, her old PA.'

They gathered around the computer screen, reading Ellen's press release about the numerous similarities between her blog and Sadie's new release. They startled at a knock on the door. Ned was there, phone in hand, wearing the same stupefied expression as Diana.

'This doesn't look good,' he said, sending her a worried glance. 'And I hate to say it, but your guests are due in an hour.'

Forcing aside her questions, Diana nodded, and called her family. Five minutes later, Penny, Angus, Lara and Toby joined them at the dining table, launching into damage control. Unlike her role in the garden, and at the helm of her household, Diana felt lost as Bron, Penny and Toby batted around media, marketing and publicity terms. She moved to the bench, making tea on autopilot, her mind swirling with the implications not just for Sadie, but her business too.

How many times had she raved about the course, the book, the launch party? How many posts had she linked back to Sadie's account, and vice versa? The enormous pride she'd felt in being singled out by Australia's most influential woman in the flower world was now tainted by hurt and anger.

I've been such a fool. This is the opposite of authenticity and there is every chance I'll be tarred by association.

Standing in her kitchen in the special dress she'd bought for the occasion, and staring out at the fancy marquee, Diana buried her head in her hands. Her thumb twinged painfully, as if to remind her that even that wasn't a good option. She struggled with the clip on the sugar jar. The latch finally sprang open, scattering sugar over the bench.

Damn it! She squeezed her eyes shut, fighting against the overwhelming thoughts. First the injury that had nearly ruined Valentine's Day, now this. They'd dodged failure then, could they possibly escape it twice?

'Hey, how are you holding up?' Ned reached for the dish-cloth, quickly clearing the mess. 'Want me to help?'

Diana could only nod. She'd always known he was a good man, but as he spooned sugar into the mugs, remembering who liked it sweet and who didn't, then checking how Bron took hers, she thought of how much he'd sacrificed for a shot at happiness with her. He'd been unfailingly polite even after she called it off, working his guts out to ensure her flower farming dreams didn't go down the gurgler too.

I've stuffed up, big time, but is it too late to fix? With a soft sigh, she looked out the window to the empty seats that wouldn't be brimming with people tomorrow. *Of course, it's too late. You made your bed, now you have to lie in it.*

Cameron strolled into the room, stopping in his tracks as he registered the mood.

'What's up?'

Diana took a deep breath, unsure how to articulate the loss, humiliation and shock, when Ned stepped in.

Cam listened, and to her surprise, clapped Ned on the shoulder. 'Let me know if you need anything, Ned.'

He rubbed Diana's arm. 'You too, Mum. Looks like you've got the dream team onto it though.'

Diana looked back at the table. Lara had commandeered her printer from the office and Angus was plugging in power cords. Before long, they were passing Diana printed speeches and media statements for her approval.

A crow cawed in the tall gum trees and a sparrow harassed one of the honeyeaters feeding on the vibrant red bottlebrushes, oblivious to the sombre mood. Ned stood on Diana's right as Bron greeted the handful of journalists and read them the statement she'd prepared about the unexpected cancellation of tonight's and tomorrow's events.

Ned could feel Diana trembling when it came time for her to read the Darling Dahlias statement. The last time he'd seen her look so desolate was in the paddock, when she'd called things off a month earlier, and just like then he wanted to draw her into his arms, bear her pain.

Ned took his hand out of his pocket and, as it brushed against hers, he felt her fingertips curl against his. It was her good hand he grasped, giving it a gentle squeeze before Toby passed her the speech he'd written on her behalf.

She drew in a sharp breath and looked to her family for support. He wondered if she knew how strong, determined and beautiful she looked.

'Thank you for coming and apologies for the change of plans. My name is Diana McIntyre and my dream of starting a flower farm became a reality after attending my first Sadie Woodford workshop. Like thousands of other gardeners, breeders and floral designers, I've been dumbfounded and disheartened by today's news. Here at Darling Dahlias, we had no prior knowledge—'

Ned watched as Diana paused, then folded the paper. He bit back a smile at the sight of Bron's worried look. Diana gave the journalists a grim smile.

'Regardless of the plagiarism, I still agree with Sadie's other values. Her advocacy for the grown-not-flown movement, empowering home gardeners to follow their dreams, and the push for country-of-origin labelling for flowers are vital keys to the growth of the local floral industry.'

She turned to Ned and it felt like she was speaking directly to him. 'Everyone makes mistakes, and I'm sure those responsible will look at this moment and wish they'd handled things differently.'

Ignoring a journalist's question, she turned and walked straight towards him, her gaze never leaving his.

'I wish I'd handled things differently too, Ned.'

The guests, the flowers and the hired event equipment melted away as she closed the gap between them and drew him into a fierce embrace. And when she pulled away, and looked up at him, he saw regret, hurt and hope in her eyes.

Hope.

'I just wanted to—'

He became aware of the hushed conversation and clicking cameras around them, and wanted to beg them all to be silent.

'Just wanted to what?'

He smiled, his gaze going to the paddocks of flowers where they'd worked so well together, the city photographers who'd come for a scoop and captured something altogether different, then back to Diana, who was asking him for a second chance.

He studied the woman he knew he had fallen for. Devoted mother, determined flower farmer, grieving widow, obliging daughter-in-law, sexy Christmas elf, loving sister and daughter. She was all those things, and so much more. She was the woman he loved and he couldn't waste another moment without her in his life.

He heard the cameras again as they locked lips, but Ned didn't pay them any attention. They could print it on the front page of the *Herald* for all he cared.

36

Ned strode across the kitchen the next day, pulling a home-spun knit over his grey shirt.

'Not quite as warm as we'd planned,' he said to Doug, sending him back to his room for a jumper.

'Has anything about this launch gone to plan, Edward?' Maeve laughed, sliding the glass door open.

'Hardly! Righto. Who's coming with me to Darling Downs and who's going with Uncle Jonno?'

Willow raced to the Land Rover ute, while Doug climbed into the dual cab, leaving the front seat for his grandmother. They travelled to the flower farm in convoy, and instead of the flash city cars bumper to bumper along the tree-lined driveway, there were so many dusty utes and mud-splattered four-wheel drives that Ned had to park near the front gate.

'Looks like all of Bridgefield is here,' Willow said, waving cheerfully at some of her school buddies.

'Wow, check out that big tent,' Doug said.

Ned spotted a family unloading picnic rugs and hats from a Toyota Troopy.

'Plenty of room in there,' Ned said, pausing to admire the ex-army vehicle.

'It's more like a tank,' the bloke said with a wink. 'Or a slab of wood on wheels. Great for big families, though.'

Ned glanced at Willow and Doug. 'Sounds right up our alley.'

He'd miss Colin's old Land Rover, with its idiosyncrasies, but a proper car would represent a new chapter of his life. His heart lifted at the sight of Diana at the garden gate, welcoming locals to the slightly revised celebration. He corrected himself. *A new chapter of our lives.*

Doug and Willow loped off to explore the marquee.

'Hey!' Ned said, smiling at the sight of Diana's sparkling eyes. She lifted up and kissed him quickly on the lips. Harry rattled the bucket in his hand.

'Gold coin entry, Ned. All money goes to a great cause,' Harry said, pointing to a small chalkboard. Ned laughed at the sound of coins clinking as he read the neat handwriting. 'Bridgefield family picnic. Donations go towards a new town playground.'

'A very good cause,' he said, tucking a twenty dollar note into the sealed bucket.

Bron strolled across, carrying a plate loaded with slices, sandwiches and mini quiches. 'This was a brilliant idea,' she said. 'I'll need to tap into the CWA catering for future events.'

'The publishers were all right with you using the gift bags and catering for this instead?' Ned asked.

Diana nodded as she waved to another local family, whom he recognised from the Christmas concert. 'They just wanted it all to go away. They would have been happy enough for us to feed it to your chickens.'

'Not on my watch,' Pearl Patterson said as she strode across the field, proffering a delicious platter. 'We'd never let good food go to waste. Now, Maeve, can I trouble you for a moment's help? It'll only take a minute or two.'

Diana and Ned waited until they were out of earshot before bursting into laughter.

'Maeve doesn't know what she's in for,' said Imogen, who had appeared by their side with Jonno not far behind, then Cameron and Georgie.

'What's this, the who's who of rekindled flames?'

Ned turned to see Sarah Squires and the McIntyre sisters arrive together. He felt his cheeks flush, recalling Sarah's text message he'd never replied to.

'Oh, you two,' Sarah said, landing a kiss on both their cheeks. 'I'm so glad you got over yourselves. Took a while though, didn't it?'

Penny and Lara grinned as Diana gasped and whacked her sisters with a rolled-up Darling Dahlias brochure.

'You didn't?'

Ned squirmed as he tried to untangle the situation.

Sarah winked at him. 'We did! We could see you two just needed a little push. Don't get me wrong, Ned, if Diana hadn't fallen head over heels, I would have happily pursued things.' Sarah turned to Jonno and Imogen. 'You two, on the other hand . . . I hope you learn from their mistakes and don't waste any time.'

A shy look passed between the pair, and Ned reached for Diana's hand. Valentine's Day might officially be the romantic time of the year, but March was off to a pretty good start from where he was standing.

Diana carried the last of the platters back to the farmhouse. Bonzer and Paddy raced up to her, tails going ten to the dozen, delighted to be let off the chain now the crowds had dispersed.

'Here, let me grab that,' Ned said, taking the platter and falling into step beside her.

Closing the flyscreen door firmly behind them, Diana resumed her place in the well-oiled McIntyre sister production line. Every spare centimetre of bench space was covered in leftovers, platters, containers and bottles of the special launch-party wine. Angie scraped and cling-wrapped, Penny washed, while Lara and her daughter Evie were on drying duty. Nanna Pearl buzzed in with another armload of dirty dishes.

Amid the cheerful chaos, Diana took a moment to pause at the window over the sink. The garden looked a million dollars. The grass was a rich green from all the February rain. Birds flitted between the bright red bottlebrushes, the lavender was alive with bees, and the bunches of flowers she'd picked specially for the event fluttered in the breeze.

Even though the launch party hadn't gone ahead as planned—the exclusive event instead becoming an open-invitation community celebration—she couldn't be happier with the result. She smiled, watching Ned return outside to help Tim, Toby and Jonesy pack up the hired furniture.

For so long she'd wondered whether she deserved a second chance at happiness. Maybe it was just dumb luck that she'd struck the jackpot twice. How had she ever considered ignoring what was in her heart?

The screen door creaked. Cameron carried in another armload of glasses. 'All good, Mum?'

She smiled at her son and held the door open for him. 'All good, buddy.'

Ned pulled up at Darling Downs the weekend before Easter, relishing the warmth of a late-March hot spell. Willow and Doug tumbled out of the car, their arms laden with bags.

They called a cheery hello to Diana before racing inside the farmhouse.

'Shopping trip went well, I gather?' Diana dusted her hands on her shorts, stood up and stretched.

Grass and fresh dirt clung to her bare legs. Her knees were stained green from the grass she'd cut earlier that morning, and the long-sleeved shirt was still ripped from her rose pruning session a few weeks back, but Ned decided Diana had never looked sexier.

'Let's just say, they'll look the part on Sunday morning.' He brushed his lips against hers and swept a rogue strand of strawberry-blonde hair away from her eyes.

'Well, we'll soon find out how compatible we are. If we can survive a family camping trip at your block in Byaduk, we can do just about anything,' she grinned.

'A dozen adults, a handful of children and a trio of teenagers . . . What could possibly go wrong?' he responded.

Diana rose up on tiptoes and kissed his cheek. 'Reckon it'll go just fine.' She picked up the trowel again and handed him a hose. 'I'll plant out the last of the flowers, if you can water them in?'

'Too easy,' Ned said, taking the hose.

They worked side by side until the new flowers were sparkling with water droplets, and the deep layer of mulch was damp through.

The back door opened just as he was coiling up the hose. He grinned, and nudged Diana gently. Her expression when she looked up was worth every dollar he'd just spent.

Leo and Doug walked out first, then Willow and the twins, and finally—with a pained expression on his face—Cameron came out.

'Matching bunny rabbit pyjamas! That is the sweetest.'

Cameron made a show of rolling his eyes and fussing with the torso of his jersey T-shirt, which matched the flannelette pyjama bottoms, but he still joined in the group twirl that Willow and Doug had been planning on the drive home.

'Just add some singing and they'll give the von Trapp family a run for their money,' Diana laughed.

When the children returned inside, Ned wrapped his arms around the woman he loved. 'Maybe a little more like *The Brady Bunch* than the von Trapps,' he said.

'Either way, I think we've hit the jackpot.'

Epilogue

Cameron gathered the empty flower buckets and tucked them over his arm, collected the takings from the flower stall's moneybox and used his sleeve to wipe the price list off the blackboard. He wheeled the timber stall just inside the gate, checked the mailbox and ambled back down the driveway to the weatherboard farmhouse he'd grown up in.

Elliot and Willow abandoned their backyard trampolining and hurried towards him.

'Any mail today, Cam?' Elliot asked.

Cameron nodded to his brother, waving the handful of mail as he climbed the steps to the deck and went inside. 'Sure is. Who wants to read the postcard?'

A cacophony of noise greeted him as he opened the porch door.

'I do!'

'Let me read it.'

Maeve grinned at him from the jigsaw puzzle that covered the dining table. Doug bounded off the couch at the same time as Harry.

'No, let me!'

Cameron grinned as they competed for the postcard.
'Ladies before gentlemen,' he said, passing it to Willow.
'A little hush, thanks,' Elliot called from the kitchen.
Willow turned the card, admiring the photograph of an enormous, rainbow-coloured staircase, before clearing her throat.

Hi from sunny Queensland, kiddos. Rainbow Beach is every bit as pretty as everyone said it would be. There're dolphins too, and if you're good for Gigi, Cam and Uncle Jonno while we're away, we might just bring you guys back here for a holiday next winter. Don't forget to add another sticker to our new map. Love to you all
xxx M + D

Acknowledgements

Here's cheers to the readers who have eagerly anticipated this fourth and final story of the McIntyre sisters. Writers are nothing without keen readers, and your support is both humbling and uplifting. I knew right from the start that I wanted to tell four stories relating to this close-knit family and it's a joy to know you've loved spending time with the McIntyre girls, too. I'm always grateful for your reviews, messages, and photos of my books, plus your word-of-mouth recommendations. Please keep sharing the love!

Big thanks to the book sellers, librarians, bloggers, journalists, reviewers, podcasters and bookstagrammers who kindly placed these novels in the hands of new readers—either virtually, via social media or in person. You rock! My novels take more than a year to write, and your help promoting them helps keep me at the keyboard.

As always, I'm thrilled to be part of the amazing team at Allen & Unwin. Special thanks to Annette, Samantha, Matt, Isabelle, Laura, Fleur, Rebecca, Peri and Jenn for championing my books, bestowing those early drafts with the attention they needed and answering my endless questions. I look forward

to working with you for many more books. Special mention to
Nada Backovic for creating such beautiful covers, but especially
this special cover, featuring my photos of my own garden in
south-west Victoria.

Thanks to my friends for supporting me on this journey,
travelling to far-flung events, gifting my books and voting for
them in contests. An extra special thanks to Karena for being
the best walking buddy/book confidant a girl could ask for;
Heather and Tony over the fence; Kaneana, Fiona, Léonie
and Sandie for replies to my random writerly queries and my
Zoom writing buddies at 'Not So Solitary Scribes' for talking
shop (and writing) on Friday mornings.

Much of this story is fictional, yet there were sections
that required research. My own love of gardening prompted
the main plot, but I spent many happy hours learning about the
Australian flower farming industry via the 'Dish the Dirt'
podcast. Thank you, Rebecca, for interviewing so many green-
thumbed superstars. I'm indebted to Lorelie Merton from
Florelie Seasonal Flowers for reading an early draft in 2021,
Janae Paquin-Bowden from Fleurs de Lyonville for helping me
with plot ideas in 2020 and Erica Downes from Little House
on the Dairy for sharing her sweet story about the Abraham
Darby rose and allowing me to modify it for Diana. I've also
taken inspiration from the testimonials on the Floret Flower
Farm website for Diana's gushing magazine interview and
styled an aspect of my plot on the *Makan* cookbook publishing
scandal of October 2021.

Cheers to Christine Cole in Canberra for answering my
cremation enquiry; Kate Griffith for helping me with medical
queries; Karen from Bridgestone Tyres for information on
caravan wheel catastrophes; Keely from Cricket Australia
and David Kelly from Geelong Cricket Club for explaining
how junior cricket segues into premier league; Paul Drew

and Penelope Janu for information about wills; Pete Gill for inspiring an Antarctic subplot (and then checking it for me); Bryan and Nicola for our conversation on the netball sidelines about car accidents (which was edited out); Tracey Kruger for kitten timelines; and Jaye and Elle from the Alcohol and Drug Foundation for help with information on addiction and the impacts on families. As you might notice, I've used my artistic licence with these subjects, and any discrepancies are entirely mine. On the subject, Western District locals might be surprised to read about a river running through Byaduk—yep, I made that one up!

Also thanks to Eliza in South Australia and Cindy in Western Australia for renaming Diana's father-in-law 'Reg'; Leeann and Kimberley from NSW for suggesting *Rosella Hill*, a lovely working title that morphed into *Paperbark Hill* late in 2021; and my newsletter community for being the loveliest bunch of people an author could hope to correspond with every month.

And finally, my family deserve the biggest thanks of all, especially Jase, for supporting me as I pursue my dream career, reading early drafts, being an all-round awesome husband and understanding that an author's job is rarely 9–5. To my children—Charles, Amelia and Elizabeth—thanks for getting excited about book events, wrangling animals for backyard photo shoots and designing gorgeous promo materials. Big love to my extended family too. An extra special mention goes to my 93-year-old nanna, Pamela, who still has a Wildflower Ridge tour poster proudly displayed in her dining room and loves books more than anyone else I've ever met; my beautiful mum, Julie, for reading early drafts and bringing the sunshine; and my dad, Bruce, for pressing my business cards into the hands of anyone who vaguely mentions books (and often when they haven't) and teaching me that dreams can come true if you're brave enough to chase them. Your eternal enthusiasm and encouragement keep me reaching for the stars.

If you'd like a little more writing, baking and gardening in your newsfeed, come and find me on social media @maya.linnell.writes or join my monthly newsletter for great things to read, bake and grow, as well as writing updates and giveaways. Sign up at www.mayalinnell.com

Love,

Maya